Include
Healing Sarah's Heart

The Memory of Love

TAMMY SHUTTLESWORTH

BARBOUR BOOKS
An Imprint of Barbour Publishing, Inc.

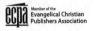
Member of the
Evangelical Christian
Publishers Association

Chapter 1

Callie Troyer watched the woman lying on the handmade wooden bed. Even from across the room she recognized the hopelessness of the situation. If she didn't do something soon, there would be two more graves in God's Acres, and the Solomon name would again mark them both.

"Child. . .comes. . .too soon!" the young woman screamed, pain twisting her delicate features into a tortured mask.

Callie hurried to Suzannah's bedside, her nerves ready to snap. What could she do? She had already administered every concoction the Delaware tribe's medicine woman—Helping Hands—had taught her how to make before the woman had returned to Pennsylvania. Suzannah was Callie's dearest friend in all the world. But Callie had not known enough to help her the last time Suzannah was with child—she miscarried—and Callie knew no more now than she had then.

Another contraction lanced through Suzannah's body, and she grasped Callie's hand, her white-knuckled fingers digging into flesh. "Make it *stop!*"

The image of two tiny graves, barely nine months old, passed through Callie's mind.

"I am trying, Suzannah," she said, squeezing her eyes shut and praying silently that they both be able to accept whatever happened as God's will.

The door to the log cabin swung open and Callie turned toward the sound, expecting to see Suzannah's husband or mother. What she saw instead left her speechless. A rugged man, cast in handsome silhouette by the afternoon sun, strode into the room as though he had every right to be there. Finding her voice, Callie moved between the man and Suzannah. "Who are you, and why are you here?"

"I have come to help," he replied matter-of-factly. He glanced around the sparsely furnished cabin as if assessing the situation. His gaze settled on Callie.

Lake-blue eyes held her doe-brown ones for a moment. His scrutiny made her uncomfortable, and she quickly looked away. Her gown was worn, threadbare in places, and was wrinkled from her long vigil. To make matters worse, her bonnet hung on a peg near the door. Nervously, she reached up to touch the blond curls that lay across her shoulders, thinking how improper it was for him to see her bareheaded.

But impropriety couldn't be a concern right now. Forgetting the bonnet, Callie swallowed her discomfort and lifted her gaze to his once again. She fixed her hands defiantly on her slender hips. "I do not need your help."

"I—I do," Suzannah gasped behind her.

His face was serious as he crossed the room, his dusty black boots kicking up straw put down to cover the dirt floor as he walked. He tossed a slouch hat through the air, settling it frighteningly close to a burning taper on the table. Shrugging off a buckskin jacket, he proceeded to dig a gnarled twig out of a large buckskin pouch he carried.

"Take this," he ordered Callie. Against her will, Callie took the twig. "Mash the end," he continued, paying no heed to what Callie thought of the matter. "Mix it in hot water." Authority echoed in the room, and he turned back to hold the other woman's slim wrist in his hand.

Suzannah did not resist him—Callie absorbed that much before she moved to do as he had commanded. *But Suzannah is not herself,* Callie thought. *She is delirious with pain and remembered grief of what happened before.* Callie paused and glanced back at the stranger. Perhaps she should insist he leave. But how? And what if he had the ability to make Suzannah's contractions stop?

Fighting churning emotions, Callie poured hot water from a kettle into a bowl. Her hands shook, but she carefully followed the man's instructions. Grabbing the end of an antler she had used earlier to mix her own remedy, she crushed the twig's bark. A bitter odor wafted up with the steam and she waved a hand at the offensive smell.

"Three minutes," he commanded.

Callie turned to look at him, thinking once again to tell him to leave. He met her gaze squarely, and when she noticed that his somber eyes flickered with warmth and compassion, she held her tongue. That did not diminish her questioning thoughts though. How had he found them? Schoenbrunn Mission was at least a four-day ride on horseback from Fort Pitt. Strangers simply did not just happen upon the settlers here, and if they did, they were usually traders. He didn't appear to be a trader. So who *was* he?

She looked at the candle's flame dancing in the pale yellow liquid in the bowl and remembered what she was supposed to be doing. He had said three minutes. She must keep track. "One hundred one, one hundred two, one hundred three. . ." she began.

"Quietly. I am praying," he requested softly.

This not only surprised Callie, it unnerved her. But she counted on silently as he transformed from a man of power to a man of prayer. His hair, blacker than his boots and wavy, was creased where his hat had rested. His face was rugged and tanned. All in all, she thought he looked rather arrogant, but a certain charm seemed to be present in his eyes as they appraised her.

Callie felt the warmth of a blush tint her cheeks. What was he looking at? The braid she had not kept up properly on the back of her head? She shook herself. The church had rules about unmarried men and women associating with each other. And she could imagine what Levi would say if he found out she was interested in this stranger. Better to concentrate on the rules than to think about the blueness of his eyes. She mashed and stirred, all the while biting her lower lip.

When the time was up, she came forward hesitantly. "Here." She handed him the bowl, wrinkling her nose at the odor; she was curious to see what he would do with it.

He took the bowl, his large, nimble fingers spanning it easily, and passed it under his nose. He dipped his hand into the liquid. When he raised it, golden drops trickled from his fingers before he smeared them on Suzannah's upper lip.

"What is it?" Callie whispered, forgetting her concerns about him for the moment.

"Just watch."

Mystified, she circled around the end of the bed and sat on the far edge.

"Are you still here, Callie?" Suzannah's words were slurred now, and she looked as if she could not hold her eyes open.

"I am here," she assured, reaching out to pat Suzannah's hand. He glanced at her as if he disapproved. Callie quickly pulled her hand back to her lap.

Silence grew heavy. She had to say something. Why not demand again that he tell her who he was? Bravely she raised her chin to do just that. She had missed her chance. Was he praying? Or sleeping? She couldn't tell, but her curiosity to know him better was overwhelming her good sense.

"The only thing wrong with curiosity is that sometimes the cat does not come home," Ruth Lyons, Suzannah's mother, always said. Surely there was no harm in watching him though. For a moment.

Dark locks of hair clung to his forehead. There were lines around his eyes and mouth, but they simply added character. *He is probably a Magicworker,* she thought. But Magicworker usually meant "black medicine." Somehow, Callie did not think this man had anything to do with witchcraft.

She glanced at the woman who had taken her in five years ago and helped her adjust to the Christian life she now led. Sleep had eased the tension on Suzannah's face, and the worry was gone from her lips. Suzannah's life, and that of her unborn child, did not appear to be in danger.

The stranger had helped Suzannah—something Callie had not been able to do. Callie felt inadequate—and irritated. But the fact that

Suzannah was resting, the dark smudges under her eyes already beginning to pale, was more important just now, Callie reminded herself.

Her gaze traveled back to the stranger. His eyes shifted to an icy blue, and she shivered as a tiny dimple at the corner of his mouth caught her attention. She was suddenly undecided about the way he looked.

"Callie?" Suzannah's hands cradled her abdomen tenderly, as if rocking a baby bird to sleep.

Callie scooted toward the head of the bed, aware the gap between her and the mysterious man had closed to inches.

She reached out to hold Suzannah's hand. "I am here."

"So. . .good," Suzannah murmured before her head rolled to one side and she fell asleep.

Callie turned a questioning look his way. She could only hope her expression did not betray the awe she felt for him. He said nothing if it did. He only smiled, a smile that said he was a traveler, a drifter, a man no one would tie down.

"She will be all right." His words filled Callie with the tiniest ray of hope.

It seemed unreasonable, this urge she felt to trust him. She didn't know him. How many times must she remind herself of that? If he was a Magicworker, he would be gone tomorrow, taking with him his knowledge and all the other wonders he had in his bag. Which would leave her here, in the eastern part of what some called "O-he-yo," with no help for Suzannah if this happened again. *If I can get my hands on some of his remedies, it will not matter if he does go,* Callie thought. *I must learn what I can before he disappears.*

"What did you give her?" she asked.

Faint laughter danced in his eyes. "Family secret," he drawled.

"You are not going to tell me?" She was not afraid, only curious, and she wondered why she felt so at ease with a man she didn't know.

He shook his head and a renegade swatch of hair fell across his forehead. He raked it back with his hand.

Callie crossed her arms in front of her. "Why not?"

"Man should never give away his secrets too easily."

"You have others?" She couldn't believe she had asked the question, but there it was, out in the open between them.

A shadow swept across his face. "Every man has things he does not reveal to just anyone." He glanced around the room and wrinkled his nose at the assortment of pouches she had left lying on the table.

"Oh," she said, her eyes tracking his gaze and seeing the piles identifying her attempts to help Suzannah. He just studied the scene, absorbing it, as if it told him everything he needed to know.

"I am not really trained in this sort of thing, you see. . . ." she started. He faced her, his jaw tightening as he peered from under dark brows. "But I am the only one we have here who. . .oh, never mind. You do not want to know that."

"Go on. I will listen," he said patiently.

Callie gritted her teeth then went on. "Helping Hands was our local medicine woman. She decided to go back to Pennsylvania, and before she did, I made her tell me whatever she could. It was not enough," she finished in a rush as tears sprang to her eyes. She couldn't help but remember how she had failed nine months ago.

"I see." He turned back to Suzannah.

Callie had other questions she wanted to ask, but her mouth refused to utter them. Why were his boots so dusty? Why were his eyes so blue? How had he happened to find the settlement they had established?

"Life is full of questions, is it not?" He unfolded his legs in front of him and leaned back in the chair.

Callie glanced at Suzannah and was about to deny she had been thinking of asking anything, when he cocked his head toward her friend.

"She will give birth early. Twins."

Air spilled from Callie's lungs and she choked back a gasp. She recovered her composure quickly. "Yes, she did," she said coolly. "Nine months ago. Little girls. We lost them."

He frowned and shook his head then pointed to the bulge of Suzannah's abdomen. "She is carrying twins now."

Callie had suspected the same thing, but had not told anyone. How did *he* know? She pressed her lips into a thin line.

"You knew, did you not?" he probed.

She could only nod and hope he didn't press her for more information.

"One of them. . ." He pressed his thumb and forefinger to the bridge of his nose, and when he did, his tattered shirtsleeve fell back, revealing a bloodred scar running down his right forearm.

Callie wondered about the injury; it made him seem even more mysterious. But she squared her shoulders and forced the question aside. "What?" Her jaw quivered. "What about one of them?"

"Not now," he mouthed.

He hadn't shut the door all the way, and cool mid-April air penetrated the room. Callie pulled her shawl tighter around her shoulders. She thought about shutting the door but didn't move.

"Shall we pray?" His hand covered hers without permission. It was a rider's hand—strong, callused, but gentle. His words echoed not only in her head but in her heart.

"Dear Lord, we commend this woman and her unborn children into Your care. We ask that You watch over them, protect them, hold them in Your hands."

Relief flashed through Callie. He was not a Magicworker, then; they didn't believe in God. At least she didn't think they did. His strong tenor floated around her. She could feel herself relaxing.

If they hadn't been praying, she would have jumped up and jerked away from him. After all, she was responsible for Suzannah's health, not him! Besides not knowing what he had given Suzannah, Callie had no idea who he was! She stiffened.

Seemingly in response, he brought the prayer to a close and released her hand. Then he crossed his legs and placed his hands, fingers entwined, on top of his right knee. Callie watched, torn between wanting to ask him to leave and wanting to know about what he had done to help Suzannah.

"Amen," he whispered, drawing her back to reality.

Callie repeated the word. She moistened her lips. Silence fell between them. In the background, Suzannah's even breathing rose and fell. A gentle breeze slipped in through the still-open door. It swirled around Callie's feet, lifting the hem of her long gray skirt.

"Survival belongs to the fit," he said seriously, his brows narrowing, becoming two slashes of brown.

What did he mean by that? She was worn out from sitting, and pacing, and hoping, and from praying that Suzannah's pains would stop.

She motioned toward her friend. "How did you know what to do?"

He leaned forward slightly. "Family—"

"Secret," she interrupted, feeling a tiny thrill of excitement that she could joke with him so easily.

He winked, long-lashed lids momentarily concealing the blue depths from her.

She let out a long breath.

"Someday. . ." His voice faded.

"Someday what?" she challenged. Why did she feel she must banter with him?

"You will see."

She hoped she appeared unruffled. "What if I do not want to see?"

An easy smile played at the corners of his mouth. The dimple she had seen earlier grew deeper. "You will," he promised.

Callie had no doubt she would. But what exactly was it she would see?

Chapter 2

Joshua watched as Callie busied herself cleaning up the table. The dreary gray dress had a bit of tea-colored lace around the neckline. Sleeves added a touch of lightness to her attire, and her slender frame was accented by an apron tied tightly around her waist. But what held his attention were her eyes, newborn fawn in hue, and no less mesmerizing now than he had found them before. They revealed every emotion Callie felt, whether she wanted them to or not.

As if she sensed him scrutinizing her, Callie wiped her hands on her apron and moved to stand at the foot of Suzannah's bed. She gazed at him for a moment before bluntly asking where he was from.

"Pennsylvania," he replied, giving up only as much as he judged safe for the moment. It hurt, not being able to reveal everything, but intuitively he sensed that doing so would ruin any chance he had with her.

Her eyebrows arched in surprise, and if the knock had not come at the door at that moment, Joshua knew she would have said she was from there also. Instead, she raced to fling the plank door open wide. A wiry, rumpled man gave Joshua a cursory glance then raced to the bedside and knelt by the woman. Out of the corner of his eye, Joshua caught Callie grabbing a bonnet from the peg and tying the strings beneath her chin before she leaned against the wall.

The emotional—the physical and mental stress of traveling across Indian territory and not knowing what he would find—had drained Joshua. He asked himself for the thousandth time if he had done the right thing—coming here, slipping through a break in the mission fence, and listening as Callie stood outside the cabin conversing with this man who now knelt by the pregnant woman. Watching. Waiting. Until he heard the woman inside cry out and knew instinctively he could help.

Mentally, Joshua berated himself. This was no time for questioning his decision. Coming here was the only thing he *could* do. He had planned this for five years, praying fervently all that time that Callie would take one look at him and remember who he was.

✍

Callie could remember how many times she had looked at him—the "stranger," as she had begun to think of him. The muscles of his jaw formed lines tears would follow, if he ever allowed them to fall; but somehow he didn't give the appearance of being soft and sensitive. Yet his powerful body moved gracefully, every movement calculated and smooth. There was a smattering of freckles across the bridge of his nose, apparently caused by being too long in the sun.

Now, he disappeared into the early evening darkness toward David Zeisberger's cabin, where she had insisted he go to properly introduce himself to the elder. Watching him leave, she was possessed by a strange urge to call him back and demand explanations. No, she wouldn't do it. She was not going to give him the satisfaction of knowing she was curious. So she had no answers.

Callie glanced over to the table where Suzannah's husband, Abe, sat. He had been in his work clothes since early this morning, and his clay-brown hair carried creases where he had run his fingers through it the last time. When she had admitted Abe to the cabin, he barely noticed the outsider as he crossed the room, sat beside his wife, and began to pray over and over, "Please, God, not again."

The same petition had echoed deep in Callie's soul as well. She had been called to the cabin that morning, fearing the worst and hoping she was wrong. The worst didn't happen, but not due to anything she had done. She shook her head to rid herself of her dark thoughts then cleared her throat. The sound apparently startled Abe, for he stretched and looked across the room at her.

"How can you be sure she will be all right?" He gazed at his wife. Asleep, Suzannah looked like a delicate flower that might fall apart in a strong wind. Cinnamon hair lay in soft curls around her neck, contrasting with her pale face.

How could she explain what she didn't know herself? But Abe was not asking about the babies, and that allowed her to speak with a confidence she didn't feel. "I am sure," she stated, averting her eyes.

Abe sighed. "Where did that fellow come from, anyway? He did not come through the mission entrance."

"No?" She had guessed Abe had directed the stranger to the Solomon home. Uneasily, Callie began to wonder about the wisdom of her decision not to challenge the man.

Abe rubbed his hands together. "No. Pretty sure about that. I was sitting out there—keeping myself occupied, you know?"

Callie knew very well what Abe meant. The last time they had been through this, Abe had sat on the same tree stump. That memory reminded her she needed to tell Abe about the twins Suzannah now carried, but Callie kept thinking of two patches of brown dirt and the words the stranger had murmured, *"One of them. . ."*

Callie wiped at her eyes, unable to find a way to say something that would cause Abe more grief than any man deserved to bear.

"You do not have to stay if you are tired," Abe admonished. He pushed away from the table before bending over and hanging his hands between his knees. "I can come get you if she gets worse."

"I will be fine." Callie looked at Suzannah, who lay with a hand across her brow. "Besides, you need rest, too. Brother David said he would put you up for the night. Why do you not go on over there?"

Brother David Zeisberger had the largest cabin in the mission. A two-story building, it had been built with extra rooms upstairs for the many friends who came from time to time. Inviting one of their own to spend the night was one way of taking care of the flock.

Abe raised his head. "I would rather be here."

Callie couldn't blame him. When he left earlier, his whole world had been falling apart. *I am sure he can scarcely believe Suzannah is not losing the baby,* Callie thought. She corrected herself: *twins.*

"He never said who he was, did he?" Abe looked at her intently.

"No, he did not," Callie confessed, wondering if that sounded as strange to Abe as it did to her. Why hadn't she asked his name? On top of that, why had she allowed a stranger to treat Suzannah, of all people? What had she been thinking? To hide her frustration, Callie moved to check on Suzannah. As she positioned herself to listen for Suzannah's breathing, a lingering bitter odor from the medicine used earlier rose up to greet her. The smell made no sense, but there was no time to explore why.

Abe paced the floor for a while then turned to face her. "What did he do?"

There was a hint of disbelief in his voice, and it caused Callie to pause momentarily. She checked Suzannah's pulse. Slow and steady, unlike her own. *How do I know it was him? How do I know what I had already done did not have something to do with it?* But she knew Abe was aware of what had happened the last time Suzannah had been entrusted to Callie's care. The memory caught in the back of her throat.

"He called it a family secret," she finally admitted.

"I am glad she is safe. . .but, a family secret, Callie? And you do not know what he used?"

Callie straightened Suzannah's bedding and ran a hand across her forehead. "Suzannah is fine now." She returned to sit at the table and noticed the candle was almost burned out. She lit another, and the haze of beeswax filled the air as the flame danced and caught.

Across the room, Suzannah stirred then pushed up on one arm. "Callie?" she called in a trembling voice.

Callie raced to the woman's side, with Abe close on her heels. "What is it?" She dreaded what she might hear.

"Pain. Again." Suzannah bit her lip, and Callie saw her own tears reflected back in Suzannah's amber eyes.

It was unkind, but Callie's first thought was that the stranger had not solved the problem after all.

✍

Joshua knocked at the door that had been pointed out to him when he left the Solomon home. It was late evening now, his favorite time of day. Soon the nighttime owls' calls would replace the sound of rain crows, and the moon would illuminate the trees.

Through the yellowed paper covering a window, the blurry silhouette of a man could be seen. Joshua knew he had found the man he sought. It had been five years since he'd had any contact with anyone in the settlement, and he was not sure how his appearance would be received.

David Zeisberger opened the door carrying a handmade candle that cast eerie shadows on the wooden frame and drew attention to the smudges under his somber gray eyes.

"Joshua! Is it really you?" David studied him as if he did not believe what he saw. "Of course it is," he continued. "No other man would dare travel so far alone! And who else would arrive at this hour?"

Joshua smiled. "I am glad you remember me, Brother David."

"You are a man not likely to be forgotten," David replied. "Except by her. . ." he added quietly as he drew Joshua into the cabin.

Joshua looked around, absorbing the room David called home. It was small but neatly kept. A spindly legged table sat in the middle, surrounded by four chairs made in the same rough style. A wooden bowl filled with porridge was surrounded by eating utensils, and the aroma of baked bread hung in the air. A handwoven throw rug lay under a sturdy shelf Joshua identified immediately as the elder's work space. A scattering of papers covered the top—notes and sermons David planned to speak from in the future.

"It is good to see you!" David's words were heavy with German heritage. "But you did not come here to visit with me, did you?" He filled mugs and offered one to Joshua.

Joshua took a seat at the plank table where David motioned. "You are right of course. I guess you could say memories could not keep me away any longer," Joshua responded, feeling the familiar twinge of regret that always accompanied the word.

"I see." David settled into his chair and sipped at his coffee. Steam wafted up, disappearing just before it reached his chin.

"My family lost everything. We couldn't keep any of the orphans. I thank God daily that you happened to be in Philadelphia during the flood. If you had not been, who knows what would have happened to them. . . ." Joshua drew a deep breath as regret once again pressed against his heart.

Am I doing the right thing? The thought slipped into his mind, forcing him to contemplate what had already happened. He had expected her to dispute his right to walk into the home and tend to the woman. After all, her quizzical expression had revealed that she had no idea who he was, and several times she had looked as if she thought to do just that. Each time she had said nothing, letting her silent gaze speak for itself.

David's eyes flashed with curiosity, and his comment was more statement than question. "You have come to stay, then."

Joshua drained the cup, which had cooled while he and David spoke. "If you do not think my presence here will be disruptive, that is my hope."

"We would have to find something for you to do."

"Do not forget that after the disaster I spent some time in medical school." Joshua closed his eyes, remembering. "I did not quite finish the entire course, but I will help any way I can. If there is nothing here for me, I will. . ."

His words faded into nothing. To find, after traveling so far, that Calliope did not remember him would be the end of all he hoped for. In his youth he had been impatient. He did not seem to have learned much patience since then.

Embers snapped in the fireplace behind him and Joshua glanced into the flames. Would the dream he had nurtured for years die when she discovered who he was? No, life would be a bitter battle if that were so. He had trusted in God to keep her safe and God had answered that prayer. Joshua had found her. But how could he tell her he had come to keep the promise she had given shortly before the flood? His good intentions had been swept away when he'd entered the cabin a few hours earlier and she'd had no obvious reaction to him.

"Finding work is not the problem," David said, interrupting Joshua's reverie. Joshua glanced to the slight-statured man who always seemed to have the time and capacity to answer any question he had ever asked. "I do not brag when I say leading a group of Indian followers is not an easy thing to do. We were fortunate to leave Pennsylvania and the pressure of white settlements, where people suspected I was forming some sort of Indian revolt."

"How many accompanied you here?" Joshua asked.

"Five families last spring. A hundred more people joined us last fall, taxing our meager stores throughout the winter." David waved a hand in the air. "But that is not the point of our discussion. We were talking about finding work for you, were we not?"

Joshua nodded.

"We are not exempt from illness. But it would mean—"

"I would have contact with Calliope," Joshua interjected. "Is that what you are afraid of?"

The corners of David's eyes flared. "Calliope? I had forgotten that was her name before. . ." David straightened his shoulders and folded his arms in front of his chest. "How did you find her? We left no trail that I know of."

Joshua noticed David had not asked how he had found *them*. Just her.

"Martin Mack." Joshua had run into Martin when the missionary made a fortuitous trip to Philadelphia. David and Martin had worked for years converting Delaware Indians, and anyone else they could, to Christ before David had led his group away from developing hostilities.

"Did he know what you really were looking for?" David asked pointedly.

Joshua was hurt that David would think he had hidden the truth.

"Do you think I would lie to him?"

"Forgive me. I did not mean to imply you had." David gave Joshua a half-smile. "It is just. . .having you suddenly show up. . .I am not sure what it will do to her."

"She has already seen me." He explained the situation with the Solomon woman and his attempts to help her. Joshua shifted against the wooden slats of the chair, which suddenly seemed hard and uncomfortable. "And she did not remember who I was. Does that make it any easier?"

Callie sipped the remains of a cup of tea she had brewed. She propped her elbows on the table and watched as the dull light outside the window began to brighten. Bread crumbs lay on the tabletop, and she swept them into a pile. Suzannah was asleep again. Abe paced back and forth; his worried steps making soft crunching sounds on the straw-covered dirt floor.

Hours ago it had all seemed so hopeless, Suzannah panting and crying in pain, twisting her arms around her distended abdomen as if she could arrest the delivery. Now, Suzannah's face was calm; and though her springy curls lay limp against her forehead, she showed no signs of discomfort. Whatever the stranger had given Suzannah had worked. But for how long? Callie wondered. And what would happen if he left and she had none of the medicine he had used?

She couldn't let him go without bargaining for some of his potions, Callie decided. She would do whatever it took to present her friend with two beautiful living infants to replace the ones Suzannah had lost.

"Since she is resting, I am going home, then to service," Callie said softly. "I will return after that." She glanced at Suzannah one more time to assure herself the crisis was over.

Abe's eyes followed hers. "All right."

Strolling down the path, Callie recalled how the stranger had marched into the cabin as if he had a right to be there.

The sounds of awakening children carried through the walls of the log cabins sprinkled about the hilltop where the mission stood, and she pictured the children rising and racing outside to play before eating. Interspersed among the sturdy cabins were simpler, temporary structures built of saplings and bark laced together. Callie and Sarah were fortunate to have one of the finished homes that had ended up being too small for families, and it was toward this structure that she was heading.

"Morning." A deep rumble jolted her from her thoughts.

"Good morning," she replied automatically, though the resonance of his voice sent her pulse racing. She put a hand up to shield her eyes from the early morning sunlight. He hadn't gone! Hope rose within her as she realized she still had the opportunity to ask him to leave some of the medicine that had helped Suzannah behind when he left.

"The woman?" His voice had turned flat, with no trace of the compassion he had shown last night.

"Sleeping. And her name is Suzannah." Callie didn't know why, but she wanted him to call the woman by her name.

"No problems?"

Callie thought back to what she had done shortly after he left. "Not really," she hedged.

He inhaled sharply. "She needed another dose, then?"

Callie paused then answered. "Yes. She did."

He rested his hands on his hips while he looked at some distant point. "Powerful medicine should be used sparingly."

Callie paled. If she had done anything she shouldn't have, she would never forgive herself. "Did I hurt her?"

"I would not have left it if it could cause harm." He reached out to touch her arm in what she assumed was a gesture of friendship. Friendship or no, his touch was warm, and tingles surged through her. She struggled to look calmly up into those magnificent blue eyes.

"I did not get a chance to ask last night. . . ." she began. "Who are you?"

He left his hand on her arm while his gaze swept the length of her plain dress, stopped at her wrinkled apron, then traveled on to the worn moccasins on her feet.

I should be insulted by his scrutiny, Callie thought distractedly. But she wasn't. She had the eerie feeling she knew him, but that was impossible, wasn't it? If she had met him during the last five years, she would have remembered. A shadow covered her heart. *What about the years before that?*

He was staring at her shoes, and Callie remembered the moccasins she had thrown on in haste yesterday morning. He pointed to them. "Your shoes?"

"I made them." She wondered why he was so interested in her footwear. The moccasins were soft and supple and worn by nearly everyone at the mission. "It is just something I learned from the Delawares," she said, as if it did not take weeks of hard work to make a pair just the right size.

He lowered the saddlebag from his shoulder to the ground, and she watched as his eyes roamed over the settlement. A small smile flirted with his mouth as he watched some children tossing sticks into a pile near the clearing.

"Did you introduce yourself to Brother David?" she asked. If he had, she would run over there and find out. She could not call him Magicworker to his face.

"Aye-ya."

No, she told herself, she was twenty-three. She would not run to Brother David. "Who did you tell him you were, then?"

Morning sun highlighted a patch of gleaming black hair and brought out his ruddy complexion. "Joshua."

She stared. "That is it? Just Joshua?"

"Just Joshua." A grin crinkled his lips.

"I suppose the rest is a family secret, too?"

"Could be," he drawled.

He was enjoying dragging this on, she realized. She wasn't. This family secret business was becoming frustrating. But she did like talking with him, liked the way he cut his sentences short as if there were better things in life to move on to.

Move on! There was that thought again that he might leave. Why did it dismay her so? *It is because of what he knows about medicine,* she told herself.

He chuckled suddenly. "No. There is more. It is Johnston."

"What?" She was so convinced he was leaving that the name had thrown her off balance.

"Last name is Johnston."

"Oh. Your name. I thought you meant that is where you are going." Callie posed a finger under her chin. "Joshua Johnston." She liked the way the words rolled off her tongue. She reminded herself that she should be on her way home to wash up and change then off to church, before returning to Suzannah.

"Going to check on Suzannah," Joshua said, withdrawing his hand from her arm. The spot he had been touching grew cold.

Callie stepped back. "Me? No. I am on my way home."

They stood quietly for a moment, and under his scrutiny she lost track of her thoughts.

"No. Me. That is where *I* am going," he said.

Callie could not resist smiling a little. It seemed to amuse him.

"Good thoughts?"

"Only that I hope Suzannah will be all right," she assured him. "What did you mean when you said, 'one of them?'"

"She will." Joshua said it so softly she had to lean forward to hear him. "Sometimes a double birth is difficult, as you indicated had already happened."

"I hope so."

"Your name?" He held a finger in front of his lips.

A look of confusion drew her brows together.

"Going to work with you, so might as well know your name," he quipped in a way that said he did not care if he learned it or not.

She crossed her arms in front of her. Should she tell him? She knew his name, and a fine one it was.

"Callie Troyer. And what do you mean work with me?"

He was leaving, wasn't he? That's what men of his sort did. They floated in and drifted out, leaving only a memory and gradual healing behind. Why did the thought of him going seem so depressing?

"Your elder asked me to stay."

Callie swallowed hard. Brother David, staunch Christian and Moravian missionary, had asked him to stay? What did Brother David know that she didn't? Did he expect an epidemic? Or worse, did he not trust her to care for the settlers anymore?

There is an advantage, she told herself. If he stays, then she would have access to his medicine, and that would help Suzannah and anyone else who might come down with an illness she couldn't handle.

She frowned, motioned down the path. "You know where the Solomon cabin is. Her husband is with her," she snapped.

"Where a man should be when his wife is in danger," Joshua said.

"You do not think that is strange?" Most men had little to do with their wives when illness or childbirth happened.

"Absolutely not."

"You should be going, then. To check on Suzannah, I mean." She stepped back to indicate she was finished.

"On my way." He picked up the saddlebag and slung it over his shoulder. "And Callie?"

"Yes?" she replied, telling herself she should not look so eager.

"Have you not remembered me yet?"

Chapter 3

Callie squinted into the sun to explore his face. "Remember you? I surely do not think so." Yet, inside her ran a tremor of hope. If he knew her. . .

His brows narrowed, drawing the small lines around his eyes tighter. His jaw was covered by a light dusting of beard that she hadn't noticed last night. Beneath the work shirt he wore, his shoulders looked a yard wide.

Not sure what to say, she added, "I do not recall ever meeting you." She spoke evenly, hiding the thread of excitement that ran through her. She would definitely have remembered him if she had ever met him.

"I thought not." Joshua shifted the bag on his shoulder.

"But I should?"

He nodded, a brief dip of his head that caused a tuft of hair to escape from beneath the brim of his hat. He took off the hat and tossed his head to return the lock to its rightful place. The movement was simple, yet sunlight caught and danced in his eyes.

"From where?"

"Pennsylvania."

A giant hand squeezed her chest. "I did live there—once. Before. . .well, before I joined up with the Moravians."

He stared at her as if he expected her to continue. She didn't.

"So did I," he admitted, settling the slouch hat on the back of his head at a jaunty angle that she thought framed his face nicely.

"I think perhaps you have confused me with someone else." She laughed. It felt so easy to talk with him. And he was a traveler, someone who would leave soon. Surely she could risk a few minutes of joy with someone she would not see ever again once he was gone.

Joshua's eyes held her prisoner. "No. I have the right person. You lived in an orphanage, right?"

"Yes," she muttered. "But that was five years ago. Since then I have traveled and lived with Brother David and his flock."

Joshua crossed his arms in front of him. "I know when you joined them."

There was pain in his words and she wondered why something like that would cause him so much hurt. She looked nervously around the mission. "You knew Brother David then, before this morning?"

He nodded. "I helped after the flood."

"The flood." Callie sighed and shook her head. "I do not recall much about that part of my life—only what my sister Sarah remembers. Since she is younger than I, she is not much help." She didn't remember anything from before that, either, but Joshua didn't need to know that.

"I figured as much." He stepped toward her.

Tendrils of worry stirred in the pit of her stomach. She turned to a safer topic. "I have heard the west end of Philadelphia was swept away."

He set his lips in a grim line. "It was terrible. No warning. Heavy rains. People were lost. We saved those we could."

A shadow veiled his consistently warm eyes. Something had hurt him in the flood—Callie sensed it instinctively. Not wanting to drag up memories she didn't possess but he obviously did, she offered, "It must have been quite a shock."

"You could say that." He turned away, leaving her feeling as if she had touched on a sensitive area that she should have stayed away from.

"If there is nothing else, I must go." She started walking toward her home then turned around abruptly. "Oh! I have not said a proper thank-you for what you did for Suzannah last night."

"That is not necessary. It is what I have been trained to do." His words were strained. Why did everything she said make him uneasy?

"Callie!" Sarah rushed toward them, her strawberry-blond braid flopping up and down as she ran. A smile curved Callie's lips in welcome as she momentarily forgot about Joshua.

Sarah was sixteen—gangly, awkward, and likely to say whatever crossed her mind. But knowing she could have lost Sarah made Callie love her that much more. As Sarah came to a stop, Callie reached out and patted her cheek.

"I want you to meet someone who once lived in Pennsylvania, Sarah," she began, turning to introduce her sister to Joshua.

But he was gone, half the settlement away, and knocking on the Solomon cabin door. Callie felt as if she were watching the scene from far off and gave Sarah a weak half-smile. "Guess he was in a hurry," she said. "You will have to meet him later."

Sarah gazed at the handsome figure he cut, his head coming almost to the top of the doorframe. "I will make it a point to. He looks mighty good from this distance."

Callie held up a hand, but Sarah rushed on. "Do not bother to chastise me for thinking that. By the light in your eyes, your thoughts are exactly the same."

"Why, I never!" Callie exclaimed, though a red tinge of a blush filled her cheeks.

"Have you been at the Solomons' all night?" Sarah asked, changing the subject. "Is Suzannah all right? Is there a baby?"

Callie straightened Sarah's braid. "One at a time," she said gently. "I was just on my way home to tell you. She will be fine. No baby yet. Which is a good thing, I might add."

"No baby? What did you use? Last time you said you did not have anything to make her pains stop."

Callie's stomach curled into a tight knot. "Actually, he gave her something to make her sleep." She rubbed her arms, which suddenly felt as if she had been swimming in an icy river.

Sarah kicked at a pebble and her head bobbed as she watched the stone hop across the grass. "Levi came looking for you a few minutes ago."

Callie stiffened, the knot in her stomach growing even larger. "I thought the hunters were not due back for another week?"

Sarah shrugged. "Got back early." She grinned. "Says he has

something important to ask you."

Two days' worth of tiredness washed over Callie. "No rumors, Sarah. I am not marrying him."

Sarah smiled dreamily. "He thinks you are. And is it not about time you settled down?"

Yes, it probably was about time she settled down. Most women her age had been married for five or six years, but Callie could not see spending the rest of her life with Levi. There was nothing specifically wrong with him. He was Suzannah's brother and could outhunt any of the Delawares in their mission. However, hunting was not high on her list of requirements for a mate.

Her thoughts stopped as quickly as they had begun. She had no right to categorize what she wanted in a husband. God put man here first then added woman to walk with him. She should be thankful Levi seemed to care about her, especially since others in her life had found her relatively easy to cast off.

"How about breakfast?" she queried to change the subject.

"Already ate," Sarah said. "You going to church?"

"As soon as I clean up."

"I told Levi he would probably find you there." Sarah giggled as she hurried away.

Callie clasped her hands in front of her and stared at them. Levi Lyons was back. He had something important to ask her. She knew what that would be. Why did the thought scare her so?

Marriage was a blending of souls, a merging of dreams. It was having someone beside you through good and bad. Someone who cared about you, someone who believed in God, and you, and made you more than you ever thought you could be by yourself. The problem with Levi Lyons was that he did not do those things for her.

She wanted a love like Suzannah and Abe had. A love that knew no bounds, encouraged hope, and made tomorrow seem like an exciting promise instead of just another day. And there again, Levi did not measure up.

Perhaps there is something wrong with me, Callie mused. Maybe, in the end, it was best she not fall in love. Even though it meant she would be alone, at least she would not have to face carrying a child for nine months only to lose it.

Joshua's rugged profile haunted her and she tried again to remember him. The attempt was fruitless, but she vowed that the next time she saw him, she would demand he tell her more about what he apparently knew. A colt whinnied, and Callie walked across the path and stroked his mane.

"Hey, fellow," she said to the bay whose head reached almost to her shoulder. "You hungry?" The colt tossed his head and Callie chuckled at his seemingly human response.

People were moving about, headed toward the meeting house for the morning service. She forced her feet to carry her home to the sparsely furnished cabin she and Sarah shared. Home to eat, to change clothes, to put on something a little more respectable than this worn-out, dingy gray dress.

✍

The morning service lasted long enough for a few hymns and a short sermon. Most Moravian congregations were separated into "choirs," which consisted of groups of single men, single women, widows, widowers, and married couples. The Delawares refused to be separated from their families in such a manner, so they were allowed to scatter as they wished throughout the building.

Callie arrived at the meeting house as Brother David strode in a back door. Sliding onto a bench in the back, she glanced around the building that was the first permanent structure always built at a Moravian mission.

Love, sweat, and laughter enabled the settlers to assemble the logs that became a thirty-six-by-forty-foot worship center. No windows were included in the design, and candles positioned down the walls every five feet provided soft golden light by which the settlers prayed, worshipped, and had fellowship.

The sleek dark heads of the Delaware Indians, called "Praying Indians" by some, filled the seats ahead of her, their broken English mingling with their native language. Almost a year had passed since she had traveled with Brother David and his flock to establish the settlement they called Schoenbrunn. The name meant "Beautiful Springs," and Callie was not alone in thinking it perfect.

Deep in the wilderness where a bear roamed occasionally and wolves howled at night, Schoenbrunn Mission sat on top of a rolling plain with a roaming river not far away. Grace was abundant here, for the mission thrived on loving Jesus and the freedom to do so.

Callie admired the way the whole village worked to overcome obstacles and concentrate on the positive. No one talked about it, especially the Delawares, but danger lurked. East and north of them, the French and British were hoarding land and running out natives who had lived there for generations. Even though the Moravians had located miles from white pioneers who Brother David said would keep pushing farther west until they ran out of land, it worried Callie that they might not be safe even here.

Several of the children she worked with in Sunday lessons smiled at her, and their broad-faced grins affirmed for her that they were doing the right thing. They didn't seem to mind that she was one of few whites living here. Nor did it matter that they had only known her for five years.

At the front of the room, Brother David raised his arms and bent his head. His coat fell open to reveal a gray vest over a white shirt and knee-high moccasins. "Shall we pray?"

Callie bowed her head while the elder thanked God for His blessings, Jesus for His sacrifice, and the congregation for their belief in God's grace. She added her own plea that Suzannah carry the twins closer to term before giving birth.

Her thoughts of Suzannah were pushed aside by Brother David's enthusiastic "Amen".

She raised her head and readied her mind to concentrate on the elder's message. When she looked at David, she caught sight of Joshua in the front row. He looked peaceful and rested, which annoyed her. Having spent most of the night with Suzannah as she had, she had expected him to look tired. And hadn't he been traveling yesterday? She knew he must have been, yet he didn't look worn out at all.

Levi Lyons slid into the seat beside her, and her thoughts retreated. Levi liked to do things that were shocking to most, and today was no exception. He gave her a broad smile as he stretched out a hand to squeeze her shoulder briefly. Remembering how Joshua had covered her hand before he prayed last night, she compared Levi's hand to Joshua's. Levi's hands could aim at a deer with surety or skin a beaver with confidence, but when he moved his hand away and let it drop across his thigh, Callie was relieved.

"Sorry I am late," he whispered. "I overslept." His curly red hair fell in disarray over his ears and his eyes were blurry with sleep.

"I am glad you are back," she acknowledged and turned to the front of the room.

Levi leaned toward her to say something, but Callie discreetly pointed to Brother David, who was just beginning to speak about the need for forgiveness. Levi seemed uneasy. He shifted and squirmed in his seat until the elder was finished. Callie didn't think it was because he was uncomfortable with the elder's message. More likely, he was getting up the courage to ask her that "important question."

The last words of praise faded into the rafters and a rare smile played on Brother David's face as he approached the stranger sitting in the front row.

"I would like everyone to meet the newest member of our settlement," he began.

Joshua stretched to his full height and faced the congregation. Every move he made seemed calculated to get the most from his energy. With his buckskin coat slung over one shoulder and that slouch hat dangling from one hand, Joshua commanded respect. The blurry image of a memory tugged at Callie but shifted just out of focus. She twisted her hands together.

"This is Joshua Johnston," Brother David said excitedly. "He will be staying, and I have invited him to use his medical training to assist Callie." David's gaze moved through the crowd until he found Callie. "We know what a difficult time she has keeping one hundred sixty people well," he added.

Several heads bobbed in agreement, but darkness engulfed Callie. She felt the beginnings of discomfort at Joshua's appearance. He had asked if she remembered him. Did that have something to do with him coming here?

The elder continued, his rich baritone echoing around the room, drawing her away from her thoughts about Joshua's intentions.

"Joshua seeks to aid us in our quest for health and happiness. Some of you will call him a Magicworker, but what he brings to Schoenbrunn is God's healing. I know you will welcome him," he finished, motioning to Joshua that it was his turn to speak.

Callie had no trouble envisioning Joshua curing sickness; he had already stopped Suzannah's babies from coming too soon. He did not, however, appear to be a man who would settle for simply helping her. She wished she knew more about him.

Joshua addressed the room, and the majority of the settlers pressed forward to welcome him. Levi took advantage of the momentary confusion to escort her outside. He grabbed her arm a little too abruptly for her liking, but she followed since the meeting house hardly seemed the place to make a scene.

"Does Brother David think you do not know what you are doing?" Levi grumbled. "I do not like the way that fellow looks."

"I do not see anything wrong with him. There are times when I do need help."

Her dress stuck to her back, where beads of perspiration had formed, and she glanced longingly toward one of the lush shade trees that lined the mission.

"You have never complained before." Levi's voice rose a notch.

"You mark my words. He will be trouble."

"Mr. Johnston will be a fine addition to our mission," Callie stated calmly. "Should we not let him prove himself before we begin belittling him?"

"What do you mean by that?" There definitely was displeasure in Levi's voice now.

When he started courting her, she would let him have his say. But after a time, a pocket of confidence formed deep inside her.

"He stopped your sister's childbirth last night," she informed him, successfully hiding her irritation that the stranger had been able to do so when she had not.

Levi's eyes widened.

"You did not know, did you?"

"No," he growled. "I got back late. After. . .not going to lose. . ." He turned away.

Hiding tears? Callie didn't think so. Nothing appeared to touch Levi's heart. He had dug the graves for his angelic nieces nine months ago without emotion, while she watched, unable to hold in her own sorrow.

"Suzannah is fine now." She regretted not stopping to think that he might not yet have heard. Levi mumbled something then sped in the direction of his sister's home.

Callie sighed. She spotted her sister ahead of her on the path, and she hurried to catch up with her. Callie reminded Sarah that she needed to finish the leggings she had been working on. She assured Callie that she would head home right away to do so. Hearing that, Callie turned her steps toward the Solomons' cabin, hoping Levi had already left there.

With morning in full bloom, the sun kissed the treetops and the roosters had fallen silent. In the clearing where future log homes would be built, men who had hurried from the service spoke animatedly with one another.

Callie loved being outside, where blue jays darted back and forth, the rush of the river could be heard in the near distance, and where the world seemed as right as in the Garden of Eden. She undid the ties that held her bonnet under her chin and let them trail across her shoulders as she walked the remainder of the way to Suzannah's.

☙

Joshua sipped from his cup, swirling the remains at the bottom. After checking on Suzannah and shaking hands with those in the meeting house who welcomed him, he had returned to the elder's for the morning meal.

Though he had been in the home earlier, he had missed noticing the front of the house actually had two small rooms: one for eating and one for sleeping. An archway opened onto a back room, where a door led outside to a covered walkway connected to the meeting house.

Joshua glanced at the man who was like a father to him. He wanted—no, he needed—the elder's support as Joshua attempted to free himself from the demons that had chased him for what seemed like decades. Their previous conversation had only given him a place to stay and a job to do.

"You do not think I have made a wise decision by coming here, do you?" Joshua tried to keep his voice respectful.

David opened his arms in a questioning gesture. "I think I know what you are trying to do," he began. "And I will admit that I am uncomfortable with it."

Joshua struggled past the knot forming in his throat. "I asked Calliope this morning if she had remembered me yet. Do you know what she did?"

Despite the loyalty he had for the man who had shown him Jesus, Joshua's gaze sought the security of his coffee mug. For a moment he glimpsed the Calliope he remembered lying on the ground, a piece of a quilt tucked under her chin and blond curls plastered against a deathly pale face.

The dark liquid in the cup reminded him of her eyes so long

ago—empty, blank, containing nothing of what the two of them had shared. *Just like last night in the Solomon home,* he thought. *She does not recognize me.* The realization scared him. His mouth grew dry. What if she never did?

"She is Callie now," David gently reminded. "What did she say?" He leaned forward, his brow pulling his gray eyes tighter together.

Joshua pushed away the last image he carried of a younger Calliope. David was right. She was Callie. She had survived. That should be enough, but it wasn't.

"She looked at me without any emotion on her face whatsoever." Joshua swallowed hard, his Adam's apple rising then falling. "How could she not remember?"

A silent, masculine tear brushed the edge of his eye. He ignored it.

David pushed an unruly tuft of hair behind one ear. "How long do you think it will be before you tell her the truth?"

"I do not plan to come right out and tell her," Joshua insisted. "I came to see if she had survived."

So many times he had thought about that night. The screaming, the crashing, the loss. He was committed now. Until he put it behind him, one way or another, there would be no sense of closure, no loosening of the bonds that tied him to this woman everyone here called Callie.

David's expression lightened. "I believe you. And if it is of any help, you are not in this alone. But how long do you plan to stay? When will enough time have elapsed?"

He knew David had spent years planning, shaping, and forging new dreams, but time meant nothing to him anymore.

"When she remembers me, then I will deal with the rest." Did the words have to drag his heart out with them?

David leaned back, slowly shaking his head from side to side. "She will not be easy to convince."

Joshua's voice thickened. "I know." He felt drained, his entire being saturated with exhaustion. "But I will do it. It is the only thing

I can give her that means anything anymore."

David's fingers tapped reverently on his Bible. "It is a good thing you are a praying man, for you will need to walk with God now as never before."

"You once told me faith made all things possible, David. Does it not apply to this situation also?" Joshua covered his brow with one hand.

"Hebrews eleven," David said. "'Faith is the substance of things hoped for, the evidence of things not seen.'" He stopped talking for a minute. "Faith makes things possible, Joshua. It does not make them easy."

Joshua snapped his head up. "If love were easy, it would not be worth having."

Chapter 4

Sarah looked across the room as Callie entered the cabin and deposited some logs by the door. While the days warmed quickly, the nights held a chill that could only be chased away by a fire. "Well? What did you find out?"

"He is from Pennsylvania," Callie muttered as she dropped onto the edge of a chair. She had just come from a meeting with Brother David and Joshua. "In fact, he lived at the same orphanage we did."

Why did it sound so unbelievable, even though she'd repeated it at least a hundred times to herself?

"The same orphanage!" Sarah slipped into a seat across from her sister, settling the folds of her long skirt neatly on her lap. "That is exciting, Callie!"

Callie struggled to remain calm while recalling the visit. She had been summoned to Brother David's and had gone thinking he wanted to discuss the illnesses sweeping through the mission. Joshua had been waiting when she arrived.

Despite every bit of common sense that told her she should pay no attention to him, Callie thought Joshua looked quite noble. The fire drew out auburn highlights in the thick dark locks that hung splendidly over his ears. He sat casually in a chair, his legs stretched out to their tremendous length in front of him.

As she listened to Brother David tell her he expected her to give Joshua her full support, Callie remembered Levi's reaction when he returned from the hunt and found Joshua would be working alongside her. Levi had certainly been displeased but wouldn't explain why. Sometimes she didn't understand Levi, more so lately than ever before. Why had he warned her to stay away from Joshua?

Callie sighed. The way things were, she would never know. Levi would think it disgusting if she challenged him to explain.

"I would not call it exciting, Sarah. I would call it. . ." What would she call it? Confusing? Worrisome? Why had Brother David asked Joshua to assist her? It was quickly becoming a muddle, and she saw no way to solve it.

"I cannot wait to tell MaryBeth!" Sarah pulled a bonnet out of an apron pocket and smoothed it into place over her curls.

"No, Sarah." Callie's voice turned brittle. "This is not something you are to talk about." Why was she warning her sister? What was there about Joshua that made her so skittish?

"But I have got to share this with her," Sarah whined. "I would think you would be delighted that someone has shown up who knew you before the flood. I have never been much help, since they kept me on a separate floor, but this," Sarah clapped her hands excitedly, "is what you have always wanted. Is it not?"

"I used to think so." Callie drew a deep breath. "Now I am not so sure. That is why I do not want you to speak of it to anyone just yet." She looked pleadingly into her sister's eyes, whose color reminded her of tanned buckskin. "Do as I ask. Please?"

A look of disappointment flitted across Sarah's round face. "I will not tell MaryBeth. Or anyone else."

Callie eyed Sarah closely. "Promise?"

Sarah nodded, her long braid bobbing as she did. "God's promise. That is better than just a plain promise."

So it was, Callie thought. People might fail, but God's covenants stood fast. At least *that* she could depend on.

"I have one question though." Sarah's voice dropped to a whisper. "What?"

"Do you remember him at all? This Mr. Johnston, I mean."

Callie shook her head, trying to dispel the image of Joshua in Suzannah's cabin that had just erupted there.

"I am not sure I want to. It is all rather confusing just now."

Sarah looked away. "It will all work out for the best. Isn't that what you always tell me?"

"Yes," Callie agreed. "I just wish I knew his real reason for coming here."

Why was she questioning his motives? Since arriving, he had taken part in both morning and evening services. Brother David had announced this morning that Joshua would preach the Sunday sermon. He was her brother in Christ, but something about him stirred uneasy feelings deep inside.

"Why do you not simply ask him?"

Sarah's question intruded in her thoughts. "That would hardly be proper. Do you not remember a woman's place in the world? We are to be seen, not heard. Whatever his reason, he will choose when he can reveal it. It is not my place to pry." She threw Sarah a warning glance. "Nor is it yours."

Sarah raised her hands, palms out. "I am going to see MaryBeth. I will not talk about *him*. Do not worry about the noon meal. I will eat with her."

"Fine," Callie replied. She would use the time to rearrange the herbs and roots in her bag before she went to sit with Suzannah.

With Sarah gone, Callie laid out her meager herb collection. Fragrant aromas drifted up as she arranged and checked the contents of each of the small deerskin pouches. Concentrating on the array of cures Helping Hands had insisted Callie memorize before the Delaware woman left the mission, she didn't hear the knock at the door. As the door swung open, it scraped against the frame, and Callie snapped her head toward it.

It was Levi. His work shirt was stained, his normally curly red hair thick with sweat and bits of tree bark. He bluntly canvassed the inside of the cabin, which took about four seconds since it was only two small rooms.

"Are you going to ask me in?"

Callie brushed her hands together to remove traces of the herbs. "You can see Sarah is gone. It is more proper that we sit under the tree."

In the time it took to walk outside, she took stock of him. No one could say Levi Lyons didn't do his share to help Schoenbrunn survive. Not only did he help clear land, he went along on hunts for game that would provide them with food and furs. Since the last hunt, something had changed him. Levi no longer seemed the courteous man he had been before.

He motioned toward a gnarled root that grew aboveground. Callie lowered slowly into place and smoothed out her skirt. Levi squatted next to her, rubbing his neck.

"Has your workload lightened since the healer came to stay?" He sounded perturbed.

"He has only been here a few days. That is hardly enough to make a large difference." She brushed at a faint sheen of perspiration that dotted her forehead.

"You need to relax, Callie. Take some time and go on a picnic with me." Levi leaned over and trailed his fingers lightly along her forearm.

His touch was familiar, and it was widely accepted that they would be wed. But Callie had never been comfortable with outward displays of affection and shifted out of his reach.

"I do not know," she argued. "There is so much to do, and it never seems to end. I should stay close in case something happens to Suzannah again."

What would she do if her friend, Levi's sister, threatened to miscarry again?

Levi sneered. "I am sure the mysterious Joshua can handle any crisis that crops up."

He leaned toward her. He had been burning brush, and the acrid smell of woodsmoke clung to his shirt. She wrinkled her nose.

"I am sure he could," she answered hastily. "But that does not mean I can forget my responsibilities."

Levi's glare sent a chill up her backbone. "Do not do it, Callie," he said sharply. "Do not push me away. We have always been able to talk before. Why have you changed?"

Callie had no choice but to look at him. His green eyes seemed to bore into hers. "I am not the one who has changed, and I am not avoiding you, Levi," she insisted. "Running back and forth between houses takes a lot out of me."

Levi pressed his lips together. At the base of his neck, his pulse jumped. "I do not like it. I want to see you, spend time with you."

"That is almost impossible as long as there are people who get sick. You know that."

Levi's shadow shielded her from the sun peeking through a tangle of tree branches. He said *she* had changed. Didn't he realize it was he who was acting so strangely?

"Then we will have to find a way to make it possible, will we not?" His tone matched the tight set to his jaw.

Callie curled her fingers around the root by her side. "I will try to make some time tomorrow," she bargained. "Perhaps Sarah can sit with the Killbuck boy."

"His mother can do it. Is that not what mothers are for?" He walked a few steps away, his hands balled into tight fists at his sides.

Callie was annoyed at the way he suddenly thought she should drop everything and rush away with him.

"Besides the fact that she has been up with him almost constantly, helping out around here is my duty." She paused. She had known Levi ever since she came to live with the Moravians, and he had never acted like this. What was bothering him?

She kept her gaze locked with his. "What happened on your last hunt, Levi?"

Levi drew back. The sun sculpted the tight muscles of his neck and illuminated the shallow circles around his eyes. "What happens on a hunt is not a woman's concern." He glanced toward the clearing, where a man was shouting and waving at him. "There will be a picnic, Callie. Just you and me."

The danger she heard in his tone shocked her. But Levi was stamping away, long, angry steps putting a distance between them that she did not understand or want to explore at that moment.

Behind the meeting house a tangle of brambles began where a small clearing ended. Squirrels and other chattering animals frolicked among the branches overhead. Brother David and Joshua sat on an old piece of buckskin that had been laid out in the late April sun.

David stretched his legs out in front of him. His coat was open, revealing a brown vest over a white shirt. "You were surprised by Callie's question this morning, were you not?"

"Stunned is more like it," Joshua confided. "It is so painful to look at her and remember. . ." He swallowed the rest of his comment. David knew the depth of his pain. There was no need to elaborate.

"Not only God works in mysterious ways." David twirled a blade of grass around his finger. "Sometimes the mind does also."

The brim of Joshua's slouch hat slipped toward his eyebrows. He pushed it back. "Are you saying she may never remember everything about us? That cannot be true! Why would God do that to me?"

"God has His reasons, Joshua. I do not have to remind you of that. It has been hard on her not remembering her life before the flood."

"And you think it was easy for me to let her go? To not know what was happening to her for five years!"

David placed a hand on Joshua's arm. "If you want what is best for her, you may have to do more than face that fact. You may have to let her go."

Joshua watched a hawk sail overhead. He had never thought about the possibility his Calliope might be lost to him forever. "I will not leave here until it is clear there is no hope she will ever remember what we had."

Bittersweet words, but he would never hold a woman to a promise she could not recall. Fear wrapped a hand around his heart. Why had he left her in the first place? If he had stayed with her and forgone the medical training his father had insisted he receive, this might not be happening now.

He had never been one to stand up to his parents, and he wondered if the relationship he had with them would have been ruined had he done so then.

David rubbed his forehead as if he was searching for the correct words. "Even if it means you live out the rest of your life here?"

"If that is what it takes, then I am willing to wait." Joshua rose. Thinking about how long it might take to win Calliope back frightened him. Surely, he thought, if he were patient and made daily contact with her, she would eventually remember. Wouldn't she?

Patience had never characterized Joshua. Sure, he had waited five years to search for Calliope, but most of that time was spent helping his parents and then attending medical school in Philadelphia. How long would it be before he said something to her he would regret?

⚭

Callie watched Sarah put a loaf of fresh-baked bread on the table to cool. A pot of thin corn soup bubbled in a kettle over the fireplace. The yeasty smell, mixed with the seasonings in the kettle, started a small rumble in her stomach. With so much happening to Suzannah and those who were ill, she realized she had not eaten much in recent days.

"Did you take a nap?" Sarah asked. She had come home from MaryBeth's to find Callie lying on her bed and had left her sister alone while she prepared the evening meal, for once without being prodded to do so.

"No. Levi came by and we talked for a while." Callie said the words quietly, not mentioning his appearance.

"He wants to marry you! I knew it!" Sarah squeezed her hands together in front of her.

"Do not start planning a wedding," Callie warned. The words stuck in her throat like musty bread.

Sarah absently pushed a clump of straw on the floor with the toe of her shoe. "Why do you not like him?" she asked. "He seems very nice to me."

"Love does not come just because someone is nice." Callie smiled apologetically at her sister. "I am sorry; I should not have barked at you. I just meant that love takes time to grow, to develop into something that will last forever."

She felt strange defining love. As an orphan, love came in the simple servings of soup and sometimes potatoes she had gotten for meals. Being a relatively new Christian, love meant trusting in God's grace and Jesus' sacrifice. But love between two people? She knew next to nothing about that aspect of life, despite Sarah's insistence that Levi was destined to be her mate.

"Can we not talk about Levi right now? There are too many other things on my mind."

Sarah stirred the soup. "How is Storm?" She gave her sister an encouraging smile.

"No better. His mother keeps asking when he will be able to get up and play. What am I supposed to tell her?"

Callie had spoken the question aloud without meaning to. She had hoped to spare Sarah the devastating news that she didn't think three-year-old Storm would survive the high fever he'd had for a day.

Sarah crossed the room, paying no attention to the wooden ladle she had let fall into the soup. She took Callie's hand in her own and turned it back and forth a few times before patting it.

"You can tell me the truth. You are afraid we are going to lose him, are you not?"

Callie fought the tears forming in her eyes. She was supposed to be the strong one. When had Sarah become so perceptive? She had never paid much attention to what went on around her before.

"Whatever happens is God's will."

Sarah dropped into the chair beside Callie's. "Sometimes I do not understand this God we worship," she said. "He took our parents away and tore our family apart, but you insist He loves us. How can you say that, Callie?"

Callie's shoulders hurt and her legs were tired, but she met her sister's gaze squarely. "Because God is love, Sarah. It is not our place to question why He works the way He does."

"I think He could go a little easier on us sometimes."

"He has His reasons."

Callie didn't understand why she could remember only the past five years of her life, and she didn't know why Joshua had shown up now, but she was determined to trust God to reveal the answers at the right time.

Sarah sniffed the air. "Soup is ready."

Callie chuckled. "It does not smell like you have burned it this time."

Sarah rolled her eyes toward the ceiling. "You will never let me forget that, will you?"

"One thing is sure," Callie said with a straight face. "If you do not improve your skills, your future husband may starve."

After a shared chuckle, they sipped the thin broth that would be much better once the vegetables in the garden began to produce.

Chapter 5

"Will it help?" Kukara Killbuck, Storm's mother, asked between sobs.

Callie waited breathlessly for Joshua's response. The depth of pain in Kukara's eyes made Callie wish she had summoned him sooner to treat little Storm. The boy's life now hung in the balance because of her pride.

Her heart staggered in her chest. How could she have done this? She thought back over the last four days. Storm's fever had risen steadily, no matter what she tried. When she finally realized her treatment was not helping, she called on Joshua. He had given Storm a potion, and they waited now for signs that the medicine was helping.

"We shall see," Joshua offered. His solemn tones underlined the seriousness of the situation.

Callie looked at him, willing him to understand how sorry she was. He glanced at her, but the familiar spark in his eyes that she had begun to look forward to was missing.

She watched Kukara's hand as the slender woman caressed her son's face. Her face was strained, and worry lines etched deep grooves around the edges of her almond-shaped eyes.

How did women endure it? Giving birth and thinking of the hundreds of things that could go wrong? Knowing the small babe you held in your arms might never grow to adulthood? The thoughts unsettled Callie.

Forcing herself not to concentrate on the depressing situation in her midst, Callie tried to find a substitute. Her eyes flitted around the cabin, searching for something familiar. What she found was Joshua staring at her. She would have given almost anything to know what he was thinking.

His face was carved stone, his jaw clenched and his brows drawn together. Then, as if he couldn't look at her any longer, he turned away and watched Storm's chest rise in deep, rasping breaths.

Joshua had grimaced at his first sight of the ill young boy, and Callie had withdrawn into a corner of the cabin rather than face him. She knew he must be disgusted that she had let the child suffer for so long.

"You must do something," Kukara wailed. "He is my only child!"

The agony in her words jolted Callie. What if Storm didn't make it? Panic stirred in her soul. Why hadn't she acted sooner? Would God call her to task when she stood her judgment day? What would she have to say for herself: "I am so sorry I worried more about what Joshua Johnston thought of me than I did about the boy's illness"? No, she didn't think God would approve of that excuse.

"He is doing all he can," Callie heard herself say, despite feeling that her eternity was now condemned to something other than heaven.

Kukara's glance skittered between Joshua and Callie. "There must be more!" She threw a hand against her lips, and the rest of her wail disappeared into her palm.

"Storm is in God's hands now," Joshua admitted.

Kukara grabbed Joshua's elbow. "You are Healer." Tears ran down her cheeks and formed splotches on her deerskin garment. "Save him."

"Kukara." Joshua shook his head. "It is God who can save Storm, not me." He dipped a rag in water and laid it on the boy's forehead, his fingers pressing lightly against the fevered brow.

Callie moved to stand behind Kukara and placed a comforting hand on her shoulder. This was so difficult. *Please, God,* she prayed silently. *Help me say the right thing.*

"We must trust in God," she began, "and in His will." She had tried to sound compassionate, but the grating sound of her voice hung in the air.

"His will takes too long! I want answers now!" Kukara threw

herself across her son's limp body, her cries muffled by the thin blanket covering him.

"God's grace comes when He decrees." Joshua backed away from the bed and stood by the wall, but nothing in his manner indicated scorn or discouragement as he leaned against the logs. "Nothing we do, except prayer, will change that. I must leave; there are others I must tend to." He settled his hat on his head and picked up the saddlebag he carried everywhere.

Callie swallowed a lump of disbelief. He was leaving! How could he, when Storm might be about to die!

Kukara lurched away from her son and clutched at Joshua's sleeve. "You not leave now. You stay with Storm."

Callie held her breath. What would he do? What would she do without him?

He laid a hand over Kukara's. "I will be back after I check on the others. Would you have them go without treatment?" He looked straight into the night-brown eyes of Kukara. "The medicine is working. Listen."

Callie did. Storm's breathing did seem less labored than it had been earlier. His face was still pasty though. She knew the worst was not over.

"You stay," Kukara repeated. She slipped away and pulled a small pouch from under a wooden crate. "If you go, I use this." She raised her hand and shook the container. Keeping one eye on Joshua, she withdrew a handful of dirt and moved toward her son, where she slowly raised her hand above the boy's head.

"Do not!" Callie and Joshua spoke together, their eyes meeting then breaking away to return to Kukara. Tears streamed down the woman's cheeks, creating tracks on her bronzed skin.

"I must give back to Earth-Mother what Earth-Mother gave to me." Kukara's voice held a strand of courage as ancient as the Indian heritage she came from.

Joshua clenched his jaw. Sprinkling dirt on the boy was Kukara's way of committing his soul back to the earth. She was giving up, something he would not let her do.

"We must allow God to do His work," he began as he moved slowly toward her.

Callie noticed how calm he appeared, and silently gave him high marks for his ability to remain unruffled. She certainly was having a hard time maintaining any semblance of control.

Kukara chewed her bottom lip while her hand edged out to hover over her son's chest.

Joshua's sharp glance at Callie stunned her. Was he pleading silently for her to help? She struggled to keep her emotions in check as she tried to figure out what she could do. She hesitated too long. Joshua moved his gaze back to Kukara.

"Have you been doing this all along?" he asked. David had mentioned to him that upon conversion to Christianity, the Delawares had promised to give up their tribal ceremonies and beliefs. He didn't like it, but he could understand how, when faced with tragedy, some might turn back to the comforting traditions they had dismissed.

Kukara appeared torn between wanting to answer him truthfully and giving him the answer she thought he wanted to hear. Though one hand bravely hovered above her son's chest, the other was wrapped tightly in a band of fringe that traveled the length of her long buckskin dress.

"Callie knew," she murmured.

Oh my, Callie thought. There would be no avoiding Joshua now. She cringed as Joshua jerked his head around to peer at her.

"Is that true?" he demanded. "You are supposed to encourage these people in their new life. How could you allow something like this?"

Her eyes grew tearful at his criticism. Somehow, she had expected him to remain distanced from anything that happened. The fact he had not was disturbing, but she could not put her finger on the reason why.

"I. . .I did not think. . .it would hurt." She had thought she was encouraging Kukara. Yes, the woman had threatened before to return to her old beliefs, but Callie had never taken her seriously. And what did Joshua know of reaching within himself and finding resources he did not know he had to help others?

"You did not think. . ." Joshua blurted. As quickly as he had allowed his irritation to show, he closed his eyes and rolled his head heavenward. "Pray with me."

Callie was grateful for the interruption. At least it meant his accusing eyes were not piercing her. She dropped her head without checking to see what Kukara had done. Joshua's solemn tones filled the room, slowing Callie's heart rate and forcing her to concentrate on something other than the small boy on the cot.

When the prayer ended, Callie did feel calmer, but she saw Kukara's hand shaking as the dirt drifted out in a tiny stream on Storm's chest. Had the woman not been listening to anything Joshua had just said?

An ominous silence filled the cabin. Joshua reached out and gently guided Kukara's trembling hand toward the pouch he now held. Indecision seemed to filter through her eyes. Then, slowly, her hand turned over and dirt sifted from her palm into the pouch.

Joshua smiled cautiously. "Put it away, and promise me you will not use it again."

Callie could see Kukara struggling with his request. His large fingers spanned the woman's shoulders easily, and she watched as he focused solely on Kukara. Some monumental bond of trust appeared to spring between them. Kukara nodded.

Storm whimpered and Callie raced to him, trying to still her own quivering shoulders. She bent over the boy, running her hand across his brow and pushing the tangled mass of thick black hair back off his forehead.

The thump behind her startled her, and she swung her head around to find Kukara collapsed on the floor.

⟡

Callie watched Joshua carry Kukara to the other bed across the room. It was strange seeing him take care of people who had been her patients. She waited until he backed away, then moved to do what she could. She dipped a cloth in water and wiped the day-old tears from Kukara's face, keeping a safe distance from Joshua. For some reason, she had to concentrate extra hard on the task at hand.

"She will come around," Joshua said over her shoulder.

She hadn't heard him approach, but she gathered her scattered wits and nodded her acknowledgment. "What about Storm?"

"Trust in God."

His voice echoed in the cabin's utter stillness. Icy fear twisted her heart as she recalled he had said the same thing to Kukara earlier. "Then you do not have the answers to every crisis we have here?"

Since she was not looking directly at him, she felt confident in her ability to question him. One look into his lake-deep eyes and she would have forgotten anything but how he had dashed to her rescue— or rather, Storm's rescue, she reprimanded herself.

"I have answers, Callie. But not to the questions you are asking. Only God has those." His eyes narrowed and he touched a finger to the brim of his hat.

She knew he expected her to pursue the conversation, but she didn't feel up to it. "How long have you believed in God?"

"Five years," he replied.

Five years! She would have been eighteen, newly homeless, being cared for by compassionate Moravians, and just discovering she had no memory of her life before the flood.

"You?" His voice dropped to a soothing level and she understood why so many villagers were enamored of him. He was easy to talk to and seemed genuinely eager to listen.

"About the same," she mumbled. Not too long after Callie was taken in by the Moravians, Brother David and some of the women had spent several weeks in in-depth Bible study with her and Sarah. When faced with the overwhelming evidence of what Jesus had done for her, Callie had readily agreed to baptism. Sarah had, too, but much later.

So why did the length of her life as a Christian concern him?

He smiled. "Then we share that in common."

"What does it matter what we share in common?" She motioned to Storm. "He may not live through the day, and Kukara's exhausted. How can you talk about something as trivial as what we have in common?"

"Because our belief in God is not trivial. It is a vital part of our lives." Joshua motioned around the cabin. "Or do you not truly believe?" The hard edge to his voice was unmistakable.

Callie squared her shoulders. "How dare you question my faith. God will never fail me, unlike others who. . .who. . . never mind."

Darkness crossed Joshua's face and she wondered what she had said that caused him to react so. But more important were her own emotions. She might not recall the actual event, but the pain of knowing she had been abandoned was not something she had been able to put behind her. She didn't think she ever would.

"Not everyone betrays a trust intentionally." Joshua studied a section of chinking in the wall that had come loose. "You must have someone on whom you can depend?"

"God is sufficient."

He laid a hand over his heart. "Then I pray that brings you peace. Perhaps someday we can discuss this further." There was a challenge in his voice she could not ignore.

"I am at peace," she assured him.

"Good. I would not be able to stand it if you were not."

Exactly what did he mean by that? Callie started to ask, but he removed his hat and with the fingers of one hand pushed his long wavy hair toward the back of his head. "I am going now," he said. "Call out if you need me. Otherwise, I will check on the boy this evening."

She watched the door in disbelief. He really had gone. When that fact had sunk into her scrambled brain, she swallowed the agony growing inside and turned her mind to Kukara. The woman was now awake and questioning again what would happen to her only child.

It took great strength, but Callie assured her there was nothing else they could do for Storm but pray.

"I will stay with you," she promised.

As time wore on, they talked about Pennsylvania and about how Kukara missed the family she left behind. Callie knew the woman's nervous chatter diverted her mind from worry, so she let Kukara prattle, content to listen with one ear while musing over her conversation with Joshua.

Despite his apparent distaste of her handling of Storm's illness, perhaps he was not such a bad sort. He had responded quickly to her request to tend to Storm, and he had been gentle in his dealings with a distraught Kukara. So why, then, at times, did he seem so distant? He spoke to her, but it was never as if he talked *with* her. In the wilds, people relied upon one another for assistance, for survival. Did he not know that?

She decided Joshua Johnston would have to change his ways if he had any plans of remaining with the settlement, and she promptly turned her mind back to Kukara, who was in the middle of asking a question.

The beauty of the Pennsylvania hills was at stake. Callie countered with the idea that this "O-he-yo" land also had some lovely scenery. She had just promised to go on a long hike with Kukara, as soon as Storm was able, when someone pounded at the door.

For a moment her pulse raced as she thought it might be Joshua returning. But the gruff "Open up" could only belong to one person— Levi. Callie hesitated, weighing the consequences of letting him in with Kukara still lying on the bed.

"Company is always welcome," Kukara said, though Callie caught the break in her voice and wondered where the woman found the courage to pretend all was well.

She ignored the black cloud threatening to cover her heart as she pulled the heavy door open. Levi pushed past her into the cabin and cast a basket onto a spindly table before turning to glance around.

Three candles sat near each bed, but the light they gave off barely pushed back the darkness. As a result, his face was shaded, making it hard for her to see his expressions.

"What a surprise," Callie managed. "May I ask why you have come?" She sat on the edge of Kukara's bed.

Levi stood in front of the fireplace. The low flames behind him did not illuminate his face, but she sensed he was glaring. "Do you really have to ask? Is it not enough that I have taken the time to fix that?" He nodded toward the basket.

Callie swallowed her retort. This was not the Levi she knew. Her heart slipped into a frightening rhythm, and her hands dampened with sweat. "You apparently are not aware of the severity of Storm's illness," she said. Her gaze slipped cautiously to Storm as she tried to decide which of them needed her protection the most, Kukara or her son.

Levi's eyes narrowed into slits of fiery green as he glared at Storm. "He is sleeping." He pointed at Kukara. "And she looks well enough to handle anything that might crop up."

Behind her, Kukara had pulled herself into a sitting position. She was pale. Callie wanted to dispute Levi, but her own wits were slightly disoriented. She wished Joshua would come back. Now.

What am I thinking? she chided herself. *I do not need Joshua to fight my battles!*

Callie issued a silent prayer before she spoke. "She could become afflicted again at any moment," she insisted. "And Storm is sleeping because Joshua gave him a potion." Her heart quaked at the thought of a different kind of sleep that might overtake Storm if his fever did not break. Could Levi not sense at all what was so vivid in her own mind?

"Suits my plans." Levi started toward her. "If he is asleep, you will not have to worry about him."

He reached out and grabbed Callie's elbow. She tried to wrest her arm from his grasp, but he held tighter. Callused fingers pressed the material of her dress into her skin.

"I will thank you to let me go. Right now."

What was he planning to do? Didn't he remember Kukara and Storm? What if the child awoke and saw them struggling like this?

His grip tightened. "After our meal, you can do anything you like." He gave her a huge grin, as if the thought of being with him should be her only concern at the moment.

"You are saying that if I go with you, you will let me come back here?" She couldn't believe it could be that easy.

Without realizing it, she had allowed Levi to draw her to her feet. Her stomach churned and her knees wanted to collapse. But that would only serve to let Levi know how weak she felt. And she was not weak! She would handle this as well as she could handle most anything that came along.

"Of course, Callie. What kind of a man do you think I am?" He spoke softly, but cold amusement glittered in his eyes.

"Do not go, Callie," Kukara pleaded weakly.

It was not in her to abandon her patients; they meant too much to her. But if Callie could get Levi out of the cabin, he would be less likely to upset Kukara more than she already was. Which was better? Stand her ground and risk Levi running amok even more than he already had, which by the look in his eyes would not take much, or appease him and go along, hoping nothing would happen that she couldn't control?

Could she handle him if he began to rant and rave? His eyes were hard and dark, and the shadow of a beard he continually tried not to grow haunted his jawline.

She couldn't refuse him, not when his state of mind seemed so tremulous and her own pulse faltered at the idea he might do something horrible to Storm or Kukara. Her chest felt as if a grizzly had sunk his claws into it.

Maintaining a shaky semblance of control, she whispered to Kukara, "Storm is sleeping. You will be fine until I return."

"But. . ." Kukara's concern stretched between them as her gaze slipped to her son.

"He will sleep for a while yet." She issued a silent prayer, only to feel Levi tug on her arm.

"Now." His eyes searched hers, daring her to deny him.

Feeling her world collapse beneath her, she nodded acquiescence. Levi hid the smug look that flitted across his face as he grabbed the basket with one hand and ushered her to the door. Callie stepped off the distance, her heart dragging in her chest. The words to part of the Twenty-third Psalm echoed in her mind: *"Yea, though I walk through the valley of the shadow of death, I will fear no evil. . . ."*

I must trust in God. He will protect me. She took one last look at Kukara before Levi pulled the door closed between them.

⟋⟍

Joshua watched as Levi entered the Killbuck cabin. He didn't know Levi well. In fact, he had stayed entirely out of his way since their first meeting—when Levi had made it clear that he intended to wed Callie one day.

Thankfully, there were few at the mission who had been with Brother David in Philadelphia when the Moravians adopted Callie and her sister. So far, Joshua had been able to keep his background, and his earlier relationship with Callie, under wraps.

Joshua had tried to keep his feelings for Callie hidden, but he sensed Levi had figured out there was, or had been, something between them. Joshua didn't like being at odds with anyone and hoped to find a way to ease the tension between Levi and himself.

Telling himself that Levi would hardly dare to cause trouble now with others present, Joshua put the young man out of his mind. It was useless to worry about a situation that he couldn't control. "Give it to God, son," Brother David would say. "He knows what is best."

Lifting his eyes skyward, he passed off this burden to his heavenly Father and then turned toward home. "Home" was a building set aside for storing extra supplies, but it would do until more cabins were built or until he decided it was time to leave.

Upon reaching the small building, Joshua sat down on the doorstep and attempted to sort out what he should do about Callie. He had been able to deter her from any further questions about Philadelphia, but he sensed it was only a matter of time before she became curious enough to want to know more. After all, if he were in her position, he would be anxious to learn of his life before his loss of memory.

His thoughts turned to the green valleys and rugged mountains he had traversed to find the Moravians, and he was surprised when he heard Brother David's rumbling voice.

"You have no work today?" The elder stretched out a hand in welcome, hitching one hand under a set of suspenders he wore.

"Plenty of it, in fact," Joshua replied. He rose and took the other's hand. "I am only resting until I begin my next round." He spoke calmly, yet his eyes drifted toward the Killbuck home.

"Do you find the work what you expected?" David asked as he settled himself on a tree stump left from clearing the land for the cabins.

"This is what I was meant to do," Joshua affirmed. "Taking care of sickness, chasing death away from the door." While that might be true, there were moments when he knew he would have given it all up if Callie had come through the flood without losing her memory. His desire would have been to be married as swiftly as possible and to go about creating little laughing Johnstons—children he would have taught to love God first, then others, then family. His eyes burned at the thought.

"I have heard good comments from your patients."

"I am glad they are satisfied." Joshua thought of Storm, who might not live. There was nothing else he could do. Did Callie know that? What would happen if they lost the boy? She would blame herself, and he didn't know how anyone could convince her that it was not her fault.

"Joshua? You seem miles away from here. Are you regretting

having left Pennsylvania? Perhaps you are not happy with the position you have here?"

Joshua cleared his throat and framed his reply carefully. "I suppose I am the sort who is never satisfied with what I attempt."

Joshua caught movement near the front door of the Killbuck cabin. Callie and Levi. "That is strange," he commented, watching as the couple headed to the fence line across the path from the cabin they had just left.

He told David what had transpired at the cabin and about the condition of Storm when he had left the child just minutes earlier.

David's eyes drifted toward the couple and followed them. "I do not think Callie would leave had she not had a good reason," he assured Joshua. "She is very cautious, that one."

"Yes, well, perhaps I will go check for myself." Joshua could not push away the finger of doubt that nudged his heart.

From everything he had seen, Callie was dedicated. Why, then, had she apparently deserted her charges? It made no sense. But neither did the man racing across the mission, waving and shouting at Joshua.

Both Joshua and David jerked to their feet just as Abe reached them. His face was white and his breath came in labored gasps. "Suzannah. Time."

Chapter 6

The seven-foot-high log fence surrounding the mission seemed little protection to Callie as she and Levi walked along beside it. The hewn wood gave off a sticky-sweet smell, and nettles grabbed at the hem of her skirt. Overhead, clouds covered the sun. The usual bird sounds were missing, lending the day a depressing air that matched her disposition.

Callie and Levi had made it almost to the far end of the fence, where it disappeared into the woods, before she dared ask where they were going.

"The spring." He was walking behind her or, rather, pushing her ahead of him. His hand gripped her elbow with brute strength, and his voice seemed to blast away at her with the sureness of an expert hunter's aim.

She leveled her shuddering shoulders and forced herself to take a deep breath. She had feared he would take her somewhere else, like toward the river, where people seldom ventured. At least the spring was visited frequently. And though she would be embarrassed if someone discovered them there, embarrassment was secondary to safety—she wanted them to be found.

She was upset at the way Levi barged into the cabin and demanded that she accompany him, but doing as he asked had seemed the lesser of two evils at the time. But now that she was here. . .

At that moment, Levi slid into place beside her, and she gave him a quick sideways glance. His green eyes were darker than normal, his red hair more unruly than she had ever seen it. His jaw was clenched, and the lines around his eyes seemed more apparent than ever. A muscle jumped along the side of his neck.

Callie had heard talk among the men at the mission about the French and British soldiers and what they were likely to do if they continued to press westward in search of more land and more furs. She had grown to dislike those who might uproot what she had been striving to attain: freedom and peace.

With Levi holding her arm as if he did not trust her, the same feeling stormed her heart. Peace and freedom seemed like butterflies that had escaped their cocoons and forgotten to land somewhere. Regardless of all she had been taught about a woman's place in the world, no man had the right to treat a woman like this!

"Quit dragging your feet," Levi admonished her as she attempted to summon the courage to question him.

"I did not realize I was," she muttered in apology, not caring how insincere she sounded. The look in his eyes made it clear that to disobey would place her in even more jeopardy.

Levi peered at her from beneath uneven brows, looking like a hawk ready to swoop upon some hapless field mouse. She tried not to stare at the angry slash of his lips, for they only frightened her more.

"You were," he snapped.

I must go along with him, she told herself. She knew he was the sort that liked to be in charge, to have everything his own way.

"Then I will walk faster." She hoped this would pacify him and checked to see his reaction.

The whites of his eyes flared as if he suspected she was ready to bolt. Callie wondered if she had said the wrong thing. The last time she had seen him like this had been when an albino deer hide he had brought back on a hunt had been ruined. He had spent a week ranting about the carelessness of the young Delaware Levi had entrusted with helping him preserve the skin. Despite Brother David's interference, the young boy had been devastated by Levi's reaction and now stayed as far away from him as possible. Levi did not allow anyone to speak of it now, preferring that the episode be forgotten.

The dreary thought crossed her mind that this might be a similar incident, one she might have to work at forgetting. Callie recalled the hate showing on his face during the first few days after the hide had been ruined. She had no wish to see Levi repeat the horrible lack of common sense he had exhibited then. For that reason, she renewed her silent vow to do whatever she could to please him.

He stepped up the pace and she stumbled, her shorter legs no match for Levi's long, powerful ones. He just clutched her arm tighter, as if he thought it might encourage her to be more obedient.

Distaste settled in her mouth as they neared the glen. At first glance, it appeared to be a perfect spot for a couple to enjoy time together. It was heavily shaded, and some of the trees dipped their branches into the stream as it coursed over a rock shelf in a pleasant waterfall. In a pond at the bottom of the waterfall, water babbled over rounded stones the settlers called "river biscuits."

"We are here." Levi's announcement was unnecessary.

Callie's knees weakened at the peril she heard in his voice. She tried to move out of his grasp and settle onto a boulder, but before she could, Levi grabbed both arms and spun her around. He stared into her eyes then drew her against his chest.

His breath escaped his mouth in hot, short blasts, while he held her with terrifying force. Her ability to breathe seemed lost somewhere between her head and her lungs. She wanted to push him away, but his arms clutched her close.

Callie closed her eyes. If she didn't look, it wasn't happening. She had never been in this position. It was not allowed of those who were unmarried.

Levi relaxed his crushing hold but did not free her. His hands encircled her slender forearms like the chains she had once seen on slaves destined for a Southern plantation.

"Please. Do not." She was embarrassed that she had to plead, but if it would break the spell he seemed to be under, she would do anything.

Levi's chuckle drifted across her cheek. "I am not going to hurt you. I just need to talk with you."

"Good," she whispered.

He draped one arm casually across her shoulder and pursed his lips while staring down into her eyes.

Regardless of how quickly he had composed himself, Callie didn't trust him. She wanted to be away from him, back at the mission where there were good, proper men like Brother David and Joshua. Her mind bounced around trying to form a plan.

Eat. Escape. Head home.

Perhaps she should scream and hope someone heard? But who would? The spring was a good half-mile from the western edge of Schoenbrunn. No one but Kukara even knew she had left the mission.

Levi released her without warning and she stumbled back a step. Indignant at his treatment, Callie recovered her balance and tilted her chin up, jamming her hands on her hips as she did.

"You have made a mistake, Levi." Her chest heaved with exertion, pain, and mistrust. Once those words were out of her mouth, she felt slightly more assured that she might be able to control what was happening. If she could keep him off balance, perhaps he would forget what he intended.

"Mistake?" He appeared confused as he lowered his head toward his chest, but he kept his eyes locked with hers. "I do not think so," he jeered, but his arm fell away from her shoulder.

The lessening of the bond between them freed her. "I do," she stormed uncharacteristically. "You are treating me as if I am a common bed jumper, like. . .like those women we met on the way from Pennsylvania."

The thought of those disgusting women made her physically sick. Ever since his family joined the Moravians, three and a half years earlier, Levi had claimed to be a God-fearing Christian. But the look in his eyes and the way he had drawn her to his chest made her wonder if perhaps she really didn't know him after all. How strong had his faith been on that trip a year ago?

Levi shoved a hand through his riotous curls and reached out toward her cheek. She swallowed hard.

"I know you are not one of those, Callie. You are uncommon. Can you not see I need to speak with you?"

She felt as if someone were pushing her over a cliff and she had no way to keep from falling. He loved her. No! Love was not supposed to happen like this. Love was soft and quiet, strong and gentle, not pushy and blustering.

Fury built inside her. She repressed it. One of them had to maintain control emotionally. It must be her, since Levi did not appear to be thinking straight.

"You have a strange way of getting my attention," she protested. Even the few steps she put between them did not lessen the feeling that he was squeezing the very life out of her.

"You are so busy taking care of the sick, what else could I do?" A little-boy-lost look softened his features.

A momentary surge of sorrow for him surprised her. Then she recalled how he had treated her—barging into the home of her patients and sweeping her away.

"You did not have to force me." Her voice carried throughout the glen. She wished someone would find them, despite the fact that there would be gossip later. Anything was preferable to standing here looking at his eyes of flint.

"You are right." He kicked at a rock and watched it scamper into the brush.

She was relieved he might have come to his senses, that escape might be within reach. A sense of determination pressed her next words from her. "You act as if I am a trinket to play with," she began before stopping abruptly.

How far could she go and not upset him? Strangely, she didn't care. She wanted him to understand she was not someone he could push around at his whims.

"I am a human being, Levi. I have feelings. I have dreams. What you did was not proper." She hugged her arms around her waist. She had never felt so desolate.

In the distance, a mockingbird called out to its mate. Levi moved away from her and threw a hand across his brow. The basket lay on the ground between them. When he had dropped it, a loaf of bread had fallen out. A sparrow flitted around as if trying to decide whether or not to land and attempt to eat it.

Callie watched the bird instead of glaring at Levi. Here she was, struggling to hold her temper and to get away from Levi, while one of God's creatures was taking time out to find its next meal. If what was happening to her was not so momentous, she would break into demented laughter. Perhaps she would anyway and see how he reacted. The thought soothed her jangling nerves.

"Survival belongs to the fit," Joshua had told her that first night when she had known only enough to call him "Magicworker." Where was he now? Tending to the sick while she was here, fighting to survive. Callie was overcome by the desire to rant at Joshua for leaving her alone in the cabin without making sure she was safe. No, she told herself sharply, her safety was no concern of Joshua's, no matter how often her mind turned to him lately.

Levi took a step toward her, his arms stretched out in front of him menacingly. Her breath rasped in the back of her throat. A thousand different images flashed through her mind. She saw herself fleeing without facing the threat, turning tail and running as fast as she could. How many times in the last few years had she allowed the relationship between them to progress against her will? And where had that passiveness gotten her?

Callie kept a wary eye on every movement Levi made while she considered what to do next. She had to make him see what he was doing, not just because she was furious with him for acting so foolishly, but because she needed to make sure she could stand up to him and survive. For all she knew, in the past she may have been as timid as a field mouse hiding from a night owl in search of its supper.

Callie decided at that moment that no man was going to tell her what she would or would not do. For if he did, she would lose the new self she had worked on becoming since the flood swept away her past.

She ground her teeth together and glared at him. She would not allow Levi to make her feel insignificant.

"Did you hear what I said?" she prodded.

Levi didn't answer right away. Instead, he straightened and looked as if he were considering how they had come to be standing here so at odds with each other. Confusion glittered in his eyes briefly then was replaced by something Callie could not define.

"I am not a trinket to play with," she repeated, more for her benefit than his. The words were a small comfort, coming as they did in such a meek tone.

She cleared her throat. Birds quarreled in the distance, forming an apt backdrop to what was going on here. The sun peeked through the heavy tree cover, warming her skin. The damp earth around the spring emitted a rank odor that wafted around her.

"I heard." His voice had changed. Gone was the malice she had heard earlier. Now there was gentleness and remorse. She could almost believe he was the old Levi she had known not long ago.

The Bible spoke of people doing strange things because evil had inhabited their bodies. Was it possible Levi's actions were directed by demons? No, she would not believe that. Levi alone was accountable for his behavior. And because he seemed so skittish, she must remain polite and courteous. Not to mention determined to find a way out of this without damaging her virtue, which she suddenly felt was what he intended.

"I will not mention this to anyone," she offered, her pulse pounding in her ears. There was no going back now.

Levi didn't answer for a moment. He took advantage of her discomfort to cross one ankle over the other and dig the toe of one boot into the ground. He stared at her as if seeing her for the first time. His expression clouded, and he pounded a clenched fist against the side of his leg.

"I am so sorry, Callie," he said heavily. He ran a hand through the too-long curls on the back of his neck. "I only wanted to talk to you. Will you forgive me?"

She glanced up at the clouds gathering in the sky; they now covered the sun. Shadows filled the glade and Callie's soul. She had known Levi long enough to know something was making him behave this way. But what?

She wanted to forgive him, wanted him to be the old Levi, but she also wanted him to know he could not treat a woman, or any human, in such a way.

It took an enormous effort for her to speak. "I will work on doing that, Levi." Her tone hardly conveyed earnestness. She watched him, sure he would advance toward her again.

When Levi did nothing but stare off into the trees, she blew a sharp breath between her teeth. What was he thinking? Was he planning how to retract everything he had done? She didn't know. But she did know one thing—she was going to get away.

Levi had crossed an invisible line in their relationship. There was no going back, no going forward, not for them. Callie glanced back only once as she pushed aside a branch to begin her trek. Despite a racing pulse, she refused to run. Running was a sign of weakness, and she was not weak. Nevertheless, she had to force her feet not to hurry.

❦

Inside the Solomon cabin, surrounded by a quilt damp with perspiration and tears, Suzannah sat upright, her hands wrapped around her abdomen. Joshua took one swift look at the woman and knew she had waited too long to send for his help. Regardless of what he had said to Callie two weeks ago, he was not sure either of the twins would survive. He calculated they were at least two months early. He had learned in medical training that single births sometimes had a chance at this stage, but a double birth? Very unlikely.

"Go get Callie." His command was intended to occupy Abe

without unduly upsetting him. He described where he had last seen her headed and sent the disconsolate man on his way.

"Make it stop!" Suzannah wailed in an eerie repetition of two short weeks ago.

"We have no choice." How he wished there were some way to soften the words! He had grown up in the orphanage his parents ran, among those who had no family. His mother had always insisted that no matter what his station in life, he was to be compassionate for and understanding of those less fortunate. Yet no matter how many times he faced death or disaster, it never became easy.

Suzannah raised pain-filled, defeated eyes to meet his. "You have to! They will not live if they come now!"

They? Callie must have told her to expect twins again.

"We shall see." He patted her arm gently. "I cannot give you any more of the potion."

Suzannah produced a strip of rawhide that she bit into savagely during the worst of her pains. She twisted the thin piece of leather over and over. "I will do it if it will save my children," she begged.

He wished it were that easy—to simply administer another dose and forget the consequences. He could do it, he knew, and if something happened to her, who would be the wiser? It would be thought an accident, and Suzannah would become just another casualty of the cruel wilderness. He could leave the mission to find a new life, a new woman, a new home.

Joshua shook his head. He was not cut from secondhand cloth. His mother had also seen to that.

"You can have no more because I am not sure what will happen if we continue to use it," he said. A sudden burst of remorse flowed through him. If he had stayed in Philadelphia and finished his medical training, he would have learned more about the drug's effects. He had always thought things through before acting on them. Except this time, when finding the woman he loved had proved more important than anything else.

And now he was trying to save two infants who would probably not survive and a woman who was the closest friend of the woman he loved, Callie. And she didn't remember him.

"I am willing to risk it." Suzannah's voice was strong despite the pain and heartache written across her pinched face.

"I am not." Joshua shoved his sleeves up above his elbows, conscious of the ragged scar that ran down his forearm. "There is no telling what could happen to you or the babies if we continued."

He moved to the fireplace where water simmered in a kettle, stirred the embers, and added a log before returning to Suzannah.

She seemed to realize there was nothing she could do to convince him otherwise. "Get Callie," she whimpered.

"Abe has already gone for her." At least he could appease her on that.

"She will help me," Suzannah insisted. "You stay away."

✍

Coming through a gap between homes, Callie caught sight of Abe. Her heart fell at the look on his face. She grabbed the sides of her long skirt and rushed toward the cabin, a prayer beating in her heart. *Please, God, more time.*

She tore through the partially open door, heedless of the fact that she had left Abe standing outside. Her eyes quickly appraised the situation.

As she did, she felt Joshua's gaze rake over her. Callie gave him an accusatory stare in return, one that demanded to know why he had not worked his healing again.

He continued to look at her through dark, brooding eyes. His lips were a slash across the beard stubble on his face, and even the smattering of freckles on his nose seemed subdued. She supposed he would somehow place the blame for Suzannah's predicament on her, just as he would also point the finger at her for Storm's dilemma.

Suzannah growled, a deep, agonizing sound that drew Callie to her friend's side. She whispered encouraging words that she knew

Suzannah would not hear. She had to say them in order to fill her own mind with thoughts of things other than what she could not change.

"Now." Joshua's command came from behind her.

Before she could properly settle into position, there was an infant in her hands, a girl with dusky red hair. *Sophie Ruth,* Callie thought, knowing the names Suzannah and Abe had picked out for the twins once they were over the shock of learning there would be two again. The birth cord was wrapped around the baby's neck and she was a horrible blue.

"*One of them. . .*" Joshua's prediction came out of nowhere and slammed into Callie. This was what he had meant. That one of them would not live!

Callie gritted her teeth, determined to show him how much he knew. She stared into the lifeless eyes of the tiny babe, willing her to take a breath. Nothing. The infant lay like a piece of driftwood against her arm. A wave of weariness engulfed her, but she was not about to give up.

Again and again she petitioned God to allow Sophie to breathe. Time ceased to exist. She had been so determined that Suzannah and Abe would have two infants to replace the two little girls they had already lost.

"The second one," Joshua barked.

She wanted to scream, "No. I am not ready."

A glance at Sophie Ruth lying across her forearm, her color no better, her life over before it had begun, brought a bitter taste to her mouth. But Suzannah's shriek brought her back to the task at hand.

I must be strong, she told herself.

Quickly, reverently, she wrapped Sophie Ruth in a blanket before laying the infant gently on the end of the bed. It took all the determination she could muster to turn around. Joshua was watching her again. He had positioned himself near Suzannah's head and was patting her brow with a damp cloth. His hair fell in disarray, partially covering his shaggy eyebrows. He gave Callie a tight smile, which shored up her nerves, and she turned back to await the next infant.

Hannah Grace had none of the sickly pallor of her twin. She came out kicking, her lungs filling with air and her lusty cry breaking the tension in the room, reminding Callie that her own despair must wait. But the joy of hearing Hannah Grace did not remove the stain of Sophie Ruth's death from her heart. She would carry that pain with her forever.

Callie looked back and forth from Suzannah to the precious infant in Callie's arms who nuzzled against her. Frightened at the jumble of emotions within her chest, Callie abruptly held the baby away from her.

Joshua had coaxed Suzannah into lying back and she was reaching out with both hands, fingers fully extended, eyes full of tears, searching for her babies.

Hot drops stung Callie's eyes as she handed the squirming infant to her mother.

"Hannah Grace," Suzannah cooed, sensing this was the second child she had delivered. She snuggled the infant tightly against her breast. While the weary woman stared into the barely open eyes of her daughter, Callie brushed away tears that slipped down her cheeks.

Joshua moved toward Callie, a handmade quilt dangling from his fingers. "There was nothing you could do," he said.

Callie glanced at Sophie Ruth, a still, silent bundle on the end of the bed. A fresh round of tears threatened to overtake her.

"How can you say that?" Pain slashed her soul for the grief Suzannah would carry with her for years. Two brown patches of dirt would become three.

"Because if it had not been for your care in the beginning, she would not have made it this far." He spoke so low she had to strain to hear him. "Double births are rare and usually one does not survive. It truly is not your fault."

Callie wanted to believe him. She *ached* to believe him. But it had been Joshua that night who had spoken the enigmatic words, *"One of them. . ."* Why hadn't she pursued his meaning? Knowing his thoughts, no matter how speculative, might have helped prepare her for this grief that wrenched her heart.

She jerked away from the bed, crossed to the fireplace, and hugged herself, hoping to stem the fresh round of tears that stormed her cheeks. *He must not see me cry,* she said silently. She didn't ask herself why that was important. It just was.

From across the room, she heard Suzannah's shaky voice ask, "The other one? Sophie Ruth or Isaac Daniel?"

Callie bit her bottom lip until she noticed the taste of blood on her tongue. She had no words to tell Suzannah she had lost another child. She couldn't even recall what she had said last time this had happened. Desperately she flicked her eyes heavenward, hoping the heavenly Father would assist her in her time of need.

"Do you not know," Joshua began, "that 'in heaven their angels do always behold the face of my Father'?"

His calm, gentle voice softened the edge of her grief as Callie recognized the words were from Matthew, chapter eighteen, verse ten. But she felt Suzannah's torment as Joshua continued. In phrase after phrase he talked about the wonders of heaven, the golden streets, the freedom. "No tears fall there," he whispered. "There will be only joy and reunion with our loved ones."

Callie sought solace in staring at his dusty boots. She wondered how she would ever face Suzannah and Abe again. She had failed them terribly. Joshua was now gently informing Suzannah of the truth, but someone would have to tell Abe. And the grandparents. And the rest of the mission. Who would do it? Callie? Never. She had done that once before and she would never forget it.

Callie's shoulders shook as she understood the burden God had given her. She would have to do it. A stranger should not be asked to do something of such significance. It was her place, her responsibility.

She stared down absently and only realized after a few moments that a pair of boots had come into view, obstructing her view of the straw covering the floor.

Her name came to her as a whisper. Then she felt his fingers gently nudge her chin upward so that her gaze would meet his. Bright blooms of color burst upon her cheeks, but she was unaware of that as she lost herself in the solitude of eyes bluer than an April sky after the rain.

Silent messages passed between them, as if they were two souls who had found a way to communicate without speaking. She felt her fears subside.

They stood like that for an eternity, each willing the other not to speak about what had just happened between them. Joshua's fingers rested just behind her chin in a soft hollow she had not been aware of before now. Tiny ribbons of enjoyment raced through her. . .until she remembered the woman lying on the bed behind them.

What was she doing? Her pulse raced. Her hands were damp, her insides churning. What power in the universe had led them to this? Callie pushed away the curious feeling that left her insides turned upside down. No matter how much she wanted to continue exploring the craggy features of his face, no matter what his touch had done to her, she could not forget he knew things about her that she didn't remember. That frightened her more than anything else.

✍

Joshua stood aside and gave Callie time to grieve with Suzannah. It had been reckless of him to reach out and touch her, but he had not been able to will away the desire to do so. It was becoming increasingly difficult to fight what came naturally to him: the desire to take care of the person he loved above all else. The fact that she didn't know the depth of his feelings only made it more difficult to appear detached.

He studied her, his gaze lingering on her fragile shoulders and the tendrils of slightly blond hair that had crept out from under her bonnet. How the Calliope he had known had changed. She was no longer a carefree young girl. She was Callie, woman of the wilderness, helper to those in pain.

He ached to hold her against him, to feel the strength of her heartbeat. But how could he? She had no idea what they had planned years ago. And he had no right to tell her, to drop it in her lap like a too-hot potato. No, he had promised David he would bide his time and wait. And he would pray she would remember who he was, who she was, what they had been to each other. And no matter what, he would carry with him forever the memory of her soft brown eyes staring into his as if she remembered every vow they had ever made to each other.

Abe's rap at the door interrupted Joshua's misery. Joshua admitted him, feeling useless as the rangy man bent in sorrow by his wife's bedside.

Joshua heard Callie explain about the loss, his admiration for her bravery growing as she did so. It seemed that only a few moments passed before she joined him at the table. Her petite oval face was flushed, her eyes fringed with crimson, clearly a result of her grief. Again Joshua wanted to touch her, to assure himself that five years of waiting was over.

"I must thank you," Callie said after she settled onto a chair. She used both hands to smudge away the tears she had cried as she spoke with Abe.

"It is you who deserves the credit," he replied. He was amazed at her ability to put aside her pain and attend to those who needed her compassion. Without thinking, he reached out and squeezed her hand, suddenly realizing that her reaction would likely be shock.

Callie didn't pull away. She only looked at him with huge dark eyes. She was the most beautiful woman he had ever known, but he was sure she viewed him through eyes of friendship, not love, something he was powerless to change. After arriving at the mission, he had learned she was expected to wed Levi. Joshua didn't care for the situation, but he would not damage what she and Levi had established together.

As if uncomfortable with his gaze, Callie abruptly stood and went over to the hearth, where she prodded the embers of the fire. When she turned back, he was gone.

Chapter 7

"We will be all right," Abe said, nudging Callie toward the door. "Love will see us through."

Before leaving, she gave Suzannah one last look. Then, finding words insufficient, Callie closed the door behind her and walked out into the bright sunshine.

At home, she prayed God would be with the Solomons during this tragic time. Thoroughly drained, she collapsed into a rocking chair in the corner, and that was how Sarah found her.

"I am so sorry, Callie," her sister said, resting her hand on Callie's shoulder. "I heard about. . .the babies."

Callie rubbed at her eyes before answering. "I. . .we did all we could, but there was nothing. . ." Her voice caught and she raised tear-filled eyes to Sarah. Why did she have to go through this again? More importantly, why did Abe and Suzannah? What was the purpose in giving life if it was to be snuffed out before it could begin?

Sarah patted her shoulder. "You do not have to talk about it. I know how you felt the last time this happened."

Callie threw both hands over her face. "I do not know that I can ever talk about this. There is too much pain. . . ."

The pain was not only due to losing Sophie Ruth; it also was caused by Levi's ungentlemanly behavior at the Killbuck cabin and the spring.

"I am sorry. It must sound lacking, but that is all I can say." Sarah rubbed her arms. "I will light a fire. Perhaps the warmth will cheer us up."

"There is no fire on earth that can take away death's chill, Sarah."

"I know that," Sarah rejoined, but she moved toward the hearth anyway, keeping her face turned away from her sister.

Melancholy hung over them for the rest of the afternoon. Sarah tried her best to lighten the mood with bits of news she had picked up. She mentioned Storm, in case it might shock Callie into remembering that life must go on.

"I stopped by the Killbucks'," Sarah said, her voice firm and steady. "Storm is still weak and feverish."

"Then there is no change?" Callie didn't know why she had asked. She hadn't expected there to be, but she hoped.

"No, none. Your Joshua came by while I was there."

"He is not my Joshua!" She should have been the one to check on the boy, not him. A fresh round of despair moved through her.

Sarah nodded. "Whatever you say. He administered another potion and said to tell you not to worry about going there tonight; he will take care of Storm."

"How nice." Callie's words were laced with irritation. He had brushed her off without any regard to her involvement. For a few days she had forgotten that in the beginning she had thought he had come to take her position away from her. Now that concern resurfaced.

"Yes, it was thoughtful of him," Sarah went on. "We had a little chat, and then Levi walked me home."

"Levi picked you up?" Shock propelled her words from her mouth.

Sarah clucked her tongue. "It was harmless, Callie. All he did was walk me home."

Sarah might think it harmless, but Callie was concerned. She must tell her sister about the way Levi had behaved that morning. But how? Sarah would no doubt take it the wrong way and point out that Levi was apparently becoming bored waiting for Callie to decide to wed him.

"I am glad you had an escort," she finally said.

"That is all it was. No harm in that, is there?"

"No." Callie clasped her hands in front of her. What was Levi up to? And why couldn't she just tell Sarah about what he had done that morning?

Sarah and Levi? She could not let that happen! Sarah was sixteen and had no idea of the intricacies of a man-woman relationship. And Levi, hunter-lean Levi, whose actions this morning had proven to her once and for all that she could never stand beside him as his wife. . .what was he up to? She had plainly told him not to count on her for any future relationship. Any chance for closeness between them was now gone.

But Sarah? How quickly he may have switched his allegiance after the fiasco at the spring.

Sarah's brows narrowed and a quizzical expression appeared on her face; it was as if she could read Callie's thoughts. "You must be tired. I promised MaryBeth I would come see her, so I had better be going."

"Sarah?" Callie began, deciding she must at least warn her sister to be careful.

"Yes?" Sarah turned and gazed at Callie with such innocence, Callie found she could not speak.

Perhaps if she just stood back and watched, things would work themselves out. "Be careful," she finally said.

"I always am," Sarah replied.

The day's events had drained Callie emotionally, and as she recalled them, her heart surged with renewed grief. Thoughts of the little blue infant would not leave her. The tears she had been fighting for most of the day filled her eyes. This time she did not try to stem the flow.

⟡

"We could not save both," Joshua explained to Brother David across the table. He had sought out David after leaving the Solomons' cabin and checking on Storm.

"It is sad when we lose a soul, especially when the soul is untried," David commented.

"Sophie Ruth is with Jesus."

David nodded. "Yes, but we must not forget the parents. Their road has been paved with loss." He wiped at the corners of his eyes. "They have one they can hold, but the memories of the others will

75

always walk with them."

"It is hard to lose someone you love," he agreed. Joshua had never lost a child, but he had lost Callie.

David removed his ever-present Bible from under his arm and laid it on his lap. "How are things between you and Callie?"

The only thing Joshua had left was the open wound of an aching heart. "I am not sure I can continue this way," he admitted.

"I do not believe that," David replied. "You waited five years for this and now you have changed your mind?"

"I do not know." Joshua jumped up and began to pace.

David settled back in his chair. "You are the only one who does know, Joshua. Are you telling me you are giving up?"

Was he? David had told him Levi and Callie had planned to wed someday. Where would that information lead him?

"I am not giving up. I just never imagined how difficult this would be when I decided not to tell her who I really am. And you have enlightened me as to Levi's expectations for her," he added.

"I will not preach to you, Joshua, but sometimes we make decisions that seem entirely wrong. We must trust God to work out any good that can come of them."

"So you do not believe I am wrong?" The question gouged a canyon in his heart. He did not really need David's approval. He had made his decision long ago to find Callie and pursue the promise they had made, despite the obstacles that might entail.

David cocked his head to one side. "You still believe she will look at you and remember who you are and who she is, do you not?"

"Yes. Well, I—"

"I will say this," David interjected. "At the risk of sounding pessimistic, I do not think that will happen. She has come a long way. She has risen above challenges that would have made many strong men turn tail and run. She lost her parents, and then she lost her home at the orphanage. And if that were not enough, Callie followed me to this lonely piece of wilderness." David crossed his arms.

"It was not as if she had much of a choice, David," Joshua said. "I was there. She did not know who she was. You offered safety. What else could she have done?"

David studied him silently. Long moments passed. Finally, with a look of exasperation on his face, the elder offered his opinion. "Have you considered why she did it? I think in her heart she thought it would distance her from what had happened."

Joshua mulled over David's words. "You sound as if you have spoken with her about this."

David shook his head. "It is in everything she does. She is gentle and patient with children, yet she never gets too close to them. She loves being around elderly people, yet she does not socialize with them much. She is happiest when she is alone, or with Sarah; but she gives freely of herself to any needy person in our midst. Do I have to tell you why?"

"She sees them as outcasts from their former homes also," Joshua mused. "Since God loves them, she believes no one but He can accept her for what she is since she does not know who she was."

David nodded. "Everyone here expects her to marry Levi someday, but I do not think so. The man who marries Callie will be the one who can help her build new memories." He paused and glanced into Joshua's eyes. "He will show her that yesterday does not matter. Above all, he will accept her for who she is now, not who she was before."

Joshua stared out the window. He loved that woman. But was it the Calliope he had known in the orphanage or the Callie he had found here in the wilderness that his heart longed for?

"You were not worried about her when she went to the spring with Levi because you trusted her judgment," Joshua reflected.

Why hadn't he realized that before? Because he had been too caught up in seeing her with Levi that all he could think of was the worst—that she had deserted Kukara and Storm.

David leaned forward, keeping his arms crossed in front of him in the manner Joshua was learning meant the elder had something important to say. "I knew Callie would do the right thing. What about you, Joshua?"

✍

It was all Callie could do to roll out of bed after a restless night. Her stomach was queasy and every muscle between her neck and her ankles ached. In fact, her entire body felt as if it were a piece of buckskin that had been stewed in hot water all night long.

Without waking Sarah, she visited those who were ill then returned home, preferring the silent condemnation of the log chinking to facing well-meaning men and women who would want to talk about Sophie Ruth and how sorry they were she and Joshua had not been able to save the infant.

Escape was not that easy. Even after she had returned home and flopped on her bed, her mind kept revisiting what had happened yesterday. The incident with Levi. Then Sophie Ruth. Hannah Grace. Suzannah's wail of grief. And when those memories had played themselves out, the image of Joshua kept coming back to her. Joshua bravely explaining to Suzannah about Sophie Ruth. Joshua touching Callie's hand in friendship, looking at her across the table through those endless blue eyes, eyes she had compared to the color of a lake just a few short weeks ago when he had first joined them at the mission.

Then, she had thought him mysterious, perhaps intent on taking her position away from her. But after watching him as he worked with her fellow villagers, Callie knew there was nothing mysterious about Joshua. He was kind and more than willing to share what he had with those who had little. He did everything he could to ease a person's pain.

So where did that leave her? Since the day she asked him where he was from, Joshua had avoided any further conversation about the orphanage or why she should remember him. But at the Solomons' cabin, when he sat across from her and reached for her hand, she had felt something stir between them. Something unfamiliar. Something bothersome. It made her wonder if there had ever been anything between them. . . .

Callie shook her head. She was thinking like Sarah, imagining things that weren't there. She was just worn out from all that had happened.

"You do not know how to relax," Sarah had told her a few months ago. She had been running back and forth to almost every home in the mission, trying to prevent a round of influenza from taking root and wiping out half of the mission's population. "Take some time and just be yourself."

Callie wanted to, but she didn't know who she was supposed to be, apart from someone who tended to Schoenbrunn's ill. The only thing she knew about herself was that she was a castoff her parents had not wanted. Brother David and the others at the mission didn't see her that way. It was her viewpoint, but a view so firmly ingrained that it was all she knew. If her own parents had not wanted her, then why would anyone? There was only God, the supreme being of total understanding.

Frustrated, Callie clenched her fists then let her hands drop into her lap. How would she ever find out who she had been? Joshua. His name erupted into her consciousness like an answer to prayer.

He knows. He can tell me. Her pulse beat out the words and battered them against her heart. Callie shoved them away. From all appearances, he did not like talking about those days in Pennsylvania. And it was not proper, no matter how much she wanted to know, for her to demand he tell her what he knew.

Callie felt as if she were trapped in a circle, the questions bouncing around in her head until the only thing she could think of was that somehow, some way, she must convince Joshua to explain what he knew about her.

"You awake?" Sarah called.

Lost in her own thoughts, Callie hadn't heard her sister slip across the room. *I must not let Sarah know what I have been thinking,* she thought as she rolled over and opened one eye halfway.

"I have already done my rounds. For now, I am going to rest. Yesterday took a lot out of me."

A look of surprise crossed Sarah's face. "What about morning service?"

"I am not going anywhere," Callie explained.

"Not even to Sophie Ruth's funeral?" Sarah asked.

"Just let me sleep," she answered. She turned away, hoping Sarah would not probe for her reason.

Sarah patted her shoulder as she was apt to do when she had no words with which to reply, then puttered around the cabin until Callie heard her leave for the morning worship.

Try as she might, with Sarah gone, Callie could not avoid the cabin's silence pressing in on her. In the past when she faced a tragedy, she had done so alone. Since she had found God, she had sincerely tried to allow Him to take her burdens and show her the answer. Sometimes, though, she felt it took God too long to reveal His will.

She had Sarah, and though they were natural sisters, she had never felt as close as she thought sisters should be. The seven-year age difference was one thing, but Callie also suspected it was due to the fact they had been kept separate at the orphanage.

The whoosh of her front door swinging open jerked her away from what was quickly becoming a depressing line of thought.

"Callie? Coming in. Stay where you are."

Ruth Lyons's voice preceded the tiny woman into the room. Ruth was Levi and Suzannah's mother. Her gray-silver hair was covered by the bonnet common among the Moravians. Age lines around her eyes drew attention to sullen smudges beneath them. The dress she wore was tattered and much patched, typical of a frontier woman.

"Sarah mentioned at worship that you were not feeling well. I have come to sit with you." Ruth breezed across the small room.

Callie had known Ruth the entire time she had been with the Moravians. Ruth would go out of her way to make others feel better.

Callie knew she had no choice but to submit to the woman's ministrations. She motioned Ruth to have a seat as she pushed herself up and leaned her back against the wall that served as her bed's headboard.

For the first few moments, Ruth made small talk, as if hesitant to bring up the subject of the twins. Then Callie watched helplessly as Ruth shoved a hand against her mouth and sobs poured forth.

No one blamed Callie or Joshua, Ruth insisted. They were all thankful one infant had survived.

Callie shifted position, trying to ignore her exhaustion. "Is there anything I can do?"

Ruth seemed to measure how ill Callie looked. "Levi is worried about you," she commented.

"Tell him thank you." Callie wanted to ask if Levi had said that or if it was just Ruth trying to make her feel better. Ruth didn't know what Levi had done, and Callie was not about to raise that subject. Memories of that ugly episode and the baby's death hung around her heart like a dead weight.

"He is digging the grave," Ruth added. Her voice caught at the end, but she did not break her gaze with Callie.

Callie tried to keep her distance when small children were lost. This one, though, seemed to have destroyed her resolve.

She asked again what she could do to help.

Ruth's lips trembled. "Pray for Suzannah," she said. "And. . ." She glanced around the cabin as if she expected to find someone there listening. "And stand with us—with our family—tomorrow as we give Sophie Ruth to God."

A hollow feeling settled in Callie's stomach and a roar filled her ears. "Is there not something else I could do?" Callie asked. Standing with them, hurting with them, watching as they lowered the tiny body into the earth. How could she do that?

Ruth patted her hand. "It would mean so much to us, to Suzannah," she added. The look in her eyes ripped Callie's heart and made her feel even worse.

"I will think about it," Callie murmured.

"I must go check on Levi and then to Suzannah's." Ruth gathered her skirt folds and brushed Callie's cheek with a kiss.

Callie watched the humble woman leave and realized she was relieved that other than to ask her to stand with them at the burial service, Ruth hadn't really spoken much about the infants.

She dozed off until Sarah returned from MaryBeth's. They passed the rest of the day carding wool and kneading bread, being careful not to talk about Sophie Ruth. After eating, Callie began to feel better physically, and Sarah caught her up on the goings-on at the mission, at least the ones important to her young mind.

Callie's weariness returned by evening, and her meal consisted of a slice of bread with butter on it. Her arms and legs felt as if she had been dragged for miles by a horse-drawn wagon; and as soon as she lay on her bed, she fell into a deep sleep.

It seemed she had no more than closed her eyes before she was awake again. Dawn's soft light had climbed the yellowed paper covering the one window. In the distance she could hear the familiar crows of roosters welcoming the day.

Swinging her legs over the bedside, she wished she had not awakened so early, as it only gave her more time to decide if she would go to the funeral. She had no real reason to stay home. The nausea she had experienced yesterday had passed and all that remained was bone-weary despair.

Callie's subconscious pleaded with her to remember what Suzannah must be feeling. In the end, the thought of her closest friend saying farewell to another child convinced her she must go. She would stand with the family as Ruth had asked, regardless of the pain she felt herself.

Chapter 8

"Y" our eyes look sad," Sarah commented as they made their way north on the hard-packed dirt trail to the cemetery called God's Acres.

"Thanks for not mentioning how red they are," Callie replied. Once she was up and about, she had spent the morning crying for Suzannah and the children she had borne but never had the opportunity to love.

She didn't know which was worse, losing a child or losing your parents. It was a question she had often asked over the last few years. *How can you mourn what you cannot remember having?* she often scolded herself as she lay tossing and turning in her bed.

She glanced down at the dreary gray dress she wore. It seemed to mirror the low clouds that encompassed as much of the sky as she could see, and was even plainer than normal today without its slash-of-white bib that she had taken off as a sign of mourning.

She joined the quiet crowd gathered around the tiny wound in the earth. Most of them wiped at their eyes periodically and sent short glances down the path as they waited for the grieving parents to arrive.

For lack of anything better to do, Callie took the opportunity to examine the land she had come to call home. Tall, elegant oak and walnut trees seemed to bow under the weight of the sorrow they were witnessing. Only a gentle breeze filtered through them, as if they knew a harsher wind might undo the shattered hearts in attendance.

Then the Solomons could be seen coming, and an ominous silence settled over the gathering. People moved into place, hands linked with hands. The words of the mercifully short service Brother David preached trembled through Callie's heart. She stood to Ruth Lyons's right, holding her own sorrow at bay by concentrating on the way Ruth conducted herself.

She had marveled more than once at how someone who had lost grandchildren could remain so serene as they huddled in a light drizzle to lay another babe to rest in Jesus' arms.

Callie's heart melted twice; once when she saw Abe's arms tenderly surround his wife, and again when she heard Hannah Grace's soft mewing sounds in the background.

First the family, then the others who could bear to do so, threw handfuls of dirt on top of the cradleboard wrapped in several layers of buckskin as they passed by the hole in the earth. All too soon a patch of brown dirt joined the others in the section reserved for female children—set apart by tradition from the men, women, and boys.

Callie viewed through misty eyes the two earlier graves of the Solomon children, noting that grass had refused to grow on them. *There should be flowers,* she thought, renewing an earlier vow to plant something there. As she stared at the plot allotted to Sophie Ruth, all she could think was that the three Solomon children were together in death as they had never been in life. And she had been present at each of their births, unable to change the tragic outcomes. Her heart contracted brutally at the thought.

She started to ease away from Ruth's side when a hand came to rest lightly on her upper arm. She turned, thinking it was Sarah. From the moment she first gazed into the anguish she saw in Joshua's gaze, she was lost.

"Are you all right?" he asked.

She forced a tight smile as she tried to recover from the hurt she saw on his face. She hadn't given a thought to how deeply losing the child might touch him, but the evidence was there for all to see. His normally bright blue eyes were twilight dark, and his characteristic smile was missing. She realized she did not like seeing him without that smile.

"I will be all right," she finally responded. "Why do you ask?"

"Because Sarah mentioned yesterday that you were not feeling well."

"You do not have to worry about me." She glanced around to find her sister chatting with friends. "And Sarah says too many things she should not say."

"That is possible, but I. . ."

"Yes?"

"I worry about you."

Joshua's words surprised her, but with them a strange sense of comfort settled over her tattered soul; she tried to ignore it.

"Well, there is no need. I am fine."

She lightly brushed with her hand at a stray curl that had fallen from her bonnet and wondered silently if he was staring at her red eyes or at the warm color she could feel splashing her cheeks.

"I have done this before, you know," she said.

"Yes, but that does not mean it does not hurt."

At a loss for words, Callie gave him a cursory glance. Joshua's lean frame was attired in a mud-brown jacket and trousers. He had shaved this morning, and a small cut ran under his chin. She had the urge to reach up and smooth her finger across it. She resisted.

Anyone looking at him would see a well-mannered individual with deep worry lines creasing his forehead. He was no longer the stranger he had been a few short weeks ago. With the slight beard he had been growing gone, he somehow looked more mature. And her feelings toward him were not as clear as they had been when he first came to town.

Realizing that he, too, must have suffered through the last few days, Callie almost admitted how desolate she felt. She stopped short. To do so would be to admit to him that she couldn't handle this on her own. And she *could*, she reminded herself; she did not need others to help her make it through tough times.

"Dying is a fact of life," she said. "Especially out here in the wilds where there are so many things that can go wrong."

Joshua arched his eyebrows. "That is true, but there is more to death than dying. And having said that, are you coming to the meeting house for the gathering?"

"The meeting house? I do not think so." If she did, she would end up having to speak with Suzannah, and she was certain she wouldn't be able to think of a thing to say.

"Afraid someone will point at you and say it was all your fault? There were two of us there, Callie. You were not at fault on your own." His words left her shaken.

A rustle of bodies pressed toward them. Callie knew the rest of those gathered there were preparing to leave. She sought her sister and found her immediately, standing with Levi and staring up into his eyes with admiration.

Callie also caught the disgruntled glances of several other women who were looking Sarah's way. Callie tried to catch her sister's eye by waving her hand, but failed. Sarah was oblivious to everyone else.

"She is not doing anything wrong," Joshua interjected. "I suspect she is just trying to be an adult and make others feel better."

"She is my sister and I will thank you to let me tend to her," Callie said.

She instantly regretted her outburst. He had only meant to help, but whenever he was around she seemed unable to think clearly, something she had to work on immediately. She was a grown woman, responsible for the health of over one hundred sixty people. She simply could not allow herself to be bowled over by a good-looking man, regardless of how compassionate and disheartened he looked at the moment.

Joshua bowed. "You are right. I apologize if I violated your duties."

Callie clenched her teeth together. Is that how he saw taking care of family? As a duty? *Then he is no better than Levi*, she thought, recalling Levi's comments about Storm's mother being the one to care for her sick son.

"I need to talk to you," Joshua continued when she failed to speak up.

"Talk? We have nothing to talk about." Callie couldn't keep the sarcasm out of her voice. "There is nothing you could tell me that would make me feel any better." Even as she said the words, she knew they were false.

"What if I said it was about you?"

He put his arm on her elbow and steered her toward the trail, pointing in the direction of the meeting house, where grief was softened and morale bolstered.

"A—about me?" She didn't mean to stammer, but hadn't she been thinking about this very thing lately? "I suppose we could discuss it on the way," she offered. Where were her good intentions now, she asked herself. Why were her knees suddenly resisting holding her up?

"Somehow I do not think that will be a sufficient length of time to say what I have to say, but. . ." Joshua halted as Brother David walked past. They exchanged greetings, and when the elder had departed, he began again. "I have never been one to turn down the offer of having a fair-haired woman on my arm. Shall we?" He held out an arm to her and motioned down the trail with his other hand.

Callie swallowed hard. Her heart was racing in her chest, which was hardly an appropriate reaction for someone who had just attended a burial. Oh, why had he chosen now to want to speak with her? Why couldn't he leave her alone? Since he didn't appear about to do so, it was up to her to control herself. She was weak, just as the Bible said.

But didn't the Bible also say, *"There hath no temptation taken you but such as is common to man: but God is faithful, who will not suffer you to be tempted above that ye are able; but will with the temptation also make a way to escape, that ye may be able to bear it"*? a little voice in her head argued.

What harm could come of her talking with Joshua? He said he planned on enlightening her about some of the things she wanted to know about the orphanage, about herself. Smiling more broadly than she could control and forgetting for the moment how upset she had been at seeing Sarah ogle Levi, Callie slipped her arm naturally through Joshua's. Her fingers lay lightly across his muscular forearm, and she inhaled sharply as he smiled down at her. She had rarely touched Levi in this fashion, but with Joshua it just seemed so natural.

It was not a great distance to the meeting house, a half-mile or so. The grass along the pathway poked green tips through loamy dirt, and here and there a robin searched for food. Crows mingled at the tree line, screeching and performing some sort of ritual walk.

A thunderstorm could have erupted overhead and Callie would have paid it no attention. She could only concentrate on the man beside her. He towered above her, rugged and strong. Other men had walked beside her, but she had never felt as protected as she did with Joshua.

"Brother Joshua," she began as seriously as she could. It was the only way she could maintain her perspective while walking with him.

When he lowered his head to look at her, a warm smile crinkled his blue eyes. "Yes?"

"What brought you here?" She hadn't planned on being so forth-right, but she did want to know, if only to satisfy a small portion of her curiosity.

"I have wondered when you would ask."

She thought he might slow down the pace of their walk, but he didn't.

He did, though, reach up with his free hand, remove his hat, and hand it to her. She took it without thinking, watching as he ran his fingers through the locks of thick black hair that chased across his forehead.

"It is a long story, and one I have not shared with many. But since you asked, I will tell you. I fell in love with a woman and planned to marry her. A situation arose and she, well, she was not free to marry me."

Callie pulled back and almost dropped his hat, which she was carrying in her right hand. Why was he confiding in her? She gazed into those blue eyes of his that lately seemed so very capable of upsetting her world.

"That is terrible, but I hardly think you should be telling me this." Did she look as confused as she felt?

"I have no one else to tell," he went on in a whisper. "It is such a relief to finally share it. You see, I carry my love for her in my heart, waiting for the day when she realizes I will never forget her."

Callie pondered his words for a minute, while his fingers tightened a bit on her forearm.

"You make it sound as if she is here, in Schoenbrunn." She flashed a glance at the log cabins of the mission that lay ahead. "That cannot be. No one here has ever mentioned being in love or running from someone."

His eyes narrowed. "Perhaps you are right. Wherever she is, she no longer knows how I feel about her."

"Then you should find her and tell her that instead of hiding out in the wilderness."

Callie had forgotten he was supposed to be talking about her. She marveled he would search so far for a woman he loved.

Joshua smoothed the lines on his forehead. "That was my intent when I began my journey, but certain events have changed my mind."

"Then you have given up your search?" Was she being too inquisitive? She watched him carefully.

He lowered his eyelashes briefly then shook his head. "I am rethinking my approach. I had planned to confront her and demand we wed immediately." He closed his eyes. "I have decided that will not do at all."

A burst of envy for the woman he loved coursed through Callie. Imagine having a man who would do anything, go anywhere, to find the one woman he wanted above all else.

"I hope you find her one day, Brother Joshua," she said.

Sarah and Levi strolled by, their arms linked lightly and slight looks of astonishment on their faces. Callie recalled that she had not yet spoken with Sarah about Levi's behavior at the spring. She made a mental note to do so as soon as they were alone tonight. The way they were looking at each other made her very uneasy.

As Sarah and Levi followed the trail of tears headed toward the meeting house, Callie turned her thoughts back to Joshua. She admired his determination in the face of adversity, but she did not feel she should tell him that. It seemed too personal, too private. He was holding her arm while they walked and had given her his favorite hat to hold for some strange reason, but she hardly knew him.

Joshua regarded her quizzically. "So do I."

He guided her back onto the path, and she watched as he compressed his lips into a tight line. Clearly, their discussion was over and she had not learned a thing about herself. Instead, she had listened to him speak of the fact that he loved someone whom he had come in search of. Someone who had left him? Turned him down? Did not love him? She could hardly pry further. Why did she always find herself in these situations where she couldn't ask what she most wanted to know?

As they walked, Joshua did not take hold of her elbow as he had before. Callie missed his nearness more than she was willing to admit. Just having him touch her had made her feel warm and safe, so different from being with Levi.

She turned her mind back to what he had told her. He had loved, or rather, still loved, a woman who no longer returned that feeling. And he seemed determined to find her again, which meant he would one day leave Schoenbrunn. Had she hurt him, Callie wondered, the woman responsible for the silent mask of pain on his face?

She sighed. It was a tragic tale, but what could she do? Other than the "family" she had established here with the Moravians, she had no basis on which to judge love that occurred between a man and a woman. Early in life, before she was old enough to understand, her parents had cast her away. She had decided in recent years that no one would ever hurt her that way again. Strangely, Callie now found herself questioning that vow.

A shiver ran up her backbone as she remembered what Levi had proclaimed he felt for her. She might be lacking in actual experience, but she was sure that could hardly qualify as love. Other than seeing him with her sister after the burial, she had not seen or spoken with Levi since the episode at the spring. She was convinced he would not pursue her any longer. No, she assured herself, their relationship, if there had ever been one with Levi Lyons, was over.

But why, then, did she feel such a deep sense of loss for Joshua? Because he had come alone to Schoenbrunn? Because he had confided his search for the woman he loved? It was her nature to care deeply when others were hurting, though she had learned how to keep their pain at a safe distance from her own heart. That way she would survive, just as she had been doing since her accident, and probably as she had been doing all her life but just couldn't remember.

She thought back to what Joshua had entrusted her with as they had stood off the path. The fact that he had given her a quick look at a small part of his past secretly thrilled her. Perhaps others would think it improper that he had confided in her, but since he had brought the issue up, she'd had no choice but to allow him to continue.

After all, he was a man and she had learned that sometimes men did strange things. Yet, there was an emptiness inside her that left her feeling as if they had left things unsaid in that short conversation. And he had not talked about her as he had suggested; he had talked about him. It all made no sense, so she pushed it away, saving it for a later time when she could concentrate.

"So you finally made it," Brother David greeted as they walked around the side of the meeting house.

While Joshua replied automatically, Callie took a last long look at him. He really cut a handsome figure, she decided. She had returned his hat to him, and she admired the way the brim sat low on his brow and cast shadows in the hollows of his cheeks. How blessed the woman was that he loved!

Unbidden, another idea formed before she could stop it. She looked forward to the day when she might find a man who cared enough for her to search through wilderness for her. Surprised at the notion that wedged a twinge of jealousy in a corner of her heart, Callie shook herself. Then as if she knew that was not enough, she issued a quietly stern warning to her heart to stop wishing. Had she not just persuaded Levi that she was not ready to marry?

She caught Brother David staring oddly at her and realized he must have asked something and was waiting for an answer. Hurriedly, she offered her thanks for the beautiful ceremony he had preached.

"It is the least I can do," he said calmly, making Callie wonder if Joshua had said much the same thing while she had been gathering wool.

"Do you have to help?" Joshua asked as Brother David moved toward the bereaved parents.

Did he want her to stay with him? She was tempted, but her reply was curt. "Usually I hand out coffee and cakes."

Adults congregated in solemn circles and children played in the open area to one side of the meeting house. Tables of baked goods and other food offerings sat along a wall. The sun had come out, burning away the mist that had fallen intermittently throughout the burial service. Its brightness lent a delicate touch to the dismal emotions reflected on the settlers' faces.

Joshua left her to pour coffee, and she watched as he ambled about among the crowd. His height made him an easy target to follow, and she found she could not keep her eyes from straying to him as he stopped and spoke with various groups.

Abe and Suzannah stayed near the worship building, appearing grateful for the attention that helped take their minds off their loss. Callie eyed them discreetly. Every so often, the one holding Hannah Grace would hand the baby to the other, and when their eyes met over the well-bundled infant, there passed an unseen bond.

She had yet to speak with Suzannah. Several times she thought to do so, but each time she held back, frightened of being unable to find words that would convey her despair and her helplessness without further upsetting her friend.

The hollowness inside her was a constant reminder of how she had failed Suzannah—not once, but twice. She could not imagine how Suzannah could ever trust her again.

Suzannah seemed to echo her sentiments, for she rarely glanced in Callie's direction. Finally, the line for coffee tapered off, and with nothing else to do, Callie grabbed a piece of jerked turkey and a mug of coffee for herself before joining her sister.

Sarah gestured toward the piece of dry meat in Callie's hand. "I see you are still not eating much."

There was an aloofness about her sister that Callie had not noticed before. Perhaps this was harder on Sarah than she wanted others to know. If that was the case, she would let Sarah work out her emotions on her own.

"I am not hungry right now," she explained. "What do you and MaryBeth have planned for today?"

Sarah appeared to have difficulty swallowing the bite of venison she had just put in her mouth. "Nothing. We are arguing."

Callie sighed. So much happened in her sister's life that Callie did not find out about until afterward. She patted Sarah's arm. "I am sure it will pass. You have had your differences before."

She thought briefly about telling Sarah then about Levi and what he had done the other day, but decided against it. Something of that import was better left for when they were in private.

"It is not me," Sarah returned, dropping her eyes to her food. "We just do not see things the same way anymore."

"You will work it out."

"I am not so sure we will this time," Sarah argued.

Before Callie could ask for an explanation, a loud wail clamored over the muted voices around her. She dropped her food and raced toward the sound, intent on helping in whatever way she could.

Joshua arrived before she could, and she stood back, watching him brush away a young girl's tears who had apparently tripped over a tree root. Joshua ran his forefinger over the scratched skin on the top of her foot.

"You will be fine," he assured the little one.

The child wiped at the side of her face, looked down at her foot as if to see how he had fixed the damage, then beamed a toothless smile up at him. Joshua smiled in return, and the girl pulled her moccasin back on and scampered off toward the children she had been racing with.

He is so good with little ones, Callie thought once the crisis was over and she had moved back to sit beside Sarah. Sarah looked unsettled about something. Callie assumed it was the rift with MaryBeth and said nothing.

The rest of the day passed quickly. Finally, the children collapsed in exhaustion on old deerskins that had been laid on the ground. Adults alternated between eating and talking and watching over the children.

On the spur of the moment, Brother David decided to hold the evening service outside, offering prayers not only for the Solomons but for the entire settlement. Tomorrow's work was parceled out, good-byes were hugged all around, and the last "Amen" was said as the sun slipped behind the trees at day's end.

Callie put aside the mending she had been working on as Sarah joined her in front of the fireplace, where the snaps and pops of the fire offered a measure of cheer. The rain from the other day had gone, but a chill remained even though it was late May.

"We must talk about your behavior after the funeral the other day, Sarah."

She had truly meant to have this conversation earlier. One illness after another had prevented her from finding the time to do so. The one good thing that had happened in the last two days had been little Storm Killbuck regaining his health. She knew she should congratulate Joshua for that accomplishment, but she hadn't had the time to approach him either. The two of them had been kept extremely busy.

Sarah was rarely at home lately, slipping in at the last moment to go to sleep. What her sister did around the mission, Callie didn't know. She hoped she had made up with MaryBeth though. The girls needed each other's companionship, as all humans needed someone in whom they could confide. She had had Suzannah once. It seemed a very long time ago.

"What was wrong with my behavior?" Sarah asked as she tucked her legs beneath her and tugged at her skirt to pull it around her knees like a blanket.

"You were, well. . . .it's the way you were carrying on with Levi."

"And what was wrong with that? He was hurting and I was trying to help." Sarah unpinned the braid wrapped around on the back of her head and flipped her strawberry curls until they tumbled down her back.

"You were doing a little more than that!" Callie pointed out.

"You taught me to be considerate of others," Sarah exclaimed. "Are you now telling me I did something wrong even though I saw you doing the same thing with Joshua?"

Callie cleared her throat. "I am not questioning your motives. You are not yet of the age to make weighty decisions such as—"

"Here we go again," Sarah groaned, rolling her eyes.

Callie held up a hand. "Do not get defensive. It is my place to bring you up correctly."

Sarah stared at the fire.

"I am trying to do the best I can," Callie added.

The chill in the room was not only because the fire had not been burning long. Callie knew Sarah disapproved of her speaking this way. She had shown it before, both in words and actions.

A heavy sigh escaped Callie's lips.

"Look, let us not argue," Callie backtracked. "It is the one thing I could not take just now. But in the future, promise me you will behave with more restraint. You know we women are to be seen, not heard."

Sarah turned her head to glare at her, her lips disappearing in a grim line. "Just because you do not know how to have fun, you do not like it when anyone else does, either, do you?"

Callie stiffened at her sister's accusation. She had heard that statement before. "Fun has nothing to do with this. You have got it wrong."

"I am not you, Callie. And I am growing up regardless of how long you try to think of me as your little sister." Sarah tossed her head. "I have done everything you have asked. I came with the Moravians to this godforsaken place. I traveled for weeks, sleeping on cold, hard earth, eating nothing but pemmican and stale bread. Do you know how sick the thought of that stuff makes me?" Sarah grabbed at her throat and acted as if she were choking.

It was not the first time Callie had listened to Sarah rage at the heavens for casting her into this lonely bit of wilderness. She could see an immense struggle taking place in her sister's eyes. She waited, patiently allowing Sarah to work out whatever was tumbling through her mind.

When she spoke, Sarah's words rushed out in an uneven stream. "I even accepted Jesus to keep you from pestering me."

Callie couldn't believe what she had just heard. Pain thudded in her ears. Even as Callie leaped from her seat she was telling herself to stem her reaction. But the anger burning her cheeks and the wave of sickness cresting in her stomach would not fade. And the look in Sarah's eyes said she was serious.

Beneath the enormous burden Sarah had just laid on her, Callie struggled to breathe. Sarah's words thundered in her mind like a horrible storm, shattering her hopes that her sister would grow stronger in Christ.

She grasped the back of the chair. She would not, could not, allow Sarah, who was not yet seventeen, to fall from grace.

"Would you care to explain that for me?" She hated the venomous tone of her voice, but shock prevented her from concentrating on how she spoke.

Sarah shrugged. "It is simple. If God were truly good, He would not do to us what the one you believe in has done."

Sarah's pitiful voice reminded Callie of all the times on the journey to Schoenbrunn that her sister had complained about her lot in life. Callie had passed it off as childish whining, sure it was prompted by the newness of the journey and by the fact that they had just lost the only home they had known.

Hands clenched at her sides, she closed her eyes and prayed for the strength to deal with Sarah's revelation. But while she could shut her eyes and lock out the sight of Sarah sitting in the chair, the phrase *Sarah does not believe* echoed in her mind.

"You are the only person she has to show her the truth," a voice whispered from deep within.

Yes, but how? she argued back.

"By showing her love and compassion, by being understanding."

Callie swung away to regain her composure, bidding her tears to subside and her racing heart to slow. What could she say to erase the pain of what Sarah had just confessed? Her fingers dug into the wooden rung of the chair back, and she clung to its surface, holding tightly as if it were the very length of wood that had held her Savior as He breathed His last. When she turned around, ready to speak, Sarah was no longer in the cabin.

❧

Joshua faced the men who had come to the meeting. Weariness pulled their features tight across their high cheekbones, and for those who had been searching all night, their bloodshot eyes testified to their lack of sleep. Joshua himself had not slept in the last three days, but some inner force compelled him to stay awake, as if by doing so he would find the answer to Levi and Sarah's disappearance.

He drew a deep breath and composed his thoughts, which was not easy to do. The images that filled his mind were of Callie and the devastation she must be experiencing because of her sister's actions. A devastation he could only imagine, since she had shut everyone out since that night.

A brief twinge of guilt that he had taken Sarah's side during the incident at the funeral struck him. He shoved it away. Like so many other things, what had happened was history, and he could not change it. What he could change, or at least attempt to, was the way the future looked for his beloved, even if she wanted no part of human contact right now. So, putting aside his own frustration, he straightened his back and motioned around the room.

"This morning some of you brought word of hoofprints along the riverbank north of here," he began. "I know you are thinking we do not know what lies that way, other than more wilderness and French or British soldiers, but it is not our safety at issue here."

He looked around the room, expecting some reaction from the dark-skinned faces. There was none. The glow of the candles hung intermittently along the wall softened the sharp edges of stress on the men looking back at him, but it did not take away the concern on their faces. It was the same concern he was experiencing, but one he tried doubly hard to ignore. If he let himself get muddled up in why he felt it was so important to find Sarah and Levi, he might regret ever coming to Schoenbrunn in the first place.

That, he vowed silently, was something he would never do. Even if nothing came of what he and Callie had once shared, he would relish the fact that he had at least been able to see her again. He turned his mind back to the task at hand.

"We have combed the hillsides, and I think it safe to say that Sarah and Levi, for some unknown reason, have headed north. We have no choice but to follow them."

He stopped, knowing he did not have to remind them that the couple had taken one horse between them, and no one knew what provisions.

"I am going," Joshua announced, his voice echoing off the rafters of the meeting house. "If you are willing to go along, I would appreciate your company."

A barely man-sized voice responded from the back of the room, "I will go."

Joshua turned in the direction of the speaker. Shadow, a young Delaware who had recently given his life to Christ, stood near the back, waving his hand over his head.

"She cannot be allowed to do this to her sister. Or to the rest of her Christian family," the young man added.

Joshua first thought to decline the offer of help from one so young. At fifteen summers, Shadow would have more energy than common sense, but he also had the stamina of youth. He smiled at the boy who was trying to appear mature enough to make such a decision. He was eager, too; but no one except Brother David knew why.

Once Shadow spoke, three others quickly followed suit. After very little discussion, it was decided they would each be outfitted with a horse, a musket, and sufficient dried food for a week's journey. If they had not found the couple by then, they were to return.

"Bring them home safely," Brother David admonished when the men were done planning. "And remember, it is not our place to serve as judge." The elder had sat quietly throughout the meeting, putting his implicit trust in Joshua's ability to handle the details.

"We will bring them home," Shadow retorted. "Whether they want to come or not." He folded his arms in front of him as if he dared anyone to dispute him.

Joshua glanced at David, who gave him a slight nod that said, *Be patient with him and teach him what you know.* He thought of his father, whom he had not seen in over a year, of how he had insisted Joshua learn to ride and track, though he'd had no idea of how Joshua's knowing those things would ever prove useful. Would he ever see his father again to thank him for those lessons? With thoughts of family crowding his mind, he was reminded of the necessity of finding Sarah for Callie.

He dismissed the men to say farewell to their families and headed toward his own cabin to pack. Strolling up the path, his thoughts turned to what had happened the night before last.

He had been treating a patient, so what he knew about the incident was secondhand, imparted hastily by Brother David before the first group had ridden out to the south, toward their sister mission downriver. By that time, the remaining Delawares had broken into small parties with various destinations in mind.

The elder had been terse while telling him of the disappearances. "I believe they will head toward civilization."

Joshua had agreed with that thinking but voiced the opinion that he thought Sarah and Levi would avoid any settlement where there would be Delawares present.

"After all," he had pointed out tactfully, "they have left this mission under the cover of darkness. Why would they seek the protection of a settlement where they believed people in it might report their whereabouts to us?"

Other than to stroke his chin thoughtfully, Brother David had given no reply.

The sun glinted on Joshua's face, snapping him out of his reverie. He was surprised to find he was not on his way east toward his house. His footsteps had carried him to Callie's door instead. He stared at it for a moment, trying to reconcile within himself why he had unconsciously come here.

Except for Brother David and those who were ill, she had kept her contact brief with everyone in the mission since the night she discovered her sister missing. She was so intent on hiding away that she rose before dawn to make her morning "sick visits" then returned home before anyone else was up and about.

An indistinct pain clawed at his heart. He should not have promised to avoid telling her more about who he was, Joshua thought irritably. He knew what he had said to her after the burial had been risky, but he had been so sure that if he gave her a hint, she would remember.

He had stopped short of revealing the whole truth only because it would more than likely have destroyed whatever she had begun to build for herself. He would not do that, no matter how much he was tempted to.

How did Callie feel about Levi deserting with her younger sister? The question had plagued him since the moment he had heard about it. Unfortunately, it was one to which he was never likely to discover the answer.

Before he could leave without at least seeing how she was, he rapped at her door. He had spent the last two nights wondering how much of their conversation after the infant's burial Callie had truly heard. The whole time he had been telling her about loving a woman and being unable to wed her, he had hoped she would realize she was the woman he sought. When she had not reacted, he had been forced to admit she might never recall those days they had shared.

Callie opened the door a scant inch, looking as if she had not slept in a week. He wanted to be the balm to her soul she so obviously needed, instead of the source of distress he felt he was for her every time he saw her.

"Yes?" Her voice wavered.

"I have come to check on you." He pushed away words of comfort that were about to burst from his mouth.

"I am fine."

Her response was not strong enough to convince him. Looking out as she was through the tiny space between the door and the frame, he could barely see one side of her face. Tiny drops edged her long lashes, causing a new wave of compassion to well up inside him.

"You do not look it," he answered.

Why didn't he just tell her how beautiful she was? How her eyes had sparkled when they found him across the huge room where the orphans ate their meals? How her lips curled up in a smile when she saw him scouting around the grounds for something to do?

She pulled the door open slightly, far enough to gaze up and down

101

the pathway, then stuck a shoulder through the opening. Her gaze hung momentarily on his face as if she were looking for something she knew should be there but wasn't.

"Look," Joshua began, "can you step outside for a moment?"

Hesitation flickered in those brown eyes of hers, but they were a moody brown now, not a laughing brown. Amazingly, she ventured out, sunlight streaming onto the slender column of her throat. Her dress was an older one, and she had not taken any time to tidy her appearance, yet he saw nothing but the beauty she radiated from within. Even the bonnet that appeared as if she had tossed it on her head looked perfect.

"You have news?" There was a scant hint of hope in her voice.

Joshua hated to disappoint her. On top of that, he had to will himself not to touch her. If he did, it would make leaving harder than the last time he had said good-bye.

"I wish I did."

He felt so inadequate where Callie was concerned. He knew this was no time for regrets. They surfaced anyway. If he had told the whole truth in the beginning, they might be man and wife by now. He would be free to hold her head against his chest and comfort her. Joshua turned away those thoughts before they resulted in some foolish action. Pressing his fingers into his palms, he gazed down at her.

Callie's eyes shifted to the ground. "Then why are you here?"

"To tell you I am going to look for them." He wished there were some way he could erase the heartache she must be feeling.

"Others have done so," she scoffed. "They were unsuccessful. What makes you think you will do any better?"

Joshua didn't blame her for being sour. Life for Callie had been turned inside out. And not for the first time.

"Because no one else has gone so far north," he answered. "There are five of us heading out. I for one am not going to stop until I find them."

"Five?" She seemed to consider the number. "For how long?"

"A week. They will return then."

He held his breath, but she appeared to miss the implication that he might not be with them.

"Godspeed, then," she offered, pushing loose curls away from her brow.

He could tell it was taking tremendous effort for her to talk to him. He offered a silent prayer of thanks that she had come out of her cabin for him when she had not for anyone else. Was it meaningful? Had she reached a point where she was beginning to trust him without knowing why?

He ground his teeth together. He was leaving, leaving her behind so he could seek out her runaway sister and the man everyone had thought Callie would marry. Where was the justice in this world? Just as the woman he loved might be realizing there was something significant between them, he was going away.

"Brother David usually says a blessing for those who are going out. Has he done so?" Her voice was so small, yet her words moved him.

"No," he admitted. "Will you come and pray with us, then?" It was bold of him to ask, and he held his breath while he waited for her reply.

Beneath the gray lines of her dress, her shoulders tightened. A burst of color on her cheeks made her pale skin look even more delicate.

"I cannot. There will be people there, and they. . ." She bit her lip.

Joshua raised his left hand, intent on letting it rest on her shoulders to provide encouragement. Callie stepped back and, seeing her prepare to move, he lifted the hand to the wooden frame of her door and leaned against it instead.

He motioned toward the cabin door with his other hand. "You cannot hide from them forever. They are concerned about you, about what has happened."

"Are they? Or are they gossiping?"

"Surely you know your family better than that?"

Her eyes widened as if she were weighing the word and she had nothing to compare it to. "Family? Oh, my Christian one. Yes, I trust them. It is just that. . ." She straightened her shoulders. "I am not keen on being the object of gos—"

"It is more than gossip, is it not?" Joshua cut in. "People want to help you. That is why we are going out. Does that not prove anything?"

It proves I love you. His plea was silent. The urge to reveal everything was stronger than ever. *If only I could tell you, we would be done with this hedging. And no matter what would happen, it would be worth it to finally say those words to you after so long.*

"It proves you are a fool, going north into unexplored territory," she retorted. Her words faded into nothingness, but there was a spark in her eyes he had not seen since that night at the Solomons' cabin weeks ago. It was there only briefly, and she concealed whatever followed by gazing toward the cemetery.

"Tell me what you are thinking."

He didn't know if saying that made him courageous or foolish. If he could draw her out for a few more minutes, he sensed he would win some sort of battle. But to what end? He was going and not returning until he had information about her sister.

How long that might take was not something Joshua wanted to ponder. Since Callie didn't know who he was, perhaps it was best they end like this. Here, alone, two souls without any apparent bond to each other. Perhaps this was what God had planned after all—to allow him to find Callie, to assure himself she was all right, and then to lead him away before he could hurt her.

A subtle burning pulled at his eyes as he stared at her, willing her to read his mind to see how much he cared for her, had always cared for her, and would continue to do so.

Her eyes locked with his, the power in them such that Joshua knew the moment would be etched in his memory forever. "I am thinking nothing," she replied.

"Your eyes disagree. So, I think, does your heart."

Dare he hope there was a small bit of sadness inside her that he was leaving?

"I am tired," she explained. "You would be, too, if your sister had run off with someone you had least expected, right after she had. . ."

Heedless of the consequences, Joshua put his hands on her shoulders, feeling every slender muscle beneath them grow rigid.

"Right after what, Callie? What have you not shared with us?" He peered at her, trying to force her to divulge what she knew.

Callie glared back, her mouth quivering. "I have told Brother David what I know about finding Sarah gone," she insisted.

To push further would ruin whatever he had managed to accomplish. He let the weight of his hands rest gently on her shoulders. She didn't pull away. Rather, he thought there might be a slight willingness to share her sorrow with him. He would gladly take that load and anything else, if she would only let him.

"We are departing in two hours. If there is anything we need to know, you must tell us."

"I have already said 'Godspeed.' That is all." She stared at a distant point on the horizon.

His hands fell to his sides. He missed the contact between them immensely. Belatedly, he realized she would think he had come as a friend, not as anything more. He didn't know if that would be enough to sustain him on his trip. But if it was God's will that this is what he would carry with him forever, then he would accept it.

Looking at her now, her shoulders slumped as if the welfare of the world rested on them, he couldn't help but wonder if she was strong enough to go it alone. First the loss of Sophie Ruth, then her sister. How much more could she take?

He checked the sun's position and realized he had just enough time to pack before leaving. Since he couldn't stay and watch over her, he would ask Brother David to keep an eye on Callie and pray for the best. Surely God would keep her safe just a little while longer. . . .

Callie heard Joshua's footsteps plodding away from her. She continued staring at the sky, hoping the blue expanse of God's handiwork would help her sort through the emotions warring within her. Crows squawked and cattle lowed nearby, but she was not aware of it—nor of anything else happening in the vicinity.

Why had Joshua come to tell her he was leaving? Did he think that was what she wanted? Had she run him off by her unpleasantness? She had watched him treat ill people with whom she normally would have worked. She had listened patiently to his confession about a love gone wrong. She had conversed with him occasionally, but always came away feeling as if he did not approve of her.

Though tears moistened her eyes, she told herself she did not need Joshua's approval. She had Jesus. That was all she needed.

Yet, if she had been a friend to Joshua as a Christian should, would he still be so eager to leave? Callie wrung her hands together. What had she done? Had she forced Sarah into Levi's arms by being overbearing when all she had meant to do was direct her sister's footsteps in the right direction?

She sobbed. She had not meant to hurt any of them, not Sarah, not Levi, and not Joshua. But they were all gone now. The salty tears that trickled down her cheeks added to her misery. Perhaps Sarah had been right; a loving God would not allow life to be so sour.

Unable to reconcile herself to what the future now held, Callie entered her cabin and flung herself on her bed. She kept telling herself that keeping secret Sarah's admission of her disbelief would not in any way hamper the search party.

Without knowing why, several times she almost caved in and ran to Joshua to inform him of her sister's desertion from God's path. Each time, she quailed at the thought of what he would then think of her. He would question her ability to teach others about God and how to love Jesus. He might also think she was unable to treat those who were sick; and if he returned and decided that, she might find herself out of work at the mission. That would mean she must leave, for she could not bear to stay where she wasn't wanted.

Callie blamed herself for Sarah's departure. She should have identified the change in her sister's behavior, sensed something momentous was about to happen, before it was too late.

That didn't prevent her from grasping the edge of her blanket as she realized how alone she was. A ragged knot formed in the back of her throat, and frustration rippled through her shoulders. Her eyes seemed blistered from the frequent crying she had been doing since she discovered Sarah and Levi missing.

"It is not fair, God. You could have warned me this was going to happen. You have taken everything I ever cared about away from me. Why did You do it?"

Callie didn't stop to consider that she included Joshua as part of the "everything" she cared about. But she did recall some of his last words: *They will return in one week.* Did that mean he would not?

Chapter 9

The search party gathered by the meeting house to begin their journey. Wives and youngsters held tenaciously to their loved ones, reluctant to let them go. The horses carried saddlebags filled with jerky, corn bread, and dried nuts and berries. Water would be taken from the river they would follow as they headed north.

No one found it easy to leave. Joshua eventually slapped the reins against his horse's neck and pulled on the leather strap of a bridle, and in doing so, assumed command of the group. The horse he rode was the same mount that had brought him to Schoenbrunn a few months earlier.

Noah was a large bay who had seen better days as a plow horse, but Joshua trusted him. The horse tossed his head, and his creamy mane bounced up and down as if he remembered what travel was all about and was anxious to begin.

"Be safe," several people called out while husbands leaned down from their horses to give their wives one last hug.

"Go with God," Brother David encouraged.

Ruth Lyons stood directly behind the elder, leaning against her husband's shoulder. One hand held tightly to her husband's, and the other shaded her eyes from the sun.

"Bring my son back," she said quietly.

Brother David turned and nodded. "They will," he replied. "We have prayed for them."

While the men began their trek, Callie fretted in her cabin. She had wanted to be there to see them off but had been unable to make herself go. She was too afraid of overhearing something that might be said of her, and she didn't want to admit how much it hurt to think of Joshua leaving.

The worry that had coursed through her when he came to tell her he was going had been unlike any emotion she had ever experienced. But somehow she had reached inside herself and found the strength she needed to stand quietly and let him go without saying anything.

Though she couldn't bring her feet to walk through it, she had left her door partway open. Now she could hear the whinny of anxious horses and the calls of the rest of the mission population bidding farewell as the men started out.

She moved quickly to the doorway to watch. Joshua, astride a bulky mount, was easy to spot, and her eyes lingered on him. He raised a hand to wave at the crowd gathered around the meeting house, and discomfort worse than that of riding in a buckboard wagon weighed her down.

As if he sensed what she was contemplating, Joshua turned and glanced toward her cabin. Callie stumbled backward, not realizing the shadows of her home hid her. As she watched, his eyes seemed to tarry on her half-open door, perhaps inviting her to step outside into the open and wave farewell. There was an enormous tug on her heart, and for a moment, her knees weakened.

Nonetheless, as she remembered why he was leaving, her cheeks burned with shame at the memory of having to tell Brother David she had found Sarah missing. And that was just the beginning. It didn't compare to how she felt when they began to suspect Levi had accompanied Sarah.

Callie inhaled sharply. The panic she felt when she had found Sarah gone returned, slicing through her stomach with the claws of a mountain lion. It was made even worse by the fact that she had done nothing but sit in a chair and wait for her sister to return.

Wrapped up in her own disavowal of Sarah's confession, she had thought her sister had run to MaryBeth's and would come back when the two girls had caught up on whatever it was they talked about.

A new wave of helplessness assailed her. Why hadn't she remembered that Sarah had admitted she and MaryBeth had had a disagreement? That Sarah had said she doubted she and the girl would ever work it out? How much of a head start had her failure to act given the couple?

Bitter recriminations stung her eyes while the word "disgrace" echoed in her mind. Sarah had humiliated not only herself but the entire mission by running off with a man and leaving no note of explanation or farewell. Callie tried hard, but at this moment she couldn't see how she could ever forgive Sarah for this. Somehow, she didn't think Sarah wanted her forgiveness anyway.

After all, Callie couldn't help thinking, hadn't Sarah admitted she had confessed Jesus only to pacify her sister? There was no denying Sarah's words. They had poured out of her like water sliding off a cliff. Callie rubbed at her temples where the pounding seemed to hurt the worst.

Where would it end? Would she ever see Sarah again? Or was she destined to remember her as she saw her last—strawberry curls tumbling around her pale face, brown eyes stricken with the deception she had been hiding for who knew how long.

She rose, not bothering to straighten the top of her dress as she usually did after sitting, her weary steps tracing the beginning of a worn trail in the straw on the floor.

"You cannot change history," Brother David had told her shortly after he and his flock had taken her and Sarah into their fold after the flood. "Nor should anyone ever want to, for it makes us who we are today and who we will become tomorrow. If we follow God's path, we can never go wrong."

Remember those words, she told herself. *Cling to them now while my heart is heavy with what Sarah has said and done and the knowledge that Joshua has gone.*

She passed the window and rose up on her tiptoes in the hope of catching a glimpse of the party Joshua led, though they certainly were out of sight by now, having left several minutes ago. Then, realizing the uselessness of her action, she wrung her hands together, hunched her shoulders, and went back to pacing.

✍

Callie's days and nights were oppressed by an agony she could not eradicate from her soul. As she had shortly after Sarah's disappearance, she refused to see anyone, ignoring well-meaning knocks on the door and anxious voices shouting through the wooden planks that had been firmly laced together.

She watched the hours stretch ahead of her, rotating from pink, empty dawn through the day to an even emptier purple night. Bible verses flitted through her mind, but she began to question their truths and promises.

After one particularly harrowing day in which Callie burned her hand on the kettle over the fire and stubbed her toe on a stone barrier put in front of the hearth to help catch stray embers, she collapsed on her bed in tears.

The sound of her door scraping across the wooden frame jolted her. She wiped the fuzziness of tears from her eyes and looked up to find Levi and Suzannah's mother, Ruth, standing over her. Ruth had her hands settled on her hips and a grim look of determination on a face that was tired and drawn.

"What are you doing?" Callie asked. She was about to demand that Ruth leave her alone so she could continue to wallow in her misery without contaminating anyone else.

"Someone had to tell you, and I figured it might as well be me." Ruth settled into a rocking chair near Callie's bed and gave her a look that warned Callie to listen without interrupting.

"MaryBeth has confessed that she knew Sarah had been planning something," Ruth announced without any trace of the sunshiny-bright tone she normally used.

Callie absorbed the statement, feeling the slightest glimmer of hope begin to build inside her. She should have thought to ask

MaryBeth herself if she knew anything, instead of hiding away from everyone. But the glimmer lasted only a moment. No, she was better off alone. To depend on others was not something she could do. She would face this just as she had learned to face the orphanage and what had happened afterward. Alone.

"How do you know that is not some story MaryBeth made up to get people to quit pestering her?" she contested.

"No one is doing that," Ruth replied. "Perhaps she did not realize Sarah was serious. You know how it is with young people, they sometimes. . ." Ruth's words faded, and a pained expression crossed her face.

Callie had stayed under her covers in her bed. Now she pushed herself up and pulled the blanket up to her chin. "Perhaps that is the problem. I do not understand young people any more than I understand myself."

Ruth covered her face with her hands. "First Suzannah and the baby, now Levi. . ." Sharp agony was apparent in the woman's sobs.

Callie hadn't thought about the fact that Ruth, who had just lost a third granddaughter, had now lost her only son also.

"I am sorry, too, Ruth, but what am I supposed to do? Sarah obviously did not wish to remain here, and so she. . ."—she gestured helplessly—"she talked Levi into doing something insane."

Ruth twisted her fingers in the seam that ran alongside her dress. "It might have been Levi's idea. You cannot blame just Sarah."

Callie struggled to hold her tears in. "I think Sarah sees this as a game. She told me that since I had never had fun, I did not know how to let her do so."

Ruth raised her eyebrows. "I am sure she did not mean it. You know how Sarah is, always chattering on and on without meaning much."

"Yes, well, she took us all for fools, did she not?" There was tartness in Callie's tone.

The idea that her sister had deserted her—and with a man, no less—and she had not suspected it, had been eating away at her. She wanted to shout at the heavens in much the same way Sarah had on the trip from Pennsylvania to Schoenbrunn. Instead, she crumpled her hands together in her lap and looked at Ruth.

Ruth's ebony eyes shone bright over her pinched lips, making Callie feel awkward. Here Callie had been feeling sorry for herself, forgetting that the woman across the table had lost so much. Had she no sense of compassion? No, she could feel Ruth's hopelessness as if it were a tangible thing.

"Sarah began acting strangely not too long ago," Callie said without prompting. "Now I see she was leading up to this. I did not press her because she always got so tired of me telling her what to do."

The tears were getting closer. She could feel them filling the lids of her eyes. "All I wanted was to bring her up properly. You understand, do you not?"

And it was all a farce, a little voice inside her head said. *Nothing you did proved to be any good. Sarah is gone!*

Ruth moved to Callie's side. If the woman was desolate, she hid it well. "No one blames you. You did the best you could."

Callie moaned. "But my best was not good enough. She is gone and Levi is with her, and now we have sent men off to explore a part of the wilderness no one knows in order to find them. What if Sarah does not want to be found? What if something happens to her and Levi?"

She didn't say his name out loud, but the concern she had for Joshua was uppermost in her mind, almost pushing away the worry over her sister.

"We must trust God to lead them home."

Callie stiffened. "The whole mission is in an uproar and it is my fault. I would not blame Brother David if he asked me to return to Pennsylvania tomorrow."

Ruth laid a hand on Callie's shoulder and squeezed gently. "It is not in an uproar and you are not leaving. You tend our sick." Ruth's hand trembled, and Callie felt her own weariness mingle with the woman's.

Ruth went on. "Have you forgotten that when we think the world is against us, we must ask God to make it right?"

"So I am allowed to stay because I have skills the mission needs?" Callie asked, deflecting the part about praying. "That is comforting."

She turned tear-drenched eyes toward the woman standing beside her. *A mother would do this,* she thought. *A mother would hold, and hug, and tell me it will be better tomorrow.* But she had no mother or father. She had only substitutes who had their own families and lives to worry about.

Ruth shook her head. "You are staying because we love you. And because you love God. It is His grace that has brought us to this point. The trials we face on earth are designed to make us stronger in the end."

"But Sarah—" Callie began.

"Shhh." Ruth ran her fingers through Callie's hair, arranging the tousled curls into some semblance of order. "Now is not the time to worry. Now is the time to pray."

"God will hate me for saying this, but I cannot. The words will not come." Callie's voice was rife with painful emotion. Without thinking, she threw herself against Ruth's ample frame.

"There, there." Ruth smoothed her hand across Callie's forehead and looked into her eyes. "God will not desert you. Nor will He desert Levi and Sarah, no matter what they do. He is always there. And there is nothing you or they are going through that He does not understand."

"Do you really believe that?"

A look of surprise flitted across Ruth's face. "Do you think I would have agreed to come to this wilderness if I did not?"

Callie pulled away from Ruth. "Why *did* you come? You and Zeke must have given up a lot to do this." It felt good to think about something else. She was tired of worrying over Sarah—and Joshua.

"There are times in your life when you have to quit looking back at who you were and start looking ahead to who you can become. Zeke and I had our troubles early on, and many times we almost caved in and allowed Satan to control us." She shivered. "How glad I am we did not."

"You mean you almost left Zeke?"

"No. We almost left Jesus."

"What happened?" The question was out before Callie could stop it, but Ruth's arm was around her shoulder and it made her feel more secure than she had in a long time.

Ruth sighed. "You might as well know. Perhaps it will help in some way."

"If you do not want to share, I will understand," Callie said, even though she was very curious.

"Brother David and his flock had camped not too far from our home," Ruth began. "We were young then. Suzannah was a wee babe and Levi was just beginning to kick within."

Ruth's eyes misted over and Callie drew her down onto the bed beside her. Suddenly Callie was the comforter, not the comforted, a role for which she was more experienced.

"We went to one of his fellowship meetings, mainly because he promised a free meal. Nothing was growing in our garden, and hunting did not bring much to our table. We had sold about every piece of furniture and hand-me-down we owned to buy a cow so we had milk."

Callie brushed a speck of straw from Ruth's sleeve. "That is terrible."

"It would have been, had we allowed ourselves to continue." Ruth swallowed hard. "Zeke had taken to traveling around the countryside and snatching stray chickens. I begged him not to, but it meant eating."

"Did you not have relatives who could help you?"

Ruth nodded. "There were kinfolk—lived not too far away as a matter of fact. But they tossed us out when Suzannah was born two months early. Said they knew what we had been doing before we married." Ruth wiped her eyes then pursed her lips. "We had not. She *was* early, but both sides refused to see us or help us. Said we had made our bed, we could lie in it."

Suzannah's tendency to have her babies early might just run in the family, Callie realized. She shifted on the bed. "Your families disowned you?"

"That is about the size of it."

"How did Brother David make such a difference?" She knew how he had helped her after the orphanage had been destroyed, how his flock had taken her and Sarah in, provided them with shelter and food, and love. And now Sarah had turned her back on that. The memory stabbed afresh in her heart.

"Brother David showed us what God's love is really all about. After we had been to one meeting, we found ourselves going back. The women in the group would take Suzannah so we could listen to the sermons. It was like being home, Callie. No one condemned us for what they thought we had done. They accepted us as we were, no questions asked."

"They loved you. That is what you are saying." The words slipped naturally from Callie's lips. She had known the same kind of acceptance when she had first been introduced to the Moravian flock.

"Yes, but more importantly, they showed us that God loves us and always will."

"Sarah does not think a loving God would let bad things happen," Callie admitted. She could say that much without telling Ruth what else Sarah had said about not believing.

"Suzannah was like that once," Ruth replied. "She did not believe it either."

"Suzannah rebelled? But she is such a strong Christian now."

"You might not recall doing so, but it seems to me that most young folks rebel at least once in their lives. They listen to their minds not to their hearts."

"So you think Sarah might return to God one day?"

"I cannot tell the future, but I do know that since you two joined us, you have given her a solid foundation to build on. It may sound cruel, but if Sarah chooses otherwise, you cannot let that destroy your life. Do you understand me?"

Callie shifted her gaze to the fireplace for a long minute before she looked back at Ruth. "It is the same with Levi, is it not? You brought him up the best you could, but after a point, what he chooses to do is his decision?"

Ruth nodded. "I think there is a young lady you need to visit. MaryBeth has been worried day and night that you will never speak to her again."

"She should not be. It was hardly her fault." Callie was suddenly aware of the truth of that statement. It was not MaryBeth's fault Sarah had run off. There was no one to blame but Sarah and Levi. That included herself, though she was not ready to let go of her guilt yet.

The knowledge didn't change the fact that no matter what she had tried to do, how she had tried to raise her, Sarah was gone. With Levi, who had not so very long ago taken her to the spring and insisted he had to talk to her. Something was not quite right about the whole thing.

Callie thought back, trying to re-create exactly what Levi had said. Had his actions even then been part of his plan to run away with Sarah? Since that day, he had been strangely detached. On top of losing his niece, Callie supposed she had given him plenty to think about when she spouted off about her not being a trinket to be played with. A lump settled in her stomach. But if she had not pushed him away, he probably wouldn't have taken Sarah and fled. That would mean it *was* her fault.

Ruth touched her elbow and she realized she had been preoccupied. MaryBeth knew something about her sister. She hadn't gotten past the shock of thinking of Levi and Sarah alone together on the trail, but she could not bear to push all thought of her only surviving relative aside.

Callie stood on MaryBeth's doorstep, wishing the last five days had been one of the bad dreams that kept plaguing her.

"Why did you not tell me what Sarah was planning?" She tried not to sound too accusing.

The girl looked at her through eyes as red from crying as her own. "I did not know she really meant it. She mentioned taking a trip a couple of months ago, but how was I supposed to know she was serious?"

That sounded like Sarah, Callie admitted to herself. Her sister had often made comments about wanting to leave the mission, needing to return to Pennsylvania. It would do no good to rail at MaryBeth. The poor child was trembling in her shoes as it was.

Callie inhaled slowly. "MaryBeth. . ." she started then stopped. The girl was devastated; even in Callie's own emotional state she could see that. "I do not hold it against you. It is. . .I had such hopes you might. . ."

MaryBeth fell toward her, her giant sobs tearing to shreds any piece of Callie's heart that remained unbroken. She embraced MaryBeth, her chin resting on top of MaryBeth's head. If she could not have Sarah, she could at least try to make MaryBeth feel better.

She raised her eyes and looked at the sky. White clouds darted, their wisps looking as if someone had run a giant brush through them. The sun shone with such force, it was almost blinding. Somewhere miles from here, men from the mission were traipsing after her sister and Levi. Joshua was with them. All she had been able to say to him was "Godspeed." She had even refused to go to the meeting house for the farewell prayer. Her heart faltered, and a sinking feeling fell over her.

She thought about the unknown territory her sister and Levi, and Joshua and the search party, were venturing into. Would they make it? All of them? *Any* of them? Despite renegade Indians, overanxious soldiers, hungry wildlife? What would befall them?

MaryBeth's sobs quieted as she leaned against Callie's chest. Callie felt awkward holding her. Sarah had never allowed such closeness. Her pulse drummed away, pushing away her fears for the moment as her own emotions produced wet trails down her cheeks. Despite how she felt about Sarah running away, she desperately hoped that someday she would once again see her sister.

Chapter 10

The nightmare woke her again. Three times in the past four nights she had bolted from sleep where she battled dark demons—faceless, voiceless shapes pressing in on her; just hands reaching and grabbing for her.

The heat had been so oppressive, she had found it hard to sleep. And the ever-present dread and anxiety that clung to her as she thought of Sarah did not contribute to a pleasant state of mind either. Perhaps that is why the terrible dreams had come.

She shivered as she swung her legs to the floor. She had experienced dreams of this sort after the flood and her accident. Then, Brother David had appointed different women to sit with her throughout the nights, to help chase away the screams and horrendous sounds. Why had they returned? It had been well over five years, and she had always associated them with her head injury.

She reached up and fingered the knot located just inside the hairline on the left side of her head. It was the only outward indication of her accident that remained. The bumps and bruises suffered as she was swept along by the raging flood had faded, leaving only a gaping hole in her memory, much as the waters left destruction behind as they receded.

She wished Sarah were here, for then the cabin would be filled with the scent of coffee brewing and stew warming. Sarah had always been first out of bed and had done those tasks.

There will be no more days like that, Callie speculated, as rain began hitting the roof, providing a chilling accompaniment to her morose thoughts.

For a moment she watched the drops cascade down the oiled paper covering the window. The paper had been rubbed with bear fat to help it repel water. Suddenly cold, she grabbed a blanket and tossed it around her shoulders. It was all so depressing—the nightmare and thoughts of Sarah and her deceit.

Her eyes tracked the water sliding down the window covering. She welcomed the rain after the stickiness of the last few days. It meant her rounds of the sick would be delayed, but she had no serious illnesses at the moment to care for.

After Ruth's visit, and her own with MaryBeth, she had resumed working with the mission's ill. Ruth had been right: Brother David was astonished to hear Callie thought she would be asked to leave.

"No one wants you to go," he had exclaimed when she confessed to him that she no longer felt worthy of staying. "You have done nothing to warrant our asking you to depart."

Callie had mumbled that she didn't deserve to be around those who loved God, but the elder would have none of it.

"The events of the last few weeks have depressed you, sister. Give it time. It is just as before, when you recovered from the flood. Your heart knows what is right." He had patted her hand and given her one of his most encouraging smiles, as if that were all that needed to be said on the matter.

It felt good to be wanted, and Callie did so want to believe he was right. But inside she no longer thought she was good enough to be a Christian. After all, she had failed in her effort to teach her sister to live a proper life. She had not been able to save three of the four Solomon children. On top of that, her un-Christian thoughts and words toward Levi proved she was not worthy of God's love.

Perhaps if she were wiser, or older? Callie rubbed at her eyes as tears threaded her lashes. Perhaps if she had had parents who hadn't abandoned her? She whisked the thought away and tried thinking of the garden plot where seedlings stretched their shoots skyward. This was much needed rain for them. She pictured the plants welcoming the refreshing drops.

Thunder suddenly rolled across the village. The room grew dark. She lit a candle and straightened her dress, noticing a small tear in the hem and making a mental note to mend it later.

Thunder cracked again, closer this time, splitting the air with its might. Following it came an eerie roar she could not place.

"I should get fresh water from the spring before the rain becomes too heavy," she murmured to herself.

Half rising from the chair, she heard the rain begin in earnest. Lightning flashed, so close that it brightened the room. She had never liked lightning, and now as twigs snapped on the oak tree beside her cabin, her pulse quickened. In the year they had lived here, there had been few storms that had sounded so ferocious. After one strong storm, Callie had spent the next day picking up leaves and branches. Sarah had helped her, laughing and giggling as they worked.

Sarah is gone, she remembered, the thought throwing a pall over everything. *She deserted me just as our parents did.* The torment that flowed through her matched the roar of the wind outside, and she collapsed into the rocker, oblivious to nature's fury.

Joshua drew his horse to a halt and looked back at the tree-laden terrain they had just climbed. The hill was covered in a soft blanket of early green and led to a valley full of trees that would turn butter yellow and flaming red in the fall. Birds flitted among the treetops. Meandering through the lowland was the river that would lead them back to Schoenbrunn, which they had left six days ago. Or rather, it would lead the rest of the party back.

Noah tossed his head in the air and snorted. They had been together so long, Joshua barely had to guide his mount, which gave him plenty of opportunity to think, to probe his heart and decide what he wanted above all else. Each time, the image of Callie inserted itself in his mind, and just as quickly, he forced it away. To remember the pain in her eyes was worse than not being able to do anything about it. Being on the trail, at least, was a tangible way he could help.

In order to return safely once he left the group, he would need to keep his wits about him. He studied a line of ominous black clouds to the south.

"Looks like we are in for a bad one," he called to the men who had accompanied him. "Let us find shelter and bed down for the night."

"What about the others?" one asked.

Shadow and another had gone ahead to scout for tracks. The plan was for the group to meet up each night. With the storm heading in, they had no choice but to abandon that for now.

"We will catch up with them tomorrow."

He was proud of the distance they had put behind them. Following the muddy brown river had not been difficult. Very little brush grew along the banks, allowing them to keep the horses close to the water.

Joshua had not liked agreeing to let Shadow and the other man go. He would have preferred they all stick together, but as Shadow had pointed out, "We can search better if some of us are looking for tracks while the others come along behind, carefully scanning the terrain for Sarah and Levi."

Joshua had nodded, and after a quick prayer in which he beseeched the heavenly Father to guard their footsteps, he had sent them on their way. Each evening, they selected a resting place and waited for Joshua and the others to join them.

The decision to stop now had not been easy. A forbidding tremor worked up his spine, but he passed it off. What choice did he have? The cloud bank was bearing down on them faster than he had realized, and if they didn't hurry, they would be caught out in the open.

The anxious looks on the faces of his fellow searchers said they, too, were worried about not meeting the other two as planned. He gave them a quick smile.

Forks of lightning split the sky and he pulled on Noah's reins. "Let's find cover, boy." He clucked to his mount and Noah picked up his heavy hooves and began to move hurriedly back down the hill.

❧

Callie was unaware of the problem until someone pounded on her door. "There has been a storm," came the shout.

Flying down the footpath, her anxiety rose as her eyes traced the storm's destructive path. After sweeping across the east end of the garden, it had torn through a once sturdy pole fence then pounced upon four cabins, erasing their roofs as easily as children cleaned their slate boards in school.

Branches and leaves were scattered across the greening grass, and chunks of chinking were strewn about. The storm had moved on as rapidly as it had arrived, allowing brittle sunshine to illuminate the mission. Fear roiled in her throat, but she thrust her head up, determined to meet this disaster head-on.

"The wounded are at the meeting house," Brother David called from across the clearing where he was already tugging at logs that had been carelessly tossed about by the wind.

She patched minor cuts and bruises, reassured all those she treated that everything would be fine, and wandered back to the entrance. Now that she knew no one had been seriously injured, the sun's glow seemed softer, as if God had lessened the blow.

The worst she had treated had been a bump on Levi's father's head, a wound he sustained by falling over a chair leg in his haste to see the storm's damage. Callie selected a quiet place off to one side from which to watch the activity. Raindrops glittered in the debris-strewn grass and the dusky sun warmed her skin, but there was a hollow feeling in her soul.

The families whose homes had suffered the brunt of the wind huddled together, staring wide-eyed at what was left of their lives. Brother David ran back and forth, seeming to be everywhere at once. A faded gray shirt thrown over his shoulders and a look of fatigue on his face, he hollered directions and paced among the damaged cabins. Someone near Callie called out to him. He hurried over. She watched as he cocked his head and listened to the man explain something.

The elder straightened and looked about him, assessing the situation. Reeling off names, he pointed to the front of one of the cabins.

"See what we can salvage and pile it out of the way."

His gaze met Callie's. He didn't seem at all surprised to see her but gave her a slight nod of acknowledgment before turning back to his damaged dream.

Callie surveyed the storm's hopscotch method of reclaiming for nature what had come from nature in the first place. The sight left her nauseous, but she forced the queasy feeling away.

A handful of men joined them, their sleek dark hair pulled away from their faces and plaited in tight braids down their backs. They stared together, their jaws tight as they surveyed the scene.

"We must gather whatever we can that is still usable," Brother David said, dismissing the group.

Soon, a pile of usable roof slats stood as a silent tribute to their will to begin anew. Farther away, another pile was growing—it consisted of damaged boards and materials that they would later burn.

While the men worked, the women, led by Ruth Lyons, were inside preparing a meal. Callie joined them. Ruth bustled around, heaping mounds of thin pancakes onto a wooden platter and directing Callie to stir the maple syrup she was warming in a pot over the fire.

The sugary smell of overdone maple filled the cabin. Callie helped collect the sticky sap each year. Some of it was used to make sugar; the rest was boiled down until it became the sweet-tasting liquid in Callie's pot. She took a deep breath, filling her lungs with the pleasing scent.

When there was nothing else to rescue from the damaged homes, the men headed to David's cabin to eat. Sitting out back, eating flatcakes, they discussed how they would reroof the cabins. With full stomachs and aching muscles, they returned to their labors.

Callie checked on the injured she had treated earlier, then went home. She tried to put out of mind the rhythmic thudding of axes that meant restoration of the mission was under way. She realized with a start that Joshua's home had been one of those that had lost its roof.

What would he do now? Where would he stay? Would it matter? Perhaps he would see this as a sign he should not stay at Schoenbrunn. Somehow, the thought filled her with gloom.

Ruth Lyons called out, pulling Callie out of her misery. Without much enthusiasm, Callie motioned for the woman to enter. Strands of silver hair hung from the bun that was usually tightly wound against the back of the older woman's neck, and Ruth's gray eyes were bloodshot.

Callie shifted clothing from a chair to the table to clear a seat. After some small talk, during which both women politely avoided talking about Sarah and Levi, their conversation turned to the storm. Callie recounted the injuries.

"I am so grateful they were not worse than they were," she finished after describing everything she had treated.

Ruth's face brightened. "If it were not for that fool husband of mine, you would have had next to nothing to treat, is that not true?"

Callie agreed, though with little spirit in her words. As if by mutual agreement, they speculated on how long it would take to fix the damaged homes. They determined it would be at least a full week, barring any work on the Sabbath three days hence.

Ruth sighed. "If I know my husband, he will be growling for food again soon." She moved to the door. "Is there anything I can help you with?"

Callie shook her head and watched as Ruth departed.

She was glad Ruth had come by, for now, without anyone to speak with, memories of Joshua ran through her heart. The way he had stood, poised and confident, as he prepared to leave to search for her sister and Levi. The way he had appeared to want to reach out and push away her fears but held back as if he were afraid she would shove him away.

Thinking about him did no good. It would not bring him back, nor would it bring Sarah and Levi back. Despite her best intentions, she continued to see Joshua's laughing blue eyes staring at her. Finally, disgusted with herself, she headed back to the damaged portion of the settlement to again offer her help.

The men had reconstructed a roof frame for one cabin, and with grunts and groans, they were raising it into position. Using a blunt mallet, they forced the notches together where they did not line up just right. A hatchet in someone's hand thudded on the opposite end, chipping off a segment that was too long.

In minutes, the skeleton was in place. All that remained was to fill the gaps with lengths of bark then add mud and let the sun's heat dry it. Men were sent to the river to collect yellow clay for the chinking. Months of experimenting had proven the yellowish, tacky earth made the best filler.

While the workers were gone, mugs of cold spring water were prepared. When the men returned with the clay, they mixed it with the water and busied themselves spreading the mixture between logs.

Callie contemplated why she had returned to watch the men. *So I can tell Sarah what is going on,* she thought, until she remembered that Sarah was not at the mission, and then she had to wipe at the tears that formed.

Abe Solomon and another man tugged at a log protruding tenaciously from the earth where high winds had planted it. Brother David had a portion of another log wedged under the buried end and was trying to pry the first one out from the hole it was buried in. The only thing they had succeeded in doing was making the mire around the hole slipperier than it had been when they started.

Abe threw his weight against the log. At the same time, the elder pushed down. Abe slipped and fell, splashing mud and bits of bark over all of them. There was a moment of strained silence. All who were watching held their breath. Then the men moved away from the log, holding their sides and laughing.

Before long, a mud-slinging contest had ensued.

"If you cannot beat them, join them," David's baritone rang out. He slung a particularly gooey mass of mud at Abe.

The ruckus brought youngsters, who rapidly realized a game was in progress. Even the most timid child was soon picking up grubby handfuls and heaving them, not caring who they hit. A glob landed on the elder's forehead and dribbled down his eyebrows, giving him the appearance of having raccoon eyes.

A rich peal of laughter rang out. For half an hour the men tossed mud with abandon while the women watched from a safe distance, some with smirks on their lips, others enjoying unrestrained laughter, a rarity for them.

Ruth Lyons launched a double-size handful of mud at her husband. The sight of the demure woman aiming at and hitting her spouse generated a spontaneous roar from those who were not participating. While the men destroyed the once green ground, Callie watched, knowing that once their joy was exhausted, they would turn back to more serious things. Even so, a small chuckle worked its way out of her own mouth.

⁂

The search party returned two days later, announced by the squeals of children racing through the settlement and accompanied by the grunts of horses who knew they were home. Pushing aside the dress she had been mending, Callie's heart jumped to an unnatural rhythm. Not because she would see Joshua, she told herself as she patted her curls under her bonnet, but because Sarah might be with them.

And if Levi were with her, she would, well, she would find a way to handle that. She'd had a week to think, and after spending the first few nights tossing in her bed, she had come to the conclusion that Levi had taken Sarah with him because Callie had made herself unavailable.

Speeding toward the meeting house, she barely noticed that spring seemed to have fled along with the search party a week ago. The May afternoon was warm, filled with sunshine and trees now in full bloom. She tried to stroll, but it didn't work. She was too eager. She imagined Sarah standing there—humbled and repentant—and her steps quickened.

She found herself rounding the meeting house along with other settlers, her feet barely skimming the ground. The riders were off their mounts, their arms enveloping their families. The horses pawed the ground, giving notice that they, too, expected attention.

As she entered the area where the horses were tethered, she could not help but count the animals.

No! That was the wrong number!

She counted again.

Four.

Her footsteps slowed while shivers danced on her spine. Four horses were too few to have returned with her sister.

Around her the laughter of riders hugging their way through reunions pierced her heart. Her mind refused to accept what she already knew—that she was not looking for Sarah as much as for a lanky frame. But there was no dusty slouch hat topping a head of wavy black hair among those who had returned.

She stood motionless for an eternity before Brother David's arm went around her shoulder in a fatherly way, and he spoke softly, drawing her away from the back of the meeting house as he did.

"The men say Joshua refused to come back."

She wrenched away and covered her ears with her hands.

The elder was not deterred and continued. "It is not what you think. They found tracks. The others knew they were expected, so. . ."

She whipped back to face him.

"But they did not find them," she said. She scowled at her feet and ground a tuft of grass into the dirt with her shoe.

He shook his head as if it were the last thing in the world he wanted to do. "Not yet. That is why Joshua stayed on the trail. He ordered the rest to come back without him."

"Why?"

If he was out there alone, how much danger was he in? At least Sarah had Levi with her.

"He told the others it was something he needed to do," Brother David said.

"By himself? Who does he think he is? He has no help. No food.

He could become hurt." She tried not to sound too alarmed but failed miserably. Her words certainly did not overcome the ominous pang in her stomach.

"He is a man driven by the desire to do the right thing, just as you do, as any of us will do, when faced with a crisis. I admit he is in dangerous country. The reports about the soldiers who seek to control the rivers and streams for furs are not good. Nor are the reports we are hearing about the Indian raids that have begun." He heaved a deep sigh. "We must pray that God will keep Joshua safe."

Prayer! What had that gained her lately? It had not helped Suzannah, nor had it brought her sister or Joshua back. Her stomach clenched.

"I have prayed since the day I discovered Sarah missing," she blurted. Only she knew how many petitions she had whispered.

"Then you have been faithful. Now you must wait for God to reveal His response at the time He chooses."

"What if His answer is that none of them comes back alive?" she asked, barely able to fight off the fear revealed in her eyes.

He did not attempt an answer.

"Where do I go from here?"

"You go nowhere, Callie. This is your home."

Home? It was where she lived, where she prayed, where she hoped. But home? No, she had no home. Home meant family, happiness, hope. She had none of those left.

Chapter 11

The next few weeks passed in a fog. Several travelers arrived from the sister mission downriver, Gnadenhutten, known affectionately as "Ja-nade-den." The German name meant "Huts of Grace." Most of the Mohicans living there had traveled with Brother David on his initial pilgrimage out of Pennsylvania and knew almost everyone at Schoenbrunn.

Like their Moravian brothers and sisters, they were a serious folk, struggling to achieve perfection and looking toward the future with hope. Most had left behind family members and understood the loss Callie endured.

Though the two settlements were separated by a scant few hours of travel, they did not gather together often, and when they did, there was much to catch up on. They shared stories of crop planting, participated in worship services, and helped to clear the land.

The women fussed over Callie, encouraging her without mentioning Sarah's name. Callie didn't bring it up, either, for to do so might bring up Joshua's name, which she could not seem to sweep from her thoughts.

Occasional joys reminded Callie that life went on. For example, there was excitement over a new convert baptized into Christ and happiness over the birth of a babe to a family from Gnaden. But even that last was bittersweet, for the birth brought back memories of Joshua assisting Suzannah when they had lost Sophie Ruth.

Callie had cleaned up the red and squalling infant and abruptly handed it to the mother before hastening away, unable to stay because she was not comfortable.

The days seemed hopelessly long without anyone to talk to. Quite often she went to the base of a tree near the cemetery and sat, staring off at the distant rolling hills as if being around those at peace would in some way soothe the ache in her breast, an ache that she realized could be attributed to the fact that she wished to see Joshua one more time, if only to ask him about the orphanage.

One day, she dug scraggly dandelions from a patch growing wild and planted them carefully on the three Solomon graves. Her tears mingled with the clumps of dirt as she patted the earth into place around their roots. Occasionally she looked toward heaven for an answer.

God seemed strangely silent, and she couldn't help but wonder if He had forsaken her much as Sarah had turned from Him.

July was half over when Brother David announced plans for a fellowship day. According to the nineteen rules of conduct each member of their society had agreed on when they established the mission, dancing and drinking spirits were not allowed. The children played games in the newly cleared pasture, and the adults spent the day feasting and moving about among the small groups that formed.

Contentment flowed among the settlers, but their happiness did not improve Callie's outlook. Soon it would be fall, and Callie knew no more of the whereabouts of Joshua, Sarah, and Levi than she had when they left. Unaware, Joshua's name had gradually crept to the forefront of her thoughts. When winter arrived, how would he stay warm and dry? What would he eat? And most of all, she wondered if he ever thought about her.

✍

Callie had volunteered to watch Storm, the young Delaware who Joshua had helped to save, for a few hours, and she took him to sit under the large oak near her cabin to eat lunch.

Since recovering from the fever that a few months ago threatened his life, Storm had literally grown by leaps and bounds. He was a strong-willed, energetic child with no signs that his illness had weakened him. When he was on the move, Callie had to struggle to keep up with him. While infants continued to frighten her, she was comfortable with those who walked upright, and she enjoyed answering Storm's curious questions.

She hastily prayed a blessing then handed Storm two slices of bread with creamy apple butter slathered on them. He ate as if he had not yet eaten that day, despite having finished his morning meal just a few hours earlier. When he was finished, he toddled off. Callie leaned back with her palms behind her on the blanket of soft green grass and watched him. Thick black hair dangled around his face as he shouted in glee at the caterpillar he had found crawling up the tree.

"Put it down," Callie admonished gently.

Storm dropped his head until his miniature chin clipped his chest. "My bug."

"It is God's bug. Put it back on the tree so it can climb."

"I climb, too." His eyes shone.

Callie knew he was recalling the walk they had taken yesterday when she had allowed him to totter across a fallen tree. She had kept his hand firmly clasped in hers, but he had thought he had done it all by himself.

She patted her lap. "Sit here and I will tell you a story."

Storm loved stories, for his mother insisted he learn his heritage, even if she could no longer practice what had once been essential ceremonies. Callie smoothed her skirts after she got the child settled. Her fingers traced the features of his sloped jaw, his baby-soft skin tugging at her heart. She wondered what a child of Joshua's would look like.

Heat flamed in her cheeks. What was she doing thinking about Joshua and having children? Children brought heartbreak, if not through dying before they could live, then they might contract a fatal illness or grow up to run off as had her own sister. She would do well to put the idea of what a young version of Joshua might look like out of her mind.

"Do," Storm ordered impatiently.

Thankful for the interruption that pulled her away from dangerous thoughts, Callie began the well-loved tale of how Rabbit got his tail. Storm listened intently, begging her to repeat the part where bits of fluff like feathers fell from the sky and startled Rabbit so much that he began to run around and around.

When she talked about the fluffy stuff falling thicker and deeper, Storm clapped his hands together, though he quieted when the fluff stopped and Rabbit looked around.

As she whispered how Rabbit slept and woke to find himself at the top of a tree, Storm relaxed against her, but she could feel him hold his breath as she talked about a hawk diving toward Rabbit.

"The hawk had huge wings, and though he was after Rabbit, those frightful wings were so big they knocked Rabbit off the branch."

Storm hugged her, bringing a swell of emotion to her heart. By the time she finished the story with Rabbit's ears stretching as branches tugged at them and how his front feet got shorter when he landed on them first, Storm had dozed off.

Callie gently maneuvered him off her lap and onto the blanket, absentmindedly patting his back and feeling his chest rise and fall. Giving in to the peace she was experiencing, she closed her eyes and let the unseasonably warm sun bathe her face.

"You seem to be quite the picture of contentment, Sister Callie." The male voice startled her until she realized it was Abe, Suzannah's husband.

She opened her eyes guiltily. "Uh, yes," she replied, checking Storm to see if he had slipped away while she had been indulging in reverie.

Abe's weathered face was covered with a fine sheen of dust acquired when he worked with the oxen to dig a new garden patch.

"I heard you have given up teaching the small ones in Sunday lessons," he began. "It is good to see you have not totally given up being with children."

Not too long after losing Sophie Ruth, Callie had begged off working with the toddlers. Did Abe know that since they had lost Sophie Ruth, she was terrified to be around helpless infants?

"I am so sorry. . . ."

Abe held up a hand. "I did not come to get your apology. I came to ask a favor."

"A favor?" What could she do that no one else in the mission could?

He gave her a solemn nod. "I want you to go to Suzannah."

Callie twisted her hands together under her apron so Abe would not see. Go see Suzannah? They had once been the closest of friends, but in recent months Callie had looked for ways to avoid her. The thought of having to look Suzannah in the eye, knowing she had failed her, settled like a boulder in Callie's stomach.

"I do not think that is. . .something I can do." The words strangled her.

"I think it is." There was a subtle plea in his tone.

"But what will I say?" She had thought that over many times without ever finding an answer. She could share, but she could not understand the depth of the other woman's pain. After all, Callie had never had a child and never would. All she had to compare motherhood to were her feelings surrounding the loss of Sarah, something she still struggled with and found easier to ignore than to think about.

"You know her well enough that the words will come naturally. I only ask that you do not tell her you are sorry. Neither of us wants to hear that." He cleared his throat. "And do not ask for our forgiveness. There is nothing to forgive. What happened was God's will. We have made our peace with it, even if we do not fully understand." His jaw tightened momentarily.

Callie knew the longer she postponed going to Suzannah, the harder it would be. Had she really thought she would never speak with Suzannah again? No, she had always understood that she would someday have to but had thought that day far off in the future. The issue was easier to deal with that way.

"So it is time for me to make my peace?" she whispered, the words catching in her throat.

"Yes, Callie. It is time. Suzannah knows the pain you are experiencing. She knows the grief you feel. By sharing, you will help to lighten your load and hers."

Brother David once told her joy and disaster were to be shared. Joy brought smiles, while disaster refined the gold hidden deep within each person. What was the rest of that verse in First Peter? She had forgotten it.

"Perhaps I will go after I have returned Storm to his parents." She glanced at the boy who continued to sleep.

Abe rubbed the side of his neck. "No. Please go now. I will watch him." He looked at Storm, whose thumb had crept to the circle of his mouth, and a brief twinge of pain crossed his face.

Callie cringed. She felt as if she were drowning; but if it was something Abe wanted her to do, she would do it. Somehow.

"Is she in the cabin?" How Callie could even enter that cabin, she didn't know.

"No. At the graves." His shoulders sagged. "Did you plant the flowers?"

Callie nodded.

"I told her that, but it just seemed to go over her head. She has been spending all her time there. I do not know what to do. She is so different than she was before. . .the last time. She will not leave Hannah Grace with anyone. She will not do any sewing. No cooking. Nothing. It is as if she is a hollow shell."

I feel the same way when I think about Joshua, Callie thought, but it was a thought better kept to herself.

"Perhaps she is just tired, Abe." She had not seen Suzannah in a while, since the burial service, actually. How long ago had that been? Days? Weeks? No, four months!

"Every woman is tired for a time after giving birth, but that is not it," Abe said. "It is something else." He threw his hands up in the air. "I do not know how to say it. She is not herself, not the Suzannah I love. Will you go to her?"

Abe looked so sure she would refuse that Callie couldn't turn him down. Hadn't he had enough disappointment in his life lately?

"Of course I will." She rose and dusted off her hands. *But what will I say to her when I see her?* That, too, she kept within her.

Chapter 12

Joshua muttered under his breath as the rope bindings around his wrists were cinched tighter. Raw and burning, his arms were tied behind him and felt as though they would fall off at the shoulders. If they did, it would be a relief.

Two British soldiers had taken him hostage. The one glaring at him now did so through a whiskey-induced haze. How men tolerated what spirits did to their bodies and minds Joshua would never understand.

Though their accent was heavy, he could follow what they said and he did not like the sound of it.

"The man will be proud when we drag this fine catch in," the heavy-set one with a double chin crowed.

Joshua contemplated the use of the word "man." Not once had they given any clue as to who "the man" was. Perhaps it was better he not know.

"Aye, he will," agreed the lanky, bearded one that had been Joshua's downfall. His piercing eyes glared at Joshua.

The one behind Joshua guffawed and shoved at him. "Get a move on, mate. We have miles to cover before ye rest now."

Turning to his partner, he snorted. "And we thought we would not find anything worth bringing in once we missed that fiery young lass and her man last week."

Ignoring the way the rope cut into his skin, Joshua focused on what they were saying. He had been close to Sarah and Levi for some time, but he was always one settlement behind, a week too late. These men who had captured him had apparently been hoping to waylay Sarah and Levi. What they probably would have done with Sarah, he wouldn't wish on his worst enemy.

Be that as it may, he would have no opportunity to catch up with the couple now. No, all he could do was pray as he had since the day the Moravians had taken Callie away with them: unceasingly.

Callie found Suzannah kneeling in front of the three little mounds of dirt that contained the children she grieved for. A light breeze gusted occasionally, tossing crinkling leaves around as if they were children's playthings.

Normally, Callie enjoyed seeing the colors of autumn. Today she had no interest in her surroundings, not even in the shrieks of children who had just been let out for a break from school. It was simply background noise to her now.

She studied the huddled figure. Suzannah had her legs tucked under her, her hands clasped in prayer. She was back to her normal thin self, though her dress appeared to hang on her more than it ever had before. A handwoven reed basket sat off to one side. It was Hannah Grace's sleeping place. A swift stab pierced Callie's heart.

"Suzannah?" She muttered the name from a distance, thinking that if she was not heard, she would turn around and leave. The hope was short lived.

Suzannah jerked upright and turned her head, while wiping away crystal drops that were bursting from her eyes. She stared at Callie for a moment then slowly rose from the soft earth.

"You have come."

It was as if the woman had been waiting for her forever. The words slashed into Callie. Her shoulders shook as she was overcome by guilt for having deserted her best friend when she most needed her.

"Suzannah, I. . ." There were no words. She had searched for them many months ago when Suzannah's twins were born dead. She had done the same after Sophie Ruth, but she had not found them then either.

There was a rustle of long skirts and the crackle of dried leaves underfoot. Suzannah flung her arms around Callie's shoulders and emitted tiny sobs, which disappeared into the woven material of Callie's dress.

There was nothing she could do but stand and allow Suzannah her grief. Her own feelings were unsettled right now; and if she spoke, who knew what she might say. Instead, she raised a slender hand to stroke Suzannah's hair.

"Yes, I have come," Callie whispered, feeling even more overwhelmed by guilt than she had imagined. The tremor that passed through Suzannah's body was matched by one of her own.

Suzannah raised her head and put on a brave face. "Do not ever leave me alone again," the woman begged, her hands clasping Callie's and squeezing hard.

Callie returned the pressure, her eyes as bright as her friend's. Without speaking, they strolled to a nearby walnut tree and settled themselves upon the ground. They were not far from Hannah Grace's basket, and Callie felt relieved that Suzannah had not insisted on bringing the sleeping baby with them.

When the significant hush around them seemed too much to bear any longer, she began bravely, "I have been a fool."

She wanted to be honest, to rid herself of the horrible lack of good sense she had exhibited when she deserted Suzannah in her time of need.

Suzannah shook her head. "We have no fools at Schoenbrunn. You did all that you were able to do, and the rest. . ."

But Callie wanted to take the responsibility for her actions. "I came here to tell you. . ." She broke off when she realized she had been about to say she was sorry. It was the one thing Abe had warned her *not* to say.

"To tell me you are sorry," Suzannah finished for her tightly. She patted Callie's hand. "I know, and we need speak no more of it."

Callie saw there were very few tears in Suzannah's eyes. Enormous relief flowed through her. Without much having been said, they seemed to have breached the gulf between them. Surprisingly, the burning behind her own eyes seemed on the verge of going away for the first time in months.

"Thank you," she said quietly.

Above them, a gaggle of geese announced their impending departure to a warmer climate. The sun silhouetted the fowl as they flew on, two pairs of eyes riveted on them until they became specks in the sky. The sharp scent of burning wood drifted to them from a fire burning where the men were clearing another section of woods.

"I have often wondered what it would be like to be up there," Suzannah mused, still looking at the sky. "To see the world as God sees it. It must be breathtaking."

Callie glanced toward the spot in the sky where the geese had disappeared.

"You would go up there if you could?" For some reason she had never imagined Suzannah having any desire other than to be a wife and mother.

"If I knew I would return to those I love," she confirmed. "Do you not have a dream you wish to see fulfilled more than any other?"

Yes, to see Joshua, Callie thought.

"I do want to see Sarah again, even if she chooses not to stay or to explain why she did what she did," she admitted. No tears pressed at her eyes, and she marveled at how serene she sounded.

"I know. It is as if you have lost a part of yourself and know you will never recapture it." Suzannah's eyes drifted toward the graves, and she studied them with deep concentration. "But beyond that, is there anything else you truly wish to do or have in your future?"

"I suppose that someday when I am old and withered and gray I will wish I had found someone to wed, to share my days with, but there does not seem much hope of that."

She closed her mouth as rapidly as if she had just swallowed a pesky gnat. Where had that come from? She had never thought about regretting she had no one beside her. Why had that answer popped out so readily?

"You do not see what is under your own nose, do you?" Suzannah chuckled. "It is so plain to the rest of the mission, and yet you. . ." she threw Callie a slightly amused look, "you do not see."

"See what?" Callie demanded. What was there to see that was so obvious?

"That Joshua traveled here because he loves you!" the woman exclaimed, her eyes shining as if she had just revealed a well-known secret.

"Where did you come up with that foolhardy notion?" Callie asked with more than shock in her voice. She gave Suzannah a long sideways glance. "I think you have been sitting in the hot sun too long."

Suzannah returned the look, unable to hide the smile flitting across her face. She said nothing, though, and Callie thought about what she had just heard. Silently repeating the words, she found they had latched onto her heart and refused to let go.

Without warning, the conversation she'd had with him after the burial flashed into her mind. He had confessed to her that he was in love with a woman who had met up with circumstances that prevented them from marrying. Was it possible the flood that had taken her memory was the circumstance he referred to? The tiniest flicker of delight shuddered in her soul.

She had naively taken his comments to mean he was searching for that woman, and she had been jealous he would travel alone through dangerous wilderness to find the woman he loved. Even though she knew he had come from the same orphanage she had grown up in, she had never thought his sudden appearance at their mission might be because it was she he was looking for.

Astounded, she searched for answers. Had he truly stayed because of her? Her heart did a quick but strangely comforting bounce. She had no memory of him, no recall of anything he might have said to her before the flood. That was true, but hadn't she felt at ease with him since the very beginning? Hadn't she missed him dreadfully while he had been gone?

Yes, she could not deny it. Since the night he had entered the

Solomon cabin and given Suzannah, and herself, a reason to believe that at least one child might survive, Callie had detected something familiar about him.

But she didn't remember him! How could she care deeply for someone she didn't know? She shook her head, willing away the disturbing truth pushing at her. Determined to ignore what was staring her in the face, she turned back to Suzannah, who was watching her as if she followed every twist Callie's mind was taking.

"Will you help me plant more flowers over there?" Suzannah motioned to the graves. "I must add something to what you have already done. It will be my way of saying farewell."

"Flowers will not grow in the winter!" Callie exclaimed. Strange how quickly Suzannah had turned the conversation away from Joshua.

"That is true," Suzannah agreed, "but while I was hurting, you took it upon yourself to try to brighten up my babies' resting places. It is only fitting that I do something to build upon your love. After months of listening to well-meaning speeches by Abe and a hundred others, perhaps it is time to put this behind me and move on."

"You mean. . ."

"I cannot change the past, Callie, no matter how hard I pray, how many nights I fail to sleep, or how many tears I cry. God meant for me to have these children even though He was going to take them away." Suzannah swiped at her cheeks. "Just as we all must face the truth someday, I have found it is time to move on. I will never forget them, but I can try to put the past behind me."

Abe had been worried that Suzannah was at a breaking point from which he could not draw her back. Suzannah was much stronger than most, Callie realized, stronger than she was herself, because she still held to a past she couldn't remember.

"I will help you."

She watched as Suzannah found a small patch of wild clover that still clung to life, though there had been several nights of light frost. Scooping it from the ground with her hands, Suzannah brought it to the graves and divided it into three segments.

"This way they will all share something." She patted the last bits of earth around the wilting green stems.

"There is something missing though," Callie said. She leaned over and whispered something in Suzannah's ear.

Suzannah grabbed the basket holding Hannah Grace and together they raced toward the river. They returned a short time later, their aprons laden with the small rounded stones known as "river biscuits."

Callie arranged the stones at the heads of each of the sites.

"There," she said, when tiny semicircles were completed and she had brushed her hands off on her dress. "In case anyone here doubts it, now they are earth's angels as well as heaven's angels."

"You have given them halos!" Suzannah's gratitude was commingled with sobs, but they were not painful ones; they were tinged with acceptance and struck an answering cord deep in Callie.

Peace seemed to flirt with her, and she squeezed Suzannah's hand. No matter what happened in the future, they would share the bond that had sprung anew between them. A tie that bridged yesterday's friendship with tomorrow's hope. She admired Suzannah for having the strength to deal with her loss and move on. She only hoped someday she could do the same.

⁂

"Did you think I would not see through your plan, Suzannah?"

Callie walked to the far side of the room, crossed her arms in front of her, and waited. When she had hoped to learn to put the pain of the past behind her, she had not meant for it to happen just days after wishing for it.

Suzannah paid no attention to Callie until Hannah was nursing quietly under a blanket. "I only did what I had to do. Otherwise, you would have avoided her for who knows how long."

"So you admit you planned it then?"

"I had to or you would not have learned I trust you with her."

"I thought we settled the trust part at the cemetery?"

"Between you and me, yes, that was taken care of." Suzannah peeked at Hannah and settled back with a smile on her face.

"Quit playing with words, Suzannah. What exactly are you saying?"

"I am telling you it is time to quit regretting what has happened to you."

"I picked her up while you were gone. Is that not what you wanted me to do? Hold her so I would face the demons associated with her birth?"

"Only because she was wailing so loudly that I could hear her over at my mother's house."

That was true. Callie personally thought Hannah's screams had been loud enough to frighten away enemies within a day's travel.

"Then why did you not come running to see what was wrong?"

"You figure it out, Callie. I really do not feel like going through this again."

"You cannot lead me into a conversation and then just drop it! It is not fair."

Callie moved to the table and placed her palms on the top so that she was looking directly at Suzannah.

Suzannah returned her stare. "What is not fair is you acting as if it were a great imposition that I trusted you with my child," she replied.

"Watching Hannah was not an imposition," Callie rebutted.

"It was. . ."

Why was Suzannah being so obstinate?

"What are you looking for? You want me to say it was a joy? A pleasure?"

"Well?"

"Suzannah!"

Why was she having such a hard time admitting the truth?

"It was a. . ."

"Oh, all right," Callie snapped. "It was not so bad. In fact, once she stopped screaming, it was, well, comforting that I had gotten her to stop."

It had been unsettling at first, but one look at that tiny scrunched-up face and she had swooped Hannah into her arms without thinking about the twin that would never enjoy life. Which was exactly what Suzannah had planned.

"I see," Callie murmured, unable to tell Suzannah she sensed she was right.

"I am tired, Callie, but I will say this. God does not judge us by our yesterdays. What He does is watch to see how we learn from what happens to us and what we are going to do with tomorrow."

Callie pondered the words. Suzannah had done the only thing a true friend could—force another to face her pain so that she could move on.

"Someday I will thank you for this, but right now I cannot think of when that will be."

Suzannah smiled, a smile that filled her whole face with joy. "It will be when you hold your own child and know that no matter what happens, you will always love them."

Strange that Suzannah's announcement echoed the very thing Callie's heart seemed to be saying.

Chapter 13

"C allie? Brother David says you must go to sickroom."

Shadow's use of the English language had improved enormously in the last year, but she watched his face as he spoke. Something did not look quite right, though she could not figure out what.

"Who is it this time?" For the last three weeks she had run herself ragged treating one family after another as they suffered through a stomach illness. Just the thought that someone had been sequestered in the cabin set aside for the most serious of illnesses did not bode well.

Shadow shrugged. "Cannot say. He just say you come."

With no idea what to expect, she grabbed her medicine bag, tucked her braid under her bonnet, and donned a cap donated by a handsome raccoon.

Hurrying down the path, she tried to ignore a gust of wind that whipped heavy flakes against the ripening color on her cheeks. Ahead of her, Shadow's lean form seemed to blend into the frozen tapestry of the mission.

As they fought to stand upright in the wind, the thought surfaced that perhaps Sarah had returned and Brother David was granting them privacy. Something clutched at the back of her throat. She didn't realize she had slowed down until Shadow shook her arm.

"Callie? He waits." He motioned down the walkway covered with a lacy blanket of snow.

He? Who? Brother David?

No, if it were Brother David, Shadow would have told her so. Besides, she had seen him this morning at service and he had looked as healthy as ever.

Levi?

It must be. Her heart fell to her feet, which felt as if they were encased in blocks of ice. The tears in her eyes were caused by the bitter cold, she told herself, not because she was afraid of who waited for her in the cabin and what he would tell her about her sister.

Then why couldn't she shake the sense of impending doom? A cold chill unrelated to the weather shook her from head to toe. Something had happened to Sarah.

Suzannah's words of a few weeks ago came back to her. *"God watches to see what we will do with what we have learned."*

What would she do if Levi had brought bad news? How would she deal with that?

Trust in God. He will see you through. She appreciated the fact that the little voice in her head seemed encouraging.

The sound of Shadow pushing the heavy plank door open jerked her to the present, and she searched the interior. Facing away from her on the other side of the room sat a man. Midnight-black curls tugged at the neckline of his jacket. One leg was propped across the knee of the other, and one of his hands twirled a slouch hat crazily around in a small circle.

The jolt to her heart was sufficient to cause her to gasp and drop the bag of herbs she had brought along. Shadow gave her a gentle push from behind, as if he knew she would not make it across the room any other way. With knees as sturdy as a pile of mashed corn, she wobbled toward him, trying to convince her now wildly tumbling heart to behave.

Gracious God, thank You. The words were silent, filled with praise.

She was vaguely aware that Shadow had remained by the door and that the floor was covered with hastily spread dried grass that was disturbed in several places. She barely noticed that there were no tables or shelves, only a few chairs upon one of which sat. . .

"Joshua?"

Had she said his name or simply mouthed it?

She wanted to touch him to assure herself he was real, but she was so stunned to see him that she couldn't move. Her breath was frozen in her chest. A roaring fire cast a soft glow over his silhouette, scattering sparks and ashes as a fine stream of smoke erupted from a log.

He turned partway toward her, his profile made bold by the firelight and strengthened by the time he had been away.

I need strength, Father. I cannot do this alone.

"Calliope. I am glad you could come. Will you sit so we may talk?"

It was not Levi. The relief was immense. Joshua was back! She clasped her hands in front of her apron. Looking at him was just a small pleasure, but if it was all she would get, she wanted it to be a memory that would last the rest of her life. The lake-blue gaze that had upset her world from the beginning was doing the same thing to her now.

"My name is Callie," she said, ignoring the excitement that swirled through her as she moved to sit in the chair across from him. She fiddled with the folds of her skirt, glad she was wearing the dress that was not as faded as the others. Finally, unable to bear not looking at him, she did.

"You are injured!"

"It is good to see you, too."

He is back!

"I, well. . .of course, welcome back." Her eyes traced the set of his mouth. "But you have a bandage on your cheek, and Shadow said Brother David asked me to come to the sickroom, and the only people we put in here are those who are suffering greatly and—"

"You are concerned about how serious it is. Do not be. It is minor in the overall scheme of things."

Nothing would ever be minor where he was concerned.

"Brother David has granted us time to speak privately, or as privately as we can with Shadow as an escort. There are things I must say, and I will not be deterred from saying them."

He is back!

"Will you listen to me without judging too harshly?"

"What is it about?" *How outrageous I sound!*

"Different things, all of which I should have told you before now. But I need to know you will listen."

She nodded, unable to bring herself to say anything else for fear it would be the wrong thing.

"You were Calliope long before you became Callie."

"Calliope?" She pronounced each syllable as slowly as he had.

"Yes."

Her name sounded so good when he said it that she had to suck in her cheeks to prevent her dimples from blooming. *I must remember why he is here,* she warned herself. *He has come to tell me about Sarah. That, and only that.*

"You should be resting," she said.

"After we talk."

He looked as if he had not slept in a week. His clothing was tattered and worn, one sleeve practically falling apart at the seams. It made him look more handsome, but why was she thinking of that? A commotion of unfamiliar feelings twittered through her.

"There will be plenty of time for talk later."

She didn't want to talk. She wanted to sit and absorb the changes in him while he had been gone. Tiny lines radiated from the edges of his eyes. Had they always been there?

"What I have to say will not wait any longer," he insisted.

It was true. Something had happened to Sarah and he had come back to tell her. Callie shook her head to clear the threads of hope that kept crowding her thoughts. She had to focus on what he was saying instead of on what she felt when he looked at her.

"Then tell me and get it over with." She made her voice as flat as possible, which meant she had to ignore her churning heartbeat.

He's about to deliver bad news. Straighten your shoulders. Keep your head up. Put your hands in your lap. Do not let him see how much what he says upsets you.

"I came back because I had no choice."

She was right. Bad news.

"I see."

"You mean you remember me?"

Callie was confused until she recalled Joshua had asked shortly after she had first met him if she remembered him yet.

"No. I thought you meant you came back to tell me something bad happened to Sarah."

"As far as I know, she is fine. She and Levi are married and have returned to the Lord. Without their help, my captors might have succeeded in removing me from O-he-yo permanently."

Callie gave a silent prayer of thanks for Sarah and Levi's spiritual health. It no longer mattered how Levi had behaved toward her, or who had been behind him and Sarah leaving Schoenbrunn. They had asked God's forgiveness. That was what was important. She caught Joshua staring at her as if he expected her to say something. "Were you in danger while you were captured?" *What a ridiculous question!*

"British soldiers thought I was a trapper who had taken their supplies. The only way out I saw was to pray—a lot. Every time they talked, I prayed. Out loud."

Nervous laughter bubbled from her lips, but Callie so liked the fact he had called on his faith for sustenance.

"I had just fallen asleep one night when Sarah waltzed into camp," he said. "She distracted the soldiers while Levi freed me. Of course, it took some doing to get to her away from them. But it was worth it. She risked her life for mine."

Callie gasped. Sarah had risked her life for Joshua! It didn't take away the sting of her sister's abrupt departure from Schoenbrunn, but it did help ease the guilt Callie had done something wrong in raising Sarah.

"Well, if Sarah is fine, then why are you here?"

Could she be any more blunt? He must wonder if she had any tact at all.

"Because of you."

His eyes held hers prisoner, the intensity so overwhelming that she wondered if that was what was making her pulse pound in her ears.

"Because I felt I at least owed it to you to see if you had recovered from your memory loss," he finished.

She forced her face to remain calm, though it was the last thing she felt like doing. Of course that would be the reason. Suzannah had said he had come here because he loved her. Oh, for the courage to ask if that was true!

"I have not."

"I can help with some of it."

"Please do." She sounded so polite, she thought she might get sick.

He nodded. "You lived in the orphanage my parents ran. From what they tell me, your mother brought you and your year-old sister to us. Father says she meant to come back for you."

Callie was touched that he had thought to tell her that. She had always wondered why she had been abandoned. Joshua made it sound as if something had happened to prevent her mother from returning. That in itself was some comfort. Perhaps she had not been cast off as she had always thought.

"I was luckier than you, for I had my parents, but that did not mean you were not loved."

Joshua related what he recalled of living there while growing up. His mother read nightly to all of them then would hug and kiss each child before they were sent off to bed. As a giant herd, the twenty or so children that lived there would sometimes splash in the creek that ran behind their "home."

Callie sensed immediately it was that creek that had torn apart the only life she had known, but she did not interrupt him. She let him speak, admiring his eyes as they alternated between sadness and elation.

"The flood destroyed everything we owned," he continued. "I did not want to let you go with the Moravians, but my parents insisted I attend medical school. They convinced me it was for the best. I regret that choice." He paused.

Callie hoped he meant what she thought he did.

"One day," Joshua said, "Father insisted everyone should learn to ride. Trouble was, the horses he hired were much too big for the little ones, and most of them ended up standing in the middle of the porch and crying. Your sister was one of them."

He sounded wistful, as if he longed to return to those days.

"You miss him? Your father?"

"Yes, but I have faith I will see him again."

She could not keep her composure from cracking. "You are going home?"

Of course he would go. No strings, no attachments, no tomorrows.

"Perhaps, when the day is right."

When it was warmer, then. She would see him for a few more months. And at least he was honest. She had always known that about him. He had even told her about the woman he loved that did not return his love. She had marveled that his devotion was so strong and that he would wade through a wilderness to find that special woman.

Joshua had to go, Callie realized, so he could search for the missing half of his heart. Wait till she told Suzannah he had not come here for her.

"Why did you not tell me from the start who you were and why you were here?"

He had been tossing the hat around and around his fingers. Now he laid it to the side. "Call me stubborn, but once I learned you were to marry Levi, I figured there was no hope for me. I had prayed continually for the years we were apart that you would remember who I was. I thought perhaps if you saw me, spoke to me, then you would remember. When it did not appear you were going to, all I wanted was for you to be happy. If that meant stepping aside, I was willing to do so."

"I am not." She smoothed the edge of her apron.

"Not?"

"Not going to marry Levi."

A burden she had been unaware of lifted. That is why she had never been comfortable around Levi. Joshua was the man she loved.

"God is very good." He breathed the words out in a rush.

"You went after him to bring him back to me, did you not?" It didn't hurt as much as she thought it would to ask.

"Partially. But I really went after Sarah. Since she was the only family you had, I knew how important she was to you."

"Thank you."

"That is all you have to say?" He sounded as if he could not believe she did not care more.

Oh, there is more, she thought, *so much more.* "I owe you a debt of gratitude."

She owed him everything. Even as he rode away, she now knew her heart could love. But only him.

He caught her eyeing his injury.

"Perhaps I will have a dashing scar when it heals."

"If that is what you want." If she could keep her distance, it would not hurt too terribly when he was gone.

"Will it matter to you what it looks like?"

Tremendously. "Why would it?"

"Some women I have known would be terrified to look at something disfiguring."

She was drawn to it. It was a symbol of all he had done, all he was.

"I thought it was a minor scratch. And looks are not all that make a person who he is," Callie announced. "It is what is in one's heart that matters."

What is in my heart? she asked herself. *Jesus, most importantly. The belief He died for my sins.*

Anything else? Sorrow when I think about what Sarah did.

And?

She caved in, finally acknowledging the feeling of utmost comfort that expanded within her when she looked at Joshua.

"So what is in *your* heart?"

Did he have to use that familiar drawl that made her want to shout?

You. "God."

It was the same answer she had used months ago.

"That is as it should be."

Callie was suddenly glad she had not cast the Lord aside and turned her back on Him. Glad she had kept her faith when life seemed so full of despair.

"Would there be room for someone else?"

"Someone else?"

Did she sound as confused as she felt?

"Yes."

That drawl again! Good thing she was already sitting, or she would have collapsed to the floor.

"As in. . . ?"

"Me."

Callie gazed at the strong, willful face she had seen in her dreams for months. They had bantered like this in the beginning. She had enjoyed it then. She was enjoying it now. Immensely.

"You?"

Room? She would always have room for him. They would be a three-strand cord. The Lord. Joshua. Herself. She regretted that Sarah might never know this kind of happiness.

"You are thinking about your sister, are you not?" Joshua asked softly.

She was amazed at how easily he appeared to read her mind.

"If it is God's will, I would like to see her again. Someday."

She traced the angry red scar that started at the underside of his wrist and ran up toward his elbow.

"When did you get this?"

"When I rescued you from the flood."

She felt woozy, as if it were July instead of December and she had been in the noon heat too long. There was not enough air in that last breath she had taken. It all seemed to be happening too fast, yet it seemed so natural, as if Someone with more knowledge and insight than she had was in control and had led them to this point.

⁊

Joshua looked at the woman before him. Her high neckline hid the slender length of her throat. Her cheeks radiated a beauty he had remembered in his thoughts throughout his captivity. When he had watched her join the Moravians after the flood, knowing she had no memory of who he was, he'd had to trust that God would bring them together again. And here she was!

She was like a delicate flower, but even the tiniest flowers sometimes thrive in the harshest conditions. Someday he would tell her how much strength he derived from her.

"No matter what you have done, or what you cannot remember, I came here because I care about you."

"Suzannah said you did."

Were those tears in her eyes? Had he put them there?

"She was right. You are not the young woman I fell in love with, but neither am I the young man you cared for then. God taught me a great deal of patience while I learned to deal with losing you the first time. I will not let you go again."

"You mean that?" She sounded incredulous.

"I do. God brought us together again because we had not finished what He began in Pennsylvania. I believe what we have gone through was so that He could make sure we were strong enough to stand up to whatever happens in our future."

"Our future?"

He enjoyed watching her face fill with awe.

"Do you mind if I call you Liope?"

She narrowed her doe-brown eyes.

"That was the special name I had—"

"Yes, you may."

Joshua especially liked the way her brown eyes softened as she gave him that permission. It was as if a fiber of what they had shared before had come to life. No, this was nothing like what they had had before, this was new, and only something designed by God could be so fulfilling.

"Did I call you Josh or Joshua?"

He laughed. "You called me Mr. Johnston. Not once could I convince you to use anything else."

"Oh." She mouthed the word.

"Liope, I do not wish to sound presumptuous, but I have waited for five years for this. There are so many memories I have of us together, of the promises we made to each other, but it does not appear as if you are ever going to recall what we had."

"It does not," she agreed. "But suddenly the past does not matter as much as it used to."

After all this time, could it be this simple? He stretched out a hand and held his breath while she considered what the gesture meant. Slowly, she tangled her fingers with his, palm against palm, heart to heart.

The moment of silence was precious. Their eyes captured and held it so that this special time would always be theirs.

"I have to tell Suzannah thanks," she finally said. She explained what had happened at the cemetery and with Hannah Grace. "She showed me that if I allow the past to control my future, I will never know what it is like to laugh at life again."

He swallowed hard. Asking should not be this difficult. He had already asked her once to marry him. Those words seemed insufficient for what he wanted to know.

"Liope? Will you laugh with me?"

For a long moment her gaze lingered on his wound, tracing its length as if it signified all they had gone through. Panic rose in his throat. Had he pushed too hard, too fast?

"Absolutely."

She punctuated her answer by bobbing her head. Her bonnet slipped off and her braid cavorted in the air around her shoulders.

It was the answer he had been longing to hear since that fateful night when Brother David had convinced him to let her go. It did not matter that she was crying instead of laughing. Her tears cleansed and healed, preparing her heart for the months and years ahead.

Joshua dipped his head at Shadow, who still stood in a corner, trying to appear uninterested in what was happening between the two but unable to contain the merriment that filled his deep-brown features.

As Joshua unfolded himself from the chair, Liope leaned into his arms. Her head nestled against his chest while his lips brushed the beginning of her plaited curls. He inhaled the scent of winter sunshine that emanated from her golden locks and whispered his gratefulness.

"Father, thank You for allowing me the privilege of making Liope laugh. I promise to keep her safe until she crosses Your final shore and to always show her that life on this earth is nothing more than a different kind of heaven."

"I promise to spend my days making new memories of love with you," Callie said.

Epilogue

L iope brushed at the drops that insisted they had a right to cascade down her cheeks. Every time she looked at the baby who had tried to arrive on the last day of 1775, but missed by a few hours, she cried. They were happy tears, but goodness, would they ever stop?

"Except for you, my Liope, I have never seen anyone so perfect."

Barring the day they had exchanged vows and promised their hearts to each other, Joshua's words sounded more full of delight than she had ever heard. And they started a new round of tears. She smiled first at her husband of twenty-two months, then at the precious gift from God in her arms.

Joshua slid into bed beside her and curled his arm around them. "Sophie Ruth Johnston. I like the way it sounds."

"We did not name her that because of the way it sounds!" Callie exclaimed. "We named her that because—"

"We will always remember the first baby with that name, the one who taught us so much about life," he finished.

"And who taught me to believe in God's plan for my life because He knows what is best for me."

Joshua kissed the tip of her nose then the baby's cheek. "Correction, my sweet. He knows what is best for us."

Healing Sarah's Heart

Enjoy Your
Bonus Story

Chapter 1

I hope this brings better news than the last one did, sir." Jeremiah handed the pouch across the table, watching anxiously as David Williamson unraveled the leather straps.

Williamson's dark eyes perused the missive before turning to Jeremiah. "It is times like these when men are asked to give more than they planned."

"I did not think it would be good tidings when I picked up the message at Fort Pitt," Jeremiah replied.

"You are right. This brings news of another attack."

Jeremiah continually hoped the need for their group of defenders would fade. But there was no indication that would happen. Though Washington County had abundant steeply sloped hills, gently gurgling streams, and quiet meadows, it also was within easy reach of Indians, who crossed the Ohio River to rid themselves of their frustrations.

"I was afraid of that, sir," Jeremiah said. "How far away was this one?"

"About a two-day ride. This reinforces our need to find more men and to ensure they are ready to fight." Williamson paused. "Despite your insistence to the contrary, you do know that you are a great help to our cause."

Jeremiah shifted from foot to foot. "I do my part, sir, but you know my view on killing."

"I would never ask you to do something I would not do myself," the colonel assured him. "But the fact is, things are getting worse."

Jeremiah motioned to the dispatch. "What happened this time?"

Williamson gave a deep sigh. "Last week, on April nineteenth, General Brodhead attacked an Indian camp near the head of the Muskingum River. He suspected they were British allies."

Jeremiah scrubbed a hand back and forth across his neck. "Suspecting and knowing are two different things."

Williamson nodded. "Yes. Well, he went south to Fort Henry before he headed to Ohio and ended up with more than three hundred men on his side. According to this, the Muskingum River was high due to recent heavy rains, with half the tribe on the other side. The general did not capture all the prisoners he wanted. He did manage to corral twenty men, women, and children and forced them to march upriver. His men massacred the hostages not far from the fort."

"Massacred them! Did he not think about the consequences of that action?"

"Apparently the general is not one to concern himself greatly with such things," Williamson said in a carefully controlled tone. "Since we are so close to Fort Pitt, I think we need to prepare for retaliation."

"I wish there were another way to resolve this situation," Jeremiah answered. "I know warriors destroy families, burn crops, and terrorize innocent children. And I know I should be glad to halt such atrocities, yet—"

"Almost everyone in these parts believes the Wyandots are responsible for the raids," Williamson interrupted. "But I am not so sure. Something must have made the general think that he needed to attack that Delaware tribe."

"I have ridden through that part of Ohio," Jeremiah pointed out. "Some of the Indians there are led by Moravian missionaries. They call themselves Praying Indians. We cannot blame a tribe for something they may not have done."

"You know what it is like to lose a family member," Williamson responded. "Revenge often comes before rational thought. I am afraid it will not take much to get the men of *this* county thinking along those lines."

"That does not mean I have to like it," Jeremiah declared.

"No, but it is becoming a fact of life," Williamson said. "While I believe that if we were able to get that British commander at Fort Detroit to quit inciting the redskins we might have a chance at some peace and quiet, it does not seem likely that will occur."

Jeremiah placed his hands on the back of the chair in front of him. He'd ridden nonstop for two days. His back ached from the jarring motion of his horse. He wanted nothing more than a hot meal and a long night's sleep.

"There are other Indian groups in that area," Jeremiah offered. "Besides the Christian Delawares, there is a group of Mohicans. I cannot see why you think they would be responsible for the assaults."

Williamson narrowed his eyes. "I know you do not believe in violence, Jeremiah. But is that all that bothers you about this?"

Jeremiah wanted no part of killing. That was why he had considered asking Williamson to relieve him of his militia position.

"Well?" Williamson challenged. "The sooner you get it out in the open, the sooner we can deal with it."

Doom echoed in Jeremiah's heart, much as it had the night he lost Jenny. He studied the man who he knew bore the responsibility for more than two hundred lives on his shoulders. Williamson's hair and brows were a prematurely grizzled gray, and weariness filled his eyes.

"How is the muster going?" Jeremiah asked, diverting the conversation.

"Last count showed eighty dependable men," Williamson bragged. "But while you were gone, another family was attacked. It will not be the last," he added. "The redcoats will prod until they get the warriors to chase us out of here. I wish we were not so close to the Ohio River."

"We are farther east than some," Jeremiah replied, thinking again about how Indians had disrupted his own life.

"Distance will not keep our kinfolk safe," Williamson argued. "Those warriors ride till they see a home, then they strike. You know what is left when they finish."

Jeremiah wished he'd dropped off the missive and gone to his cabin. The tiny house nestled in the hills had been empty when Jeremiah arrived in Washington County. He knew why but tried not to let that bother him.

Williamson drummed his fingers on the desk. "We are going to have to take drastic measures, whether we want to or not."

"Are you sure that is wise?"

"Being in command sometimes means ignoring what others think," Williamson replied. "The settlers did not elect me because I would make everyone happy. They put me here because they trusted me to do a good job."

"Of course, sir, but—"

"They expect me to protect them," Williamson went on, seemingly oblivious to Jeremiah's anxiety. "That means I have only one choice—to go out on the trail and see for myself what is happening."

"You mentioned earlier that Major Whelp is out on patrol," Jeremiah said. "If you go, there will be no one left in charge."

"Every good leader does need a dependable backup." Williamson clasped his hands in front of him on the desk.

"So you will wait until Major Whelp returns?"

Williamson studied his hands. "You know I have a very high regard for you."

Jeremiah nodded. "You are one of the few who do not hold my past against me, sir. I appreciate that."

Williamson waved a hand in the air. "We all make mistakes. I have made plenty in my day. But what I am about to tell you is no mistake." Williamson gazed at Jeremiah. "I signed you up as a county lieutenant. I know you will do a good job."

Jeremiah bounded from behind the chair. "With all due respect, sir, you cannot do that. I promised to serve as a courier. Nothing more."

Williamson gave him a pointed look. "May I remind you that since I am in charge, I can do whatever I wish? The subject is closed."

"But sir," Jeremiah began, ready to protest this unexpected turn of events.

It was no use. Williamson had turned to examine a map on the wall. There was only one thing left to do, a habit from as far back as Jeremiah could recall.

Lord, I know I forgot to thank You for bringing me back safely on this ride. Please accept my gratitude now. If it wasn't for You, I wouldn't accomplish the things I do. I know You've led me down some strange paths before. . .but, Lord? I don't like the looks of this.

"Lieutenant Stewart!" The colonel's smile was broader than the gate leading into Jeremiah's family's pasture, showing his obvious pleasure with Jeremiah's promotion. "I like the sound of that title. How about you?"

"I do not think this is a good idea," Jeremiah spoke candidly. "Major Whelp will not be happy."

"I knew you would be. . .well, should we say less than enthusiastic?" Williamson consoled. "This is only temporary. One hundred eighty days. Come on, Jeremiah. You are one of the few people in this county who can read and write, and the men trust you."

"But what about Major Whelp?" Jeremiah repeated. "No matter what I do, he does not like me."

Williamson snorted. "Whelp could not find a tepee if someone placed his hands on either side of its entrance. He is second in command only because he finished behind me in the election." He pointed to a map on the wall. "Pay close attention, Stewart. This is what you need to know to catch up on what has been going on around here." The colonel began to point out different areas on the map.

Aren't you even going to protest? a little voice in Jeremiah's mind asked.

Jeremiah frowned. No one argued with Williamson and won. He doubted that even the Almighty could change the colonel's mind once it was made up—the stubborn streak in the Williamson family was as long as the Ohio River.

It was late April. Six months would take him to December. Did the one hundred eighty days start today? Or tomorrow?

Chapter 2

"I think this is the most beautiful country I have ever seen," Bessie Hall said with a sigh.

Sarah Lyons turned to the woman she had traveled with for seventy miles. Bessie's curly red hair tumbled about her face, but her sparkling green eyes reflected her delight.

Bessie is the closest thing to a friend I have, Sarah reminded herself. *I must be pleasant.*

"It is green for September," Sarah agreed. "I am so glad the nights of having to stay alert are over." Sarah stretched to work out the cramps in her lower back that had accumulated with the miles.

"We made it. That is the important thing," Bessie said.

Despair swamped Sarah's heart as she watched Bessie caress a wilted sprig of late-blooming posies that her husband had tucked at her bosom.

Levi will never bring me *flowers again,* Sarah thought. Yet she strove to sound unaffected. "I am still amazed your husband let you travel."

"You know how strongly Captain believes in the power of prayer," Bessie said. "He was convinced that we had to be here now."

Sarah prayed occasionally, but it had been a long time since she'd believed God answered her prayers.

"He trusted God to bring us here safely," Bessie continued, looking around. "We made it, Sarah. We really made it!"

"So we did," Sarah replied with little excitement. No matter how important this move was for her son's future, her feelings about it were as dismal as the mud-covered moccasins she stared at.

"And Samuel did not give you any of the trouble that you feared he would, Sarah. That is one fine boy you are raising. I hope my children turn out to be as mannerly as he. You must be proud of him."

Sarah glanced at her four-year-old, Sammy, who was nestled in a corner of the wagon. His thumb hovered near the "O" of his mouth. Shafts of sunlight highlighted his auburn hair. Others called him Samuel, but to Sarah and Levi he was Sammy. Sarah hoped Sammy turned out to be a fine young man. She owed it to Levi to raise their son the best she could.

Bessie's chatter drew Sarah's attention. "I wish Captain would get back. I wonder why he did not want us going in the house with him."

Sarah didn't answer; she just glanced about them. They had stopped their wagon not far from some dilapidated structures. Sarah became nervous in places she wasn't familiar with—she hoped Captain would return soon.

"I do so hope our home is ready," Bessie went on. "I am glad the colonel found a circuit opening for Captain. He might be gone when the baby comes, but Williamson is going to pay us in food and supplies. Does that bother you, Sarah?"

Sarah's jaw tightened. "You know I do not like it. Until I get my life settled I have no choice but to depend on others."

"Doing so is not that bad, Sarah. David is a good man. So many others are, too, if you would only let them prove themselves."

Sarah sighed. "I imagine so, Bessie. But right now I do not want commitments of any sort."

"I think someday you will change your mind," Bessie replied. "Oh! Did I tell you what Captain said about the militia? I cannot wait to see the men marching in their best and putting on a parade! Does that not sound exciting?"

"I did not come here to see men of any sort, those on display or otherwise," Sarah reminded Bessie.

"Perhaps not," Bessie announced. "But the people you meet here will welcome you. One day you will not hurt as much as you do now." She patted Sarah's forearm tenderly.

Sarah pulled away. She didn't want a fuss made over her.

Just then Sammy awoke. "Mama?"

Sarah smiled at her son, grateful for his intrusion. She pulled Sammy onto her lap and straightened his shirt.

"About time you arose, sleepyhead," she said, ruffling his hair. "Look! Over there is the river Captain promised we would see. And beyond those trees is where Bessie says our new home is."

Sammy glanced briefly toward the woods before turning back to her. "Go see water?"

Sarah's gaze flitted between sloppy tents and lazy horses. She must quit thinking that harm waited around every corner.

"If Bessie does not mind." She gave Bessie a questioning look.

"Go on," Bessie encouraged. "It will do you good."

Sarah swung her son off the wagon, ignoring her tears. It was silly to think that Sammy would be eager to see his new home. He was too young to realize what they'd lost.

Sammy is the only one who makes me laugh, Sarah reminded herself. *He depends on me to take care of him, to help him grow. Perhaps taking him to the river will help pass the time until Captain returns. And then. . .*

Sarah shook the thoughts away. She was just anxious to find someplace warmer to sleep than on the ground beneath the wagon. The September air in the Ohio Valley could be slightly cool or downright cold at night. Lately it had been the latter.

"Will you join us, Bessie?" Sarah asked.

"I do not think so. I will just sit here and enjoy getting kicked by this young'un." Bessie laid her hands on her rounded abdomen. "He will only be in here a few more months. Go on, Sarah. Samuel needs some pleasure in his life right now. So do you. Nothing will happen. Captain would not have left us here if it were dangerous."

Bessie is right, Sarah advised herself. *I haven't been happy lately and it has affected Sammy. I came here with the Halls to make life better for us, so I might as well start doing so.*

Sarah folded her hand over her son's pudgy fingers and matched his small steps as they strolled toward the riverbank. Leaves rustled underfoot, the product of fall's frosty hands. A few birds swooped overhead, filling the emptiness with tiny chirps. Sammy spied some twigs on the ground and giggled as he tossed them into the river.

While the distant clang of a blacksmith's forge carried to them, a soggy mass of clouds drifted overhead. The resultant shadows filled Sarah's heart with remembrance.

It might not be a harbor in the wilderness, but I miss our home, she thought.

"Twees sleeping, Mama." Sammy pointed out a barge headed downriver.

"They do look like it," she agreed. "They are taking the trees to people so that they may build houses," Sarah informed him.

Sammy jabbered some more while Sarah turned her mind back to her situation. She hadn't understood how difficult it would be to leave the area that had been her home for seven years.

She missed the land she and Levi had built a three-room home on. There were so many pretty sights—trees welcoming spring with new buds, deer coming to the natural salt lick in the valley. The trees and the deer were still there, but not their home. Sarah pushed the thought away. *Lighten your heart,* she scolded herself, *for Sammy's sake.*

"Listen, Sammy. I hear Bessie calling. Hurry now!"

Sarah chased Sammy back to the wagon, flapping her apron at him. She smiled at his squeals of joy, but as she climbed aboard behind her son, disappointment was in her eyes. Perhaps when they got settled she and Sammy would walk here. It seemed like a place of hope, of peace. Something Sarah sorely needed.

∽

"These must be read immediately, sir. Then you need to write out the requisitions for supplies. Then there is the complaint that must be handled. Now, let me think. Oh, yes. If you have any questions, the colonel said he would be back in two days. There, I think that is it."

Jeremiah stared at the stack of papers the clerk had thrust at him.

"I guess that settles what I will be doing for the rest of the evening."

"Did you have other plans, sir?"

"Of course not. And please stop calling me sir. Save that for the real boss around here."

The clerk grinned. "Sure thing, Lieutenant Stewart."

As they passed houses strung between trees like fallen pinecones, a variety of sights and sounds assailed Sarah. Men shouted, axes splintered firewood, venison grilled over open pits, and children rushed around. Sarah was annoyed, not at the sight of the children, but because she wasn't sure that trying to find a new life for Sammy and her was the right thing to do.

Perhaps I should have listened to my heart and kept Sammy among familiar surroundings.

And where was that? a voice in her mind taunted. *All alone in the wilderness in a burned-out shell of a home with a young child and no man to protect you?*

But at least it was ours, Sarah argued back. *Now, except for Sammy, I have nothing—no home, no husband, no life.*

"There's always the Lord, Sarah. You can depend on Him."

It wasn't the taunting tone of her sadness talking; it was her husband's voice drifting to her from within the tangled mist of remembrance. Levi never stopped believing that God would take care of them, even though Sarah's faith wavered as often as the sun rose and set.

"Keep Sammy safe, Sarah," Levi implored her just before he closed his eyes for the last time. "Promise you will take him to meet my parents and your sister. Promise me. . . ." Levi's words faded into the nothingness that had taken him away from her forever.

I promise, Levi, Sarah thought, renewing her pledge. She swiped at the tear trickling down her cheek. So many wrong moves, so many chances gone bad. If only. . .

Sarah turned the ache away. She couldn't think about where loving

Levi had left her; it was too hard to accept, harder still to forget. And despite Bessie and Captain's best efforts, Sarah found that pain doesn't fade easily. Sometimes, no matter how often Sammy smiled at her, she wasn't sure it ever would.

Chapter 3

S arah shaded her eyes from the piercing sun so she could gaze at the shanties huddled together. A man blowing into a horn made quite a racket. She supposed it was all part of their militia practice.

The tang of sizzling bacon filled the air. Sarah's stomach growled, for she hadn't eaten much of a morning meal. However, thoughts of food did nothing to solve her dilemma. Now, which building had Bessie said was the trading post?

Scrunching her eyes shut to help her recall didn't help. She'd been in such a tizzy, with Sammy pulling at her apron while Bessie reeled off instructions, that she had failed to listen properly. At least the trail through the trees was well marked. The trading post was another matter.

Sarah stared at the building beside the one they stopped at the other day. A blue jay perched on the roof tilted his head and squawked an obnoxious welcome. Could that horrendous building be the trading post?

She took another look around. It might be safer if she went to the building she recognized as Williamson's home. She could ask there for directions.

Sarah tossed a frightful glance toward the trees. Captain and Bessie's residence was at the far end of that stretch. She longed to hurry back to them, afraid the cost of independence was more than she was willing to pay.

She braced herself. *No, I cannot let Sammy grow up on others' benevolence. That is what I must keep in mind.*

An ear-splitting whistle penetrated Sarah's awareness. More militia practice, no doubt. Did they think that noise would deter the warriors? Sarah could tell them from firsthand experience that that wouldn't work.

She took a deep breath. *I am here to find work, to turn my life around, to help Sammy. I have to reach these goals, no matter what I run up against.*

⟡

The man who peered at Sarah over the top of heavy spectacles seemed close to her own age of twenty-five. A sparse beard sprouted from his boyish cheeks, and freckles blotched his otherwise pale skin.

Sarah summoned a friendly smile. "Good day, sir. I just arrived and am looking for a list of work folks around here may need help with."

The young man's glance took in the worn hem of her gray full-length dress before he gazed back at her. "Jeremiah said you-all was coming. Have a hard time on the trail?"

"I do not know any Jeremiah," Sarah replied. "But to answer your question, we did not run into any heathens."

"That does make the journey more tolerable. Oh my! If my mama were here she would hang her head, 'cause I overlooked my manners. Rufus Putter, ma'am. Everyone calls me Rufe, or Putt."

"Pleased to make your acquaintance, Mr. Putter. Now about that list. . .where can I find one?"

"I hate to disappoint a fine-looking lady like you, but I cannot help you."

Sarah refused to give in to the urge to just plop down in the dust and cry. Other than sponging off the Halls, she had nowhere to go. She mustered her courage, knowing this was something that must be done in order to build a new life.

"I am fairly well trained in teaching and housekeeping," she offered.

"Most folks 'round here do not believe in schooling. As for house-keeping, none have enough to pay someone—"

"Rufe?"

The voice that intruded into their conversation was so command-ing, Sarah's gaze snapped to the other side of the room. The soldier walking toward them nodded briefly at Sarah.

"Sorry for interrupting, miss," the newcomer said, "but militia business comes first." He turned back to the clerk. "I cannot find that last message from Major Whelp. Do you have any idea where it might be?"

The men debated the issue while Sarah tried not to listen. She told herself it didn't matter, but the boldness in the newcomer's voice would fill one of the Allegheny valleys she'd recently traveled through.

As the clerk and the new arrival walked toward the rear of the room, Sarah followed, studying the room with a wary eye. A crooked table held a few books and an inkwell and quill. The few pieces of furniture appeared to be on the verge of collapse.

Sarah returned her gaze to the soldier with the vibrant voice. He was tall and apparently in charge. Then *he* was the person she should talk to about work.

"Go look," the soldier directed the clerk. With Rufe gone, he leaned against a table, crossed his arms in front of his chest, and gazed at Sarah.

Sarah knew what he saw. Her hem was muddied and torn, her hair tangled from a run-in with a low-hanging branch, and her shoes almost worn through the sides. Though he stared at her, Sarah didn't think he meant to be rude. He seemed to be focusing on her eyes. They gazed at each other until the clerk cleared his throat.

"Sir?" Rufe prodded.

"What?" the soldier snapped. "Is this a lassie of yours and you need to finish making plans to meet with her later?"

The idea that she could be anyone's lassie made Sarah want to giggle. She took a good look at the soldier again. His hair was beyond midnight and full of soft curls that whirled over his brow. She had a sudden urge to push them back away from his eyes, much as she might her son's tousled mop.

"I am not his lassie," she said, finding it difficult to quit looking at him.

If his hair was beyond midnight, his eyes reminded Sarah of a morning mist, with a smidgen of mischief in their depths.

He looked between her and Rufe and chuckled. "You do not know what a relief it is to hear that, miss. If you were, it would not say much for your character. But seeing that you deny knowing this scalawag we call Rufe, you must be a good sort."

Sarah sensed that the soldier was joking. Still, his praise warmed her from head to toe, and she drew in a deep breath to stay focused.

"Since you appear to be in charge, perhaps you can help me," she said. "You see, I just arrived with the Halls, and Bessie. . .er, Mrs. Hall, sent me to the trading post to see if anyone might have need of help. I am very adept with children. I can also teach, if there is need."

"Did you memorize that or just make it up on the spur of the moment?" he teased, slanting the clerk an amused glance.

"I assure you I am well qualified in these areas," Sarah replied briskly.

He held up his hands in surrender. "I do not doubt that. I am surprised to see you here, that is all."

Sarah frowned. "You make it sound as if few women ever come here."

"From what you said earlier, it sounds as if you are in search of the trading post," he said. "This is David Williamson's home—or, rather, this end is his office. We mostly see volunteers for the militia in here. Have you come to volunteer?" The twinkle in his eyes accented his grin.

Sarah's face warmed. "Oh! You think that I thought this is the trading post. Well, I did not see a sign to indicate that building. I thought someone here would point me in the right direction."

His smile aimed right for Sarah's lonely heart. "So you are looking for what we laughingly call the 'post with the most'?"

Sarah didn't want to stammer, so she simply nodded.

"I will escort you there," he offered. "I have been in Washington County awhile. I have not lost a young woman yet who has been directly in my care."

"What about your militia business?" Sarah managed.

"You would be doing me a favor," he assured her. "I am tired of studying plans that make no sense. Not to mention trying to decipher correspondence that seems written in a foreign language."

Relief flowed through Sarah. It wasn't her. He wanted a break from his demanding workload.

"I will take her, boss. You can get started on your reply to Major Whelp," Rufe said, holding out the misplaced message.

"No. Since the colonel left me in command, I feel it is only proper that I escort the lady."

Sarah wasn't sure about being alone with this soldier; his presence seemed to swamp her soul. Her good intentions wavered. It would be nice to have someone as brawny as he at her side. Perhaps it would curtail the rude comments some made when they saw her alone.

He settled a wide-brimmed hat on his head and motioned for her to precede him. Sarah swept in front of him, reminding herself that at the very least she must thank him for his help.

❦

Outside the building, Jeremiah drew her to a halt.

"Before we go any farther, I feel duty bound to introduce myself. County Lieutenant Jeremiah Stewart at your service. My duties include providing protection to pioneers who search for freedom and land in this area, along with a few other choice things that I am not at liberty to discuss."

"That is quite impressive, sir. I am Sarah Troy. . .er, Lyons."

"Troyer-Lyons," he repeated. "Is that one or two words?"

"One." Oh dear! That wasn't the truth. She had not used her maiden name of Troyer in years. Why did it slip so naturally to her lips now?

"Mighty pleased to meet you. It is miss, correct?"

"Miss is only appropriate for those who have not wed," Sarah answered. "That is not true of me."

Her reply curtailed any hope Jeremiah might have about getting to know her better. Which was a good thing, he reminded himself.

With the colonel off on a family matter and Major Whelp out in the field, he was in charge. He didn't have time for lollygagging around with women as Rufe liked to do.

"So you are married, then." Jeremiah motioned for Sarah to step along. "Just my luck. I meet a beautiful woman, and she is unavailable."

"Oh, but I am not. . ." Sarah fell silent as a blush crossed her cheeks.

"Available or married?" Jeremiah scolded himself the moment the words were out. He must forget the way his heart leaped when he looked into Sarah's eyes. Only one woman had made him feel so. . .alive.

"Married," Sarah replied. "Not anymore." A hint of memory slowed her words.

"I am sorry," Jeremiah responded. "I did not mean to bring up something that appears to pain you greatly."

Sarah fussed with her dress sleeves, giving Jeremiah a chance to study her. Hair the shade of ripe summer grain dangled down her back in some sort of fancy braid. High cheekbones accented exquisite brown eyes that Jeremiah found it easy to lose himself in.

Forget it, Stewart. No one will ever take Jenny's place.

Sarah raised her chin, insecurity glittering in her eyes. "Thank you for. . .your concern. Losing my husband is something I am still getting used to. I do have a son, though, and that is why I am here. To search for a way to provide for him."

"I admire you for that." Jeremiah watched her eyebrows rise at his compliment.

Sarah cleared her throat. "I made a mistake earlier," she said. "Troyer was a slip of the tongue. It was my name before I wed." Her gaze moved to the pasture, where several horses grazed.

Jeremiah reminded himself that he didn't have time for this sort of folly. As a matter of fact, he should have insisted Rufe escort her to the store. He had too many things to do and not enough time to do them, before the colonel returned.

"Well, Mrs. Lyons, let me officially welcome you to our humble village. I hope you find what you are looking for. It is not often we get a lady like you here."

"Mr. Stewart," Sarah began with perfect diction, "I am here because the Captain and Mrs. Hall talked me into coming along. With my son of course."

"Captain and. . .why that means. . . How old is your son?"

"A few months beyond four, but Sammy was well behaved on the trip. I am rather pleased for Bessie, I mean Mrs. Hall. . . . Being with child, well, she needs all the rest she can get."

"Mrs. Hall is with child?" Jeremiah gasped. The next time he saw Bessie, he would wring her neck. After she presented him with a niece or nephew of course.

Sarah wrinkled her forehead. "Do you know her?"

"Yes. Quite well."

"Captain said they had family in the area."

"They do," he affirmed, mentally making plans to visit his sister. He'd been out yesterday when they arrived. Upon his return, Rufe had thrust a mess of paperwork at him, insisting that Jeremiah take care of it before he did anything else. By the time he finished, it was well into the night.

"I was only recently promoted to the rank of county lieutenant," Jeremiah said as they began their walk to the post. "I hope that is not disappointing to you."

"No. Why should it be?"

The confusion on Sarah's face told him she had no idea why he'd brought that up. Jeremiah didn't know either. He was fortunate she was so proper, for he was making eight kinds of a fool of himself. He would have to keep his distance, despite the attraction he felt for Sarah.

He motioned toward a tumbledown building. "Here is where you made your mistake. You should have gone past Colonel Williamson's home before you stopped."

"Someone should have erected a sign, but thank you." There was a small admonition in her voice, but Sarah's gaze lingered on Jeremiah's.

A group of soldiers exited the post and spilled out onto the path. Some had learned this morning that passes to see their families had been denied. They glared at Jeremiah and Sarah.

He realized that the men resented him. *So be it,* he told himself. *I might not like my current assignment, but if they don't get their training straight, this whole territory will disintegrate.*

"I will take care of erecting a sign immediately," Jeremiah promised, moving so as to shield Sarah from the glaring looks tossed her way.

"Watch your step." Jeremiah placed a hand on her elbow and guided her around some horses. "Things are rather difficult around here. I am not sure anyone will be able to hire you. What was it you hoped to do again?"

"Preferably something that allows me time with my son without causing trouble for my employer—if any such thing exists, that is."

Sarah didn't sound very hopeful. Jeremiah was sorry that he'd squelched her expectations.

"Allow me." He opened the door and waited for her to go ahead. "I did not mean to sound skeptical. Perhaps you will find someone who will be happy to give you work."

"You do not have to apologize. I am used to men who think women are unable to fend for themselves. Let me tell you something, Mr. Stewart. I have been the sole provider for my son for almost two years, and I will continue to do so. If that causes a problem, perhaps I should go back to. . .where I came from and not contaminate this piece of land."

Jeremiah didn't blame Sarah for sounding aggravated; he'd spoken before he'd thought. That was something he was going to have to work on. Suddenly he wanted more than ever to succeed, especially around Sarah Lyons.

Chapter 4

Sarah trudged back to the cabin. While she watched Captain and Bessie unload the wagon, she gave her new home an impassive glance. The walls gave only a hint of solidity, the door hung crazily on its frame, and the chimney appeared as if it were tired of seeing the same sights every day. But with some fresh chinking, the cabin would keep the elements out, which was more than could be said of the house she'd left a few weeks ago.

Sarah watched as Bessie gave directions and Captain did his best to follow them. *That is what a family is supposed to be like,* she thought, ignoring the brutal twisting of her heart.

Sammy spied Sarah and threw himself against her. "Mama! You back."

Sarah hugged Sammy, knowing that he grew anxious when she was not with him all the time. "Yes, dear. I hope you were good for Miss Bessie while I was out."

Captain wiped a fine line of sweat from his forehead and joined Sarah and Sammy near the wagon. "Samuel is one fine boy. He did quite well carrying things into the house. He also picked out his room and said his mama would help him with it later."

"Thank you for watching him," Sarah said. "I do not know what I would do without you two."

Bessie joined her husband, leaning against a barrel of flour still tied to the wagon.

"Are you feeling better?" Sarah asked. When Sarah left earlier, Bessie was suffering from queasiness.

"I am now," Bessie answered. "I thought women only got ill in the beginning of their childbearing time."

"I guess we are all different," Sarah said.

"That we are," Captain affirmed. He drew Bessie against him and planted a noisy smack on his wife's cheek. "I am so glad this one is mine."

Bessie placed her hands on her hips and tossed him a mock frown. "Why do you say that, Daniel Hall?"

"Because you are good for a person's spirit." Captain sneaked another kiss.

Though Sarah saw them like this often, she marveled that two such opposites were man and wife. Daniel, known to most as Captain, was more apple-shaped than anything. The silver sifted through the brown at his temples made him appear twice Bessie's age. Bessie was generally outspoken and devoted her days to taking care of her husband. Sarah frowned. She and Levi had enjoyed the same sort of camaraderie displayed by the Halls until—

"Did you find the post, dear?" Bessie's query disconnected the chain of thoughts that might have sent Sarah into tears.

Sarah held Sammy close. "I ended up going to the Williamsons'. A very nice militiaman showed me the correct place to go though."

"A very nice militiaman? What did he look like?" The peskiness in Bessie's tone could only mean trouble.

"You know I do not pay attention to those things." Sarah waved off the question, yet the memory of Jeremiah's misty eyes hovered in her mind.

"You ought to," Bessie said frankly. "A woman should not be alone these days, what with the war and all. Besides, our Lord made woman so man would have a companion. Right, Captain?"

He nodded, about all a man *could* do when Bessie got started.

"I appreciate your concern," Sarah said, "but I have been alone for so long, it seems like it has never been any other way."

Not long enough to forget though, Sarah's heart reminded her.

"You are never alone," Bessie contributed. "Whether you believe it or not, the Lord steps right along with you everywhere you go."

"You know, I have not seen much evidence that God is anywhere near me lately," Sarah replied. "Now, please, can we leave it at that?"

"Yes, of course. Did you find work?"

Sarah shook her head. If she spoke, she might regret what she said.

"I was so sure you would," Bessie said. "I guess the war changed more than just the men who fight it."

Sarah gave an inward groan. She understood why Bessie chattered on about some things, but the war? Sarah knew it had something to do with the colonists wanting their freedom from England. At sixteen, she joined a group that fled Pennsylvania, in 1772, to settle in eastern Ohio. Nine years had passed since that time.

Does Callie still live in that Christian settlement? Fear stirred in Sarah's stomach. She'd promised Levi that she would take Sammy to find their relatives. What if she finally got there and they weren't there?

No! I have to believe I will find them. This move is a step toward that end.

"You know we counted on you staying with us," Bessie interjected. "We have four rooms. Besides, I think Captain likes your singing voice more than mine."

Sarah silently agreed. Bessie's best effort sounded like a wounded screech owl falling out of a tree. "I just do not want us to be a burden."

"We enjoy having you and Samuel with us," Captain inserted.

"We would not have asked if we did not," Bessie agreed. "Perhaps we will help you past that sorrow that haunts your eyes. We will pray for you. That will help."

Bessie grabbed a handful of tablecloths and moved toward the house. Captain followed behind.

Sarah gazed around at the open trunks and quilt-wrapped dishes representing Captain and Bessie's marriage.

I don't envy Bessie because she has a husband and a child on the way, Sarah admonished herself. *I don't.*

᧰

"You could at least have written and told me I was going to be an uncle," Jeremiah said as he released Bessie from an almost rib-shattering hug. He leaned down and offered to shake hands with the small boy who ducked behind Bessie's skirts. The child jerked back, sending a stack of kettles clanging to the floor.

Bessie patted Samuel's head then squatted to pick up the items. "Captain believed the Lord called us to travel when we did. If you had known about it, you would have insisted we wait until after the baby's birth."

"You know me too well, little sister. Now, tell me how things are going in your life."

"I will admit that times are rough, but seeing you makes our trip worthwhile, Jer. Though Captain was certain we would be fine, I feared we would not make it here safely."

"Well, you did, so let us not think about what could have happened." Jeremiah motioned toward Bessie's growing midsection. "You look good. Marriage to Captain agrees with you?"

"It does." Bessie clasped Jeremiah's arm. "I need to thank you for the support you gave me when—"

Jeremiah pressed a finger over her lips for a moment. "It was not me who pulled you through, it was the Lord. You know that."

"True," Bessie confirmed. "Now it is your turn, Jer. If you will allow Him, God will send the right woman to heal *your* heart."

Jeremiah cleared his throat. "Let us get one thing straight, Bessie Josephina. The condition of my heart is not available for discussion."

"I will drop it. For now," Bessie added with an impish tone. "By the way, Captain checked for you when we got in. No one seemed to know where you were."

"Out rounding up more men for the colonel's militia. I am glad you made it here safely. Makes my day a whole lot lighter."

"Those we care about generally do that," Bessie responded. "Where is your house, by the way? Is it close enough for me to walk to?"

Jeremiah told her he lived two valleys and a creek away. The first owners had tired of worrying about whether or not the Indians would choose them as their next victims.

"It is not a home, though, if you know what I mean," he finished.

"They never are unless there is love in it," Bessie advised. "How is Pa? You heard from him lately?"

"Got a letter last week, only he did not write it," Jeremiah replied. "A woman named Hazel signed it. She said they got hitched a few months ago, and we were—"

"Pa got tied again?" Bessie interrupted. "But he said he would never marry again."

Jeremiah had nothing to say. Other than losing Jenny, their mother's death was the most horrifying experience of his life.

Jeremiah decided to steer the conversation to a safer area. "Who is this little fellow who keeps hiding behind your skirt?"

Bessie moved aside and smiled down at Samuel. "This is my brother, Jeremiah. Can you say hello to him, Samuel?"

Samuel laid his head against her leg and refused to speak.

"Be patient with him, Jer," Bessie explained. "Strangers make him nervous."

"But who is he? You did not just pick up a small boy and cart him off."

"I would love to have a house full of children like Samuel. He belongs to Sarah, the woman we brought with us." Bessie gazed around the trading post. "Now where did she get off to? I wanted you to meet her."

Jeremiah raised his eyebrows. "Sarah?"

"Yes, Sarah Lyons. It is a long story, Jer. She lost her husband almost two years ago. She was living with some friends of ours. Captain and I could not see leaving her on her own any longer. We are determined to help her put it all behind her, but I do not know. Sometimes Sarah seems stuck with memories that I fear she may not ever be free of."

"Indians?"

Bessie nodded. "Sarah will not yet talk about it."

"I understand."

"I knew you would, big brother. You lost the apple of your eye.

Speaking of Jenny, you cannot let what happened to her ruin the rest of your life. After all, I put Martin behind me."

"Jenny did not destroy me," Jeremiah insisted. "Yours is a different story. Besides, it seems to me you have enough to worry about with that little one on the way, that you should not be fussing over me. Have you forgotten I am older than you and that I can take care of myself?"

Bessie wagged a finger in the air. "If that is true, when did you last sit down to a home-cooked meal?"

"I do not get those often," Jeremiah admitted. He wouldn't have traded his memories of growing up with Bessie for anything, but sometimes Jeremiah wondered why the Lord put them in the same family. Bessie would have been better off with seven sisters so they could cackle over new quilt patterns.

Bessie grinned. "Mmm-hmm. That is what I thought. And that is exactly why you must eat with us tonight." She swished her skirts. "So there, Jeremiah Stewart."

"I have work to do, Bessie—you know that. Wait. You do not know, do you?"

"Know what?"

Jeremiah told her about David Williamson's election as commander. "You remember that I mentioned in my letters that he sometimes does crazy things?"

"So?"

"Believe me, Bess, I feel awkward about this, and I do not like it one bit."

"Tell me what it is." Her voice grew in pitch.

"Are you sure?" Jeremiah couldn't help dragging out the suspense as he'd done in their childhood.

"As sure as I am that if God does not hold this against you on your judgment day, I will. Let me hear it."

"Well," he drawled, "if you insist."

Bessie stomped a foot. "Now, Jer!"

He chuckled at her aggravation. "Williamson came up with this notion to make me a county lieutenant."

Bessie was never this quiet.

"Did you hear me?"

Bessie glanced around. "But you are. . .how in God's great world did he pick *you*?" Despite her disbelief, pride shone in her eyes. "How could he do that? I mean, you are not even. . . I thought all you did was deliver messages."

Jeremiah hooked his thumbs into the pockets on his jacket. "Williamson does anything he sets his mind to. I believe, dear sister, his exact words were, 'This is my county and I will. . .' oh, never mind. Suffice it to say that the colonel can do pretty much whatever he wants."

"Then you are definitely coming to eat with us tonight. Anyone with such high rank must be properly fed in order to work at his best. I will be able to brag to your nieces and nephews someday that I fed their uncle, the next commander of the Washington County Militia. Supper is at six o'clock. My house."

"I will not be the next commander," Jeremiah began. "I only have a few months left, and—"

His words fell on deaf ears. Bessie was waltzing away, her hand wrapped around little Samuel's. Jeremiah wasn't upset with Bessie. She always acted this way when she considered a conversation finished.

As he watched them walk away, his heart ached for the youngster at Bessie's side. Perhaps he should have made more of an effort to get the child to say something? No, if Bessie had thought that necessary, she would have seen to it. She always knew when to push and when to leave things alone. Jeremiah admired that in his sister.

Perhaps it wasn't so bad having Bessie for a sister after all. She just might put a few pounds on his slender frame!

⟋⟍

"Is the pie ready yet, Sarah?" Bessie dashed around the tiny area she considered the "eating room."

"Yes. I tossed a dash of sugar on top before I took it out. It looks as good as it smells."

Sarah finished placing plates, utensils, and tea-filled mugs on the table. She was glad it was almost time to eat, for Bessie had been a bundle of nerves all day. Sarah didn't know what her part in the evening was to be. Since she was indebted to the Halls for giving her and Samuel a place to stay, she would do her best to not embarrass them.

"Could you get the door?" Bessie called. "Our company has arrived. I am not able to leave the stove."

"On my way," Sarah assured her, smoothing the front of the dark blue dress Bessie had foisted on her.

Sarah fixed a welcoming smile on her face and swung open the door. The man who'd been so kind as to show her to the trading post filled the doorframe.

"You? What are *you* doing here?" Sarah spouted.

Jeremiah swept his hat off and bowed. "Good evening, Mrs. Lyons. Of course it is me. Whom did you expect?"

"Bessie. . .er, Mrs. Hall, did not tell me who was coming," Sarah admitted.

Jeremiah chuckled. "That sounds like my sister."

"You are Bessie's brother?" Land sakes, she found it hard to concentrate when those gray eyes of Jeremiah's stared at her.

"For the last twenty-three years," he confirmed.

"But she never mentioned. . ." Sarah peered around him. "Where is your wife? Will she be along later? She is not ill, is she?"

Jeremiah gave a short chuckle. "I take it Bessie has not told you much about me."

"Such as?"

"I am not married." Jeremiah's tone was suddenly sharp, as if he didn't want to talk about it.

That was fine with Sarah. The subject of marriage didn't appeal to her either. *I have no ties to anyone.* The words echoed in Sarah's mind.

"I am sorry," Sarah murmured, wondering why the fact that he had no mate seemed to stick in her mind.

"Sorry I am not married?" Jeremiah stepped in, pausing to scrape his boots across a rug. "I have nothing against those who choose to wed. It is just that I have decided that marriage is not for me."

Bessie's entrance saved Sarah from having to comment.

Chapter 5

Jeremiah hugged Bessie and murmured a greeting. "You get prettier each time I see you, sis," he remarked.

Bessie laughed. "That is because there is more of me, Jeremiah. I am so glad you finally get to meet Sarah." Bessie gazed between the two of them.

Jeremiah gave Sarah a friendly smile. "Actually, I met Mrs. Lyons the other day when she searched for the trading post."

"'A nice young militiaman,'" Bessie muttered, her eyes moving between Sarah and Jeremiah.

Jeremiah studied Bessie. "Why did you not tell her I was your brother?"

Bessie shrugged. "I suppose there were too many things going on, with the move and all. I have to sit down; my feet are killing me." She plodded away.

Jeremiah shook his head. *Bessie is about to play matchmaker again, and if I'm not wrong, the pretty young widow is oblivious to Bessie's scheme.*

As Jeremiah trailed after Bessie, he reminded himself that he wasn't looking for commitments. His memories of Jenny served quite well to fill his lonely hours.

"Jer? Would you mind. . ." Bessie glanced over his shoulder. "Where is Sarah?"

"She scooted down the hall as soon as you came in here, Bess. If I did not know better, I would say she does not want to be around me."

Bessie finished stirring a pan of gravy and tapped the wooden spoon on the side of the pan. "Nonsense, Jer. Sarah needs to be around people like you. That is exactly why we brought her here. Someone has to help her get over those appalling memories she carries."

"If you do not keep your voice down, she will hear you," Jeremiah cautioned.

"Perhaps that would be best."

Jeremiah spun a fork in a circle. "There are some things you cannot force people to forget, Bess."

"And as you well know, there are some people you cannot force into doing what is right for them."

"Well, that settles that." Jeremiah grinned. "You cannot fool me, Bessie. That look in your eyes says you think we can help each other get over our grief."

"I would never encourage two people to get to know each other if they are not good for each other," Bessie stated.

Jeremiah feigned surprise. "Let me guess. You think Mrs. Lyons and I would make a handsome couple."

Bessie shook the utensil in her hand at him. "What is wrong with that? You think there will never be a woman to take Jenny's place. You are right, Jer, but you cannot spend your life looking for a copy of the woman you loved. You have to accept the one that the Lord sends. Even I know that."

"I do not believe there is anyone out there who could take Jenny's place, Bess. But should Mrs. Lyons ever feel the need to divulge her troubles, my shoulders are broad enough to take whatever she wants to share."

"Captain said much the same thing. So far Sarah has not shared much about what happened to her, so I cannot say what she will think of your offer. It does make *me* feel better though."

Good thing it helped his sister, because Jeremiah didn't like the way Sarah had already woven herself into his thoughts. If he didn't watch it, he'd be first in line to do as Bessie asked, to help Sarah get beyond her pain. He might not like it, but he was a soldier, at least for another few months. He didn't have time for a woman, especially one that did not seem impressed with him.

Bessie put aside Sarah's concern about joining them for the evening meal by saying, "Samuel did not take a nap today. He will be fine playing all by himself. I took a plate back to him and he seems quite happy. Quit worrying about him."

Sarah thanked Captain for holding her chair and listened as he offered the blessing. She added a silent plea of her own that she would not say something humiliating. The aroma of steaming beef and buttered potatoes soon filled the small room.

Sarah listened to the others converse about the growing tensions. She wished she'd paid more attention before when Bessie spoke about the war.

How was I to know I would end up sitting next to a soldier? I don't want to impress him anyway, she fumed to herself.

The evening meal passed with laughter and smiles passing between Bessie and Jeremiah. It was obvious that they'd grown up in a house full of love and that both had missed seeing each other over the last few years.

Captain finished eating and pushed his plate aside. "I believe I have forgotten to congratulate you on your promotion, Jeremiah."

Jeremiah sighed. "I will be honest. I do not like what Colonel Williamson did one bit."

"He must have had a good reason to choose you," Captain said. "I cannot imagine he would put just *anyone* in such a delicate position."

"He said he needed someone the men could trust, that I was one of the few who could read and write. Still. . ."

"But that speaks highly of you, Jeremiah. From what I have heard, Williamson's word is law in these parts, so there is no chance anyone will rebut what he has done."

"Only Major Whelp, who is gone right now."

"It does not sound as if you can change the way things are," Captain said. "If you do not feel comfortable with the task given you, I trust you are praying?"

"Daily," Jeremiah commented. "I am committed to staying until the end of December. I know I cannot walk away from the job because that would leave everything in an uproar. Besides, there are several messages recently that have come in about the Praying Indians. Someone has to deal with them."

Sarah's spoon clattered to the floor. She dove toward it before Jeremiah could assist, but she felt his eyes follow her every move as she recovered it.

Captain went on as if he hadn't noticed. "Sometimes the demands of the job are discomforting, especially when we feel unprepared to handle them. I imagine there is someone who is helping you learn the way things are done."

Jeremiah nodded. "Rufe Putter, the colonel's clerk. We have become close friends since we started working together."

"Ah, yes. Rufe. I met him shortly after we got here," Captain said. "He seems to be a wise, though sometimes immature, fellow. As far as the militia is concerned, I am sure he knows things that you do not."

"He seems to," Jeremiah concurred.

"Sounds to me as if you are afraid of responsibility," Sarah blurted out. She munched on the inside of her cheek. *Will anyone notice if I climb under the table?*

Jeremiah's mouth curved in a small smile. "Perhaps wary would be a better choice of words, Mrs. Lyons. There are so many things to keep straight, I am worried that I might forget something important."

"Call her Sarah, Jer. That other sounds so stuffy."

Sarah jerked her glance across the table, where Bessie primped one side of her upswept hair, oblivious to Sarah's discomfort.

"May I?"

Sarah snapped her head toward Jeremiah. "Sarah will be fine," she said tersely.

"Then you must call me Jeremiah."

"I will," she agreed. There were few with whom she was close enough to use their first names. The thought of such familiarity settled within Sarah like lead.

Jeremiah's gaze held hers. "I believe Sarah was Abraham's wife's name."

"Good point, Jeremiah," Captain said. "I admire the Old Testament Sarah's patience while she waited for the Lord to bless her."

"Amen to that," Bessie seconded. "It is my opinion that the Lord provides exactly what we need when we need it. We only need to accept what He sends."

"What do you think, Sarah?"

Jeremiah sounded sincere, but he gazed at her as if she'd sprouted carrot tops behind her ears. Sarah patted her hair. All seemed well, but why were her fingers shaking?

"Yes, that Sarah was a rare woman," the present-day Sarah concurred. She regretted that she did not recall much about Abraham's wife. It had been so long since she had actively studied God's Word, that much of what she knew had withered away. Her heart flinched uncomfortably.

Over the next few hours Sarah listened as Bessie and Jeremiah shared more stories from their childhood. She refilled coffee mugs and sat quietly until Captain exhorted Jeremiah to tell what he could of events in Washington County. When Jeremiah spoke of a few incidents and politely skimmed over the barbarity involved, Sarah's soul experienced anew the devastation associated with the Indian attacks. She chewed on her bottom lip to keep from saying anything.

"Some say the Praying Indians in Ohio are the ones we must keep an eye on," Jeremiah finished.

"But they. . . What makes you think it is them?" Sarah knew she should not have spoken so forcefully, but she couldn't help it. She knew some of those people. They were Christians. How could anyone suspect them of murderous deeds?

"There are several reasons that I cannot discuss right now," Jeremiah responded.

Sarah kept her voice even. "I refuse to believe that those Praying

Indians are responsible for attacking innocent white families."

"Why do you say that?" Jeremiah challenged.

"Because. . .well, I just do," Sarah said. "Do not ask me to explain."
She grabbed her plate and fled to the washroom.

A few moments later Bessie joined Sarah by the washbasin. She
laid a friendly hand on Sarah's shoulder. "Are you all right? You look
peaked. Let me do this."

Sarah shoved food scraps from the dinner plate into a bucket. "I
will be fine, Bessie. It is you who should be resting. You have been
humming with activity all day long."

"I understand," Bessie said. "I will leave you alone."

"How could you understand," Sarah murmured to Bessie's departing back, "when not even I do sometimes?"

<hr/>

For the next few days no one spoke of Sarah's outburst, which made
her feel worse. She and Sammy played together, went on walks,
and searched for shapes in the clouds. No matter where she went,
there was always another family to remind Sarah of her personal
situation.

Sarah desperately wished God had taken their home and spared
her husband. She was thankful she and Sammy had not perished,
but. . .why had Levi been killed?

Sarah pushed the depressing thoughts away. If she continued to
think about her loss, she would end up in tears. She found her mind
returning to the night Jeremiah visited.

There was no excuse for her outburst at Jeremiah. He was a visi-
tor, and Bessie's brother, not to mention someone whose job it was to
protect the settlers. Sarah was in Washington County to make things
better for her son. Jeremiah did not mean any harm when he had discussed the Praying Indians. He was just passing on information. But
he was a member of the militia. If the militia suspected the Praying
Indians of the attacks, Sarah must be careful to avoid appearing too
concerned about them. If people thought she sympathized with a

band of redskins, who knew what would happen to her plans to build a new life for Sammy?

✍

Jeremiah watched Sarah and her son as they walked along the riverbank. Though it had been a week since he'd last seen Sarah, his heart stirred at the sight of her.

It is not fair to Jenny's memory, Jeremiah warned. His heart didn't listen. While he watched Samuel tossing handfuls of leaves on Sarah's head, Jeremiah let his heart dream. . .of a day when he might stand with Sarah and laugh with her as Samuel played. Of a time when he might be able to—

"Mr. Stewart?"

The closeness of Sarah's voice jerked Jeremiah out of his reverie.

"Good day, Sarah," he said, striving to sound unaffected by her presence. "Are you enjoying our beautiful fall weather?"

"Yes," she replied. "We went by the trading post, but there are still no jobs available. I thought I would bring Sammy out to get some fresh air."

"I know how demanding a move can be. Are you getting settled?"

Sarah patted her son's head. "We are. And Sammy has not had any trouble sleeping as I feared he would."

"By the way, I thought we agreed last week that you would call me Jeremiah."

"So we did." Sarah leaned down and adjusted Samuel's sleeves, apparently wanting time to think.

"I am glad you did not have trouble on the trail on the way here," Jeremiah commented. "There are so many dangers out there, and running into warriors would tend to make a trip quite troublesome."

Sarah's shoulders stiffened. Compassion for her washed over Jeremiah. *No,* he warned his heart sternly. *Keep your distance.*

Sarah rose and studied him. "It has been my experience that some heathens are good people. Or are you one of those who blame all of them for the actions of a few?"

"I do not blame an entire tribe for something a few renegades do," Jeremiah responded. "If you knew half of what I do, you would realize that there are several tribes who will use any excuse they can to attack whites who may or may not have done anything to them."

"Has anyone ever asked them why they go after helpless families?"

"Usually there is no time to ask that question," Jeremiah replied. "They are too intent on retribution for what the British have convinced them is unfair treatment by us pioneers."

"Well, I suppose as a militiaman you must do your duty, regardless of the facts."

Jeremiah cringed. He should tell Sarah that his being a militiaman was not by choice. He was stuck in this job for another three months, whether he liked it or not.

"Look," Jeremiah began, as nonthreateningly as he could. "I promise that while you are here, I will do my best to not let harm come to you or your son."

Sarah's eyes widened. She took a step backward. "No one can keep a promise like that."

"My primary obligation is to ensure the safety of those who live in our community," Jeremiah assured her. "That means I will do my best regardless of who those individuals might be or what happened to them in the past."

Sarah hugged Samuel close to her side. "I know what you are trying to say. I do not need a man, Mr. . . . Jeremiah. Men only complicate matters and cause undue heartache. Regardless of what your sister seems to think, I did not come here to find a man."

"I am simply trying to make you feel welcome," he said.

"I can appreciate your concern," Sarah replied. "But I suggest that any further contact we have be limited to discussing the weather. Agreed?"

Jeremiah wished he could do as Sarah asked. He had thought long and hard about her comments at his sister's home last week. He figured Sarah must know more about the Praying Indians than she wanted others to know. If she did, and he could learn what it was, it might help their militia efforts in some fashion.

"I cannot do that, Sarah," Jeremiah replied. "There is something you and I must discuss that most definitely does not involve the weather."

Chapter 6

Jeremiah strolled toward the office in Williamson's home, his earlier conversation with Sarah replaying in his mind. Instead of gaining her trust so she would talk more openly to him, he had pushed her away.

Perhaps that is best, he mused, stopping for a moment. A web of soft sounds borne on the wings of a bitter wind surrounded him. The only voice was that of a sentry whose duty was to shout the alarm should warriors appear.

Jeremiah felt comforted knowing the man he had chosen to watch through the hours of darkness was one of the best in the county. His heels plunked on the wooden floor of the part of Williamson's cabin that was devoted to militia business. He headed to the corner that contained a table, a wobbly chair, maps tacked onto one wall, and a very tall stack of reports.

Jeremiah took a deep breath. He must put aside thoughts of Sarah Lyons for the moment and prepare his mind for what lay ahead. In eighty-three days he would be released from the militia. Jeremiah recalled how, in April, the colonel had gathered the men around him and announced that Jeremiah was their new lieutenant.

Jeremiah secretly had hoped the men would rebel. If they had done so, he thought that would have convinced Williamson to change his mind. Instead, they had cheered their approval.

Jeremiah pushed out a heavy sigh. All right, then. He didn't like it, but God obviously intended to work another lesson in his life. He'd do his best at this job until his term ended. People—including his sister and Sarah Lyons—counted on him for their safety. He was duty bound to protect them. Not that Sarah Lyons needed any protection. She seemed quite capable of verbally handling anything that came her way.

Jeremiah groaned. Sarah popped into his mind more every day, which wasn't fair to Jenny. Jenny was the woman he had loved. Jenny was the woman who should fill his days. Jenny was. . .gone.

Let her go. Learn to look ahead.

Though he'd had those thoughts before Sarah came along, the words had echoed louder in Jeremiah's heart each day since he met the young widow.

"The past," Jeremiah mused out loud. "If not for the past, Sarah would not be here."

As if that statement had cleared his mind, he opened the journal on the table. Jeremiah leaned back in the chair, propped the book on his knees, and flipped to the opening scrawl.

✍

A few weeks later Sarah was still without work. She took it upon herself to do most of the household tasks as a way to repay the Halls for their kindness.

Shooing Sammy back from the table's edge, she rolled a steaming loaf of bread from the pan. The crusty end was Sammy's favorite treat, and he eagerly awaited it.

"Smells good, Mama," Sammy complimented in his best begging tone.

Sarah handed him the end piece and watched as he happily scampered away. At least Sammy would have a warm place to live this winter. She wondered what would have happened to them had they not moved to Washington County.

"I am so glad Captain remembered to stock the woodpile before he left last week," Bessie said, garnering Sarah's attention. "Seems like it gets colder each passing day."

"Captain does seem to remember to take care of every little detail before he leaves on his circuit rides," Sarah said. "You are fortunate to have such a caring mate." She offered Bessie a slice of bread.

Bessie patted her stomach. "I think I had better pass on that. There does not seem to be much room in here for anything but the baby lately."

They sat quietly as Sarah finished chewing her bread.

Finally Bessie broke the silence. "Do you mind if I ask a nosy question?" At Sarah's shake of the head, Bessie went on. "I just wondered if you happen to know something about those Praying Indians the men were discussing last month?"

Sarah swallowed hard. "I suppose you could say that."

"You know, it might be of some help to Jeremiah if you told him what you know," Bessie said.

"Well, Mr. Stewart will not get any useful information from me," Sarah declared. "What I know is hardly worth the trouble of asking about."

"But it might help the militia," Bessie answered.

Sarah stood up. "I did not come here to help the militia," she stated.

"If you know something, then I do not understand what you will not tell him," Bessie persisted.

Sarah drew a deep breath. "I just cannot do it, Bessie."

Bessie dropped the subject. Sarah reflected on why she didn't want to reveal her knowledge. For one thing, she refused to believe that the tribe she once worshipped with would kill a person. She knew the missionary who led them, recalled the hymns and other parts of the morning and evening worship services.

Those Indians would not kill anyone, regardless of their skin color, Sarah thought. *They journeyed to Ohio to gain religious freedom, to avoid battling white folks who wanted to pen them into a tiny area hardly big enough to support a family, let alone a whole tribe.*

Should she attempt to prevent them from being blamed for something she did not believe they could do? What could she say that would make a difference?

The solution flashed quickly to mind. She could tell Jeremiah what little she knew. No, she realized, she couldn't. If she disclosed what she knew about the tribe, Jeremiah would discover her secret. Sarah frowned. There didn't seem to be a way to convince him without revealing her past.

Though his heart wasn't in it, Jeremiah smiled at the woman at his side. The colonel's niece, Gemma Winslow, was staying with the Williamsons while her parents built a new home a few counties to the west.

Gemma had a cute pixie face surrounded by a halo of reddish-gold curls, but she was too short for his liking. As Jeremiah listened to her chatter, he added to his mental tally that Gemma also was simply too talkative. He forced himself to pay attention.

"So," Gemma said, "I said to Uncle Davy that he simply must allow the men more time to see their families. Do you not agree that is a grand idea, Jeremiah?"

"Actually—"

Gemma's beguiling look cut him off. "The way I see it, the men need to know that their loved ones support them in their venture to serve their country."

"Well, I suppose you could—"

"Uncle Davy agreed to look into my idea as soon as he can. Ah, to be married to a marvelous-looking man who fears nothing and is willing to give his life to defend this land from those dreadful heathens who insist on perpetuating those horrid atrocities." Gemma paused for a breath.

Jeremiah jumped up from his seat. "Please pass my thanks on to your aunt for the superb meal. I must go though. Militia business calls."

Gemma frowned. "But you have been here hardly a half a hand of time, Jeremiah. Surely there is someone else who could do whatever it is that you do."

"Afraid not. I really must go, Gemma. It has been a pleasure talking with you."

Gemma stood and walked to his side. "You are coming back tomorrow night, are you not? I heard Uncle Davy ask you to stop by."

Jeremiah sighed. "Yes, I will be back. To discuss militia matters," he added, just to set Gemma straight.

Sarah seated herself on the floor near the fireplace. Though the spot was overly warm, it did not chase away the cold in her soul. Sammy was abed for the night, and she planned on taking a few moments to relax.

Her thoughts circled from her childhood in an orphanage, to living with the Praying Indians, then to Jeremiah.

Why did he intrude so much in her mind? Why didn't he just join the ranks of other men she had met since losing Levi, men who had wanted nothing to do with her once they learned of her horrible past?

"I am just a lonely widow trying to set my life back to rights," Sarah said aloud. "If Jeremiah wants to know about the Praying Indians, he can ride there and find out for himself."

"He has probably already been through there when he was a courier," Bessie said. "If the issue bothers you so much, Sarah, why do you not tell him so yourself?"

Sarah realized Bessie had heard what she said. Though nervousness gripped her, she crossed the room to a chair. "I just might do that, Bessie."

"Good," Bessie said, harrumphing as she plopped into her own chair. "You do that. I know he wants to see you again."

"You cannot fool me, Bessie Hall," Sarah said. "You are playing matchmaker again, just as you did with Mary Logan and Tom Pittman. I do not like it, and I would appreciate it if you stopped."

"Mary and Tom are happily married," Bessie replied. "And despite what you think, there are decent men in this world. Matter of fact, Jeremiah is one of the best men I know."

Sarah folded her arms in front of her. "I appreciate all you and Captain do for Sammy and me, but I do not think I need to remind you that I am not looking for a mate."

"You do not, but I have to admit something. . . ." Bessie grinned.

Sarah threw her hands up in the air. This wasn't going at all like she had planned. Instead, it was as if she stood in a cabin in the middle of the Ohio wilderness with her sister, who was spouting thou-shalts and thou-shalt-nots at her. A wave of turmoil rose within Sarah. If she'd listened to Callie, she wouldn't be in the situation she was in now.

"Say it, Bessie. You will not stop until you do."

"Jeremiah is not just any man," Bessie announced.

"I do not care if he penned the Declaration of Independence," Sarah replied. "I am not interested."

"He has been hurt before—a woman named Jenny.... That is all I am going to say." Bessie grumbled as she got up heavily and marched to the fireplace where she poked at some embers.

"It does not matter to me that he has been hurt," Sarah called out. "Everyone has at one time or another."

"At least you realize that much," Bessie commented. "Do you also know that most find a way to pick themselves up and carry on? Prayer helps, and so do friends."

"Besides you and Captain, I do not need friends," Sarah insisted. "I am quite capable of making it alone."

"What about God?"

"Sometimes I do not see a need for Him either," Sarah said. "If He was a loving God as the Bible claims, He would not have disrupted my life."

"He *is* a loving God, Sarah. It is only that you chose to look at what He gave you as trouble, instead of as a test to make you stronger." Bessie clucked her tongue. "The book of Matthew says, 'Come unto me, all ye that labour and are heavy laden, and I will give you rest.' What a divine promise that is." She gave Sarah a tender glance. "You say you do not need God and you do not need friends. In that case, I pray our heavenly Father has an easy life planned for you."

"This is beginning to get old," Sarah warned. "*I* am in control of my life, no one else."

"That is where you are mistaken," Bessie replied. "God always has everything to do with your life. You just have to learn to trust Him again."

Sarah jumped from the chair. "How can I trust Him when I know what He took from Sammy? I may sit and listen, Bessie, but that is why I do not participate in Captain's Bible studies. I find it hard to believe in Someone who allows such cruel things to happen."

Did I truly mean that? Sarah was so flustered, she didn't know. Nothing seemed to work the way she wanted; perhaps nothing ever would. Going it on her own couldn't be any worse than walking with God, could it? Two years ago God let her down one too many times. Everything since that night only proved her need to stand alone. Why couldn't Bessie see that?

"That is exactly why I believe in Him, Sarah," Bessie said. "I have no doubt that He is always with me." Bessie patted the child within her. "Yes, God sometimes takes away that which we love the most, but if we are patient, He will send us other blessings. Not to make up for the ones we lost, but to show us that we are His children and that He loves us."

Sarah shook her head. "You cannot tell me you are content to sit around and wait for God to work a miracle."

"Captain is a miracle, as far as I am concerned," Bessie said. "Someday, when you are ready to listen, I will tell you what happened to me. And I am convinced that no matter what tribulations God allows me to endure here, He will make up for my difficulties in the Great Beyond."

"You are the most stubborn person I have ever met," Sarah replied.

"Guess that is why I survive what life throws at me," Bessie said. "Jeremiah is the same way."

"He does not look as if he has survived that woman you mentioned," Sarah commented.

"So you did notice him." Bessie grinned like a cat who just caught the last available mouse.

Alarm tightened Sarah's throat. "You do not have to raise your voice, Bessie. What I noticed is that Jeremiah appears uncomfortable around me," she explained.

"Why would a man who is not afraid of going out into the unknown to fight something he does not understand be uncomfortable around someone like you?"

"Why are you asking me? You should ask Jeremiah that question."

"I think you should ask yourself that, Sarah."

Chapter 7

This man wants the job, Lieutenant Stewart."

Jeremiah pushed aside the journal to scan the candidate for courier who stood beside Rufe. Tall and rangy, he was just shy of being gaunt. Black hair spilled over his ears, and his features seemed fixed in a perpetual sneer.

With Colonel Williamson out again, Jeremiah had no choice but to acquaint himself with the only applicant. He introduced himself.

"Just call me Shade," the newcomer stated.

"Has Rufe explained the responsibilities of the job?" Jeremiah asked, thinking that the man's name certainly matched his solemn features.

"Yes." The man kept his dark gaze locked with Jeremiah's.

Jeremiah felt uneasy, but he continued. "You do not have any questions?"

Shade shook his head.

"Why are you so willing to work with us?"

Shade shifted his weight to one hip. "Call it evening the odds."

There was an air of edginess about Shade. *Just what I need,* Jeremiah thought. *Someone who is out for revenge.* "You do not talk much, do you?"

"No need to talk. Action is better."

"We do not pay much," Jeremiah offered, intrigued by the confident air Shade possessed.

"Don't need much."

Jeremiah didn't have much choice. The colonel had announced the job to the men, but none had stepped forward to accept it. "Well, then, I reckon you will have to do," he told the man.

"Reckon I will," Shade answered.

Jeremiah narrowed his brow. Rufe had done the preliminary work;

all Jeremiah must do now was confirm the selection. He recalled Captain telling him to trust the clerk's judgment. Jeremiah would do that, but a prayer that this wouldn't be a decision that would haunt him couldn't hurt.

The interview over, the new courier gave a two-fingered salute to his brow and eased out the door with the elegance of a mountain lion. Rufe followed him.

Jeremiah's gaze returned to the journal. He'd have to finish it later. There was another matter he had to take care of first, one that had developed over the last few days, no matter how hard he tried to ignore it.

"Rufe, I am headed to the trading post. Got a few things to take care of."

❧

Sarah dashed into the house. She almost tripped over Sammy, who played with his blocks in the middle of the floor. After assuring herself that her son was fine, she shouted for Bessie.

"Miz Bessie upside down," Sammy contributed. He made a V with his fingers to show his mother what he meant.

Oh dear! Had Bessie fallen? Sarah's heart bobbled to a halt. *What should I do?*

She realized she must find Bessie and see what had happened. Sometimes the woman poked her nose into places where it didn't belong, but Sarah didn't want anything to happen to her. She shouted Bessie's name again.

Bessie's reply came from the back room. Sarah rushed down the hall. She found Bessie leaning over and holding her ankles, exactly as Sammy had shown with his hand motions.

"What are you doing? You are over seven months along. You could hurt yourself." Sarah bent down to peer at Bessie's flushed face. "Have you no sense?"

"I only wanted to see my toes before they disappeared," Bessie explained. "I did this last week and did not have a bit of trouble getting back up. But now look at me!"

Sarah had done the same thing when she carried Sammy. Levi had joked with her and told her that if she'd been any shorter or further along, she'd have been stuck in that position. Sarah was glad Bessie wasn't huge, otherwise she could imagine that very thing happening to her.

"You do not hurt anywhere, do you?" Sarah perused the V-shaped woman.

"No. I just cannot seem to get the motion going to stand back up. Will you help me?"

Sarah moved in front of Bessie, grabbed both arms, and tugged gently upward, ready to counterbalance if need be. When Bessie stood upright, her eyes shone like lanterns on a winter night.

Bessie fanned herself. "How embarrassing. Please do not tell Captain. He would skin me alive if he knew I did that."

"I did something similar once," Sarah confided in a burst of intimacy. "I will not tell if you promise not to do it again."

"You do not think I hurt my child, do you?" Bessie looked stricken.

"I do not know, but it did not seem to injure Sammy."

"Oh! I promised I would watch him for you. I plumb forgot. Did you see him?"

Sarah explained that he was playing by the door. "How long were you like that, anyway?" Now that her initial agitation had faded, she relaxed a little.

"Not long. Honest." Bessie collapsed onto the edge of her mattress. "Whew. That was refreshing. You sound out of breath. Why were you hurrying so?"

"Well, I went to the trading post, and you know I was not really expecting anything, but there it was."

"What?" Bessie sounded suspicious.

Sarah was too excited to care. "A notice that someone wanted a laundress."

"Who?"

"It didn't say."

"You mean you do not know who you will be working for?"

Sarah frowned. "No." Not knowing hadn't seemed important until Bessie pointed it out. "The clerk at the post just said I could pick up and return the work there."

"And he gave no hint as to who it was for?"

Sarah paced the small room, chewing on her lip. "No. Do you think I should refuse since I do not know who I will work for?"

"Oh no. I did not mean that," Bessie gushed. "I am sure whoever it is has a reason for keeping their identity hidden."

Sarah caught her hands behind her. "It does sound strange, but this will allow me to contribute to the running of your household. You know how guilty I feel about accepting food and lodging from you."

"We have all known hard times. It is only proper that we help others when they need it. Captain and I would not have asked you to come with us if we did not want to share." Bessie pushed off the bed. "I think we should celebrate your hiring with a cup of tea."

"Only if you promise to sit, like a woman with child should," Sarah admonished.

"Yes ma'am." Bessie giggled as she ambled down the hallway. "I cannot believe I could not get back up. Oh Sarah. What would I have done if you had not come back just then?"

"I do not know." Bessie's gratitude tugged at Sarah's heart. She didn't need commitments like that.

Jeremiah closed his eyes and rubbed the bridge of his nose.

Lord, You know what is in the next entry as well as I do. I'm scared, Lord—afraid of what I will do when I see the words. Be with me, Lord. Help me through this.

He opened his eyes and focused on the date: *"August 14, 1779."* He knew he must read this, if for no other reason than to put it behind him. He blinked to clear the blurry words he was about to read.

"A band of Wyandots were shot not far from here by a Fort Pitt

detachment. We are positive that the heathens were responsible for the recent deaths of Jenny Townsend and her brother."

Sorrow wedged in Jeremiah's throat. He dropped the journal, not caring that it landed on the toe of his boot. Jenny Townsend—his promised, his beloved. Tears burned his eyes. Jenny, with her carefree laugh, her long, dark hair, and her way of making everyone she talked to feel more loved, more precious.

Pain dug through Jeremiah's heart. He didn't push it away. It was time he faced his loss. He could have avoided reading this and not recalled the horror of Jenny's death, but hadn't he done that for too long? Hadn't he lived within himself, not reaching out to others as he should?

Yes, he had. That wasn't how his parents had raised him.

"Blessed is the man that maketh the Lord his trust." Jeremiah's mother had quoted that verse from chapter forty of the book of Psalms at the table every morning. Later Jenny had adopted the practice herself. If nothing else, Jenny Townsend had believed in Jesus.

That's what I must remember, Jeremiah consoled himself. *Jenny may not be here with me, but she is in heaven with our Lord, and with my mother.*

Jeremiah repeated the statement until it seemed branded on his heart. With a deep sigh, he drew the book back onto his lap and hardened his heart as he reopened it.

Once past the heartache of the first entry, Jeremiah tried to make sense of other writings, which detailed the successes and failures of pioneer families. Being unable to concentrate, he slid the book out of sight and formed a triangle with his pointer fingers and thumbs.

Why did You put me here, God? What is it I have yet to learn before I move on?

He thought back on his childhood. He'd grown up content to help his parents eke out a living until he was old enough to learn the blacksmith trade. Though he barely made a success of that, he enjoyed working with animals. When the courier position arose shortly after his mother died, Jeremiah decided to apply for it.

"You are running off to war," his father had argued.

"No, Pa. I am going to help my country in its search for freedom."

"Believe what you want, son, but you will end up killing those who God put on this earth."

"I am just a courier, Pa. I will never kill," Jeremiah had promised.

In the end, after all the disagreeing, there was nothing left to say. As a courier, he thought he would not rise above the enlisted ranks. Now he was a county lieutenant, with the potential to control the fate of an entire county.

Perhaps I should write Pa, fill him in on all that's happened. Or perhaps I should wait until after the birth of Bessie's child?

Jeremiah's gaze settled on the candle on the desk. He followed wisps of smoke rising from it as they traveled toward the ceiling's gloom. It wouldn't hurt if he posted a letter to his father tomorrow. He would tell him about Bessie and the young'un on the way, about Captain and how he appeared to have helped Jeremiah's baby sister get over her grief. He might even mention Sarah Lyons, if for no other reason than to let his father know she'd suffered as great a tragedy as Jeremiah himself. The only thing he wouldn't tell his father was what he was doing in the militia—no use upsetting Pa any more than necessary.

✍

Sarah scrubbed shirts until she thought her arms would fall off. Even though the position offered her scarcely enough to buy Sammy a hard candy every week, she wanted the clothing to be as perfect as possible so she wouldn't lose the job.

Bessie still thought Sarah should ask who'd hired her. Sarah was reluctant to do so. If she was successful at this, she might garner more work. That would provide her a way to raise Sammy, and that was what was important.

Bessie had taken Sammy to see Jeremiah, as she did daily. Before she left, she insisted that Sarah use her portion of soap, as well as the hot irons. Promising to reimburse Bessie for the lye soap, Sarah agreed. She had propped the irons against the grate to heat, and glanced over to check them. Satisfied that she wasn't going to get the shirts any cleaner, she wrung out the water and hung them near the hearth. Wiping her hands on her apron, she sauntered to the large room, where she straightened a few of Bessie's knickknacks.

Noticing that the quilt across the back of Captain's chair was skewed, Sarah moved to straighten it. One of Sammy's blocks lay in her path. She stumbled over it, her hand flinging out and knocking Captain's Bible off the chair arm. The book fell, its pages ruffling. A flash of yellow drifted downward like an autumn leaf.

Sarah glanced around until she spied a sliver of yellow ribbon tied around a lock of hair. Whose was it? It didn't matter whose, she had to put it back. But where? Her sister would have stashed a small object such as this in a specially marked place within God's Word. Sarah hadn't touched a Bible in years, let alone opened one.

It's just a book, she told herself. *Just because I've decided to go it alone doesn't mean anything will happen if I open it.*

Sarah studied the volume, knowing there was only one thing she could do. Finally, she picked up the book and raised the cover. Inside, a spidery inscription read: *"Presented to Daniel Hall and his second wife, Bessie, on the occasion of their marriage. Given by Johanna Hall— December 25, 1778."*

It took Sarah a minute to recall she'd heard Bessie call her husband Daniel occasionally. But it was the phrase "his second wife" that baffled Sarah. She had not suspected that Captain had been married before. Did Bessie know? Oh, what did it matter anyway? Whatever had gone before in Captain's life meant little to Sarah.

"Was it not Psalms that Captain declared his favorite?" Sarah murmured to herself.

Thinking she might lay the tuft of hair there until she found out for sure where it belonged, she slid a finger between some pages in the middle of the book and turned to the book of Psalms. As the rustling pages settled into place, verses sprang to her mind.

"He that dwelleth in the secret place of the most High shall abide under the shadow of the Almighty."

"I waited patiently for the LORD; and he inclined unto me, and heard my cry."

They were words that had given hope when there was little else to cling to. As a new Christian, Sarah once had believed their promises. Now she trusted only herself. Misery filled her heart.

Why did I make the choices I made? How can God ever forgive me for not trusting Him as I should have all this time?

Sarah stifled a sob. Instead of concentrating on the path she'd chosen, she needed to decide what to do about the snippet of hair. She couldn't go through the Bible page by page hunting for evidence of where it belonged, could she?

Why not? Captain was out for the day, and Bessie was gone visiting. Neither would return for a few hours. She had nothing else to do until the shirts dried.

It was just her and the Bible.

With trembling hands, Sarah turned to the beginning and searched for the familiar words. *"In the beginning God created. . ."*

The fingertips of her right hand lingered on the words. The small indentations where the letters pressed into the thin paper nestled against her skin as if they belonged there.

God's Word. This was what her sister, Captain, and Bessie, and so many others as well, put their trust in. Fragile words printed on delicate paper.

"The Word of the Lord stands forever."

Sarah shook her head. "Now where did those words come from?"

The memory crept slowly to mind. It was from a sermon the Moravian missionary David Zeisberger had preached—on a fine fall day filled with laughter, sunshine, and friends—just after the group arrived at the site where they would build their wilderness mission.

"The Lord knows your sorrow, knows your pain, but He can only take

your burden if you let Him."

Who was that? Levi's mother, who did not yet know her only son had passed on. Sarah brushed away the drops that slipped down her cheeks and splotched the tiny letters.

"Stop crying," she chided herself. "Tears don't solve anything. All they do is pull my heart into my throat and make me feel as if the whole world is collapsing around me."

Sarah pressed a thumb and forefinger between her eyes and took a deep breath. Feeling composed, she turned the pages one at a time, renewing her search for something that identified where the tiny remnant of hair belonged.

⚬

Jeremiah listened as his sister argued with Rufe in the outer office. Shortly after her move to Washington County, Bessie began coming by daily. She claimed the exercise and fresh air were good for her health, but Jeremiah suspected she really wanted to check on him.

Jeremiah knew he should go out to greet Bessie, but Shade's latest delivery lay on the table, an unpleasant reminder of the newest task Jeremiah had been given.

"I am here to see Jeremiah." Bessie's loud announcement drew Jeremiah's thoughts back to the present.

"Lieutenant Stewart is busy, ma'am," Rufe replied. "He left orders not to be disturbed."

"But I am his sister. Surely he can see me."

Though Rufe was captivated by Bessie's outgoing personality, the clerk did as Jeremiah had ordered. "I am sorry, ma'am, but the lieutenant said—"

"I have some important business with my brother," Bessie interrupted. "I demand that you let me in."

Jeremiah envisioned Bessie leaning over the desk, her crazy curls falling around her shoulders and her bright eyes glaring at Rufe. It was almost enough to lighten his foul mood.

"I am sorry," Rufe began again, "but Lieutenant Stewart said no one was to interrupt him. In fact, Gemma was here earlier and he even refused to see her. Hey! You cannot go in there!"

"Jer?"

Jeremiah slowly raised his gaze. "Hello, Bess. And Samuel. How are you?" It was all he could do to keep his voice from breaking.

"Miah!" Samuel gave him a sprightly smile.

For the sake of the child, Jeremiah grinned back. "Hello, scout. Are you making sure my sister gets here safely?"

"I am," Samuel replied. He sauntered a few steps closer to Jeremiah.

"That is good," Jeremiah said. "I am glad you came with Bessie. Did your mama come along, too?"

Despite a constant hope that she would, Sarah rarely accompanied Bessie. If Sarah did, she went to the trading post while Bessie visited with Jeremiah.

"She wash shirts so she can buy me candy," Samuel explained.

"That is right," Jeremiah said without thinking.

"Jer? How did you. . ." Bessie began. Understanding dawned in her eyes. "You?"

Jeremiah nodded, hoping the young boy did not follow their conversation.

"Why did you not tell—"

"I am glad you stopped by," Jeremiah interrupted. "Can I walk you home?"

He sent Bessie a silent plea with his eyes that said, Please don't ask me to explain why I didn't let Sarah know it was my laundry.

"Sure thing. Are you ready to go, Samuel?"

Samuel looked up. "Now?"

"Yes. Jeremiah is going to walk with us."

"He stay and eat with me?"

Before either Bessie or Jeremiah could answer, Samuel raced out the door. He sprinted ahead down the path, stopping to point out moss growing on the base of some trees and giggling at a squirrel scolding them from the branches overhead. Sunshine filled a cloudless sky, and as they walked, Bessie tucked her hand around Jeremiah's elbow.

"Go on, big brother. You might as well tell me what is bothering you."

"A spot of bad news, Bessie. That is all I can say."

"I have not seen you this upset since. . . I wish Captain were not out on his circuit. He would know what to say to you."

Jeremiah was sure Bessie had been about to refer to his behavior when he found out about their mother. It would be nice if Captain *were* here, but he wasn't. Jeremiah wanted the Whelp family to know what he'd learned before others from the community found out. The dismal burden pressed against his heart.

"I am sure Captain would be a big help," Jeremiah said, "but since he is not here, and neither is Colonel Williamson, this is something I must handle."

Jeremiah wasn't looking forward to taking the news of the major's death to his family. He hadn't liked the way Dan Whelp had pushed people around, but the man's earthly life was gone—snuffed out by a wayward arrow in the heat of conflict, for the little good that would do his widow.

Bessie studied him with a younger sister's patience. "It is about the war, is it not?"

"Look, Bess. I know you mean well, but—"

"If you promise you will pray, you do not have to walk us the rest of the way," she said.

I want to go with you, Jeremiah thought. *I want to see Sarah. And it will keep me from having to face Mrs. Whelp until I figure out what I'm going to say to her.*

"Seems as if I have been doing nothing but praying since I got this job," he admitted.

"Say no more." Bessie patted his arm.

Jeremiah wasn't quite ready to be alone. "How long do you reckon it is before your young'un is due?"

"Another couple of months. Why?"

"I thought I would write Pa. Perhaps he would like to know."

Bessie studied Jeremiah's face. "Pa is a survivor, Jer, just like us. He always told us we cannot stumble if we are on our knees."

Jeremiah nodded. There wasn't anything else to say.

Chapter 8

Bessie waited until Samuel hugged his mother and went off in search of his blocks. "Would you say all that again? I must have missed something."

Sarah repeated her story. "I tried to go back through a page at a time to find out where this tuft of hair went."

Bessie gave the item a quick glimpse. "It is not the Bible I am worried about, Sarah. It is you. You look different."

"What do you mean?"

"I do not know, but something about you has changed."

Sarah sought something else in the room to look at besides Bessie. She thought she knew what Bessie was referring to. As she'd leafed through the Bible, occasional passages had grabbed her attention, reminding her of the times when God's Word had soothed her troubled heart. Since she'd lost Levi, believing was so hard to do.

Sarah held up the lock of hair again. "I thought perhaps you could tell me where it belongs. I will return it to its rightful place, and I promise never again to pick up that Bible."

"That Bible belonged to Captain's grandmother," Bessie responded. "She carried it across the ocean when she settled here. Pick it up anytime you wish to. As a matter of fact, I would like you to do so. When Captain is gone, I do not get to hear the stories I love. You can read, Sarah. Would you?"

"Would I what?" Sarah asked cautiously.

"Read to me," Bessie said, caressing her abdomen. "I want my child raised in the Lord so he knows there is a reason for everything that happens in his life. This way he will get a head start."

Sarah's throat grew dry. "I do not think that is a good idea. I do not read very well."

"There is only one thing that is better than your reading, and that is your singing. It would mean so much to me. Please say yes." Bessie seldom begged, but she was doing it now.

When Sarah was with child, Levi had done everything he could to please her. Sarah didn't know why exactly, but making Bessie happy seemed important.

"Perhaps I could read a few verses a day," Sarah offered.

"You are so wonderful," Bessie squealed. "Captain will be over the moon. He has prayed for someone to study with me. I am so glad it will be you. Can we start right now?"

Sarah swallowed her discomfort. "I suppose now is as good a time as any, but what about this lock of hair? You still have not said where it goes."

"I think Captain keeps it in the book of Isaiah," Bessie said. "Just slip it in there somewhere. He will set it to rights when he gets home."

Sarah felt awkward just "slipping it in there somewhere," as Bessie suggested. Sarah recalled that one of her sister's favorite Bible chapters was Isaiah 40. She paged to it and tucked the hair away, silently reading a sentence there: *They that wait upon the Lord shall. . .mount up with wings as eagles; they shall run, and not be weary. . . .*"

"Wait upon the Lord," Sarah repeated to herself. Doing so probably couldn't hurt. She'd waited for something to happen that would give her hope for the future since the day she had lost Levi. Perhaps there was something more meaningful that she needed to think about.

"Do you think you could start somewhere other than 'In the beginning'? I know it is important, but I am anxious to hear about Jonah, and Ruth, and Daniel."

Sarah drew a deep breath. Reading the words of the prophet Isaiah, she'd experienced a brief memory of comfort. She thumbed her way through the Bible so she wouldn't have to think about it. "How about Jonah first?" Sarah asked. "It is short and will not take us long."

And it describes exactly what I am feeling just now, Sarah realized, *as if I have been swallowed by an animal much larger than myself and have no means of defense.*

Bessie smiled. "I just love the part when Jonah finally realizes God is in control. How about you?"

_꧁_

Jeremiah entered the office, stamping his feet to rid his boots of the dust collected on his trip to Fort Pitt. He'd enjoyed the brief time on the trail, though he knew he wouldn't have gone if Dan Whelp were still here.

Jeremiah frowned as he scanned a note lying on the desk. Colonel Williamson had been in while Jeremiah was gone. He left an invitation for Jeremiah to meet with Gemma tomorrow night, with a postscript indicating that he was again gone to the farthest reaches of the county.

Sometimes I think the colonel only wants the glory of being the commander, not the hassles or heartache that go with it, Jeremiah thought. _No, that's not fair,_ he corrected. _The colonel does what he can._

Rufe cleared his throat and Jeremiah forced his mind back to the task at hand.

"What am I supposed to do with this mess?" Jeremiah pointed to a pile of papers on the desk.

Rufe shrugged. "You have done pretty well up to this point. Just tell me where to start, and I will get right to work helping you compose the answers."

Jeremiah studied the heaps. Five months as county lieutenant had done nothing to relieve his awkwardness at being a leader. He made decisions and wrote requisitions for supplies, but mostly he prayed.

"Want some time to look through them before you write the replies?"

"I suppose that will be best," Jeremiah said. "Especially since I might be tempted to quit if I wrote right now."

He stared at a hand-drawn map on the wall. Miniature red dots marked Indian attacks up and down the Ohio River and several points to the east. With each attack, the red circles marched closer to their settlement.

Jeremiah tried hard to follow two principles his father had taught him: Study a problem from all angles and figure out the best way to solve it. But he still doubted his ability to make the best decision. Perhaps all the trip to Fort Pitt had accomplished was to point out that he missed hitting the trail and taking messages to leaders who would decide what to do next.

That's what it was. He'd never had this much responsibility before. He just carried others' decisions to those of higher rank. Perhaps that was part of his problem; he needed to take a step back and consider what it was he really wanted to do in life. That wasn't going to happen anytime soon. Not when the colonel refused to spend any time at home.

The next time Williamson returned, Jeremiah would insist Williamson select someone to fill Dan Whelp's position. Then Jeremiah would take a few days off, time he needed to clear his head. Perhaps he'd visit the grave he hadn't visited in so long. Then again, perhaps not.

You don't need to resurrect pain you've already buried, Stewart, he admonished himself.

Pain. At least a benefit to staying busy was that he had little time to think about Jenny. All the way to Fort Pitt and back he'd thought of. . .Sarah.

Sarah, who had the same hollow look in her eyes that echoed how Jeremiah felt when he thought of how wrong his life had gone since losing Jenny. Sarah, who appeared to feel that she was the only one who'd experienced great tragedy and would never find anyone else who understood.

Jeremiah understood, though he didn't like talking about it. Some things were better left alone. Scars healed faster that way, covering wounds that would otherwise always hurt if continually exposed. That's why he kept thinking of Sarah Lyons. Not because she was beautiful. Not because the sad look on her face dug furrows in Jeremiah's heart every time he saw her. Jeremiah buried his head in his hands.

Lord, what is it You would have me do? I do not understand why You have put me here, or what purpose I have in Sarah's life. And speaking of Sarah, do You think You might find a way to take away her hurt? When I see her standing off to the side where she thinks no one is watching, it's as if she sees something horrible run through her mind, over and over. Perhaps she does not know it shows, but it does. I trust You. Please help her, Lord.

Jeremiah opened his eyes to find the red circles on the map staring at him.

"Figure it out yet?" Rufe asked from behind him.

"Not yet, but I reckon that is why I do not sleep much. Gives me more time to ponder things."

"I will fire up the lanterns and stay with you," Rufe offered.

"What?" Jeremiah quizzed. "I thought you would probably go see that young lady you have been crowing about lately."

Rufe shook his head. "It did not work out. Seems the only one worth going after would be that pretty miss that wandered in here by accident a few months ago. But I got the feeling she wanted nothing to do with men."

"I think you are right, Rufe," Jeremiah said, ignoring how painful that understanding was.

⟋⟍

Jeremiah glanced across the table. Gemma's cheeky stares were beginning to get on his nerves. He tried not to let his irritation show, but the more time he spent with her, the less he wanted to.

"You look so dashing tonight, Lieutenant Stewart," Gemma cooed. "I just adore the way that dark blue jacket brings out the gray in your eyes."

Jeremiah coughed. Mrs. Williamson glanced at Gemma but returned to sipping her soup without comment.

"Thank you, Miss Winslow." Jeremiah wished he'd gone to Bessie's instead of coming here. The colonel's request that he visit Mrs. Williamson and Gemma was not a military order, but Jeremiah felt bound to do as the colonel requested.

"Did you know," Gemma began, "that Uncle Davy has insisted that I spend the whole winter here? Now, is that not just the most wonderful news? I miss my parents, of course, but to stay here with Aunt and Uncle is an opportunity that I cannot put aside."

"How nice," Jeremiah murmured, though it really didn't matter. Once Gemma started talking, she didn't need encouragement from anyone. His sister sometimes chatted incessantly, but Bessie was family—he *enjoyed* listening to her. Gemma, on the other hand. . .

"And so," Gemma went on, "since my mother just absolutely has no skills where cooking and sewing are concerned, I plan to learn those sorts of housekeeping details from Auntie while I am here. Must be prepared to be a proper wife when the day arrives, you know." Gemma flashed him a coy smile.

Jeremiah lowered his gaze and grimaced. Gemma left little doubt as to whom she expected to be a wife to.

✍

Sarah opened the door to Jeremiah's knock. Her surprised look told him that he was the last person she expected. Jeremiah didn't know how to relieve her distress, so he simply asked if he could enter. While Jeremiah took a seat at the table, Sarah rushed to find Bessie.

"Bessie is taking a nap," Sarah announced as she returned. "Is there something I can do for you?"

"Yes. I came to deliver an invitation. There is going to be a Winter Supper," he said. "For everyone in Washington County. The main purpose is to fellowship and to celebrate the birth of our Lord. Will you pass the word on to Bessie and Captain for me?"

"I take it I am not invited."

You certainly handled that well, Jeremiah chided himself.

"Of course you are invited, Sarah. I meant that since Bessie is not available right now, I wanted you to let her know about the gathering."

"I will tell her," Sarah said. "But you can count me out."

"You have something against getting together with others to celebrate the birth of our Lord?"

"No," Sarah replied.

"I think Samuel might enjoy seeing everyone," Jeremiah urged. "I hope you will reconsider. The supper is designed to encourage the men of the militia and give the ladies a chance to dress in their finery."

"Well, Mr. Stewart, you will have to do without my presence," Sarah said. "The less I have to do with militiamen, the better. After all, if your counterparts at Fort Henry had responded to my late husband's request for protection, I would not be here today."

This was not going at all the way Jeremiah had planned.

"Point taken, Mrs. Lyons. I will not let your comment pass without saying that our military companions downriver operate under different rules than we do. Please don't assume that I or our force here would have done the same. May I also add in our defense that if people would quit settling so far from others, there would be less chance of renegades, Indians or otherwise, upsetting their worlds."

"We thought we were out of the way," Sarah retorted, her voice rising in pitch.

"In this day and time there is no place that is truly out of the way," Jeremiah replied. "It becomes doubly important that we all help and encourage one another when we get a chance."

"That might be," Sarah acknowledged, "but I do not see a need to get myself involved in others' lives right now. I will not attend the supper."

⟡

"Tell me a story, Mama," Sammy demanded, climbing onto her lap and disrupting her line of thought.

She did as he asked, but Sammy soon fell asleep in her arms. While he dozed, Sarah stared at the whorl of hair on the top of Sammy's head. She placed a soft kiss on his brow.

"No matter how I try, Sammy, I cannot change what happened to us. Your pa and I planned for our lives to be filled with love and laughter. And that would have come to pass if those horrid Indians had not attacked us. I miss your pa, Sammy. Sometimes I miss him so much I cannot imagine how I am to go on without him. At least I still have you. I hope I can find a way to help you grow to be a man your pa would be proud of."

Chapter 9

Jeremiah figured he'd be pressed into escorting Gemma to the supper, something he definitely did not want to do. He wondered if perhaps he might convince Rufe to escort the colonel's niece and decided that he would discuss that idea with Rufe later.

With the colonel back and demanding an update, Jeremiah pointed to an area on the map a half-day's ride north. "The latest report came from a family by the name of Clayton. They took the wife and two girls."

Williamson indicated some other dots to the south. "What about these?"

Jeremiah shook his head. "I just do not know. They usually are not this scattered. When they attack, they hit one or two close together then disappear."

Good thing there is less than a month of my commitment left, Jeremiah thought. *I cannot wait till the Winter Supper, for I'll be released shortly after.*

"You are in charge while I am out in the field," Williamson said. "You read all the reports. Give me your input as to what you think is happening, Lieutenant."

Jeremiah thought for a moment before he spoke. "I think the group of Indians responsible for the raids is getting nervous. They do not know what is going to happen, since their alliance with the British is becoming more apparent."

Williamson folded his arms in front of his chest and rested them on his portly middle. "A good analysis. I would like to add that after this latest trip of mine, I firmly believe the Wyandots are not the ones we need to worry about."

"Why not?"

Williamson glanced to the dots spiraling out along various creeks that fed into the Ohio River. "You read those journals Rufe's father loaned to us. If I am not mistaken, it seems he believes the Praying Indians are the prowlers."

Jeremiah studied the colonel. Feeble candlelight gave him a sallow appearance and drew attention to his somewhat rumpled shirt.

"Those Indians are Christians, Colonel. I cannot believe that they are to blame. Besides, I think that Colonel Brodhead out of Fort Pitt stirs them up on purpose."

"Brodhead is just trying to defend his territory, Jeremiah," Williamson replied. "Did you read the last report he sent out?"

"Yes," Jeremiah growled. "All that bragging about how they took three hundred men and killed fifteen warriors then dragged the old men, women, and children away. They murdered most of them before going back to Fort Pitt. What is the world coming to?"

"My mother would say, 'Nothing good,' " Williamson offered. "Sometimes we can only react to an action. We do not control our fates. We do what we are pressed into doing."

Jeremiah flexed the fingers on his right hand. "They killed forty warriors they said were drunk and highly dangerous. Those braves were probably scared and running away. Brodhead didn't have to pursue them. I wonder if he had proof that they were guilty."

"Brodhead is on our side, Lieutenant. What is the matter with you?" The colonel pinned him with a hawklike gaze. "Getting cold feet?"

Jeremiah raked his fingers through his hair. "I believe that as Christians, Zeisberger and his flock will not kill. Nor will I." He sought to remind Williamson of his promise not to take part in any such thing.

"I think there is something more than Brodhead killing warriors bothering you."

"Rufe's father wrote everything he could in those journals." Jeremiah hoped to turn the conversation away from death and dying.

Williamson nodded. "So?"

"I think I will read them again and see what else I can find out about those Moravian missions. If that fails, I may just take a short trip to Fort Pitt to see what I can find out from them."

"It will not change my mind, but do what you think you need to. I think they are guilty. That is all I need to know." Williamson's words were filled with bitterness.

⁊

Bessie waddled through the door with Samuel pushing her knees from behind as if she couldn't make it under her own power. She was not far from giving birth, and though it wore her out, she insisted on going out each day for a short walk. Sarah remembered that awkward time when her body felt like a fruit that stayed on the vine too long. But the end was worth it—holding your child and realizing that God's blessings often came in the form of babies. As if he knew the joy he brought her, Sammy launched himself into Sarah's arms.

"Missed you, Mama." He planted a smack on her cheek.

Sarah's heart spun in her chest. Sammy looked so much like his father that she wanted to cry. What if she couldn't keep Sammy safe long enough for him to grow up?

"I missed you, too, Sammy." Sarah smoothed his hair behind his ears. "Looks like we will have to cut your hair soon."

"No haircut. I want hair like Miah." Sammy pouted.

Bessie chuckled. "Guess I ought to tell you so you know what Samuel means. You know those daily strolls we take?"

Sarah nodded. "I do not understand how you can continue to go out every day. I sat at home and did nothing but wait for the big day."

"Family means a lot to me, and so I go to visit Jeremiah. He has been rather gloomy lately, and I do so want him to cheer up. You know that Major Whelp is. . .gone. Well, actually, I guess his dying is only part of the story."

Bessie had the geese ready to head south again, prattling on about things that made no difference to what she had started talking about. Sarah snuggled Sammy on her lap and prepared to stretch her patience.

"I am sure you remember Captain telling us about Dan Whelp being killed," Bessie continued. "I heard he wasn't well liked, God rest his soul, but anyway, with Colonel Williamson back, Jeremiah is upset because now he does not see any way out of this militia business. He only did it as a favor for Williamson, and in the beginning Williamson told him it was only for six months and now he says longer. That has Jeremiah all worked up. I just hope he does not do something he will regret later."

Bessie rubbed her arms. "Where was I? Oh, yes. Jer sent off some letters without telling the colonel about them. He requested that they appoint a replacement for Major Whelp. They—I forget who 'they' is, but they did not answer yet. In protest, Jeremiah decided he will not cut his hair until he is out of the militia. Says he is not made to be a militiaman and does not know what God is trying to do with him. Sarah?"

"Go on. I am listening." Sammy squirmed as if he were tired of hearing Bessie go on and on like a crow with a piece of corn stuck in its beak. Sarah let him down, knowing he would toddle off to his blocks. She considered joining him.

Bessie smirked. "Have you seen him lately?"

"Colonel Williamson? I do not even know him."

"Jeremiah, you ninny. Who do you think I have been talking about? You have not been paying attention, have you?"

"Partially," Sarah admitted. "He should hear soon, I would think," she said, responding to a part of the chatter that she recalled.

"He hopes it will be soon. He says this has been the longest year of his life."

"From what I have seen, I think he has done an admirable job," Sarah said.

"Shall I tell him you said that?"

"Why would it matter to him?"

"Jeremiah would be thrilled to hear it, but I will not let him know if you do not want me to."

"Let him know what?" Sarah glanced at Sammy. He played with his blocks near her feet. The way he leaned against her legs made Sarah feel as if she could conquer the world. Then she remembered that night a few years ago when she had failed Levi, and she went back to thinking the world often conquered her.

Bessie sidled to the washtub and swished some clothing around in the soapy water. "That you care about him."

In her haste to stand up, Sarah practically bounced Sammy off her leg. She checked on him before she replied.

"Owls and loons, Bessie. Jeremiah and I have nothing in common. We want none of the same things from life, and neither of us wants an involvement with someone else. We simply are not interested in each other."

Bessie tsk-tsked. "Jeremiah does not share those sorts of details with just anyone."

Sarah shook her head. "Other than the fact that he is not interested in marriage, he did not share anything with me. I simply guessed that is how he feels."

"Well, it was a mighty fine guess, because you are right on the mark. And you know what that means. . . ." Bessie turned away and hummed a tune Sarah hadn't heard before.

Sarah reached for a small piece of composure. "What *does* it mean, Bessie?"

"It means what I have thought all along. You two are meant to be together."

Sarah threw her hands up in the air. "I give up."

"I do not." Bessie swung around with her hands clasped around her midsection. "But I think we will put any further discussion aside, because it appears this young'un is anxious to make his appearance."

✍

"Shade dropped this off, Lieutenant. Do you have time to read it before you go see your new niece?" Rufe handed the missive to Jeremiah.

Jeremiah wanted to see the tiny angel God had blessed Bessie and Captain with, but he knew when duty came before family. He unfolded the parchment and spread it out in front of him.

> *Eyes see the big man across the lake. He supports missionaries' plan to bring the Gospel to Indians, but he still thinks they are guilty of treason. Captive Indians now stay south of Delaware village, south of the big lake where they build homes to stay through the winter. Many want to leave but are forbidden to. Rumor says some will attempt a return to Muskingum Valley in the spring—they want to collect the harvest left behind when they were captured in August. Prepare for attack from those who return.*

Jeremiah rubbed his forehead. *"The big man across the lake"* must refer to none other than the British commander at Fort Detroit.

"What did it say, boss?" Rufe moved toward Jeremiah.

"Please do not call me that," Jeremiah snarled. "That title belongs to Williamson."

"Sorry." Rufe backed off. "Must be some powerful stuff in there to upset you so."

"There is, but no signature to tell me who it came from. Go find Colonel Williamson. Let him worry about it. I am off to see my niece."

And Sarah? his heart asked hopefully. *Of course not. She doesn't want anything to do with me.*

His heart gave a huge sob.

Chapter 10

Jeremiah pressed a package wrapped in brown paper into Sarah's hands before disappearing down the hall. Sarah thought it a gift for the baby and laid it on the table.

She checked on Sammy and then gave a hurried peek into Captain and Bessie's room. There she caught sight of Jeremiah holding the new baby. The miniature bundle lay snuggled in his arms while he spoke with Captain.

Sarah slipped back down the hall. As she began ironing, she recalled Levi's excitement the night Sammy arrived.

"We got us a boy, Sarah. May he grow to be strong and true. May God help us raise him correctly."

Sarah paused to think about Levi's words. No matter what disaster befell them, Levi always trusted God to bring them through. If God was so loving, why didn't He save Levi from being killed? Now Levi would not see Sammy grow up. It was up to her to make the decisions that would influence Sammy's upbringing.

Anxiety whirled through Sarah. She wasn't the first woman to be left to raise a family, but she often felt like it. Other women had lost their mates to the Revolution or to marauding Indians. Most of them lived near family who helped them through difficult times. Without family near, Sarah bore her grief alone.

"I believe the first of December is a fine day for a birth. What do you think?"

Sarah gazed across the room to find Jeremiah settling into a chair.

"Yes, it is a fine day." Sarah noticed that Jeremiah appeared tired. She offered him tea, but he declined.

"Bessie and the baby are sleeping," Jeremiah said after a moment of observing Sarah while she pressed a shirt.

"New mothers need all the rest they can get." She flipped the shirt over to begin working on a sleeve.

"I have heard that many times," Jeremiah replied. "Do you agree it is grand that God brought Captain back in time to see the babe during her first few hours?"

"The timing does seem fortunate." The crease in the sleeve refused to line up correctly. Sarah frowned at it.

"Those garments do not have to be perfect, you know," Jeremiah stated. "A small crook in the sleeve will not hurt."

Sarah straightened the sleeve and settled the unwieldy iron on it. "I appreciate your comments, but I prefer them to be as flawless as I can get them. Since you seem to be in no hurry to leave, I take it there is nothing pressing, as far as slaughtering Indians goes, demanding your attention?"

Jeremiah laced his fingers together and laid them on the table. "You know what, Sarah? This may sound strange, but I really do not go about hunting down Indians to kill. When I began working with the militia, it was with the explicit understanding that I wanted nothing to do with killing."

Sarah arched her eyebrows. "Then why do you not just quit?"

"Because I promised David Williamson that I would stay until the end of December, and I will, even though there are times when I wish I did not have to."

"Do you know what you will do when you leave the militia?"

"I was a blacksmith before, so I imagine I will return to that trade. By the way, Sarah, did you give any more thought to going to the Winter Supper?"

"I thought I made my choice clear earlier," Sarah said.

"So you did, but a man can always hope. Perhaps you will not want to go with me anyway, after what I am about to tell you."

Sarah's throat tightened. "And that is?"

"I came today not only to see my new niece but to check on how my shirts are faring."

Sarah gazed at the garment in front of her as if it were a snake. "*Your* shirts?"

"Yes. Bessie and I have discussed my decision not to tell you many times recently. She will be pleased that you finally know the truth."

"But. . .why did you hide it from me to begin with?"

"Bessie told me what little she knows about your history, Sarah. She said you were trying to build a life for yourself and your son. I wanted—"

"Bessie had no right to. . ." Sarah began in a shaky voice.

Jeremiah appeared at Sarah's side and laid his hands on her shoulders. "Bessie worries about you. She is concerned that if she does not get you involved with people, you will destroy yourself, and your son."

Sarah took a step back. "I did not ask her to fret over me. For your information, Sammy and I are quite fine without anyone's help."

"People worry because they care," Jeremiah said softly. "Why is that so hard for you to accept?"

Sarah turned from Jeremiah's probing gaze. She wanted to share the reason with him. If she did, though, she sensed he would become another in a long line of those who didn't understand why she had once lived among Indians.

Jeremiah strode back to his seat and stretched his legs beneath it. Sarah wished she could join him, let her heart reach out to him. To do so would invite danger. She shuffled some drying pots and pans.

"I did not hide the fact those were my shirts from you on purpose," Jeremiah offered.

Sarah faced him. She hoped her confusion did not show too plainly. "Then why did you have me drop them off and pick them up at the trading post? The way you did it makes it seem like charity."

Jeremiah shook his head. "I guarantee it is not charity."

Sarah relaxed. "Good. For that is the last thing I will take from anyone."

If I stay here on the other side of the room, I'll be fine, Sarah told herself. *Of course, leaning against the butter churn isn't comfortable, but I will not move.*

Jeremiah propped his elbows on the table. "You needed a job. I provided one. If you do not want it, I will be glad to find someone else."

"No! I need. . .er, I will keep it. I just cannot bear to be beholden to folks any more than necessary." Sarah wished she didn't sound so anxious.

"It is just a job, Sarah," Jeremiah said. "I am not asking for a lifetime commitment. The Bible directs us to assist widows and young children. That is all I am doing."

Perhaps that is the problem, Sarah reflected. *Despite the fact that I want to be independent, something about Jeremiah makes me want to reconsider that issue.*

Levi's face drifted through her mind. Sarah missed him, not as drastically as she had in the fresh days of grief; the pain had softened since she met the Halls. . .and Jeremiah.

"I feel guilty about taking a job someone else might need more than I do," she said.

"I did my own laundry before you came. You did not take anyone's job."

Sarah wrinkled her forehead. *He did his own laundry? Well of course. Living alone in the middle of who knew where, all men in the militia probably did so.*

"I feel better knowing that." Sarah warned herself to keep her feelings about Jeremiah to herself, no matter how difficult that was when he was around.

"Me, too. I already told you I am not interested in women. But can we at least be friends?"

Sarah's heart sputtered. Besides Bessie and Captain, it seemed like forever since anyone cared about her in a personal way. She and Levi lived far from civilization, and they'd had only themselves to depend on. A lot of good that had done them. Being alone was awfully lonely.

She knew that much after being around Bessie and Captain the last few months.

"I am not sure about being friends with anyone," Sarah confided. "Once you trade your life history and tell others things you consider important, they push you into corners where you do not want to be."

"I would never push you," Jeremiah said. "You are the only one who can put yourself in a corner, Sarah."

⟨❧⟩

Jeremiah reminded himself that he had come here today to visit his sister and see his niece, not to spend time with Sarah. Yet, the offer of friendship had come so naturally from his mouth that he wondered why it had taken him so long to make it.

"Friendship is all I *can* offer," Jeremiah said, hoping Sarah didn't think he was asking too much.

"I suppose it is hard for someone who has always had people close to him to understand," Sarah said, "but I am not like normal people."

"You are as normal as you let yourself be," Jeremiah replied.

Sarah shifted her stance. "I was abandoned by my parents when I was very small then raised in a Philadelphia orphanage." She spit the words out as if they might do irreparable damage.

"I knew others who grew up without parents," Jeremiah replied. "They did not let that stop them from living and having friends."

"I also lost that home when a flood swept it away."

"Where did you go then?" Jeremiah recalled that he had once told Bessie his shoulders were broad enough to take whatever Sarah might wish to share. He sat up a little straighter.

"The orphanage owner knew a missionary, and his flock willingly accepted me. When they headed west, I went with them." Her words trickled with sadness.

"A missionary?"

"Is there something wrong with men who instruct others in God's Word?"

"No." Jeremiah thought of the missive he had read before coming to see Bessie and the baby. It mentioned missionaries. How many missionaries were there in Ohio? Only the Moravians that he knew of.

"Then why do you sound as if you disapprove?"

"I did not expect you to say something about them."

"I knew it!" Sarah paled.

"Knew what?"

"You are just like all the rest."

"The rest who?"

"Men!" Sarah crossed her arms in front of her and stared at him.

"How can you say that? You do not even know me."

"I know you well enough to know that all you think you have to do is snap your fingers and people will die!"

"Sarah, I have already explained that is not something I am comfortable with," Jeremiah insisted.

"Then why did you not tell me from the start it was your laundry I was doing? Were you afraid I would refuse it if I knew it came from you?"

"That is not it at all." Jeremiah couldn't figure out why Sarah changed the subject from the militia back to the laundry.

"Do not move from behind that table or I will scream so loud everyone within the county will come running."

"You do not have to scream, Sarah. I will leave on my own." Jeremiah moved toward the door, careful to keep as much distance between them as he could.

"Do me a favor," Sarah directed as he reached the passage.

Jeremiah was relieved Sarah had not called him Mr. Stewart. And he was absolutely crazy to ask what the favor was. He should leave this woman alone, since that appeared to be what she really wanted.

"What, Sarah? Tell me."

"Concentrate on your profession and quit worrying about the little people who make no difference in your life."

"Do what?"

"You heard me. Forget about those of us who do not matter to you. We are really quite capable of surviving on our own."

Jeremiah thought Sarah looked too pale, but what could he do? She obviously did not want any assistance from him. He hardened his heart, since it was the only way he could see to deal with Sarah's demand. "I thought we just agreed to be friends."

Sarah glared at him.

"All right, but no one survives alone very long, Sarah. However, if that is your wish, I will do my best to uphold it."

Chapter 11

Jeremiah patted Sarah's neck with his hand. "Come on. Wake up, Sarah."

When Sarah mumbled, the feeling of helplessness that had overcome Jeremiah initially when Sarah collapsed began to fade.

"Please, Sarah." Jeremiah brushed a lock of hair off her brow.

"Jeremiah?"

"Yes. It is me."

"What happened?"

"Well, I guess the only way to say it is. . .you swooned."

Sarah pushed her way up to a sitting position. "I will have you know that I never swoon. I thank you for assisting me, Mr. Stewart, but I am fine."

Sarah sounded determined, but she was shaking. "Are you sure?"

"Of course I am." Sarah shrugged her shoulders and shook her hands in front of her. "See? I am fine."

"What is going on out there?" Bessie's piercing question traveled down the hall.

"Nothing to worry about, little sis," Jeremiah called out.

"If you do not leave soon, Bessie will be coming out here to find out what happened," Sarah said. "She should not be up, having given birth only yesterday."

"I just want to assure myself that you are all right before I go," Jeremiah insisted.

Sarah rubbed the sides of her head. "Will you quit arguing with me? You are giving me a head pain."

Sarah did *seem* to be herself. When she had slumped to the floor, he hadn't moved fast enough to catch her. He had worried that Sarah might have seriously injured herself.

Jeremiah thought himself strong and capable, but the sight of

Sarah lying on the floor had twisted through him with vicious force. Without thinking, he brushed his hand across her forehead again.

Sarah shoved his hand away. "Bessie told me once that you are persistent. I guess she is right, but I honestly do not need someone to fuss over me. I am capable of taking care of myself."

Sarah wished Jeremiah would leave, for his arm around her shoulder felt too comforting as he helped her to a chair.

"I only want to help you," Jeremiah replied. "I am sorry if you think that what I am doing is wrong."

"It is not," Sarah said. "I am just tired of telling people that I am the only one I can depend on."

Jeremiah searched her face. "As far as I am concerned, leaning on others signifies courage, and there is nothing wrong with doing so. No matter what, I know of only one ultimate source of peace. I need to pray, Sarah. Will you join me?"

Jeremiah stretched a hand toward her and closed his eyes. He began to offer a prayer of thanks that Sarah wasn't seriously injured. When he felt the tentative brush of Sarah's fingertips on his own, he thought his soul would never stop singing.

❧

How could things go so wrong? Jeremiah thumped his fist against his thigh. He thought sure he'd argued his point successfully, but Colonel Williamson refused to appoint Harry Ray to replace Dan Whelp. It appeared Williamson was bent on making Jeremiah the replacement instead.

Jeremiah shuddered. He could not, no, *would* not, accept the position. He'd voiced the fact that he did not believe in killing to the colonel several times during the last year.

But that wasn't Jeremiah's problem right now. Shade was hanging his outer garments near the fireplace; he surely did not bear good news. Weariness was evident in Shade's face as he turned toward Jeremiah.

"Eyes are again on the Praying Indians," Shade said, rubbing his hands together for warmth.

"What now?" Jeremiah grumbled inwardly that Williamson always seemed gone when something of import happened.

Shade frowned. "British commander accused Zeisberger of treason last summer because missionary is in constant contact with colonials at Fort Pitt. Missionary says he is friendly to both British and colonials and that he only want to be left alone with his Christian converts. British commander agreed Zeisberger could do so, as long as they stayed in the Wyandot village near the Big Lake."

"What else?" After dealing with Shade for several months, Jeremiah knew there was always a reason for everything Shade said. Sometimes Jeremiah just had to wait until later to figure it out.

"So now they stay in old Wyandot homes and search for food. The British promised them supplies, but the Praying Indians turn it down."

Jeremiah leaned against the table. "Mighty brave of them, since they were not allowed to carry much with them in the fall."

Shade's face grew solemn. "They brave people."

"Do they realize how fragile their situation is? They have the British pulling at them from one side and half of their own clan squealing on them. Not to mention that most of our militia is convinced they are heathens."

"They know what life means, and they believe God provides."

Jeremiah understood the strength in that. "Is there anything else?"

"One moon ago Zeisberger met with British commander again. Outcome a surprise to all there."

"I am beginning to see that anything the British are involved in does not turn out the way we expect," Jeremiah said. "What is the rest?"

Shade shook his head back and forth as if to the beat of a war drum. "Wyandot leader full of lies. He told British the missionaries were his friends. Not so. Wyandot and British are dangerous. Will cause the Christian Indians to die. Soon."

Uneasiness stole through Jeremiah's heart. "How soon?"

"Shade's bones feel sorrow."

Jeremiah paced back and forth between a chair and the hearth. "What do you really think is going to happen?"

"Your militia will be involved," Shade said. "Stop them."

"They are not my. . . Oh, never mind." Jeremiah tossed his hands in the air. "How will the militia be involved?"

Shade sighed. "Danger will decrease your friends. The settlers will insist army protect them."

Jeremiah's soul hit the bottom of his feet. "You mean there will be more attacks?"

Shade grimaced. "More vicious ones."

"It has been quiet here lately. I hoped they were afraid of our weapons, or that the weather was too cold for them."

"Except Great Spirit, real warriors are not frightened of anything. They will come again."

"I do not know how you know that," Jeremiah countered, "but I will warn everyone in the county to be more watchful. Let's suppose our men, and we are well over one hundred now, do want to fight. How do I stop that many?"

"You are wise man," Shade said. "Find a way. Remember, the eyes of all miss nothing."

Jeremiah sighed. He would definitely have to sort this out later. "Who are 'the eyes of all'?"

"Some men see but miss the important things," Shade replied, donning his jacket.

"So?"

Shade kicked at his moccasins. Clumps of half-melted snow fell onto the warm hearth and spat like an angry cat. "Not all tribes happy with whites in Ohio wilderness. Not all whites happy they in Ohio wilderness."

"That does not make sense," Jeremiah stated. "What are you trying to tell me?"

"Be wary of what others ask you to do, for not all are on your side.

I must go." Shade eased from the room.

Jeremiah rubbed his neck. He propped his chin in the palm of one hand and studied the lines in his other palm.

What if Shade is right? What if there are more deaths? What if I get caught up in an upsurge of hate and Colonel Williamson orders me to kill someone? Oh Lord, don't desert me if such a thing comes to be!

⟡

At least I still have Sammy, Sarah thought as she watched her son play at her feet. But the years before he grew up and said good-bye would pass quickly, then she would be all alone.

"Is everything all right, Sarah?"

Sarah looked up to see Bessie raise Elizabeth to her shoulder and pat the infant's back.

"I know this must be a bad time of year for you," Bessie added. "Is there anything I can do?"

"No. I was just thinking that perhaps my sorrow is not so bad this year. Why?"

"I know it cannot be easy." Bessie gazed at her newborn. "No matter what people say, often time is not enough to heal our wounds. Just the other day you read chapter fifty-eight in Isaiah to me. Do you remember what it said?"

"Not really," Sarah admitted.

"If I recall, it goes something like, 'Then shalt thou call, and the Lord shall answer; thou shalt cry, and he shall say, Here I am.' See, Sarah? You can call on our Lord any time for any reason. He is always there, willing to love, to share, to bring you peace."

"Bessie, I hope that someday I will return to God's flock, but after the way He destroyed my life, I am just not sure how far off that day may be."

"God loves you, Sarah. So do several others. You do not know how happy it would make me to learn that you are ready to come back to our Lord."

Sarah stared at the fireplace, contemplating Bessie's words. Bessie never seemed to let events depress her. How did she keep such confidence that life would work itself out for the best?

Bessie broke the quiet. "The other day I heard you tell Captain you wanted to start teaching Samuel his letters. Do you think you could teach me at the same time? I never saw a need before, but now I would like to know how to read so I may teach my daughter someday." Bessie beamed a grin at two-week-old Elizabeth.

"It is not something you learn overnight, Bessie."

"I do not expect it to come quickly. It would not be too big a bother, would it?"

Sarah shook her head. "I did not mean to make you think that." Teaching letters would be easier than reading Bible stories to Bessie. Every story Bessie chose seemed to spur Sarah's heart.

"If we need something special, Captain can fetch it for us tomorrow," Bessie said. "That way we can begin after our evening meal."

Captain's one circuit trip since the baby's birth had ended. Unless there was an emergency, he planned to stay home for the winter.

"When I was little, we used the smooth side of a split log and a charred stick to write the letters," Sarah replied.

"If it was good enough for you, then it is good enough for me," Bessie declared. Samuel came to stand beside her. She lowered Elizabeth so he could reach out and tickle the baby's chin.

Sarah watched her son babble something to the infant in an incoherent language. With every day that passed, she and Sammy got more entangled in Bessie's and Captain's lives. When Sarah joined them for the journey here, she'd not foreseen that happening.

She thought she'd find something that would allow her to support her son and herself. She hadn't imagined how barren Washington County would be.

What will I do if I can't find something to help me support Sammy? I cannot live off of the Halls' generosity forever.

". . .telling Samuel about the music there is going to be. May even be some small treats for the little ones, you know."

Bessie's chatter intruded on Sarah's thoughts. She snapped her head toward the woman.

"I wish you would change your mind about going," Bessie said. "It will be good for you and Samuel, and that way it will all work out."

"What will work out?" Sarah quizzed, sensing something in Bessie's voice that she wasn't sure she wanted to hear.

"The seating particulars," Bessie confided with a sly smile. "If you are not there, the whole evening will be a disaster."

"Quit being so emotional. No one will notice if I am not there."

"Those who are important will," Bessie replied.

Sarah gave a troubled sigh. "What does that mean?"

"It means we are to sit at the commander's table," Bessie responded. "You have to go. Otherwise, that silly Gemma Winslow will end up sitting by Jeremiah."

Sarah's throat tightened. Gemma Winslow? She'd heard the name before but hadn't known that the woman had designs on Jeremiah.

It did not matter. She couldn't sit with men who were determined to do away with those she once lived with, even if those men included Jeremiah.

Sarah feigned indifference. "I doubt one or two missing people will be a catastrophe," she said.

"I think it would be to Jeremiah. He does not like Gemma, you know, but she seems determined to get him to notice her."

"Gemma is quite free to sit with whomever she wishes," Sarah answered, keeping her voice even.

"Well," Bessie went on, a sly smile curving her lips, "everyone knows you are staying with us. It will look strange if you are not there."

Gemma Winslow's name rolled around in Sarah's mind. What did Gemma mean to Jeremiah? Was he seeing her? Courting her? Sarah found thinking on this to be painful.

"Have they chosen a replacement for that major who got killed yet?"

"No news from that quarter," Bessie replied. "Jeremiah does know he has another ninety days to serve. The colonel talked him into it."

"You must be mistaken. The last time Jeremiah talked about it, he said he wanted out of the militia so he can go on with his life."

"Oh, Jer does not want to do it," Bessie agreed. "He told me that he prayed long and hard before accepting. He decided that God must want something special of him if he keeps putting him in uniform. It would sure make Jeremiah's night if you went."

Something nagged at Sarah. A few weeks ago she consented to be Jeremiah's friend. She hadn't been too friendly since that day. To be fair, the times Jeremiah had seen her, he had not tried to push her into anything more than casual conversation.

And don't forget, Sarah's heart reminded, *Bessie linked Gemma Winslow's name with Jeremiah's.*

"I might go, but I refuse to borrow another of your dresses," Sarah muttered.

Bessie grinned. "Jeremiah brought me a package the day Elizabeth was born. I have not opened it yet, but I think we need to take a look."

"I thought he brought it for the baby," Sarah said, recalling him handing her the parcel.

"No. If Samuel will go fetch it from the corner near my bed, we can decide what to do."

While Sammy rushed down the hall, Sarah took a seat.

"The only reason I would even be interested in going would be to see what sorts of food the women bring," Sarah said.

"We will see," Bessie replied, a mischievous glow dancing in her eyes.

❧

"Are you sure I did not miss Shade when I ran home?"

"No sir. He has not been here," Rufe assured. "Shade is always smack on time, too. Wonder what could be keepin' him?"

"I do, too." Though Jeremiah had resigned himself to another three months in the militia, he didn't like it. After much prayer, God had impressed upon his heart that the militia was where He needed Jeremiah to be for the time being.

In his courier days, Jeremiah had feared being strung up alongside a forgotten trail. Had that happened to Shade? A damp chill climbed Jeremiah's spine. No! He had to believe Shade would appear.

Jeremiah ambled to the door and peered down the wagon trail. He mouthed a verse from the fourth chapter of Philippians: "'Be careful for nothing; but in every thing by prayer and supplication with thanksgiving let your requests be made known unto God.'"

He took a deep breath. Worrying did no good. He must trust God to take care of Shade.

Rufe began dousing candle wicks. "I am sure Shade will be here soon. Perhaps we can get him to stay for the big doings?"

"I will ask," Jeremiah said. "You know he is uncomfortable around people. He only stays long enough to deliver messages."

Jeremiah studied Rufe from across the room. "You never did tell me how you found Shade."

"I did not?" Rufe appeared surprised.

"Spill it, Rufe. The way things are, ferrying messages is a dangerous job." Jeremiah wasn't bragging; he chose the occupation because it meant the chances of having to kill someone would be less than if he were embroiled in battle.

"I knew Shade when I grew up," Rufe explained. "Pa would not let me near him, because he said no man that mysterious had anything good to give the world."

"So why did you pick him?"

Rufe weighed his words before speaking. "Pa can be one-sided sometimes. He gets something stuck in his head and no one can budge him. Some folks did not think I should get the job of clerk because I am so scatterbrained. But Colonel took a chance on me. It is the best thing that could have happened. I have learned so much that I am almost like a new person, especially working for you."

Rufe was silent for a moment. "I think everyone should get the chance to prove they can do great things. This job does not ask much of Shade except to ride, which he loves, and to stay away from those who might try to stop him, which he is good at doing." Rufe's eyes widened. "You are not going to fire him, are you?"

Jeremiah shook his head. "Shade might be slow, but he does a grand job."

Rufe nodded his head. "Will that be all, then? I hoped to help set up for tonight."

Jeremiah straightened some papers. "You go on. I will wait for Shade."

"I sure hope Shade is all right."

"I do, too." Jeremiah recalled Shade's warning that there would be more attacks and that the militia would want to go after the Praying Indians because of them. What would happen if Shade got caught in something and wasn't able to think fast enough to defend himself?

Jeremiah didn't know Shade very well, but he knew the man performed to the best of his ability. In a war, some didn't return; that risk was always there. Jeremiah turned the thought away. He hoped he didn't have to hear that Shade hadn't made it.

Rufe got ready to leave. "If it helps, I am behind you every step of the way, Lieutenant."

Jeremiah gave the clerk a small smile. "I do not see how I can miss, then. With you pushing from behind and the Lord pulling me along, seems like I could just about deal with anything."

⟡

Jeremiah gave up after two hours of waiting and headed toward Bessie's to visit his niece. As he neared the Halls', he saw Sarah and Samuel making their way toward him. Jeremiah grinned as Samuel leaped across a puddle.

What a wonderful blessing God provided in the form of children, he thought.

Samuel's mother wasn't bad either. Sarah's hair cascaded down her back, and her flushed cheeks gave testimony to the length of time she'd been out in the cold. Jeremiah's heart raced. He took a deep breath to calm down, but his heart refused to listen.

A few days after her fainting spell, Sarah had sought him out. She apologized for demanding that Jeremiah not worry about the little people, and admitted that it was probably just a spell of anxiety that caused her to collapse.

While her words were spontaneous, Jeremiah thought he had detected a glimmer of something more beneath the surface. Since then, Jeremiah tried to let Sarah set the terms of their friendship. He did not think he'd gotten very far.

Samuel ran toward him. "Miah! Miah!" He proudly displayed a missing front tooth.

"Hello, scamp!" Jeremiah squatted in front of the boy.

Samuel scuffed the toe of his shoe on the ground.

"What?" Jeremiah exclaimed in mock astonishment. "I know we have not seen each other since little Elizabeth was born, Sammy. Have you forgotten me?"

"I am the only one who calls him Sammy." Sarah pulled her son close to her side. "Come along, Sammy. We promised Bessie we would be right back with the tea."

Jeremiah rested his hands on his knees. Samuel looked as if he wanted to stay but didn't want his mother to know. Jeremiah's heart caught in his throat.

"Go on, Samuel," he encouraged. "Smart men always mind the women in their lives."

"Now that is an interesting admission, coming from you, Mr. Stewart."

Jeremiah met her gaze. "I did not always believe it, but I have discovered that without the love of a good woman, many men fail to accomplish great things."

"And you claim that the same is true for you?"

Jeremiah stood up. "Perhaps I have never had the right woman behind me, one who inspired me to do more than I could alone. . . ."

Sammy pressed against Sarah's side just in time to save her. "Mother? I'm hungry."

"Yes, son. Only a moment longer." She gave Jeremiah a guarded glance.

"You better go," Jeremiah said. "I do not want the little fellow to starve."

"Yes. Bessie will wonder where we are if we are not home soon. Come on, Sammy."

"Sarah?"

"Yes?" She squeezed Sammy's hand.

"I know you recall that a few weeks ago we agreed to try to be friends. I do not feel I have done much to further our friendship, so I would like you to do something for me."

"And that is?"

"Honor me by sitting with me at the Winter Supper."

"See, Mother? Miah wants us. We can go," Sammy offered.

Sarah kept to herself how much Jeremiah's invitation thrilled her. She was tired of mourning, of holding to the past and having it drag her down. And here was a chance to make up to him for what she'd failed to do as a friend in the last few weeks.

"I will go, but you must understand that I go only as your friend." *And because it will keep you from sitting with Gemma Winslow,* Sarah thought.

Jeremiah's grin melted any ice that might have remained in Sarah's heart. "I hoped you would say that."

Chapter 12

"I f you keep moving, I will never make sure you are proper."

"Quit fussing, Bessie. It is a get-together to listen to Captain's service, eat, then come back here. One would think this is my wedding day, the way you are acting."

"If you would just open your eyes and your heart," Bessie answered, "it could be your wedding day. I must say that you look very fetching in this dress."

Sarah held her tongue as Bessie fiddled with a bunch of material at the back of Sarah's garment. Though Jeremiah had given the cloth to Bessie as a gift, Bessie pressed Sarah into accepting it for all the work Sarah had done for the Halls, both before and after Elizabeth's birth.

Bessie had used one of Sarah's old dresses for the sizing. This wasn't a drab, washerwoman style, and it wasn't the orange-brown material Sarah once had admired at the post. Sarah didn't know how Jeremiah had procured the deep-green fabric, but it made Sarah think of spring leaves, of hope, of a better time.

She glanced down at the gown. Bessie had cut off tiny wooden buttons from one of her old garments, and they marched in two straight lines up each side of the skirt. Full sleeves accented the top of the dress.

"Ouch! That hurt!" Sarah jerked away from the stab of the needle, the skirt frolicking around her ankles. If she only had something more fancy than these plain brown moccasins to wear with it, she would be happy.

"You are as frayed at the edges as some of the seams of this dress." Bessie held up a handful of bits of material she had picked up off the floor.

"I am not nervous," Sarah declared. *Not much, anyway,* she

admitted to herself. Her heart pounded in her ears at the idea of being around so many people at once. That was all. She was also thirsty, but if she sipped any more water, she'd have to disrobe to relieve herself.

"First is the worship," Bessie reminded her. "Then the feast, with as many of us as can fit into the big room off the store."

"I know. And we are to sit at the commander's table." Sarah wished that thought would quit playing so vividly at the front of her mind.

Bessie stood back and scrutinized Sarah. "Are you going to be all right?"

"Of course," Sarah replied. "I am going tonight only as a friend to Jeremiah. There is nothing between us, and I do not want you thinking that there is."

"You will have a good time."

Bessie's promise was overcome by Samuel's announcement: "Cap'n is fixin' to take us to the supper."

Sammy's eyes sparkled. Sarah knew he expected great things from the evening. In a way, so did she, despite her insistence to Bessie that she was only going as Jeremiah's friend.

⁂

A gentle breeze teased the flames of candles set along the edges of the walkway. Frigid temperatures made the sprinkling of stars in the sky shine much brighter than normal. All in all, it appeared for the moment that the settlers' tenuous hold on peace and security was safe.

Some of the men had moved the store furniture out of the way, making room for everyone who brought chairs to line them up. Captain had taken their chairs over earlier.

Inside, lanterns glowed softly, lending a special radiance to the room. Sap snapped in a corner fireplace. Sarah trailed behind Bessie, nodding politely as Captain introduced her to those she had not yet met.

Sarah knew within moments of meeting Gemma Winslow that the encounter was not going to be a high point of Sarah's night.

Gemma's voice dripped with derision. "So you are the one

staying with the Halls. Jeremiah told me all about you—and your poor little boy."

Sarah strove to sound pleasant, though she really wanted to shove a handful of snow down Gemma's too-low neckline. "We do not plan on staying here long," she replied. "Washington County is just a temporary solution."

"That is good," Gemma replied. "There is so little here for a widow. All the good men are taken, if you know what I mean."

Sarah knew exactly what Gemma implied, but Sarah was the one who would sit with Jeremiah at the supper. That provided her a small sense of satisfaction. Sarah gave Gemma a cautious glance while Gemma exclaimed over baby Elizabeth. The woman soon moved on to other potential conquests, and, with a sigh, Sarah gazed around.

The entire county appeared to be there. Sarah spent time memorizing the sights so she might pull them out later and recall the festive details.

Sammy pointed out various small discoveries. For once, Sarah bit back the desire to hush him. He meandered freely between seats where families grinned at his very proper hellos.

After an opening prayer in which he thanked the Lord for the turnout, Captain began to recite the story of the Christ Child's birth.

Sarah's Bible readings to Bessie during the last few months had reawakened knowledge Sarah thought long forgotten. Though her mind resisted, Sarah felt God's Word working in her heart. She could not pinpoint a time, but she knew it wouldn't be long until she again believed in God. She looked forward to that day when she could cast off her fears and feast on the promise of eternal life.

Captain's exuberant voice beseeched the crowd not to forget Jesus' sacrifice. As he spoke, the cross at the front of the room drew Sarah's full attention. Comprised of two saplings tied together with strips of leather, it was an amazing sight.

Sarah was struck by the significance that from trees that provided nuts for eating came a symbol that gave so many here a different type of nourishment. Her heart ached as she realized how much she had missed making that connection.

She closed her eyes, thinking that perhaps this was the night when she would allow God back into her life. But a commotion drew Sarah's attention.

She watched as Jeremiah and two other men entered the room. The older one she presumed to be Colonel Williamson. He wore a pair of dark trousers and a well-worn gray shirt. His hair looked as if he had not combed it in a week.

On the other hand, Jeremiah was smartly turned out in a pair of black trousers and a crisp white shirt, one that Sarah was proud to have pressed. Her heart raced. She couldn't help but think how splendid Jeremiah looked. She did not get a good look at the third man as the trio took their seats and the hubbub subsided.

When Captain finished his sermon, Jeremiah rose and apologized for being late. "But," he said, "I have someone with me tonight who has come to impart to us some important news."

"If he means that fool the militia has carrying messages, he belongs in the woodshed, if you ask me," a portly man off to Sarah's left snarled.

Sarah wasn't the only one who thought the comment cruel, as Jeremiah glared at the man before continuing. His gaze rested briefly on Sarah before he went on.

"Many of you are willing to risk your lives in order to keep your families safe," Jeremiah said. "But I have heard comments that place the blame for the atrocities on Indian groups that I do not believe are at fault. I asked Shade, our messenger, to explain some things you may not be aware of."

Shade stood and faced the audience. His dark hair was plaited down his back, and puffy smudges beneath his eyes led one to believe he didn't sleep much.

"Please listen to everything he has to say before you make any judgments," Jeremiah finished.

Shade spoke hesitantly, a fact that several near Sarah grumbled about. Above some rude snorts, he informed the audience about what was happening in the wilds of Ohio and farther west into Illinois. When he offered what he knew about the British encouraging Wyandot warriors to harass the Praying Indians in order to make the Christian tribe look guilty, he gained Sarah's attention. Uneasiness filled her heart.

Shade requested that the audience not blame the Praying Indians. "They serve the same God you worship here tonight," he said. "All they want is to live their lives in peace."

"That ain't true," the portly man near Sarah shouted. "They come over here and kill our folks. You never lost someone to a scalping or you would not be defending those yellowbellies."

Sarah chewed on the inside of her cheek. She really wanted to stand up and tell the blathering idiot to her left what she knew about the Praying Indians. She might have done so, but Jeremiah sat at the front of the room. She couldn't let him learn about her connection with that tribe.

Shade's features hardened. "I tell you the Praying Indians are not the ones you seek. They are being made to look like they are at fault by those who do not wish to be punished."

"Then who is it?" the man insisted.

A swell of support followed the agitator's comments. Jeremiah stood. The rumble subsided.

"Shade is here at my invitation," he said. "Treat him with respect or you will find I order double details." Jeremiah apologized to Shade.

"It is a sad day, Lieutenant Stewart," Shade said. "As sad a day as when they crucified my Christ."

The portly man erupted again. "You leave Jesus out of this. Those heathens come killin' my family and they will have to reckon with me."

Several shouted their agreement. Jeremiah placed two fingers in his mouth and gave a shrill whistle. The clamor faded.

Shade faced Jeremiah and shrugged. "I cannot change their minds, sir. It is up to you."

*

Jeremiah later thought that the Winter Supper was one of the worst nights of his life. Sarah left her son with Bessie and disappeared. Jeremiah entertained Samuel willingly, even when Gemma Winslow finagled her way into sitting at his side. He kept glancing at Gemma, wishing that Sarah were sitting there instead.

When he asked, Bessie did not know why Sarah had left early. "Give her time, Jer," she soothed. "Something probably reminded her of her husband, and she needs to sort it all out."

Thanks to the colonel, Jeremiah had at least three more months anyway. He should have turned a deaf ear to Williamson's pleas and refused to serve any longer. He would have, but he kept thinking of Bessie and Captain and their new baby, and Sarah and Samuel. He didn't know what one man could do if Indians attacked, but he felt better knowing he was at least trying to help defend them.

But if he left the militia, then what? Would he leave Washington County? Where would he go? What would he do?

Gemma's nasal tone intruded on Jeremiah's thoughts. "This is absolutely the most wonderful gathering. I do declare, Jeremiah, you went all out to make this evening so special." She batted her eyes.

Jeremiah mumbled his agreement. He didn't feel like talking to Gemma. It would have been much nicer to have Sarah beside him.

"I asked Uncle Davy when he thought he was going to promote you, Jeremiah," Gemma said. "Do you know what his answer was?"

Jeremiah shook his head. He didn't care about promotions. Three months and he'd be gone.

"Well, he said that it would all depend on how soon you and I—"

"Excuse me—sir?"

"Yes, Rufe. What is it?"

"I hate to interrupt, but it is time to go, Lieutenant Stewart."

Jeremiah jumped up, rapidly excusing himself.

"Will you be back soon?" Gemma's anxious tone followed him out the door. "We have plans to make."

Sarah tucked Sammy into bed, avoiding Bessie's questions. Once he fell asleep, she flung her dress into a corner. Myriad emotions prompted by Shade's earlier comments battered her.

No matter how she tried, Sarah couldn't remember Shade's exact words. Was he for or against the Praying Indians? Sarah thought he'd tried to convince the gathering to believe that the Christian Indians should not be blamed for any killings in Washington County.

Jeremiah said he invited Shade to speak at the supper. Did that mean Jeremiah didn't believe the Praying Indians were guilty? Perhaps Jeremiah had attempted to get Sarah to tell him about the Indians because he thought that he could stop the militia from attacking them.

Sarah scrunched her eyes shut. If she could just recall exactly what Shade had said, she'd be able to figure it out. One thing was for sure—the crowd did not agree that the Praying Indians were innocent.

Realizing she would not figure it out tonight, Sarah sighed and climbed onto her mat. She gave one last glance toward the dark corner where her gown lay. So much for dreams.

Sleep eluded her. Her mind returned again and again to Jeremiah. Would he arrive in the morning and demand to know why she had left the gathering? Sarah balled her hands into fists. If Jeremiah learned that she had grown up with the Indians that most militia members apparently thought responsible for destroying their families, then Jeremiah, as part of that company, would want nothing to do with her.

Fear pooled in Sarah's heart. Not long ago she admitted to him that she traveled with a missionary to live in the Ohio wilderness. At the time, she did not suspect that Jeremiah would connect that missionary with the Praying Indians.

Shade's comments left no doubt that Jeremiah would eventually make that link. While he might be able to accept her despite her having lived with Indians at one time, Sarah did not think Jeremiah would accept her if he learned what she had done eight years ago.

Why is that? a little voice in her mind nagged.

"Because I do not want to hurt Jeremiah," Sarah whispered. "I care about him. As a friend doing a job he does not want to do in this wilderness we live in."

Is that all? the tiny voice quizzed.

No, but I will just have to deal with the way I feel about Jeremiah as a man. On my own. Again.

✍

At the last possible moment, Sarah led Sammy down the hall to the eating room. She convinced herself that any unpleasantness about her disappearance from the assembly last night was better off dealt with and put behind her.

Captain's blessing was quick. "Bless this food to nourish our bodies. And pass the flatcakes, Bessie."

The ping of forks against pewter plates and the soft thud of wooden mugs being set on the tabletop accompanied other normal eating sounds. Sarah waited for Captain or Bessie to bring up her behavior of the night before.

"Jeremiah is gone," Captain announced after he devoured a towering stack of flatcakes and two mugs of coffee.

Bessie's shocked gaze collided with Sarah's. "When did he leave?"

"Early this morning," Captain said. "Rufe mentioned as we left last night that Jeremiah and some of the others in the militia will be out of the territory for at least a week."

A quick sigh of relief fell from Sarah's lips. Jeremiah would not be coming by to call her to task for running out on him. She drizzled syrup on her flatcakes, but she didn't think she would eat.

"Sarah," Captain began. "I hope you will forgive me for intruding, but I think it is time we talked."

The nibble of food Sarah took stuck in her throat. She glanced between Bessie and Captain. Bessie stayed quiet, as if she wished she knew a way to turn the conversation in another direction.

Sarah realized that she was not the only one who had been going through rough times. Dull shadows beneath Bessie's eyes were not only because Elizabeth refused to sleep for longer than a few hours. Sarah lost track of the nights Bessie fretted when Captain did not return home when Bessie expected him to. Even when he did, he rose early to visit with families whose men had joined the militia and were having second thoughts.

A feeling of hollowness invaded Sarah as she shoved her plate aside. "I suppose it is. First, please allow me to apologize for last night. My behavior was highly unsuitable."

"I think you should save your apology for Jeremiah when he returns," Captain said. "I wish to speak to you about something else."

"Oh? But I thought. . ."

Captain cleared his throat. "This is not easy, not just because of who you are but because some people believe sharing things of this nature isn't done unless the one addressed is in their immediate family."

"Go on." Sarah could not figure out where he was headed.

"Bessie and I promised not to press you because we realize that everyone heals differently. Neither of us wishes to make you more uncomfortable than you already are."

"Just say whatever it is you wish to say," Sarah stated. "You do not have to go slowly with me. I am strong enough to stand up to anything." She placed her hands in her lap, pressing her right thumb into her left palm.

Captain scratched at his beard. "I understand that you are helping Bessie learn her letters. Some would say that is a good work, Sarah, something that she will have with her the rest of her life."

"Did you not want her to learn?" Sarah wondered if she'd upset Captain without realizing it.

"No. I am glad you are doing it. But that is not my point."

Sammy played with his flatcake, pushing it around his plate and saying, "Gee-up, gee-up." He'd seen the militiamen say that to their mounts. Sarah laid a hand on his arm to stop him. He sulked but began to eat without any accompanying sounds.

A compassionate smile softened Captain's face. "Sometimes we make choices that we think are best based on our circumstances at the time. Now and then, even though we regret them, we maintain those decisions because we think there is no way out, or because we are afraid to admit that we made a mistake."

"I do not follow you," Sarah commented. "How does that apply to me?" Beneath the table, she began squeezing her hands together.

"Pray take this in the spirit with which I give it," Captain went on. "I am here to serve any who need it. I often speak with men who are being asked to do things they never imagined they would have to do. Many of them were raised without God. They are the most challenging to convince that if they ask Jesus into their hearts, He will heal their troubled souls. Not all accept that immediately. Sadly, some choose to ignore everything I say."

Sarah's mind whirled at his words. "Are you telling me that if I go back to Jesus, all my troubles will disappear?"

Captain's voice was firm. "Trials and tribulations never disappear completely. But I do know that since you lost your husband, you seem to have chosen to live without tapping into God's power. What I want you to think about is this, Sarah: How much more could you do if you had Him on your side again?"

Chapter 13

"Ya got tha wrong place, mister, if yore lookin' for dem Prayin' Indians. Da Brits dragged 'em all off las' fall."

Jeremiah studied the scraggly figure who said his name was Mash. He reeked of vinegar and a month without bathing. He also had a habit of picking his teeth while he talked, which jumbled his words.

Jeremiah had ridden hard in order to arrive in the Muskingum Valley in just over a day and a half. He would ride just as hard on the return trip, but not before he discovered what he could about these mission settlements carved into the Ohio wilds.

"Can you tell me anything about them, or their missionaries?"

"Don' know what 'twould be." A scowl formed along the edges of Mash's unshaven lips.

Jeremiah motioned toward the settlement. "I can tell this place was not always like this. It took some effort and time to build such log homes. It is too bad they have been allowed to deteriorate so much."

Standing at the entrance, Jeremiah could see more than forty cabins, their walls bonded with chinking. Their roofs sloped sharply toward the ground, a necessary slant that encouraged winter snow to slide off. A fence, woven around the bottom portion with dried grapevine, rambled down two sides of the mission behind the rows of homes, but portions of it were missing.

"Don't matter ta us. We're deserters from da British army. Also got some Indians who claim ta be our allies. We didn't have nowhere else ta go and dis was available." Mash spit out the pieces of bark from a twig he'd been chewing. "I only been here a few weeks. Rode in, got 'vited to share some whiskey, and ain't never left. Can't tell ya nothin' 'cause I don't know nothin'." Mash paused to wipe spittle from his beard. "Ain't got nothin' ta give, I ain't."

"I will ride on, then," Jeremiah said. "I appreciate your taking the time to speak with me." He shivered as he realized how different Mash's greeting would be if he discovered Jeremiah was on an official militia scouting trip.

Someone shouted from down the pathway. "Mash! Get yore backside over here so ya can finish da cookin'."

Mash waved off the shout. "Ya best be ridin' on if dat's yore plan."

"That is my plan." Jeremiah was glad he didn't have to stay around these ruffians. They made his skin crawl. They didn't do much for his appetite either. He turned his horse toward the tree line.

Should he go farther? He knew there was another settlement downriver, one with a name Jeremiah could never remember how to pronounce. What would he prove by going there? Likely he'd find the same hopeless sort living among homes that were once filled with prayer and praise.

Jeremiah clucked his tongue. His mount moved forward. Before horse and rider blended into the tree cover, Jeremiah took a last look back at the mission. He tried to see the settlement as it once must have been, tried to decide which of the homes might have been Sarah's.

✍

"I am tired of talking about it, Bessie."

Sarah dropped the stack of plates onto the table, hoping their clatter would get her point across. She didn't want to hear about Jeremiah, or the past, or her future.

"You cannot quit because you are tired," Bessie pleaded. "Someday you will have to face what is ahead of you, Sarah. That means you are going to have to let go of the past."

Sarah glanced out a small window to see Captain showing Sammy how to push a pine branch at the snow to clear their walkway.

"I have faced Levi's death, Bessie. Why do you think I brought Sammy here? I want to make life better for him."

"I will grant you that. You have done everything you can to make his life easier. But I have one final thing to say."

"Then please do so. I need to get to work mending Sammy's britches."

"If you faced Levi's death, Sarah, then you should now think about your own." Bessie settled her arms across her still-pudgy middle.

Sarah's eyes widened. "My own? Why, that is the most ridiculous notion I have ever heard. I do not plan on dying for years."

"None of us do, Sarah," Bessie rejoined. "Sometimes it happens earlier than we expect. Levi is a good example of that. You read to me the other night from Hebrews chapter nine. Remember? You read that it is appointed unto men to die once then to face the judgment. We both know that God numbers the hairs on our heads; we just do not know when it will be our turn. That is why you have to be ready to explain to God why you turned from Him and insisted on running things on your own."

Sarah thought about Bessie's comments. "You are right, Bessie. A few years ago, when I trusted God, I was happier. Then disaster struck, taking with it my faith—in God and humankind. I long to be the open and caring person of yesteryear, but I am not sure how to go about it."

"Happiness takes effort, Sarah. So does living when you think there is no reason to go on. God gives us heartaches to make us stronger. If we never weep, how can we know what true love really is?"

Sarah tucked a wayward strand of hair behind her ear. "God gave His only Son as a measure of how much He loved the world He created, as a sign of His trust that humans would make the right choices in their own lives."

Bessie's eyes glimmered with tears much like Sarah's. "Yes, Sarah. He did."

❧

Sarah began to pray daily for Jeremiah's safety. She was not sure that she would ever tell him what she had done eight years ago, or if he would listen if she tried. But she wanted to do so, for Sarah now knew that she wanted more from Jeremiah Stewart than friendship.

✍

Jeremiah frowned as his rap on the door went unanswered. Since thoughts of Sarah had filled his mind on his most recent trip, he was determined to discover why. Journeys through Indian land were dangerous enough without thoughts of a woman clouding his thinking. Once and for all Jeremiah planned to settle the pull Sarah had on him and get her out of his mind.

Gemma Winslow, with all her faults, might not be such a bad choice. At least he didn't spend his free time thinking about Gemma, which allowed him to accomplish what he could for the militia.

"Why, Jeremiah. You are the last person I expected to see. Come in."

He last had seen Sarah leaving the supper before Shade finished speaking. She did not act now as if she were trying to hide anything from him.

Jeremiah knew he must deal with that issue eventually, but for now he spoke as candidly as he could. "I came because there is something I have to get straight."

"I figured as much." Sarah waved him in, her eyes betraying an uneasiness at his presence.

"Is Bessie here?"

"She had a touch of stomach trouble yesterday, but I think she might be well enough to get up. Let me get her."

"No. I came to speak with you on official business. Can we sit down?"

He heard Sarah inhale sharply, but she followed him to the eating room.

Sarah spent some time arranging her skirt folds after she took her seat. "Go on and have your say," she finally said without looking at him.

Jeremiah draped his hat over the top prong of the chair. "I am not good at easing into things carefully, so I want you to know that anything I say is not designed as an attack on you."

He laid his hands palms down on the table, staring at a scar on the bridge of his knuckles. He had received the wound when he pummeled a tree shortly after learning about Jenny's death.

"You are not making much sense, Jeremiah."

"Nothing makes sense anymore, Sarah. I pray daily, begging God to provide the answers I need to do what is best. You once ordered me to forget about the little people. I did not even try, because I know I cannot do that. I might not like my position in the militia, but the little people are young boys like your Samuel, and like my niece Elizabeth. They are the families, friends, and people I see daily, even you. They are also our enemies, many of whom have no more choice in what is going on than we do. Sometimes it seems things are more confused than they ought to be."

"I thought you said you came here to discuss business."

Jeremiah sighed. "When I first took this job, I worried about learning everything I had to do."

"So?"

"I have prayed more in the last year than I have ever done in my life," he admitted.

"You must be lacking sleep, for you are talking in circles." Sarah's glance flitted past Jeremiah's and ended up on the woodpile.

"No, Sarah. It is not from lack of sleep. It is more likely because, when I think of you or look at you, words seem to flee my mind. Speaking sensibly becomes one of the hardest things I have ever had to do."

Sarah shifted position. "I do not think that is why you are really here. Is it, Mr. Stewart?"

Jeremiah drummed his fingertips against the tabletop. The fact that she had not used his given name hurt, but he ignored it. "You are right. You once told me you traveled with a missionary after the orphanage you lived in was destroyed."

Sarah raised her chin to look him squarely in the eye. "That is true."

"I am making an assumption here that may be incorrect, but did you happen to settle in the eastern part of Ohio?"

Only the continual drumming of his fingers on the table broke the silence. Jeremiah watched as fear flickered in Sarah's eyes.

"There is nothing I know of that says a person cannot move around wherever they wish, is there?"

"No, but I need to hear what you know about it."

"The mission?"

Jeremiah didn't know exactly what he was looking for. He'd seen the settlement with his own eyes. "Where it is. How many lived there. What kind of land surrounds it. Tell me anything you can think of."

Sarah jumped up and tramped around the small room.

Jeremiah cleared his throat. "Several months ago, when I served as a courier, I met most of the Indians that David Zeisberger had living with him in those mission settlements."

Sarah glared at him. Jeremiah would have preferred not to continue, but something he didn't understand forced him to go on.

"On this latest trip I stopped by Fort Pitt on my way home," he said.

Sarah pulled at her earlobe. "So?"

"The commander granted me access to the fort's journals. Those chronicles contained some of Zeisberger's actual missives to those who ran Fort Pitt throughout the last ten years or so."

Sarah's facial expression gave away nothing. "And?"

"In a letter eight years ago, Zeisberger mentioned that one of the young women he allowed to live at the mission disappeared. . .with a young man. . .Levi Lyons." Jeremiah tried not to sound harsh, but the accusation poured out of him.

Sarah paled. "Are you pestering me so that I will confess?"

Jeremiah fought for self-control. "I want to know about the mission. That is all."

Sarah studied Jeremiah. His long hair was uncombed, his lips pinched, and she thought he'd lost weight since she'd last seen him. "You want information from me to help you fight your battles with the Indians. Check your muster rolls, Mr. Stewart. I am not one of your soldiers."

Jeremiah threw his hands up in the air. "You have to tell me, Sarah. Why can you not see that?"

"Because I see a greedy man who wants me to help him kill Indians."

"I do not want the information for that reason."

"Oh? You know, Jeremiah, while you were gone I began to hope that you and I might someday become real friends."

Jeremiah took a step toward her. "I would like to discuss the friendship possibility later. This is official, remember?"

"Right. I did not mean to detain you from your militia business."

"Sarah, I do not want to do it, but I have to tell you that the missionaries and inhabitants of those missions are charged with treason."

Sarah did not blink.

"And that the British forced several Praying Indians north, away from their homes, their crops, and their freedom. All I am trying to do is find a way to keep them from being held accountable for something they probably have not done."

Sarah remained silent, but agitation flashed in her eyes.

"I am a Christian, Sarah. I do not kill people on purpose. My parents taught me to love all mankind, not just those with the same color skin as mine."

The growing sparks in Sarah's eyes were the only indication that she heard him.

"Do you not see?" Jeremiah pushed on. "I chose to deliver messages because I refused to take an active part in killing people."

"You are not carrying letters back and forth any longer," Sarah accused. "You are even more involved in the decisions to send men out after them. You might as well murder them with your own hands."

"You feel strongly about this because you knew people at that mission, and there are others in places near them that you knew, too."

"That is not. . .the reason!"

"Then tell me why you keep refusing to cooperate," Jeremiah demanded. "What is it that bothers you about Schoenbrunn, or that other place, Ja-nade-en?"

"Ja-nad-den-hut-ten," Sarah said, correcting his mispronunciation of the Christian settlement Gnadenhutten. "You would not understand."

"You do not know that. You are judging me without knowing what drives me," Jeremiah stated. "You have not given me a chance since the very first time we met, have you? You are afraid of commitments, Sarah. That is what this boils down to."

"That is not true."

"You are too afraid that what we share now might grow into something significant, are you not?"

Sarah dropped her gaze to the floor. Her heart twisted in the wrong direction, hurting much as it had when renegades had killed her husband. That couldn't be. There was only one man she loved that much, and his name was *not* Jeremiah Stewart.

"I do not have to know you to see what sort of man you are. I have met others like you."

"You have not been listening to me, Sarah. I keep trying to tell you that I am not like the other men you have known."

"Really? Then why are you, like everyone else, unable to understand that there are some things about my life that I do not wish to share? Keeping it hidden is much easier to deal with, so much less painful."

"That is fine with me. But at least tell me what type of man I am, Sarah Lyons. I want to hear it from you."

Sarah lifted her chin, meeting his gaze. "This is ridiculous. This is not business, as you professed it was to be when you arrived, nor is it getting us anywhere."

Jeremiah pretended not to understand the hurt in Sarah's eyes. "We will not get anywhere until you let someone knock that frown from your face and that pain out of your heart. I have been there, Sarah. I know what it feels like."

"You do not have any inkling of what happened to me, Jeremiah."

"I can tell that you lost something very precious."

"As if you would understand the agony in that," Sarah said.

"Yes, I w—"

Jeremiah's words were lost in Bessie's worried interruption. "What is going on in here?" Bessie bumbled into the room, rubbing her eyes. "I heard voices." She glanced back and forth between the two of them. "If this is private, I will leave."

"It is not private," Jeremiah volunteered when Sarah said nothing.

"No. It is not," Sarah granted. "I was just telling your brother farewell."

Bessie slipped to Jeremiah's side and gave him a sisterly hug. "Welcome back, Jer. Did you know you two were making enough noise to scare a herd of wild horses away?"

Jeremiah and Sarah glowered at each other.

Jeremiah jerked his head toward Sarah. "I came over because Sarah knows things about those missions that Zeisberger settled in the Muskingum Valley. She refuses to help."

"For a very good reason," Sarah inserted.

"Sarah, you have to put your own feelings aside for the moment," Jeremiah cajoled. "You might know something that will help avoid a disaster. That alone should make a difference."

Sarah crossed her arms in front of her, not caring that it drew attention to her shaking shoulders. "I have not been there in years."

"That does not matter. Tell me what you know about the people who lived there. How strong was their faith? Why did they choose that area?"

"Both of you can ask all that you want, but I will not divulge a thing."

"Jer?" Bessie stood beside her brother, though she appeared to want to be at both their sides. "Give Sarah some time. Knowing you, you sprang this on her and now you have her all worked up. I am sure that once Sarah mulls it over, she will realize that helping you is the right thing to do."

Sarah faced Bessie. "Do not tell me that you think I should assist him?"

"Eventually Jeremiah will get the information from somewhere. If you know something, Sarah, why not tell him now? It might help keep us all safer here. You do not want something to happen to Samuel, do you?"

It made no sense, but Sarah ignored the plea for Sammy's safety. If she told Jeremiah even a bit of what she knew, he would come back for more.

"I do not trust what he is going to do with it," Sarah stated.

"I am trying to help those people, Sarah," Jeremiah responded. "You have to believe me."

"I have known Jeremiah all my life," Bessie said to Sarah. "Not once did he ever lie to me or let me down. You can depend on him." She turned back to her brother. "Sarah is not going to tell you today. Let her sort things out."

Sort things out? Did Bessie think that what Sarah felt was as simple as sorting the whites from the darks for the wash? It was much more complicated than that.

"I do not need time." Sarah glanced between them. "I will not tell anyone about the Moravians."

"What if it means you might save their lives, Sarah?" Jeremiah prodded. "Will you still keep it to yourself?"

"I might."

He dropped a fist onto the table. Bessie winced.

"All right, then," Jeremiah declared. "I will not ask you again. Human life obviously does not mean much to you."

"It means a lot to me." Sarah faltered. "It does. Truly."

"Then prove it by putting others ahead of yourself for once." Jeremiah flung the words at her as he thrust his arms through his jacket sleeves.

His reluctance to probe further made Sarah wish she had confided something to him, even if it was one small tidbit—just so she knew he would come back to see her.

Chapter 14

I do not know how much more I can take." Jeremiah shoved Shade's latest delivery aside and threw his hands over his face. He cared little that he looked nothing like a man of battle.

"What now?" Rufe asked respectfully.

Jeremiah shrugged. "I knew there would be trouble when I learned that British commander ordered those Praying Indians from their homes last fall."

"You cannot change that, sir."

Jeremiah straightened a stack of papers. "I know, but things are getting worse. I have a feeling that something is about to happen, and we are not going to like the result."

Rufe slumped into a chair. "Pretty much what Shade tried to tell everyone at the Winter Supper. So what are you going to do? You cannot run to Fort Detroit. It is a British holding, and I have heard that their commander is the best they have."

Jeremiah pondered things for a moment. "Perhaps Shade can find out more about what is going on."

Rufe sat up. "To prove what?"

"I do not know," Jeremiah confessed. "I have already made one trip there, but sending Shade beats sitting here waiting for something or someone to come to us. Williamson promised I would only serve till mid-March. He said he would not ask me to take Dan Whelp's place. Well, it has been over a month and a half, and he has yet to submit a replacement name for the major's position!"

"Colonel Williamson is a busy man." Rufe clearly did not want to take sides with either Williamson or Jeremiah.

"Busy rounding up more men for his militia," Jeremiah scoffed. "Sometimes I think he moves people into the county so that he will have more men on the rolls."

Rufe propped a finger under his chin. "Perhaps you could send a message to headquarters insisting that they appoint someone. Never mind. You already tried that."

"God put me here to do something, Rufe. I just do not know what." Jeremiah ran his hands through his hair.

"Pa always says we should not bring trouble upon ourselves," Rufe stated. "He says we should look for what we can do that is good and be satisfied with that."

Jeremiah fanned the edges of the papers. "Your pa is a smart man, Rufe, but that does not ease my frustration."

"What if we send someone out to get Colonel back here? Then you could demand that he do something about replacing Dan Whelp. That is what you want, is it not?"

"Yes. No. I do not know. I am worried we are going to find ourselves being attacked by more Indians than we can handle. If that happens, we will have no choice but to defend ourselves, to kill." Jeremiah raised stricken eyes to the clerk. "That is strictly between you and me."

"Yes sir," Rufe promised.

"That must be so," Jeremiah replied. "For if anyone found out how I feel, I might be looking at a charge of treason."

⟿

Winter slipped by in a barrage of blizzards and icy winds. Sarah hadn't seen Jeremiah since they quarreled about the mission. Early on, each day she expected him to visit and question her further, but he never did.

Did she miss him? Kick a squirrel in the tail and chase it up a tree. Why would she miss Jeremiah? She should be glad he no longer dropped by as he once had. But the short winter days made for long nights, times when Sarah thought about Jeremiah and Gemma. . .together.

Sarah turned her mind to happier prospects. Bessie and Sammy's "letter lessons" were going well. Bessie had caught on quickly to the shapes of the letters of the alphabet. Sammy ran a close second with his ability to recite the letters in sequence.

Sarah knew that on days when the snow wasn't blowing too hard or the wind too chilly, Bessie bundled up and went to visit her brother. Sometimes Sarah allowed Bessie to take Sammy along. Other times Bessie went alone, leaving baby Elizabeth, or Lizzie as she was now known, with Sarah.

Sammy loved to sit beside Sarah as she held Lizzie, babbling and smiling at the infant. Sarah felt her heart warm when Lizzie charmed her with a toothless grin.

Sarah refused to ask about Jeremiah, knowing it would only lead Bessie to speculate about her motives for asking. One day, though, Sarah couldn't hide her curiosity any longer. She waited until Bessie had put away her purchases from the post.

"Is this a busy time of year for the militia?" Sarah hoped her use of the term "militia" disguised her true interest.

"Jeremiah is always a busy man." Bessie failed to hide her smug grin. "Do you miss seeing him?"

"About as much as I miss those oxen that pulled our wagon here," Sarah quipped.

"I wish you two would work out your problems. Jer is just as troubled as you are. I am sure it is because he feels you no longer care to see him."

"He is free to think that if he wishes." Sarah hoped Bessie did not mention Gemma Winslow, for Sarah didn't think she could take hearing that woman's name.

Toward February's end a huge snowfall left them homebound and impatient for the white stuff to melt. Captain read from the Bible, encouraging Bessie to try out the words she knew. Bessie's hesitant, but progressively improving, attempts gave Sarah a great feeling of accomplishment.

Sarah grew used to seeing Sammy climb up on Captain's knee, as if it were the most natural thing in the world for Sammy to do. She enjoyed listening as Captain explained Jesus and the apostles to her son.

Captain left without explanation one afternoon. Bessie fretted until he returned with a goose. He stated the gift came from a family who wished to express their appreciation to him for sharing the Gospel with them.

Bessie basted the goose with cream and hung it over the hearth. The aroma of sizzling fowl filtered through the home throughout the night. Sarah slept soundly until she was jolted awake by early spring's gusty breath lifting the roof edges and dropping them back into place.

As Sarah waited for a pan of sugared bread to finish frying, Captain entered the room. At first he said nothing. Sarah remained quiet while he flipped through his Bible. She watched as he picked up the locket of hair she had dropped that day months ago. He ran a finger along its length then flipped the pages.

Sarah swallowed hard. "Captain?"

It seemed an eternity before he glanced at her. "Good morning, Sarah. Did you sleep well?"

"Until the racket began outside."

Captain chuckled. "Those northern blasts can be quite chilling. Did you need something?"

His cheeks were plumper than Sarah had noticed recently, and though his hair appeared grayer, the youthful echo of auburn peppered his beard.

Sarah explained her clumsiness with the tuft of hair a few months earlier. "I am so sorry. I should have told you long ago. I thought Bessie already had."

Captain arched an eyebrow. "Isaiah 40 or 41?"

"Forty."

"The Lord works in mysterious ways," Captain said. "I chose Proverbs, but Isaiah is just as appropriate."

"I am not sure how you expect me to answer that," Sarah answered. "You know my faith is not exactly a shining example for others to follow."

"God's Word contains beautiful promises, no matter where you look," Captain said. "And I think you are wrong, Sarah. I feel that what happened to you was of such size that it overwhelmed you. You would not be the first to turn away from God during disaster."

"Are you saying I never quit putting my faith in God? I hardly think that is true. Look at what He did to my family. Everyone seems to forget that."

"We have not forgotten, Sarah. More than likely it is that we suffered something that pains us just as deeply, but we accepted it and prefer to look ahead, not backward."

Sarah lived with her disappointments and lost dreams every day. "I keep seeing that. . .night. . .happening over and over. I will never forget it."

Captain nodded. "I had trouble, too, until I decided to set aside a block of time each day and use that to deal with my pain. Eventually I taught myself to push the ache away until the next day."

"Seems to me," Sarah replied, "that if I made myself think about it every day on purpose, I would just recall it more."

"There is that risk, but if you truly want to become a mother that Samuel is proud of, then each day you work at making yourself think of the hurt less. You will never forget it completely, though—it is too much a part of you."

"What if I never put. . .it. . .behind me?" Sarah closed her eyes, wishing that the choices she'd made had not turned out to be so disastrous.

"You think that if you put your pain behind you, you will also put your husband there." Captain fingered the small lock of hair. "It might be hard for you to understand right now, but someday Levi will be separate in your mind from the pain."

"How do you know that?" Sarah's question filled the room.

Captain smiled. "This clip of hair came from my first wife's curls. We were not blessed with children, but I loved her, still do in my own private way. No one can ever take that from me. Katherine is gone, but she lives on in my heart. Every time a robin sings, I hear her voice, feel her love, touch again the gentle waves of her beautiful red hair."

Captain fingered the lock of hair. Sarah grasped the edge of her apron. Finally, Captain cleared his throat, brushing aside the solemn moment. "It does not make me love Bessie any less. In fact, it took me a while to realize that if I did not know the great trust that comes with loving God, if Katherine had not been abruptly taken from me, I might have missed out on Bessie and little Lizzie."

He hung his head, hiding his tears. "And that would have been a real shame."

Chapter 15

Captain's disclosure explained the inscription in his Bible that Sarah had read months ago. It also played heavily on her heart over the next few days. While Sarah didn't wish to snoop, she did want to discover more about how Captain relinquished the grief associated with losing his first wife. And, she recalled, hadn't Bessie hinted at something similar?

Speaking of Bessie, Sarah noticed that she no longer flitted about and chirped inane things as she once had done. Bessie was now an earnest young woman, devoted to raising her daughter as best she could in troubled times. Sarah found that she missed the constant chatter Bessie once had filled the days with. She decided one afternoon to have a talk with Bessie, to see if she could learn why she'd changed.

Her plans were stymied. Bessie came down with a cold. Captain stayed at his wife's side constantly, refusing to allow even Sarah to tend to Bessie. Sarah recalled how Levi always had taken care of her when she was ill. Thinking of him now didn't cause her as much pain as it usually did. She'd begun doing as Captain had suggested and hoped this was a sign of progress.

After Bessie recovered, Sarah waited until Captain left for a visit to a neighbor's home before she began the conversation.

Bessie searched Sarah's face as if looking for a clue. "I knew you needed something of me. What is it you want to know?"

Sarah swallowed. "For one thing, how do you always know I am troubled?"

Bessie spoke without hesitation. "Not long after you joined us, I learned that when you are not—shall we say *bothered*?—by something, you are more willing to talk. When something troubles you, you push everyone away except Samuel. . . . That is not what you really want to know, though, is it?"

Sarah shook her head. "I think you seem very different since Lizzie's birth."

"For the better?"

"Yes, but it is also as if there is something deep inside that you cannot resolve," Sarah replied. "I do not mean to pry, but is that true?"

Bessie sighed. "It might sound odd, but having a child scares me, Sarah. Suddenly there is this little lass who depends on me for everything. I did not know it would be so awesome."

"The responsibility?"

Bessie shook her head. "The love. I fell for Captain practically the moment I met him at a worship service—silly me, mooning over a man of God almost twice my age." Bessie chuckled then sobered. "This is a different sort of caring. You have Samuel, so you know what I mean."

Sarah nodded. That grand tenderness that filled her heart every time she looked at him, the love that was a constant part of her life but sometimes frightened her—different from the passion with which she had loved his father, but just as strong.

"A child is fulfilling," Sarah concurred. "And I am blessed that I did not lose Sammy. He is so full of joy and life that the world seems made just for him to discover. Last night I realized that even though I lost Levi, I still have a part of him with me in Sammy."

"I have said this before," Bessie added. "Samuel will grow up to be a fine man, thanks to your guidance. You let him join Captain as he reads God's Word. That is a wise decision."

"Yes, it seems more intelligent every day. I did some thinking, Bessie, and it will not do any good if Sammy learns the history of God's people and the plan of salvation if I do not reinforce it."

Bessie simply smiled, and Sarah turned her mind to the men who volunteered to leave their families, if needed, to fight battles they might never return from. And to Captain, who spread the news of redemption regardless of people's reaction to it—Sarah's included. Her thoughts returned to Bessie, who quietly displayed her own brand of hope as she rocked her wee daughter.

Finally, Sarah pondered Jeremiah—tall, confident Jeremiah Stewart. From the beginning he seemed intent on upsetting her tiny fragment of the world. Was he really? Or was that what Sarah thought because she could not believe he really wanted to help her?

No matter what Jeremiah did, Sarah pushed him away because he frightened her. Was it him or was it that when she saw him, she felt things she had resolved she would never allow her heart to feel again?

Sarah shook her head. Bessie was chattering. She rolled her mind away from Jeremiah to listen.

". . .and I told Captain that was the most beautiful thing he could ever say to me."

Sarah apologized for daydreaming.

Bessie gave her a curious look. "Captain said that if it had not been for me, he would not have understood God's plan for his life. He also said that if not for you, Sarah, he would not have shared that with me."

"What did *I* do?"

"Captain told me about how much he once loved Katherine. In all this time, he had never talked about her with me. He said that as he spoke with you, he grew convinced that when you tucked that snippet of hair away, you had chosen Isaiah without realizing it. He believes that the message of hope and comfort that speaks across the years from the prophet Isaiah called to you, asking you to place your trust in the Lord."

"Captain thinks that?"

"And much more," Bessie continued. "That is when he told me the rest. Seems that when we met, he decided to wed me because he thought I would be a help to him spreading the Gospel. I do not know why, since I was hardly a good example of the perfect preacher's wife."

Bessie grew pensive, her eyes drifting to Captain's Bible on the mantel. "I suppose I did not truly love him at first," she admitted. "I cared about him and liked him as a friend, but I think I was agog over his good looks and the way he made me feel special."

Good looks? Heavens, Bessie must be blind!

Sarah's taste ran more to men like Jeremiah, men with a hint of danger and an air of greatness about them, yet with a portion of gentleness that shone through at the most unexpected times.

"Why did you wed Captain, then?" Sarah challenged.

"I lost my first husband in a farming accident. Martin and I had had big dreams for our future, plans for a large family, and a big farm our boys would help us run. One day he went out to plow and did not come home."

Bessie's eyes filled with tears. She tightened her jaw and went on. "With no one to take care of me, I went back to live with my parents. Jeremiah was there. He had just lost Jenny. I do not have to tell you what a sorrowful bunch we were. Well, Captain came by a few weeks later to stay with us, for my parents held the church service that month."

"How long did you know him before you joined him in wedlock?"

"A few weeks." Bessie caught Sarah's glance of shock. "He was in a hurry to depart for another town. I was in as big a rush to leave home so that my parents would stop telling me they had known all along that Martin had not been right for me."

"It does sound sudden," Sarah murmured.

"Yes, but it has been worth it. I am a blessed woman, Sarah. But only because I accepted what God gave me as my lot in life."

"Can I tell you my story?"

At Bessie's nod, Sarah spoke. "I suppose my departure from Schoenbrunn with Levi was just as impulsive. We were enthusiastic about beginning our lives together. To stay at the mission would mean waiting until the elders, my sister, and his parents decided we could wed."

"Is that all?"

"No. I guess we should have done things differently, but Levi had just lost his third niece in a year. He suggested we leave immediately so that he could put some distance between that grief and himself. I went with him because I loved him. After we married, he promised to take care of me until his final day. As you know, that day occurred much earlier than we planned. You and Captain were smart to grasp what joy you could, Bessie. I envy you."

"Someday you will find another," Bessie said. "He may not be what you think you want, but he will fill your heart with his presence. He will draw you into his life without hesitation because he cares about you, perhaps even more than he realizes. If you give him the chance, he will change your life forever."

Sarah raised her eyebrows. "I take it you mean Jeremiah?"

Bessie nodded.

"I do not think there is much of a chance for that, Bessie. Not with Gemma Winslow around."

✧

"Jeremiah is coming to eat with us." Bessie passed on the news and went to her room to nurse Lizzie.

Sarah set the table then hurried to change dresses. She hadn't seen Jeremiah since the day that she refused to offer him any knowledge she had of the missions. Was it possible he missed her and was coming over to see her?

Drivel! She must be turning soft from sitting around and doing nothing. Even with Rufe coming by in the evenings so that Sarah could teach him his letters, she didn't have much to occupy otherwise empty hours. Sammy played by himself so much, sometimes Sarah wondered if it was normal.

To whom could she ask such a question? With Lizzie so young, Bessie wouldn't know what a child should do at Sammy's age. Who then? Sarah hadn't gone out of her way to foster a relationship with any of the women who lived near them. In fact, Sarah realized with a start, Bessie hadn't either.

Why not? Sarah concluded that despite Bessie's insistence otherwise, she must be ashamed of having Sarah and Sammy living with them. Well, Sarah couldn't change that now, but in the spring she would think about moving on. She'd said this move to Washington County was only temporary in any case.

Sarah donned the dress made from the emerald material. With the full skirt swirling around her ankles, she moved down the hallway, her heart pounding at the sound of Jeremiah's voice.

Sarah listened from the hall as he entertained Bessie and Sammy with tales of something Rufe had told him. They quieted as she arrived.

"Do not stop because of me," Sarah said, giving each of them a smile.

"We are not." Jeremiah rose and motioned for her to take his seat.

Sarah gazed at Jeremiah. If she left in search of her sister, she would never see him again. A part of her heart splintered. If only things had worked out differently. . . .

"I did not get a chance to tell you before, but your dress looks grand." Jeremiah's gaze swept the smooth lines of her gown.

He was, of course, referring to the night she had fled the supper wearing this same garment. Why did she think he would not raise that topic eventually?

Sarah seated herself where she did not have to look directly at Jeremiah. "I have never apologized for leaving that night. . . ."

"Perhaps we will have another chance. . .in times to come." Jeremiah's gaze followed Sarah's hands as she shifted them to her lap.

"Perhaps," Sarah replied.

Jeremiah scooted his chair around so he could face her. "I am sure Bessie told you about the wonderful food the women provided that night."

Sarah glanced at Bessie, who sat with Sammy on the floor to help him stack blocks. "No. She only mentioned that Gemma sat with you."

"Well, let me see if I can do the supper justice." Jeremiah did not mention Gemma while he spoke of the roast pork, turkey, potatoes, and vegetables. He ended by saying he devoured several slices of apple, sweet potato, and mincemeat pies.

"You ate all that?"

Jeremiah patted his stomach. "It was enough to hold me for a week."

"I see. Perhaps I should throw a few more potatoes in the kettle to ensure we have enough stew for tonight," Sarah teased.

Bessie cleared her throat, and before Sarah knew it, Bessie rushed Sammy from the room.

Sarah's brow narrowed. "Did I say something wrong?"

"No. Bessie knows that I am about to tell you I cannot stay and eat tonight."

"You cannot?" Sarah felt as if every hope she'd ever dreamed was ripped to shreds and laid at her feet.

Jeremiah traced the line of her jaw with his gaze. "No. We. . .er. . . the militia has a campaign. I have to go with them."

"I see." Sarah did not know how much she had looked forward to seeing Jeremiah until he said he was not staying.

"Do you?" Jeremiah gazed at Sarah, memorizing her looks.

Her hair was twisted into some sort of fancy arrangement on the back of her neck. Her eyes followed his, as if she were trying to commit to memory what he looked like also. Gemma didn't look at him like this. Gemma looked at him with marriage in her eyes, no matter how many times Jeremiah told her that he was not interested.

"Yes, Jeremiah. Above all else, you must uphold your military obligations."

Pain clawed at Jeremiah's heart. He wanted to sit here with Sarah. To watch her as she cooked, or baked, or sewed, or performed one of the hundred other tasks women did in a household. He would give anything for that privilege, regardless of what he had promised after losing Jenny. There came a time when a man took what God sent, thanked Him for the gift, and moved on to enjoy life with that blessing by his side.

Jeremiah suspected that was why God kept him in uniform in Washington County. So he could heal Sarah's heart.

"When do you leave?" Sarah's words were hesitant.

Jeremiah shifted his tone so that it was more professional, more appropriate for the task that was about to take him away. If he kept his distance, it would be easier to say farewell.

"Tonight. I should be back by next Sunday. Certainly no later than Wednesday of the next week."

"Is it serious?"

"It relates to that earlier discussion we had about those Ohio settlements. Have you changed your mind about giving me information?"

"In a way." Sarah searched his face. "I can tell you that when I left the Schoenbrunn mission, there were almost two hundred people living there. Most of them were Delaware Indians, people I knew. We considered another settlement downriver our sister settlement. I think there were perhaps half as many there. They were Mohicans, but Christians."

"Thank you, Sarah. I have done some thinking lately. I should not have pushed you to tell me things you were not ready to talk about. Please accept my apology."

Sarah watched as Jeremiah rubbed his hands together, then she answered, "I should not have been so stubborn. I would have told you, only. . ."

"It is all right, Sarah. You did what you thought was best. That is all I hoped for."

Their eyes met and held.

"You will be careful?" Sarah whispered.

"It is the only way I do business, Sarah."

"Do you think it would do any good if I asked God to watch over you?"

"I think God is waiting for you to talk to Him, Sarah."

"I will, then."

"I asked Him to guard you, too, Sarah."

Sarah gave Jeremiah one of the most beautiful smiles he ever saw adorn a woman's face.

"So many people think I no longer believe. Sometimes I act like I do not, but you know what, Jeremiah? Somewhere deep inside me is the Truth. When you come back, will you help me find it?"

Chapter 16

I don't believe Colonel Williamson actually wants us to do this. The entire territory seems to have gone mad. Protect me, Lord. Be with me now as You've never been with me before.

The petition's echo was Jeremiah's only comfort when his commander's flinty gaze turned on him. "Last chance, Major Stewart. We are waiting."

Jeremiah felt the cold penetrate his warmest jacket. He once had wanted to be like David Williamson—bold, well liked, able to make snap decisions. Not anymore.

Jeremiah met the commander's glare without hesitation. "I refuse to participate, sir."

"You cannot mean that, Major Stewart. I promoted you because you have the potential to be a great leader. These redskins scalped a family. We found the woman's bloodstained dress among their belongings when we searched their homes."

"Leaders do not always make popular decisions, Colonel. I think someone talked them into accepting that dress as part of a trade."

The only proof Jeremiah had of that was the startled look on the Indian's face when one of the militiamen pulled the stained garment out of a basket.

"This is not their full contingent," Jeremiah added. "If it were, there would be more than this. These folks were run out of here last fall by the British commander at Fort Detroit. The ones here only came back to collect what was left of last year's harvest. They could not have made the attacks on our county because they were not here to do it. I tell you, they are innocent."

Shade found out more than just tidbits on his last ride. Sure it had been risky sending the courier into parts unknown. The payoff was that Jeremiah now knew another part of God's design for his life.

He was to convince as many as he could not to participate in this act.

"They are murderers," Williamson insisted. "They must pay for their crimes." He pinned Jeremiah with an icy stare. "Do I need to remind you that you are now my second-in-command? You will do as you are ordered. Is that clear?"

Jeremiah thought back to the militia's arrival in this quiet Ohio valley. Colonel Williamson promised the Indians protection from the British and ordered them to surrender their weapons. Once they complied, he directed them to two cabins where they now awaited their fate. The background noise of men cleaning and loading weapons muted the hymns being sung by the prisoners not far away.

Regret surfaced in Jeremiah. There were so many things he should have done since taking over as the vice commander. He would do what he could. Williamson had pushed Jeremiah around for the last nine months. Winning this argument would make Williamson furious, but it was the only one Jeremiah thought worth winning.

"I will not do it, sir." Jeremiah spoke loudly, trying to forget what he knew was bound to happen. "There are others who feel as I do also."

Silence lapped at the valley's edge, broken only by a wild animal scurrying through the brush. The other men in the company looked anywhere but at Jeremiah or Williamson.

"I will not allow you to do this," Williamson ranted, his chest heaving.

"You do not have the power to stop me, sir. You told me from the beginning that you would not press me into doing something I did not believe in."

"That applied to taking care of things like ordering weapons and such, and you know it. It certainly did not apply to this."

"This is what I will have no part in," Jeremiah asserted. "Nor will any other man who feels it is wrong to take a life. What you do not know, Colonel, is that I posted my resignation to Philadelphia last week. I am no longer a member of your militia, nor am I subject to your rules. There were other names on that letter, too."

"That is impossible. I would know if any of these men did not want to be here." Williamson glared at his group.

"You are never around," Jeremiah pointed out. He glanced at the soldiers. "Those who earlier indicated that they wish to stand down may form up over there." He pointed to a dip in the landscape.

Shade moved first. Thirteen others followed. They formed a ragged line of rebellion, their faces pale and lined. Jeremiah gave them high marks for upholding their convictions and not lowering themselves to the ranks of those who only wanted to satisfy the fright in their hearts.

"You cannot do this." Williamson fastened an icy look on the deserters.

"We can and we will, sir. This war began with rebels who sought the freedom to worship and who believed that they could make life better. Go ahead with your plan, Colonel. We will pray for their souls, and for yours, for surely there is need of forgiveness here."

Williamson jerked on the reins of his horse. "You realize there will be a report on your insolence?"

Jeremiah nodded. He wasn't part of the militia any longer, though he wasn't sure that would protect him. At least this way he could live with himself in the morning.

"I expect nothing less, sir. It is only fair to tell you that we also posted another letter before we left Washington County. It is a detailed summary to the president of the militia as to your plans for this mission."

Color drained from the colonel's face. He scowled at Jeremiah, as if unsure whether or not to believe him.

Rufe stepped forward, his stature as straight as an oak. "It is true, sir. I wrote it myself."

Jeremiah gave the clerk an encouraging smile before turning back to the commander. "Shoot me if it will make you feel any better, Colonel. If I am gone, perhaps these men will rejoin your army."

"You are not worth wasting ammunition on," the colonel snapped.

"Let us go, men. It is our duty to destroy these heathens before they destroy us. Axes to the ready!"

The men marched toward the cabins, their pace increasing as they topped a small rise. When they were out of sight, Jeremiah realized three more had joined his group, making eighteen total who stood on the side of right. How few they seemed next to the hundred who voted to attack. He had won this argument with the colonel, but his heart filled with sorrow that he had not convinced more to join him.

Forgive me, Lord, but I did my best.

Jeremiah gathered the men in a circle and asked them to join hands. "Let us pray."

He squeezed the hand next to his and did not continue until he felt the pressure returned from the man on his other side.

"Lord, grant them immunity from the final horrors of this life as they pass into Your love. Our Father who art in heaven, hallowed be Thy name."

As the Ohio wilderness witnessed the destruction of a tribe who had only wanted religious freedom, Jeremiah and his following prayed throughout the night.

Chapter 17

"Y ou came back." Sarah grabbed Jeremiah's arm and drew him into the home, shutting out the frigid evening air.

"I told you I would help you find God. I do try to keep my promises, Sarah."

Sarah ignored the burst of happiness that Jeremiah's presence created. She sensed that something bothered him. "Was your trip successful?"

"It did not go exactly as I would like. There are several things I must tell you, Sarah. But for now, I want to hear how you have been."

As she took a seat, Sarah tried to push away the nagging fear that squeezed her heart. Jeremiah settled into a chair across from her, pushing his sleeves up as if preparing for battle.

"You cut your hair, Jeremiah. I thought you were not going to do so until you were out of the militia. Oh, listen to me prattle. I have been fine, but I would rather hear about you, Jeremiah. Tell me everything."

"The whole thing may not be such a good idea."

Sarah's stomach sank. "I want to hear it anyway."

Jeremiah gave her a small smile. "Indulge me. There are some things I do not feel up to discussing just now."

Sarah didn't push Jeremiah as she might have when she first met him. "Then I will go first. Sammy said his letters from start to finish while you were gone. Bessie and Rufe are doing quite well themselves with reading."

Jeremiah's jaw showed some lessening of the tension he had brought in with him. "I knew Samuel was a quick learner the first time I met him. Any man would be proud to claim him as his son. What else happened?"

Sarah's eyes glittered. "Captain and Bessie have studied with me."

"The Bible?"

Sarah nodded. "I know it was wrong to avoid God, but. . ."

"You are not ready to return yet," Jeremiah finished for her. "I understand, but I bet the angels stand ready to rejoice for your soul when you decide to do so."

"I do not know about singing; they might just hum."

Jeremiah laughed quietly. "Only you, Sarah. Only you."

"It has been quiet around here lately," she said. "Captain said he thinks the cold keeps the savages away. But what about you? The north wind was absolutely horrible here the other night. I wondered if you stayed warm and had enough to eat."

"I managed to survive. Quiet is good. I suppose if they do not send out detachments to look for rebels, that is a sign the militia is doing something right."

"Is that the only thing you care about, Jeremiah?"

"Not anymore."

"Not any—I do not understand."

"I am no longer a part of them."

"That is. . .good to hear," Sarah admitted.

Jeremiah spoke in a broken whisper. "As hard as I tried, I could not do what the colonel ordered. I kept thinking of you, Sarah. I knew you would never forgive me if I went along with the campaign."

A burst of happiness filled Sarah's heart. Jeremiah had thought of her while he was gone! She composed herself.

"I am the last person you should worry about," Sarah reminded him. "You should know that by now."

Jeremiah's voice was low and smooth. "I do, but there are some things in life I cannot control. One of them is that I worry about you."

"There is no need for you to do so," Sarah insisted.

Jeremiah stretched his hand out toward her. "I wish it were that easy. No matter where I go or what I do, Sarah, you push your way to the front of my heart."

"I find *I* can make myself do just about anything I wish," Sarah argued. "Just tell yourself I do not exist."

"Is that what you do? Tell yourself I am not a real person, with hurts and feelings?"

"Sometimes. It is safer that way."

⚮

Later that night Sarah realized that she had not told Jeremiah the truth. No matter how she pretended, Jeremiah was very real to her. He felt pain, and, like Sarah herself, he needed someone to help him become whole. He professed to be God-fearing. God would not keep him warm on a winter night when howling winds forced their way through the chinking of cabin walls.

Sarah swallowed her discomfort. There she went, thinking that perhaps someday—years from now—there might be a man like Jeremiah who would love her.

⚮

"Gemma, please," Jeremiah said. "We've gone over this too many times already. Your uncle and I did not agree. I took the only action that would allow me to continue living in line with God's Word."

Gemma dabbed at her eyes with a fancy handkerchief and sniffed. "Well, thank you very much, Mr. Stewart. I had such hopes for our lives as a couple. I suppose it is best that I find this out now. . .before you break my heart."

Despite Gemma's stoic words, Jeremiah knew he'd already done that very thing. If only Sarah felt this way about him. But it was better that Sarah not feel anything for him other than friendship. Now that he had resigned his commission, it was only a matter of time before he headed back east to visit his pa and figure out what to do with the rest of his life.

⚮

"Tell me you are not serious," Bessie said as she watched Sarah beginning to pack her few belongings.

"You knew my moving here was not for the long term, Bessie. There is nothing here for me, no way to support Sammy. You and

Captain have Lizzie. You should be a family and not have to worry about us."

"But where will you go, Sarah? Tell me that."

"I have a plan." Sarah neatly folded one of Sammy's shirts before placing it in her only trunk.

"Does that plan include coming back here someday?" Bessie's eyes overflowed with tears.

"I cannot answer that right now," Sarah replied. "It is time I move on and find whatever it is I am supposed to do with my life."

"Promise me you will speak with Jeremiah before you leave. I think he needs to know what you are doing."

"Jeremiah has Gemma, Bessie. I walked to the river yesterday to think things through. Gemma intercepted me there. She indicated that she and Jeremiah are. . .an item."

Bessie rolled her eyes. "But Jeremiah does not love Gemma. He loves you, Sarah. He has all along."

"Come on, Bessie, admit it. Your attempt at matchmaking this time has failed."

Bessie crossed the room and put her arms around Sarah. "If you are too stubborn to see what is in front of you, then I will not argue. I will miss you. You do not know how much help you have been. Thanks to you, I can read. Someday I will teach little Lizzie to do the same."

Sarah's eyes misted. "I am glad I gave you something that you will remember me by."

"But what will I give you? Wait! I know; I can read to you from the Bible to show you how well I can do."

"That would be nice." Sarah hoped she hid the commotion boiling inside her. There was no hope for her as far as Jeremiah was concerned. She did not think she was far enough in her journey back to God that she could bear to stay and see Jeremiah with Gemma.

"Let me pick something special," Bessie said, pulling Sarah's mind back to the present. "Meet me in the eating room."

Moments later, Bessie haltingly read from Psalm 103: " 'Bless the

Lord, O my soul: and all that is within me, bless his holy name. Bless the Lord, O my soul, and forget not all his benefits: Who forgiveth all thine iniquities; who healeth all thy diseases; Who redeemeth thy life from destruction; who crowneth thee with lovingkindness and tender mercies.'

"Are you listening, Sarah?"

"Yes." How could she not listen? The words pulled at Sarah and urged her to do the right thing, to return to her heavenly Father and accept His grace.

"I picked this verse because it says all I need to know about our Lord, Sarah. Only He serves as our ultimate protector, our source of comfort. God can heal your heart, Sarah, if you let Him. Is that not a wonderful thought?"

"Yes, it is. The words are just as you say. They combine hope, faith, and trust in a Supreme Being who accepts me just as I am, despite what I've done."

'God can heal your heart, if you let Him.' Bessie's words echoed in Sarah's mind that night as she tossed on her mat. God could heal her heart, but only if Sarah allowed Him to. Why did she not take the last step toward believing?

☙

Low-hanging clouds and a slight breeze made it feel colder than it was as Sarah headed toward the trading post. Jeremiah came from the other direction, and with the woods on either side, she had no choice but to speak to him.

They exchanged small pleasantries, and Sarah acted as if she were going to continue her walk.

"Sarah? There is something that I have to tell you." Jeremiah stuck his hands in his pockets.

Sarah's calm voice belied the depression in her heart. "You do not have to. Gemma cornered me the other day at the riverbank. I am happy that you have found someone to help you get over Jenny."

Jeremiah gave her a puzzled look. " Gemma is not. . . never mind.

How do you know about Jenny?"

"Bessie told me you loved her. That is all." Pain gouged Sarah's heart. Gemma, fortunate woman that she was, had lightened Jeremiah's burden.

"You told me that you wanted me to help you hunt for the Truth," Jeremiah said. "We did not get a chance the other night, upon my return, to begin that journey. That is why I was coming to find you."

"I do not think you need to worry about helping me with that anymore. You have other. . .other things to tend to."

"But I promised I would. At least grant me the privilege of saying what I think."

Sarah nodded her permission.

"One thing I learned in dealing with Jenny's death is that a person cannot keep their grief locked up in their heart forever, Sarah. They never get beyond it if they do."

"You are simply luckier than most, Jeremiah. You happened to find someone who means something to you." Tears threatened without warning. Sarah brushed them away. "I can keep my anguish to myself. No one but God will ever understand my feelings."

Chapter 18

Jeremiah watched Sarah turn and run back toward the Halls'. Unless she put her trust in God, he knew she would always search for something she would never find.

Jeremiah's rap on the door was too forceful, but he meant business, and it was not militia business this time. It took some doing, but Bessie helped him persuade Sarah to sit with him by the fireplace and continue their conversation.

"You have to share your burden, Sarah. That way it halves the grief."

Sarah looked as if she didn't follow his meaning. "You really want to know the truth?"

Jeremiah nodded. "We all make bad choices. It is part of God's way of teaching us to be better, to make us stronger."

Sarah stood. "Bad choices are indeed my problem, Jeremiah. If I had not insisted that Levi. . ."

Sarah's sobs sliced through Jeremiah like the flint head of an enemy's arrow.

"You keep looking for something to wipe away whatever it is you did, Sarah. Only God's grace can do that."

"His grace seems so far away, Jeremiah. I do not think I will ever feel happy and free again. Why is that?" The most ancient kind of hurt filled Sarah's eyes.

"I do not know, Sarah. I know I have been there, too. It is not easy alone. Just as you need God to help mend your heart, I need you." Jeremiah rose and wiped a tear from Sarah's cheek.

Sarah caught her breath. "What if I do not want you to need me?"

Jeremiah's voice held a note of disbelief. "I think you do want me to care, but you are so sure you might lose whatever you and Levi shared that you will not allow it."

"Levi was Sammy's father," Sarah pointed out.

"And you loved him."

"I still do."

"Do you? Or do you love the memory you have of him?"

Sarah's eyes clouded with uneasiness. "I do not want to forget him."

Huskiness broke Jeremiah's voice. "I do not want anyone to ask me to forget Jenny Townsend either. Look at Captain and Bessie. Both lost their mates, but they built a new life together. They know what it is like to lose, to have their dreams crumble into ashes."

"How did they survive? How did they put the past behind them and move on?"

"Sarah, are you asking how they freed their hearts to love again?"

"Yes."

"They gave God their hardships. They let Him restore their souls."

"How did. . .do you do it?" Sarah ventured.

Jeremiah studied her face. "At first I did much the same as you. I turned away from God. I grew bitter and spiteful."

"You are not. . .not that way now."

"I would be if I allowed my path to stray from that which is right. Now I keep God first, let Him lead me in the direction He chooses."

Sarah began to pace. "Does it help?"

"He is the only reason I can go on each day, Sarah."

Sarah stared into the fireplace.

Jeremiah spoke sincerely. "I am not good with fancy words, Sarah. Now that I am out of the militia, I do not even have a home. Thankfully, Rufe's father agreed to let me stay with them. I am just Jeremiah Francis Stewart, but I want you to be happy. I want you to care about me as much as I care about you."

"How can you say that, Jeremiah? Gemma said that you and she were going to wed."

"Gemma does not want to accept what I have told her all along. Now may I finish what I was saying?"

"Of course you may."

"I care about you, Sarah Lyons, but there are things I need to share with you about my past."

Jeremiah was uneasy about what he was about to say. Did he already regret announcing that he cared for her?

"I loved Jenny Townsend. She was everything I had wanted in a wife. She thought the world of me and would have made a wonderful mother for my children."

"So that explains why you keep coming here. You want children and I have one?"

"Let me finish. Jenny and I would have married if she had not taken a trip to visit her brother."

"What happened?" Sarah steeled her heart for his confession.

"Indians. One of our patrols found Jenny and her brother and buried them on the spot."

"I am sorry," she managed in a small voice.

"I am, too." Jeremiah sank into a chair and faced her. He shoved one shirtsleeve from his elbow to his wrist and back again, over and over. "But it is in the past, Sarah."

Sarah felt her poise dissolve. Jeremiah's loss almost matched hers. So many others also had lost loved ones. But they did not let devastation tear them apart. They learned to deal with their loss then moved on. Was it possible she. . . he. . .they could do so together?

"I believe God put me here for more than one reason." Jeremiah told her he had originally come to Washington County so that when they wed, Jenny could stay close to her ailing mother. "The only skill I knew was blacksmithing. I set up my tools and went to work. I never dreamed I would end up involved with the militia."

Jeremiah hung his head. Sarah's stomach clenched. What could she say to ease his pain?

"When I lost Jenny," he continued, "the whole world could have disappeared and I would not have noticed. I returned to my parents' home to live. That is when Bessie came home because she had lost her husband. She helped me see that things do not happen only because we make bad decisions. Things also happen because God has other plans for us. He prunes us so we will grow stronger, smarter, able to love more deeply the next time because we have lost so much."

Jeremiah wanted Sarah to stay with him for the rest of his life. How could he convince her? For just a moment he closed his eyes in silent prayer. *Lord, You never fail to deliver me from difficult situations, even though I sometimes think Your response is too long in coming. Look at me, Lord—I'm standing here trying to get this woman to reconcile her past so she can share my future. Sarah doesn't love me. What do I do now, Lord?*

"I am truly sorry that you lost the woman you loved." Sarah pressed a hand against her brow as if her head hurt.

"It took awhile for me to get over Jenny. For a long while I did not want to."

"What changed your mind?"

"You. The first time I saw you, I knew God had a purpose for bringing you into my life. I just never dreamed what it would turn out to be."

"That points out the major difference in our lives. You believed in God all along. I am just coming back to Him. What if I take the wrong path someday? There is no way we could be happy, Jeremiah. I do not want to be a stone around your neck."

"Stones have their use," he commented. "They anchor, they hold, they lock in place. We could not have built some of the homes in this county without them, but I would never call you a stone, Sarah. You are too lovely to be something like that."

"What would you call me, then?"

"I do not know. I can think of nothing right now that lifts you to the heights you deserve, Sarah. You do not think you are worth much to anyone except your son. That is not true. You taught Bessie her letters and helped her learn to read. You gave Rufe the chance to learn also. Who knows how many people your efforts will touch in the future because you cared enough to get involved today?"

Jeremiah wished that he had not started this discussion. No, that wasn't true. He loved Sarah. If he were to have any chance at her loving him, he must get her to the point where she could let go of Levi.

Jeremiah searched her face. "I cannot take away your pain, Sarah. Only God can do that. But you have to turn to Him. He does not help if you do not ask."

"It cannot be that simple. What if He will not listen to me or take me back?"

"God always listens, Sarah. Even through all those times when you were not looking at Him, He watched you. He has never given up hope that you would return to Him."

A frown marred her features. "You make it sound so easy, Jeremiah. It is not."

"I know. It is like crossing a river with your heart outside your body. You do not think you will ever get it back in place. I was at that point once. It takes courage and persistence to change. You have to really want it, not just for yourself but for those around you, especially Samuel."

"Leave him out of this. He is an innocent child who lost his father. What if something were to happen to me? Then where would he go?"

"There are quite a few around here who would gladly raise him, myself included. He is a fine boy, one you should want only the best for."

"I do. That is why I came here, to try to make life better for him."

"There is only one sure way you can do that, Sarah, and you know what it is. But do not do it if you do not mean it."

Sarah closed her eyes briefly, interrupting the tears that trickled out. "But what do I say?"

"Just start talking. If you really mean them, the words will come." Jeremiah covered her hand with his and gave it a gentle squeeze.

"Lord?" The word sounded stilted on her lips.

How could one word have so much power? It was a question

Jeremiah didn't think he would ever be able to answer.

Sarah started with a sob. "My burden—take it so that I may be free."

Jeremiah watched as Sarah struggled with her disclosure. Her eyes were ringed in red. She looked as if she had spent the past week crying.

What am I supposed to do, Lord? I know You put me here to help this woman, but what do I possess that will give her the peace she needs?

Jeremiah thought of the night sky he used to fall asleep gazing at on trips as a courier for the militia. The light of thousands of stars glowed softly, the twinkles spelling out a message he couldn't decipher. Suddenly he knew why God had provided that heavenly display.

"Sarah. I found something to compare you to."

"What?" She raised tear-stained eyes to meet his gaze.

"You are like a star. Despite the darkness that surrounds you, you shine, even as you continue your search for the perfection you know is out there. God put the stars in our heaven, Sarah. He is perfection. And peace. He is the only place you will find it."

"You said you would help me?" She stretched her hand toward him.

Jeremiah held back his smile, covered her trembling fingers with his own, and gazed into her eyes. "Go on. Let it out."

Once Sarah started, the echoes from her past spewed forth as if the earth rent a mountain and every bleak thing within escaped. Jeremiah hardened his heart against the surge of tenderness that engulfed him.

"I did something terrible," Sarah said, her throat closing around the words. "Levi and I ran away to marry. I never dreamed of what lay ahead, that he would. . .die before me. I am the only one left now, the only one to raise Sammy. Sammy deserves so much more, but I messed up his life. He deserves a father, and he might have had one had I stayed at Schoenbrunn."

Sarah's heavy sobs battered Jeremiah's soul, reminding him of his own process of grieving for Jenny. How many times had he held back his sorrow in the hope it would go away, only to find it growing by leaps and bounds with each passing day?

"Take it slow, Sarah. God will wait for you."

"God might," she whispered, "but what about you, Jeremiah Stewart?"

Chapter 19

"I will wait," Jeremiah assured her. "The weather changed early this afternoon; I think it may be warm enough for a stroll. Would you care to go with me?"

Jeremiah thought that the quiet and solitude outside would enable him to find the words he had not yet spoken.

Sarah nodded. On the Halls' porch, she pressed his arm and drew to a halt, gazing at him. Shiny tears glinted on her cheeks, giving her the appearance of fragility that Jeremiah knew was not part of her true character. He needed to see Sarah smile, to feel the spark only she could produce within his heart.

A renewed urge to replace Sarah's pain with happiness spilled through Jeremiah. "*I can do all things through Christ,*" he reminded himself, quoting from Philippians.

Jeremiah sighed. He still must tell Sarah what happened a week ago at a tiny mission in eastern Ohio, a deceptively peaceful setting where only the hills knew the truth of what the militia had done.

Jeremiah could never remember how to pronounce the name. He recalled that Sarah once called it "Ja-nad-den-hut-ten." Shade had told him it was "Ja-nade-den-hut-ten," which he said was Dutch for "Huts of Grace."

Where was God's grace on March 7, 1782? Nowhere near Gnadenhutten, Jeremiah could vouch for that. He remembered the scene, and fear shivered up his spine.

I pray their souls are at rest in Your court, Lord. I pray You gave them peace and welcomed them with open arms. If there are any who deserve Your favor, it is those who were slaughtered in cold blood.

Sarah tugged at his sleeve. "What is it? You have mumbled to yourself for several moments."

"I have?"

"Yes. It must be something terrible."

"Sarah, I fear what I have to tell you may upset you."

Sarah drew a deep breath and glanced around for something safe to cling to. They might as well be standing on a scrawny patch of spring grass. From a distance, vague sounds penetrated her awareness—an owl, a loon, a sentry calling out "All is well."

"Perhaps it would be better if we go back inside, Jeremiah. Captain and Bessie might want to hear this."

"No. This is between you and me."

Sarah met his gaze. "Go on, then. It will not be any easier if you delay."

"There has been a terrible tragedy at the Gnadenhutten Mission."

Wild fear engulfed her. Sarah stumbled, a reaction to the thought that eight years ago she and her sister lived only five miles away from there. But Jeremiah didn't know that. His militia had apparently been a part of this tragedy he spoke of. If she told him now that she had lived among those Praying Indians, what would he think of her?

Sarah schooled her features into a mask that didn't betray her terror. "Go on."

"Do you remember the last trip I took?"

She nodded.

"It was part of Colonel Williamson's plan that the militia raid that mission."

"Why would he assault a mission filled with Christians?"

"Williamson decided it was time to punish the ones he thought responsible for murdering the Wallace family."

"And?"

"He wanted to settle once and for all the question running through the minds of the people who voted him into office."

"I do not see how that applies to me."

Jeremiah narrowed his eyes. "If you have any doubt about my actions during the journey, I wrote everything down. I do not blame the militia for wanting to strike out at those who they thought were at fault, but that does not make it right."

"Did someone try to change their minds?"

His gray eyes darkened. "I did."

"But you said there has been a terrible tragedy."

"They would not listen to me, Sarah. Most of the men were too full of desire to get back at the heathens. They. . .they massacred them. All I could do was pray for their souls."

Massacred. The word settled inside Sarah like ice water. She couldn't bring herself to repeat it aloud; it was too bloody, too dirty. She knew most of those people. They were solemn Christians who left Pennsylvania years ago because whites kept tormenting them.

"I tried to prevent it, Sarah. I did the best I could."

"But. . .how many are gone?" Sarah wanted to know about the people at Schoenbrunn; her sister Callie, Levi's parents, Brother David, little Storm Killbuck. Memories of them singing praises to their heavenly Father filtered into her thoughts. Was it possible she had waited too long and would never see them again?

"At least ninety were killed, possibly more."

The time has come, Sarah realized. *I can't hide the truth from Jeremiah any longer.*

"Do you know any of their names? I mean, of the ones who were killed?" *Please don't say even one I recognize,* Sarah begged silently. *Please.*

"No. Some of us voted not to participate. We came back before the rest did. I had already tendered my resignation from the militia. Colonel Williamson did not know that until we were there and ready to begin the campaign."

"It is all so senseless, Jeremiah. Just like Levi's death. Someone reacted without thinking, did they not? Do you still claim God is in control of this world? And if He is, why did He not halt the slaughter of good people?"

"I do not know why, Sarah. But I do know this: I brought an eight-year-old boy back with me. He says his name is Abel."

Sarah grabbed Jeremiah's sleeve. "You brought an Indian child here? What do you think you are going to do with him?"

"Now that the militia has no hold on me, I am going to raise him to forgive those who took his family away."

"What makes you so sure you can succeed at raising an Indian child, Jeremiah? Sometimes I think you have no idea of what life is all about."

"I was going to ask you to marry me so we could raise him together, along with Samuel of course."

Sarah's mouth gaped. "You were going to do what?"

"You heard me. I want you to marry me."

"Me?" Everything else Jeremiah said since he arrived was momentarily forgotten. Jeremiah wanted to marry her!

"Because you are the one person who can help Abel get over his anger." Jeremiah drew a deep breath. "You left that mission under less than perfect circumstances, giving little thought to those you left behind, right?"

"Yes, but why would you think I would willingly help you bring up a child who has no parents, Jeremiah?"

"Because you grew up without them," Jeremiah said. "You told me you were an orphan. That is why you are so protective of your son, and your heart. You know what it is like to be without hope, to be lonely, to be lost, to have no relatives around to help you. Is that not right?"

Sarah inhaled deeply. "Not exactly. I do have a sister."

"Why did you not tell me that before?"

She dropped her gaze. "I was afraid that if you found out, you would track her down and tell her where I was."

"Would it be so terrible if I had?"

"Callie would have. . .told you about me. . .about what I did."

"The past is the past, Sarah. It does not matter to me where you came from, or what you did. What matters is who you are now. The woman standing in front of me is the woman I love."

"There is still something you do not know," she said.

"Then tell me so we can move on, Sarah."

Jeremiah's encouragement did little to stem the feeling that if she admitted this one last bit, he would walk away, leaving her stranded again. But once she started, the rest of her story rushed from her in a torrent.

"I chased after the man my sister was supposed to wed. When Callie did not want Levi, I took him. And look what happened. I killed him—Sammy's father—because I was jealous of my sister."

Jeremiah let Sarah's tears drain until there were no more before responding. "Levi was a grown man. He could have chosen not to go from the beginning, Sarah. You told me he loved you. I think you are being too harsh if you blame yourself for his death."

Sarah stared at Jeremiah. Was he right? Had she blamed herself all along for Levi's passing? She ached inside, but it was a hurt that relieved the pressure she had put on herself for the last two years.

"But it is for Levi's death that I do not think God can forgive me, Jeremiah."

Jeremiah leaned toward her. "If you repent, God forgives, Sarah. He does not rank sin according to size, or depth, or the person involved. A wrong is a wrong, a sin is a sin. If you feel you were wrong, then ask God for His forgiveness. Do not ever think He cannot forgive; He is the only one who can."

"I hurt my sister. . . . It is all such a tangle! How will I ever sort it out?"

"Let God guide your path."

Sarah's tears ran freely. With Jeremiah as her guide, Sarah sought God's forgiveness. Emotions burned at her eyes, but she ignored the discomfort. Inside, for the first time in years, she felt cleansed.

"What if I slip someday, Jeremiah?"

"I will be there to help put you back on the right path."

"And will you help me find my sister?"

"You do not know where she is?"

"She was at Schoenbrunn when I. . .left eight years ago."

Jeremiah dipped his head slightly. "I went to Schoenbrunn just last month. No one lives there now but renegade Indians and British army deserters."

Sarah gave a cry. "I will never find her. I knew I should not wait so long to go back."

"I know someone who is fairly good at finding information," Jeremiah said. "Let me ask Shade to help."

"That is all well and good, Jeremiah, but what happens if he cannot? Then what will I do? I have to ask Callie for forgiveness or I will never know true peace inside." Sarah held her chin at a determined angle.

"We will not stop until we discover where she is."

∽

Jeremiah caught Bessie peering through the tiny window, her face filled with quiet joy. She'd known from the beginning that something good would happen when God brought together two people like Jeremiah and Sarah. Why hadn't he believed her?

"I think it is time to return to something I said earlier. I love you, Sarah Lyons. I have since the day I met you, though I was too headstrong to realize it. Now, one more time, because I will not ask again: Will you help me raise Samuel and Abel so that they see that love is the only emotion worth pursuing in this world?"

"Samuel Stewart?"

"He will never be mine, Sarah, but he will be ours. I promise. He can remain Samuel Lyons for the rest of his life if it will convince you to marry me."

"Sammy Stewart." Sarah gave Jeremiah permission to call her son by the favored nickname only she used. "And it is about time you asked, Jeremiah."

Epilogue

Howdy, neighbor!" A flock of cackling chickens accompanied the man's greeting. Behind him was a quaint, well-built log home. A musket was slung across his body. "What can I do for you?"

Sarah clenched her husband's arm. Now that they were here, she did not think she could go through with this part of their journey. They had first gone to Jeremiah's home, where Sarah spent a week getting to know his pa and Hazel, his father's wife. Before they left, Jeremiah and Pa resolved any lingering resentment over Jeremiah having been in the militia. Hazel was a delightful woman who insisted that they return and bring their sons with them.

As if he knew what she was thinking, Jeremiah held Sarah's hand and gave her an encouraging smile. He rolled from the wagon seat, holding his hands up to show he carried no weapons.

"We are looking for a woman known as Callie Troyer. We heard she lives here."

Beneath a wide-brimmed hat, worry creased the farmer's tanned face. He drew one hand along the stock of the weapon as if preparing to flip it to his shoulder and take aim. "Depends on why you want her."

"She is related to my wife." Jeremiah motioned to where Sarah sat on the wagon seat.

Sarah's mouth grew dry. The tension knotting her stomach for the last three miles solidified into a huge mass.

What if Callie wanted nothing to do with her? Thank goodness they had left their sons, Sammy and Abel, with Captain and Bessie. *Their sons*—the words made Sarah smile despite the strain of the moment.

"That right?" The man perused Jeremiah. "Who might you be?"

Jeremiah introduced himself with a steady voice. Sarah bit her lip so hard she tasted blood.

The man raised the brim of his hat. A mass of tangled curls escaped. He was heavier than he'd been eight years ago, but Sarah would know him anywhere.

"Liope?" the man called over his shoulder. "Come on out. Your sister is here."

Liope? Sarah had never heard her sister called that before. A small eternity passed, long enough for Sarah to pray that God's will meant that all would work out.

"Josh?" The woman's voice was filled with concern. "I thought I heard you say my. . ." Her gaze traveled to Sarah.

"Sarah?" She shoved the toddler clamped around her hip at her husband. "Oh Sarah. It is you!"

Sarah met Callie halfway. Neither spoke. Their gazes held each other's, first cold with the memory of a long ago night, then warming with remembrance of all they shared as sisters.

"I had to come," Sarah croaked out. "I have to explain. . . ." Words crowded her throat.

"Nothing is important except that you are here." Callie flung her arms around her younger sister. Sarah returned the embrace. Years of worry, wonder, and waiting blossomed in her eyes and made her unable to reply.

"I thought I would never see you again." Callie held Sarah away from her. "You do not know how many times I have prayed for this day, this moment, Sarah."

Sarah grasped Callie's hands. Callie wore the years well, and Sarah could tell Callie was happy.

Cackling chickens scurried nearby, scratching and paying no heed to the two women. Near the cabin, a small toddler cried out for "Mama."

"Your nephew Isaiah," Callie said, motioning to the youngster. "His sister, Sophie Ruth, is seven." She turned back to Sarah. "But what about you?"

Sarah related the events of the years that had passed. Having Sammy; losing Levi; finding Jeremiah.

"Our Lord?"

Sarah nodded.

"Then there is nothing else we need to say. If you have asked and received His forgiveness, I can do no less than give you mine."

Callie drew Sarah against her again. Sarah laid her head on her sister's shoulder in much the same way she had when they were younger. Peace settled within her heart.

It had been such a long trek—a long, winding journey much like Moses and his people undertook. They'd wandered through a desert; her trip involved a wilderness. Along the way she learned to trust, to need, and to accept help from others.

She had restored her faith, regained her sister, and healed her heart. Sarah lifted her head and looked toward Jeremiah. He stood beside Joshua. The two of them chatted as if they had known each other forever.

A verse from Psalms crossed Sarah's mind: *"A man's heart deviseth his way, but the Lord directeth his steps."*

She closed her eyes and leaned into Callie's embrace. Being independent was no longer important, Sarah realized. She was a child of the King. She could do almost anything alone if she had to. But she much preferred being loved by the people she loved most.

Captain and Bessie, who were adding another small bundle to their family.

Abel, the wisp of an Indian boy with his lisping way of calling her Ma-Ma, and who had formed an uncanny relationship with Shade, the messenger who pointed Sarah in the direction of her sister.

Sammy, who loved having an older brother and who was helping Abel learn to read.

Callie, who had spent as many days and nights as Sarah had waiting to be together with her sister again.

Jeremiah, the man she would walk proudly beside for as long as God gave her life.

Lastly, but most importantly, God. For without Him, Sarah would be no one, no matter who loved her here on earth.

TAMMY SHUTTLESWORTH is an Ohio native who now considers Louisiana her home. She travels as often as she can to visit her daughters and grandchildren in Florida and family in Ohio. Now retired from the Air Force and teaching, she enjoys reading about and exploring Civil War battlefields and Native American historical sites. The two stories in this collection were inspired by the rich Ohio history she grew up visiting as a child.

If You Liked This Book, You'll Also Like...

Love's Story by Dianne Christner
Venture into this classic historical romance set in California from bestselling author Dianne Christner. As a female journalist, Meredith has something to prove with her big story on forest conservation. But when her heart becomes entangled, will she risk her career? Also includes a bonus story, *Strong as the Redwood* by Kristin Billerbeck.
Paperback / 978-1-63409-901-1 / $9.99

The Lilac Year by Janet Spaeth
Travel to the northern prairie wilderness where this historical romance from author Janet Spaeth is set. Mariah is searching for her nephew and a quick way to leave the frontier when she meets homesteader Ben Harris. Also includes the bonus sequel, *Rose Kelly*.
Paperback / 978-1-63409-908-0 / $9.99

Wildflower Harvest by Colleen L. Reece
Enjoy an inspiring historical romance set in Wyoming territory from author Colleen L. Reece. Dr. Adam Birchfield risks losing love in order to keep searching for his brother. Also includes the bonus story, *Desert Rose* in which a woman falls in love with a man through his letters.
Paperback / 978-1-63409-907-3 / $9.99

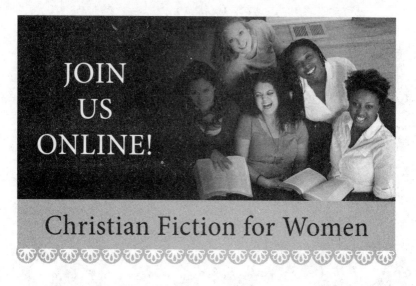

Christian Fiction for Women

Christian Fiction for Women is your online home for the latest in Christian fiction.

Check us out online for:

- Giveaways
- Recipes
- Info about Upcoming Releases
- Book Trailers
- News and More!

Find Christian Fiction for Women at Your Favorite Social Media Site:

 Search "Christian Fiction for Women"

 @fictionforwomen